Dialogues

of

the

Dead

REGINALD HILL

Dialogues

of

the

Dead

or

PARONOMANIA!

~~an Aged Worm for Wept Royals~~

~~a Warm Doge for Top Lawyers~~

a WORD GAME for TWO PLAYERS

DOUBLEDAY CANADA

Doubleday Canada and colophon are trademarks.

National Library of Canada Cataloguing in Publication Data

Hill, Reginald.
  Dialogues of the dead

Canadian ed.
ISBN 0-385-65872-9

  I. Title.

PR6058.I448D5 2002a   823'.914   C2001-902327-8

Book design by Lynn Newmark
Printed and bound in the USA
First published in Great Britain by HarperCollins Publishers/Spring 2001

Published in Canada by
Doubleday Canada, a division of
Random House of Canada Limited

Visit Random House of Canada Limited's website: www.randomhouse.ca

BVG   10 9 8 7 6 5 4 3 2 1

paronomania (pəronəʊˈmeɪnɪe) [Factitious word derived from a conflation of PARONOMASIA [L. a. GR. παρουομασια] Word - play + MANIA (see quot. 1823)]

1. A clinical obsession with word games.

1760 George, Lord LYTTELTON *Dialogues of the Dead: No XXXV BACON:* Is not yon fellow lying there Shakespeare, the scribbler? Why looks he so pale? *GALEN:* Aye, sir, 'tis he. A very pretty case of paronomania. Since coming here he has resolved a cryptogram in his plays which proves that you wrote them, since when he has not spoken a word. **1823** Ld. BYRON *Don Juan Canto xviii* So paronomastic are his miscellanea, Hood's doctors fear he'll die of paronomania. **1927** HAL DILLINGER *Through the Mind-Maze: A Casebook* So advanced was Mr. X's paronomania that he attempted to kill his wife because of a message he claimed to have received *via* a cryptic clue in the *Washington Post* crossword.

2. The proprietary name of a board game for two players using tiles imprinted with letters to form words. Points are scored partly by addition of the numeric values accorded to each letter, but also as a result of certain relationships of sound and meaning between the words. All languages transcribable in Latin script may be used under certain variable rules.

1976 *Skulker Magazine, Vol 1 No. iv* Though the *aficionados* of Paronomania contested the annual Championships with all their customary enthusiasm, ferocity and skill, the complex and esoteric nature of the game makes it unlikely that it will ever be degraded to the status of a national sport.

OED *(2nd Edition)*

Du sagst mir heimlich ein leises Wort
Und gibst mir den Strauss von Cypressen.
Ich wache auf, und der Strauss ist fort,
Und's Wort hab' ich vergessen.*

Harry Heine (1800–1856)

I fear there is some maddening secret
Hid in your words (and at each turn of thought
Comes up a skull,) like an anatomy
Found in a weedy hole, 'mongst stones and roots
And straggling reptiles, with his tongueless mouth
Telling of murder . . .

Thomas Lovell Beddoes (1803–1849)

* A word in secret you softly say
And give me a cypress spray sweetly.
I wake and find that I've lost the spray
And the word escapes me completely.

I

the first dialogue

Hi, there. How're you doing?

Me, I'm fine, I think.

That's right. It's hard to tell sometimes, but there seems to be some movement at last. Funny old thing, life, isn't it?

OK, death too. But life . . .

Just a short while ago, there I was, going nowhere and nowhere to go, stuck on the shelf, so to speak, past oozing through present into future with nothing of colour or action or excitement to quicken the senses . . .
Then suddenly one day I saw it!
Stretching out before me where it had always been, the long and winding path leading me through my Great Adventure, the start so close I felt I could reach out and touch it, the end so distant my mind reeled at the thought of what lay between.
But it's a long step from a reeling mind to a mind in reality, and at first that's where it stayed—that long and winding trail, I mean—in the mind, something to pass the long quiet hours with. Yet all the while I could hear my soul telling me, "Being a mental traveller is fine but it gets you no suntan!"
And my feet grew ever more restless.

Slowly the questions began to turn in my brain like a screensaver on a computer.

Could I possibly . . . ?

Did I dare . . . ?

That's the trouble with paths.

Once found, they must be followed wherever they may lead, but sometimes the start is—how shall I put it?—so indefinite.

I needed a sign. Not necessarily something dramatic. A gentle nudge would do.

Or a whispered word.

Then one day I got it.

First the whispered word. Your whisper? I hoped so.

I heard it, interpreted it, wanted to believe it. But it was still so vague . . .

Yes, I was always a fearful child.

I needed something clearer.

And finally it came. More of a shoulder charge than a gentle nudge. A shout rather than a whisper. You might say it leapt out at me!

I could almost hear you laughing.

I couldn't sleep that night for thinking about it. But the more I thought, the less clear it became. By three o'clock in the morning, I'd convinced myself it was mere accident and my Great Adventure must remain empty fantasy, a video to play behind the attentive eyes and sympathetic smile as I went about my daily business.

But an hour or so later as dawn's rosy fingers began to massage the black skin of night, and a little bird began to pipe outside my window, I started to see things differently.

It could be simply my sense of unworthiness that was making me so hesitant. And in any case it wasn't me who was doing the choosing, was it? The sign, to be a true sign, should be followed by a chance which I could not refuse. Because it wouldn't be mere chance, of course, though by its very nature it was likely to be indefinite. Indeed, that was how I would recognize it. To start with at least I would be a passive actor in this Adventure, but once begun, then I would know without doubt that it was written for me.

All I had to do was be ready.

I rose and laved and robed myself with unusual care, like a knight readying himself for a quest, or a priestess preparing to administer her holiest mystery. Though the face may be hidden by visor or veil, yet those with skill to read will know how to interpret the blazon or the chasuble.

When I was ready I went out to the car. It was still very early. The birds were carolling in full chorus and the eastern sky was mother-of-pearl flushing to pink, like a maiden's cheek in a Disney movie.

It was far too early to go into town and on impulse I headed out to the countryside. This, I felt, was not a day to ignore impulse.

Half an hour later I was wondering if I hadn't been just plain silly. The car had been giving me trouble for some time now with the engine coughing and losing power on hills. Each time it happened I promised myself I'd take it into the garage. Then it would seem all right for a while and I'd forget. This time I knew it was really serious when it started hiccoughing on a gentle down-slope, and sure enough on the next climb, which was only the tiny hump of a tiny humpback bridge, it wheezed to a halt.

I got out and kicked the door shut. No use to looko under the bonnet. Engines, though Latin, were Greek to me. I sat on the shallow parapet of the bridge and tried to recall how far back it was to a house or telephone. All I could remember was a signpost saying it was five miles to the little village of Little Bruton. It seemed peculiarly unjust somehow that a car that spent most of its time in town should break down in what was probably the least populated stretch of countryside within ten miles of the city boundary.

Sod's Law, isn't that what they call it? And that's what I called it, till gradually to the noise of chirruping birdsong and bubbling water was added a new sound and along that narrow country road I saw approaching a bright yellow Automobile Association van.

Now I began to wonder whether it might not after all be God's Law.

I flagged him down. He was on his way to a Home Start call in Little Bruton where some poor wage-slave newly woken and with miles to go before he slept had found his motor even more reluctant to start than he was.

"Engines like a lie-in too," said my rescuer merrily.

He was a very merry fellow altogether, full of jest, a marvellous advert for the AA. When he asked if I were a member and I told him I'd lapsed, he grinned and said, "Never mind. I'm a lapsed Catholic but I can always join again if things get desperate, can't I? Same for you. You are thinking of joining again, aren't you?"

"Oh yes," I said fervently. "You get this car started, and I might join the Church too!"

And I meant it. Not about the Church maybe, but certainly the AA.

Yet already, indeed from the moment I set eyes on his van, I'd been wondering if this might not be my chance to get more than just my car started.

But how to be certain? I felt my agitation growing till I stilled it with the comforting thought that, though indefinite to me, the author of my Great Adventure would never let its opening page be anything but clear.

The AA man was a great talker. We exchanged names. When I heard his, I repeated it slowly and he laughed and told me not to make the jokes, he'd heard them all before. But of course I wasn't thinking of jokes. He told me all about himself—his collection of tropical fish—the talk he'd given about them on local radio—his work for children's charities—his plan to make money for them by doing a sponsored run in the London marathon—the marvellous holiday he'd just had in Greece—his love of the warm evenings and Mediterranean cuisine—his delight in discovering a new Greek restaurant had just opened in town on his return.

"Sometimes you think there's someone up there looking after you special, don't you?" he jested. "Or maybe in my case, down there!"

I laughed and said I knew exactly what he meant.

And I meant it, in both ways, the conventional idle conversational sort of way, and the deeper, life-shapingly significant sort of way. In fact I felt very strongly that I was existing on two levels. There was a surface level on which I was standing enjoying the morning sunshine as I watched his oily fingers making the expert adjustments which I hoped would get me moving again. And there was another level where I was in touch with the force behind the light, the force which burnt away all fear—a level on which time had ceased to exist, where what was happening has always happened and will always be happening, where like an author I can pause, reflect, adjust, refine, till my words say precisely what I want them to say and show no trace of my passage . . .

For a moment my AA man stops talking as he makes a final adjustment with the engine running. He listens with the close attention of a piano tuner, smiles, switches off, and says, "Reckon that'll get you to Monte Carlo and back, if that's your pleasure." I say, "That's great. Thank you very much." He sits down on the parapet of the bridge and starts putting his tools into his tool box. Finished, he looks up into the sun, sighs a sigh of utter contentment and says, "You ever get those moments when you feel, this is it, this is the one I'd like never to end? Needn't be special, big occasion or anything like that. Just a morning like this, and you feel, I could stay here for ever."

"Yes," I tell him. "I know exactly what you mean."

"Would be nice, eh?" he says wistfully. "But no rest for the wicked, I'm afraid."

And he closes his box and starts to rise.

And now at last beyond all doubt the signal is given.

Down in the willows overhanging the stream on the far side of the bridge something barks, a fox I think, followed by a great squawk of what could have been raucous laughter; then out of the trailing greenery rockets a cock pheasant, wings beating desperately to lever its heavy body over the stonework and into the sky. It clears the far parapet by inches and comes straight at us. I step aside. The AA man steps backwards. The shallow parapet behind him catches his calves. The bird passes between us, I feel the furious beat of its wings like a Pentecostal wind. And the AA man flails his arms as if he too is trying to take off. But he is already unbalanced beyond recovery. I stretch out my hand to the teetering figure—to help or to push, who can tell?—and my fingertips brush against his, like God's and Adam's in the Sistine Chapel, or God's and Lucifer's on the battlements of heaven.

Then he is gone.

I look over the parapet. He has somersaulted in his fall and landed face down in the shallow stream below. It is only a few inches deep, but he isn't moving.

I scramble down the steep bank. It's clear what has happened. He has banged his head against a stone on the stream bed and stunned himself. As I watch, he moves and tries to raise his head out of the water.

Part of me wants to help him, but it is not a part that has any control over my hands or my feet. I have no choice but to stand and watch. Choice is a creature of time and time is away and somewhere else.

Three times his head lifts a little, three times falls back.

There is no fourth.

For a while bubbles rise. Perhaps he is using these last few exhalations to rejoin the Catholic Church. Certainly for him things are never going to be more desperate. On the other hand, he is at last getting his wish for one of those perfect moments to be extended forever, and wherever he finally lies at rest will, I am sure, be a happy grave.

Fast the bubbles come at first, then slower and slower, like the last oozings from a cider press, till up to the surface swims that final languid sac of air which, if the priests are right, ought to contain the soul.

Run well, my marathon messenger!

The bubble bursts.

And time too bursts back into my consciousness with all its impedimenta of mind and matter, rule and law.

I scrambled back up the bank and got into my car. Its engine sang such a merry song as I drove away that I blessed the skilful hands that had tuned it to this pitch. And I gave thanks too for this new, or rather this renewed life of mine.

My journey had begun. No doubt there would be obstacles along my path. But now that path was clearly signed. A journey of a thousand miles must begin with a single step.

And just by standing still and trusting in you, my guide, I had taken that step.

Talk again soon.

II

"Good lord," said Dick Dee.

"What?"

"Have you read this one?"

Rye Pomona sighed rather more stentoriously than was necessary and said with heavy sarcasm, "As we decided to split them down the middle, and as this is my pile here, and that is your pile there, and as the script in your hand comes from your pile and I am concentrating very hard on trying to get through my own pile, I don't really think there's much chance I've read it, is there?"

One of the good things about Dick Dee was that he took cheek very well, even from the most junior member of his staff. In fact, there were lots of good things about him. He knew his job as custodian of the Mid-Yorkshire County Library's Reference Department inside out and was both happy and able to communicate that knowledge. He did his share of work, and though she sometimes saw him working on the lexicological research for what he called his *minusculum opusculum,* it was always during his official breaks and never spread further, even when things were very quiet. At the same time he showed no sign of exasperation if her lunch hour overflowed a little. He passed no comment on her style of dress and neither averted his eyes prudishly from nor stared salaciously at the length of slim brown leg which emerged from the shallow haven of her mini dress. He had entertained her in his flat without the slightest hint of a pass (she wasn't altogether sure how she felt about that!). And though on their first encounter, his gaze had taken in her most striking feature, the single lock of silvery grey which shone among the rich brown tresses of her hair, he had been so courteously un-nosey about it that in the end she had got the topic out of the way by introducing it herself.

Nor did he use his seniority to offload all the most tedious jobs on to her but did his share, which would have made him a paragon if in the context of the present tedious job he'd been able to read more than a couple of pages at a time without wanting to share a thought with her. As it was, he grinned so broadly at her put-down that she felt immediately guilty and took the sheets of paper from his hand without further protest.

At least they were typed. Many weren't and she'd soon made the discovery long known to schoolteachers that even the neatest hand can be as inscrutable as leaves from the Delphic Oracle, with the additional disincentive that when you finally teased some meaning out of it, what you ended up with wasn't a useful divine pointer to future action but a God-awful dollop of prose fiction.

The Mid-Yorkshire Short Story Competition had been thought up by the editor of the *Mid-Yorkshire Gazette* and the Head of Mid-Yorkshire Library Services towards the end of a boozy Round Table dinner. Next morning, exposed to the light of day, the idea should have withered and died. Unfortunately, both Mary Agnew of the *Gazette* and Percy Follows, the Chief Librarian, had misrecollected that the other had undertaken to do most of the work and bear most of the cost. By the time they realized their common error, preliminary notices of the competition were in the public domain. Agnew, who like most veterans of the provincial press was a past mistress of making the best out of bad jobs, had now taken the initiative. She persuaded her proprietor to put up a small financial prize for the winning entry, which would also be published in the paper. And she obtained the services of a celebrity judge in the person of the Hon. Geoffrey Pyke-Strengler, whose main public qualification was that he was a published writer (a collection of sporting reminiscences from a life spent slaughtering fish, fowl and foxes), and whose main private qualification was that being both chronically hard-up and intermittently the *Gazette's* rural correspondent, he was in a position of dependency.

Follows was congratulating himself on having come rather well out of this when Agnew added that of course the Hon. (whose reading range didn't extend beyond the sporting magazines) couldn't be expected to plough through all the entries, that her team of ace reporters were far too busy writing their own deathless prose to read anyone else's, and that therefore she was looking to the library services with their acknowledged expertise in the field of prose fiction to sort out the entries and produce a short list.

Percy Follows knew when he'd been tagged and looked for someone on the library staff to tag in turn. All roads led to Dick Dee who, despite having an excellent degree in English, seemed never to have learned how to say no.

The best he could manage by way of demur was, "Well, we are rather busy . . . How many entries are you anticipating?"

"This sort of thing has a very limited appeal," said Follows confidently. "I'd be surprised if we get into double figures. Couple of dozen at the very most. You can run through them in your tea break."

"That's a hell of a lot of tea," grumbled Rye when the first sackful of scripts was delivered from the *Gazette*. But Dick Dee had just smiled as he looked at the mountain of paper and said, "It's mute inglorious Milton time, Rye. Let's start sorting them out."

The initial sorting out had been fun.

The idea of refusing to read anything not typewritten had seemed very attractive, but rapidly they realized this was too Draconian. On the other hand as more sackloads arrived, they knew they had to have some rules of inadmissibility.

"Nothing in green ink," said Dee.

"Nothing on less than A5," said Rye.

"Nothing handwritten where the letters aren't joined up."

"Nothing without meaningful punctuation."

"Nothing which requires use of a magnifying glass."

"Nothing that has organic matter adhering to it," said Rye, picking up a sheet which looked as if it had recently lined a cat tray.

Then she'd thought that perhaps the offending stain had come from some baby whose housebound mother was desperately trying to be creative at feeding time, and residual guilt had made her protest strongly when Dick had gone on, "And nothing sexually explicit or containing four-letter words."

He had listened to her liberal arguments with great patience, showing no resentment of her implied accusation that he was at best a frump, at worst a fascist.

When she finished, he said mildly, "Rye, I agree with you that there is nothing depraved, disgusting or even distasteful about a good fuck. But as I know beyond doubt that there's no way any story containing either a description of the act or a derivative of the word is going to get published in the *Gazette,* it seems to me a useful filter device. Of course, if you want to read every word of every story . . ."

The arrival of yet another sackful from the *Gazette* had been a clincher.

A week later, with stories still pouring in and nine days to go before the competition closed, she had become much more dismissive than Dee, spinning scripts across to the dump bin after an opening paragraph, an opening sentence even, or, in some cases, just the title, while he read through nearly all of his and was building a much higher *possibles* pile.

Now she looked at the script he had interrupted her with and said, "*First Dialogue?* That mean there's going to be more?"

"Poetic licence, I expect. Anyway, read it. I'd be interested to hear what you think."

A new voice interrupted them.

"Found the new Maupassant yet, Dick?"

Suddenly the light was blocked out as a long lean figure loomed over Rye from behind.

She didn't need to look up to know this was Charley Penn, one of the reference library's regulars and the nearest thing Mid-Yorkshire had to a literary lion. He'd written a moderately successful series of what he called historical romances and the critics bodice-rippers, set against the background of revolutionary Europe in the decades leading up to 1848, with a hero loosely based on the German poet Heine. These had been made into a popular TV series where the ripping of bodices was certainly rated higher than either history or even romance. His regular attendance in the reference library had nothing to do with the pursuit of verisimilitude in his fictions. In his cups he had been heard to say of his readers, "You can tell the buggers owt. What do they know?" though in fact he had acquired a wide knowledge of the period in question through the "real" work he'd been researching now for many years, which was a critical edition with metrical translation of Heine's poems. Rye had been surprised to learn that he was a school contemporary of Dick Dee. The ten years which Dee's equanimity of temperament erased from his forty-something seemed to have been dumped on Penn, whose hollow cheeks, deep-set eyes and unkempt beard gave him the look of an old Viking who'd ravished and pillaged a raid too far.

"Probably not," said Dee. "Be glad of your professional opinion though, Charley."

Penn moved round the table so that he was looking down at Rye and showed uneven teeth in what she called his smarl, assuming he intended it as a smile and couldn't help that it came out like a snarl. "Not unless you've got a sudden budget surplus."

When it came to professional opinions, or indeed any activity connected with his profession, Charley Penn's insistence that time equalled money made lawyers seem open-handed.

"So how can I help you?" said Dee.

"Those articles you were tracking down for me, any sign yet?"

Penn had no difficulty squaring his assertion that the labourer was worthy his hire with using Dee as his unpaid research assistant, but the librarian never complained.

"I'll just check to see if there's anything in today's post," he said.

He rose and went into the office behind the desk.

Penn remained, his gaze fixed on Rye.

She looked back unblinkingly and said, "Yes?"

From time to time she'd caught the old Viking looking at her like he was once more feeling the call of the sea, though so far he'd stopped short of rapine and pillage. In fact his preferred model seemed to be that guy in the play (what the hell was his name?) who went around the Forest of Arden, pinning poems to trees. From time to time scraps of Penn's Heine translations would be put in her way. She'd open a file or pick up a book and there would be a few lines about a despairing lover staring down at himself staring up at his beloved's window or a lonely northern fir-tree pining for the hand of an unattainably distant palm. Their presence was explained, if explanation were demanded, by inadvertence, accompanied by a knowing version of the smarl which was what she got now as Penn said, "Enjoy," and went after Dee.

Now Rye gave her full attention to the *First Dialogue*, skimming through it rapidly, then reading it again more slowly.

By the time she'd finished, Dee had returned and Penn was back in his usual seat in one of the study alcoves from which he had been known to bellow abuse at young students whose ideas of silence did not accord with his own.

"What do you think?" said Dee.

"Why the hell am I reading this? is what I think," said Rye. "OK, the writer's trying to be clever, using a single episode to hint at a whole epic to come, but it doesn't really work, does it? I mean, what's it about? Some kind of metaphor of life or what? And what the hell's that funny illustration all about? I hope you're not showing me this as the best thing you've come across. If so, I don't want to look at any of the other stuff in your possibles pile."

He shook his head, smiling. No smarl this. He had a rather nice smile. One of the rather nice things about it was that he used it alike to greet compliment or insult, triumph or disaster. A couple of days earlier for instance a lesser man might have flapped when a badly plugged shelf had collapsed under the weight of the twenty-volume *Oxford English Dictionary*, scattering a party of civic dignitaries on a tour of the borough's newly refurbished Heritage, Arts and Library Centre. Only one of the visitors had been hit, receiving the full weight of Volume II on his toe. This was Councillor Cyril Steel, a virulent opponent of the Centre whose voice had frequently been raised in the council against "wasting good public money on a load of airy nowt." Percy Follows had run around like a panicked poodle, fearing a PR disaster, but Dee had merely smiled into the TV camera recording the event for BBC Mid-Yorks and said, "Now even Councillor Steel will have to admit that a little learning can be a dangerous thing and not all our nowts are completely airy," and continued with his explanatory address.

Now he said, "No, I'm not suggesting this as a contender for the prize, though it's not badly written. As for the drawing, it's part illustration and part illumination, I think. But what's really interesting is the way it chimes with something I read in today's *Gazette*."

He picked up a copy of the *Mid-Yorkshire Gazette* from the newspaper rack. The *Gazette* came out twice weekly, on Wednesdays and Saturdays. This was the midweek edition. He opened it at the second page, set it before her and indicated a column with his thumb.

AA MAN DIES IN TRAGIC ACCIDENT

The body of Mr. Andrew Ainstable (34), a patrol officer with the Automobile Association, was found apparently drowned in a shallow stream running under the Little Bruton road on Tuesday morning. Thomas Killiwick (27) a local farmer who made the discovery theorized that Mr. Ainstable, who it emerged was on his way to a Home Start call at Little Bruton, may have stopped for a call of nature, slipped, and banged his head, but the police are unable to confirm or to deny this theory at this juncture.

Mr. Ainstable is survived by his wife, Agnes, and a widowed mother. An inquest is expected to be called in the next few days.

"So what do you think?" asked Dee again.

"I think from the style of this report that they were probably wise at the *Gazette* to ask us to judge the literary merit of these stories," said Rye.

"No. I mean this Dialogue thing. Bit of an odd coincidence, don't you think?"

"Not really. I mean, it's probably not a coincidence at all. Writers must often pick up ideas from what they read in the papers."

"But this wasn't in the *Gazette* till this morning. And this came out of the bag of entries they sent round last night. So presumably they got it some time yesterday, the same day this poor chap died, and before the writer could have read about it."

"OK, so it's a coincidence after all," said Rye irritably. "I've just read a story about a man who wins the lottery and has a heart attack. I dare say that this week somewhere there's been a man who won something in the lottery and had a heart attack. It didn't catch the attention of the Pulitzer prize mob at the *Gazette*, but it's still a coincidence."

"All the same," said Dee, clearly reluctant to abandon his sense of oddness. "Another thing, there's no pseudonym."

The rules of entry required that, in the interests of impartial judging, entrants used a pseudonym under their story title. They also wrote these on a sealed envelope containing their real name and address. The envelopes were kept at the *Gazette* office.

"So he forgot," said Rye. "Not that it matters, anyway. It's not going to win, is it? So who cares who wrote it? Now, can I get on?"

Dick Dee had no argument against this. But Rye noticed he didn't put the typescript either into the dump bin or on to his *possibles* pile, but set it aside.

Shaking her head, Rye turned her attention to the next story on her pile. It was called *Dreamtime*, written in purple ink in a large spiky hand averaging four words to a line, and it began:

When I woke up this morning I found I'd had a wet dream, and as I lay there trying to recall it, I found myself getting excited again . . .

With a sigh, she skimmed it over into the dump bin and picked another.

III

"What the fuck are you playing at, Roote?" snarled Peter Pascoe.

Snarling wasn't a form of communication that came easily to him, and attempting to keep his upper teeth bared while emitting the plosive P produced a sound effect which was melodramatically Oriental with little of the concomitant sinisterity. He must pay more attention next time his daughter's pet dog, which didn't much like men, snarled at him.

Roote pushed the notebook he'd been scribbling in beneath a copy of the *Gazette* and regarded him with an expression of amiable bewilderment.

"Sorry, Mr. Pascoe? You've lost me. I'm not playing at anything and I don't think I know the rules of the game you're playing. Do I need a racket too?"

He smiled towards Pascoe's sports bag from which protruded the shaft of a squash racket.

Cue for another snarl on the line, *Don't get clever with me, Roote!*

This was getting like a bad TV script.

As well as snarling he'd been trying to loom menacingly. He had no way of knowing how menacing his looming looked to the casual observer, but it was playing hell with the strained shoulder muscle which had brought his first game of squash in five years to a premature conclusion. *Premature?* Thirty seconds into foreplay isn't premature, it is humiliatingly pre-penetrative.

His opponent had been all concern, administering embrocation in the changing room and lubrication in the University Staff Club bar, with no sign whatsoever of snigger. Nevertheless, Pascoe had felt himself sniggered at and when he made his way through the pleasant formal gardens towards the car park and saw Franny Roote smiling at him from a bench, his carefully suppressed irritation had broken through and before he had time to think rationally he was deep into loom and snarl.

Time to rethink his role.

He made himself relax, sat down on the bench, leaned back, winced, and said, "OK, Mr. Roote. Let's start again. Would you mind telling me what you're doing here?"

"Lunch break," said Roote. He held up a brown paper bag and emptied its contents on to the newspaper. "Baguette, salad with mayo, low fat. Apple, Granny Smith. Bottle of water, tap."

That figured. He didn't look like a man on a high-energy diet. He was thin just this side of emaciation, a condition exacerbated by his black slacks and T-shirt. His face was white as a piece of honed driftwood and his blond hair was cut so short he might as well have been bald.

"Mr. Roote," said Pascoe carefully, "you live and work in Sheffield which means that even with a very generous lunch break and a very fast car, this would seem an eccentric choice of luncheon venue. Also this is the third, no I think it's the fourth time I have spotted you in my vicinity over the past week."

The first time had been a glimpse in the street as he drove home from Mid-Yorkshire Police HQ early one evening. Then a couple of nights later as he and Ellie rose to leave a cinema, he'd noticed Roote sitting half a dozen rows further back. And the previous Sunday as he took his daughter, Rosie, for a stroll in Charter Park to feed the swans, he was sure he'd spotted the black-clad figure standing on the edge of the unused bandstand.

That's when he'd made a note to ring Sheffield, but he'd been too busy to do it on Monday and by Tuesday it had seemed too trivial to make a fuss over. But now on Wednesday like a black bird of ill omen, here was the man once more, this time too close for mere coincidence.

"Oh gosh, yes, I see. In fact I've noticed you a couple of times too, and when I saw you coming out of the Staff Club just now, I thought, Good job you're not paranoiac, Franny boy, else you might think Chief Inspector Pascoe is stalking you."

This was a reversal to take the breath away.

Also a warning to proceed with great care.

He said, "So, coincidence for both of us. Difference is, of course, I live and work here."

"Me too," said Roote. "Don't mind if I start, do you? Only get an hour."

He bit deep into the baguette. His teeth were perfectly, almost artistically, regular and had the kind of brilliant whiteness which you expected to see reflecting the flashbulbs at a Hollywood opening. Prison service dentistry must have come on apace in the past few years.

"You live and work here?" said Pascoe. "Since when?"

Roote chewed and swallowed.

"Couple of weeks," he said.

"And why?"

Roote smiled. The teeth again. He'd been a very beautiful boy.

"Well, I suppose it's really down to you, Mr. Pascoe. Yes, you could say you're the reason I came back."

An admission? Even a confession? No, not with Franny Roote, the great controller. Even when you changed the script in mid-scene, you still felt he was still in charge of direction.

"What's that mean?" asked Pascoe.

"Well, you know, after that little misunderstanding in Sheffield, I lost my job at the hospital. No, please, don't think I'm blaming you, Mr. Pascoe. You were only doing your job, and it was my own choice to slit my wrists. But the hospital people seemed to think it showed I was sick, and of course, sick people are the last people you want in a hospital. Unless they're on their backs, of course. So soon as I was discharged, I was . . . discharged."

"I'm sorry," said Pascoe.

"No, please, like I say, not your responsibility. In any case, I could have fought it, the staff association were ready to take up the cudgels and all my friends were very supportive. Yes, I'm sure a tribunal would have found in my favour. But it felt like time to move on. I didn't get religion inside, Mr. Pascoe, not in the formal sense, but I certainly came to see that there is a time for all things under the sun and a man is foolish to ignore the signs. So don't worry yourself."

He's offering me absolution! thought Pascoe. One moment I'm snarling and looming, next I'm on my knees being absolved!

He said, "That still doesn't explain . . ."

"Why I'm here?" Roote took another bite, chewed, swallowed. "I'm working for the university gardens department. Bit of a change, I know. Very welcome, though. Hospital portering's a worthwhile job, but you're inside most of the time, and working with dead people a lot of the time. Now I'm outdoors, and everything's alive! Even with autumn coming on, there's still so much of life and growth around. OK, there's winter to look forward to, but that's not the end of things, is it? Just a lying dormant, conserving energy, waiting for the signal to re-emerge and blossom again. Bit like prison, if that's not too fanciful."

I'm being jerked around here, thought Pascoe. Time to crack the whip.

"The world's full of gardens," he said coldly. "Why this one? Why have you come back to Mid-Yorkshire?"

"Oh, I'm sorry, I should have said. That's my other job, my real work—my thesis. You know about my thesis? *Revenge and Retribution in English Drama?* Of course you do. It was that which helped set you off in the wrong direction, wasn't it? I can see how it would, with Mrs. Pascoe being threatened and all. You got that sorted, did you? I never read anything in the papers."

He paused and looked enquiringly at Pascoe who said, "Yes, we got it sorted. No, there wasn't much in the papers."

Because there'd been a security cover-up, but Pascoe wasn't about to go into that. Irritated though he was by Roote, and deeply suspicious of his motives, he still felt guilty at the memory of what had happened. With Ellie being threatened from an unknown source, he'd cast around for likely suspects. Discovering that Roote, whom he'd put away as an accessory to murder some years ago, was now out and writing a thesis on revenge in Sheffield where he was working as a hospital porter, he'd got South Yorkshire to shake him up a bit then gone down himself to have a friendly word. On arrival, he'd found Roote in the bath with his wrists slashed, and when later he'd had to admit that Roote had no involvement whatsoever in the case he was investigating, the probation service had not been slow to cry harassment.

Well, he'd been able to show he'd gone by the book. Just. But he'd felt then the same mixture of guilt and anger he was feeling now.

Roote was talking again.

"Anyway, my supervisor at Sheffield got a new post at the university here, just started this term. He's the one who helped me get fixed up with the gardening job, in fact, so you see how it all slotted in. I could have got a new supervisor, I suppose, but I've just got to the most interesting part of my thesis. I mean, the Elizabethans and Jacobeans have been fascinating, of course, but they've been so much pawed over by the scholars, it's difficult to come up with much that's really new. But now I'm on to the

Romantics: Byron, Shelley, Coleridge, even Wordsworth, they all tried their hands at drama you know. But it's Beddoes that really fascinates me. Do you know his play *Death's Jest-Book*?"

"No," said Pascoe. "Should I?"

In fact, it came to him as he spoke that he had heard the name Beddoes recently.

"Depends what you mean by *should*. Deserves to be better known. It's fantastic. And as my supervisor's writing a book on Beddoes and probably knows more about him than any man living, I just had to stick with him. But it's a long way to travel from Sheffield even with a decent car, and the only thing I've been able to afford has more breakdowns than an inner-city teaching staff! It really made sense for me to move too. So everything's turned out for the best in the best of all possible worlds!"

"This supervisor," said Pascoe, "what's his name?"

He didn't need to ask. He'd recalled where he'd heard Beddoes' name mentioned, and he knew the answer already.

"He's got the perfect name for an Eng. Lit. teacher," said Roote, laughing. "Johnson. Dr. Sam Johnson. Do you know him?"

"That's when I made an excuse and left," said Pascoe.

"Oh aye? Why was that?" said Detective Superintendent Andrew Dalziel. "Fucking useless thing!"

It was, Pascoe hoped, the VCR squeaking under the assault of his pistonlike finger that Dalziel was addressing, not himself.

"Because it was Sam Johnson I'd just been playing squash with," he said, rubbing his shoulder. "It seemed like Roote was taking the piss and I felt like taking a swing, so I went straight back inside and caught Sam."

"And?"

And Johnson had confirmed every word.

It turned out the lecturer knew his student's background without knowing the details. Pascoe's involvement in the case had come as a surprise to him but, once filled in, he'd cut right to the chase and said, "If you think that Fran's got any ulterior motive in coming back here, forget it. Unless he's got so much influence he arranged for me to get a job here, it's all happenstance. I moved, he didn't fancy travelling for supervision and the job he had in Sheffield came to an end, so it made sense for him to make a change too. I'm glad he did. He's a really bright student."

Johnson had been out of the country during the long vacation and so missed the saga of Roote's apparent suicide attempt, and the young man clearly hadn't belly-ached to him about police harassment in general and Pascoe harassment in particular, which ought to have been a point in his favour.

The lecturer concluded by saying, "So I got him the gardening job, which is why he's out there in the garden, and he lives in town, which is why you see him around town. It's coincidence that makes the world go round, Peter. Ask Shakespeare."

"This Johnson," said Dalziel, "how come you're so chummy you take showers together? He fag for you at Eton or summat?"

Dalziel affected to believe that the academic world which had given Pascoe his degree occupied a single site somewhere in the south where Oxford and Cambridge and all the major public schools huddled together under one roof.

In fact it wasn't Pascoe's but his wife's links with the academic and literary worlds which had brought Johnson into their lives. Part of Johnson's job brief at MYU was to help establish an embryonic creative writing course. His qualification was that he'd published a couple of slim volumes of poetry and helped run such a course at Sheffield. Charley Penn, who made occasional contributions to both German and English Department courses, had been miffed to find his own expression of interest ignored. He ran a local authority literary group in danger of being axed and clearly felt that the creative writing post at MYU would have been an acceptable palliative for the loss of his LEA honorarium. Colleagues belonging to that breed not uncommon in academia, *the greater green-eyed pot-stirrer*, had advised Johnson to watch his back as Penn made a bad enemy, at a physical as well as a verbal level. A few years earlier, according to university legend, a brash young female journalist had done a piss-taking review of the Penn oeuvre in *Yorkshire Life*, the county's glossiest mag. The piece had concluded, "They say the pen is mightier than the sword, but if you have a sweet tooth and a strong stomach, the best implement to deal with our Mr. Penn's frothy confections might be a pudding spoon." The following day Penn, lunching liquidly in a Leeds restaurant, had spotted the journalist across a crowded dessert trolley. Selecting a large portion of strawberry gateau liberally coated with whipped cream, he had approached her table, said, "This, madam, is a frothy confection," and squashed the pudding on to her head. In court he had said, "It wasn't personal. I did it not because of what she said about my books but because of her appalling style. English must be kept up," before being fined fifty pounds and bound over to keep the peace.

Sam Johnson had immediately sought out Penn and said, "I believe you know more about Heine than anyone else in Yorkshire."

"That wouldn't be hard. They say you know more about Beddoes than anyone in The Dog and Duck at closing time."

"I know he went to Göttingen University to study medicine in 1824 and Heine was there studying law."

"Oh aye? And Hitler and Wittgenstein were in the same class at school. So what?"

"So why don't we flaunt our knowledge in The Dog and Duck one night?"

"Well, it's quiz night tonight. You never know. It might come up."

Thus had armistice been signed before hostilities proper began. When talk finally turned to the writing course, Penn, after token haggling, accepted terms for making the occasional "old pro" appearance, and went on to suggest that if Johnson was interested in a contribution from someone at the other end of the ladder, he might do worse than soon-to-be-published novelist Ellie Pascoe, an old acquaintance from her days on the university staff and a member of the threatened literary group.

This version of that first encounter was cobbled together from the slightly different accounts Ellie received from both participants. She and Johnson had hit it off straightaway. When she invited him home for a meal, the conversation had naturally centred on matters literary, and Pascoe, feeling rather sidelined, had leapt into the breach when Johnson had casually mentioned his difficulty in finding a squash partner among his generally unathletic colleagues.

His reward for this friendly gesture when Johnson finally left, late, in a taxi, had been for Ellie to say, "This game of squash, Peter, you will be careful."

Indignantly Pascoe said, "I'm not quite decrepit, you know."

"I'm not talking about you. I meant, with Sam. He's got a heart problem."

"As well as a drink problem? Jesus!"

In the event it had turned out that Johnson suffered from a mild drug-controllable tachycardia, but Pascoe wasn't looking forward to describing to his wife the rapid and undignified conclusion of his game with someone he'd categorized as an alcoholic invalid.

"Mate of Ellie's, eh?" said Dalziel with a slight intake of breath and a sharp shake of the VCR which, with greater economy than a Special Branch file, consigned Johnson to the category of radical, subversive, Trotskyite trouble-maker.

"Acquaintance," said Pascoe. "Do you want a hand with that, sir?"

"No. I reckon I can throw it out of the window myself. You're very quiet, mastermind. What do you reckon?"

Sergeant Edgar Wield was standing before the deep sash-window. Silhouetted against the golden autumn sunlight, his face deep shadowed, he had the grace and proportions to model for the statue of a Greek athlete, thought Pascoe. Then he moved forward and his features took on detail, and you remembered that if this were a statue, it was one whose face someone had taken a hammer to.

"I reckon you need to look at the whole picture," he said. "Way back when Roote were a student at Holm Coultram College before it became part of the university, he got sent down as an accessory to two murders, mainly on your evidence. From the dock he says he looks forward to the chance of meeting you somewhere quiet one day and carrying on your interrupted conversation. As the last time you saw him alone he was trying to stove your head in with a rock, you take this as a threat. But we all get threatened at least once a week. It's part of the job."

Dalziel, studying the machine like a Sumo wrestler working out a new strategy, growled, "Get a move on, Frankenstein, else I'll start to wish I hadn't plugged you in."

Undeterred, Wield proceeded at a measured pace.

"Model prisoner, Open University degree, Roote gets maximum remission, comes out, gets job as a hospital porter, starts writing an academic thesis, obeys all the rules. Then you get upset by them threats to Ellie and naturally Roote's one of the folk you need to take a closer look at. Only when you go to see him, you find he's slashed his wrists."

"He knew I was coming," said Pascoe. "It was a set-up. No real danger to him. Just a perverted joke."

"Maybe. Not the way it looked when it turned out Roote had absolutely nothing to do with the threats to Ellie," said Wield. "He recovers, and a few months later he moves here because (a) his supervisor has moved here and (b) he can get work here. You say you checked with the probation service?"

"Yes," said Pascoe. "All done by the book. They wanted to know if there was a problem."

"What did you tell the buggers?" said Dalziel, who classed probation officers with Scottish midges, vegetarians and modern technology as Jobian tests of a virtuous man's patience.

"I said no, just routine."

"Wise move," approved Wield. "See how it looks. Man serves his time, puts his life back together, gets harassed without cause by insensitive police officer, flips, tries to harm himself, recovers, gets back on track, finds work again, minds his own business, then this same officer starts accusing him of being some sort of stalker. It's you who comes out looking like either a neurotic headcase or a vengeful bastard. While Roote . . . just a guy who's paid his debt and wants nothing except to live a quiet life. I mean, he didn't even want the hassle of bringing a harassment case against you, or a wrongful dismissal case against the Sheffield hospital."

He moved from the window to the desk.

"Aye," said Dalziel thoughtfully. "That's the most worrying thing, him not wanting to kick up a fuss. Well, lad, it's up to you. But me, I know what I'd do."

"And what's that, sir?" enquired Pascoe.

"Break both his legs and run him out of town."

"I think perhaps the other way round might be better," said Pascoe judiciously.

"You reckon? Either way, you can stick this useless thing up his arse first."

He glowered at the VCR which, as if in response to that fearsome gaze, clicked into life and a picture blossomed on the TV screen.

"There," said the Fat Man triumphantly. "Told you no lump of tin and wires could get the better of me."

Pascoe glanced at Wield who was quietly replacing the remote control unit on the desk, and grinned.

An announcer was saying, "And now *Out and About,* your regional magazine programme from BBC Mid-Yorkshire, presented by Jax Ripley."

Titles over an aerial panorama of town and countryside accompanied by the first few bars of "On Ilkla Moor Baht 'at" played by a brass band, all fading to the slight, almost childish figure of a young blonde with bright blue eyes and a wide mouth stretched in a smile through which white teeth gleamed like a scimitar blade.

"Hi," she said. "Lots of goodies tonight, but first, are we getting the policing we deserve, the policing we pay for? Here's how it looks from the dirty end of the stick."

A rapid montage of burgled houses and householders all expressing, some angrily, some tearfully, their sense of being abandoned by the police. Back to the blonde, who recited a list of statistics which she then précis'd: "So four out of ten cases don't get looked at by CID in the first twenty-four hours, six out of ten cases get only one visit and the rest is silence, and eight out of ten cases remain permanently unsolved. In fact, as of last month there were more than two hundred unsolved current cases on Mid-Yorkshire CID's books. Inefficiency? Underfunding? Understaffing? Certainly we are told that the decision not to replace a senior CID officer who comes up to retirement shortly is causing much soul searching, or, to put it another way, a bloody great row. But when we invited Mid-Yorkshire Constabulary to send someone along to discuss these matters, a spokesman said they were unable to comment at this time. Maybe that means they are all too busy dealing with the crime wave. I would like to think so. But we do have Councillor Cyril Steel, who has long been interested in police matters. Councillor Steel, I gather you feel we are not getting the service we pay for?"

A bald-headed man with mad eyes opened his mouth to show brown and battlemented teeth, but before he could let fly his arrows of criticism, the screen went dark as Dalziel ripped the plug out of the wall socket.

"Too early in the day to put up with Stuffer," he said with a shudder.

"We must be able to take honest criticism, sir," said Pascoe solemnly. "Even from Councillor Steel."

He was being deliberately provocative. Steel, once a Labour councillor but now an Independent after the Party ejected him in face of his increasingly violent attacks on the leadership, hurling charges which ranged from cronyism to corruption, was the self-appointed leader of a crusade against the misuse of public money. His targets included everything from the building of the Heritage, Arts and Library Centre to the provision of digestive biscuits at council committee meetings, so it was hardly surprising that he should have rushed forward to lend his weight to Jax Ripley's investigation into the way police resources were managed in Mid-Yorkshire.

"Not his criticism that bothers me," growled Dalziel. "Have you ever got near him? Teeth you could grow moss on and breath like a vegan's fart. I can smell it through the telly. Only time Stuffer's not talking is when he's eating, and not always then. No one listens any more. No, it's Jax the bloody Ripper who bothers me. She's got last month's statistics, she knows about the decision not to replace George Headingley and, looking at the state of some of them burgled houses, she must have been round there with her little camera afore we were!"

"So you still reckon someone's talking?" said Pascoe.

"It's obvious. How many times in the last few months has she been one jump ahead of us? Past six months, to be precise. I checked back."

"Six months? And you think that might be significant? Apart from the fact, of course, that Miss Ripley started doing the programme only seven months ago?"

"Aye, it could be significant," said Dalziel grimly.

"Maybe she's just good at her job," said Pascoe. "And surely it's no bad thing for the world to know we're not getting a replacement DI for George? Perhaps we should use her instead of getting our knickers in a twist."

"You don't use a rat," said Dalziel. "You block up the hole it's feeding through. And I've got a bloody good idea where to find this hole."

Pascoe and Wield exchanged glances. They knew where the Fat Man's suspicions lay, knew the significance he put on the period of six months. This was just about the length of time Mid-Yorkshire CID's newest recruit, Detective Constable Bowler, had been on the team. Bowler—known to his friends as Hat and to his arch-foe as Boiler, Boghead, Bowels or any other pejorative variation which occurred to him—had started with the heavy handicap of being a fast-track graduate, on transfer from the Midlands without Dalziel's opinion being sought or his approval solicited. The Fat Man was Argos-eyed in Mid-Yorkshire and a report that the new DC had been spotted having a drink with Jacqueline Ripley not long after his arrival had been filed away till the first of the items which had seen her rechristened Jax the Ripper had appeared. Since then Bowler had been given the status of man-most-likely, but nothing had yet been proved, which, to Pascoe at least, knowing how close a surveillance was being kept, suggested he was innocent.

But he knew better than to oppose a Dalzielesque obsession. Also, the Fat Man had a habit of being right.

He said brightly, "Well, I suppose we'd better go and solve some crimes in case there's a hidden camera watching us. Thank you both for your input on my little problem."

"What? Oh, that," said Dalziel dismissively. "Seems to me the only problem you've got is knowing whether you've really got a problem."

"Oh yes, I'm certain of that. I think I've got the same problem Hector was faced with last year."

"Eh?" said Dalziel, puzzled by this reference to Mid-Yorkshire's most famously incompetent constable. "Remind me."

"Don't you remember? He went into that warehouse to investigate a possible intruder. There was a guard dog, big Ridgeback I think, lying down just inside the doorway."

"Oh yes, I recall. Hector had to pass it. And he didn't know if it was dead, drugged, sleeping or just playing doggo, waiting to pounce, that was his problem, right?"

"No," said Pascoe. "He gave it a kick to find out. And it opened its eyes. *That* was his problem."

IV

the second dialogue

Hi.

It's me again. How's it going?

Remember our riddles? Here's a new one.

> *One for the living, one for the dead,*
> *Out on the moor I wind about*
> *Nor rhyme nor reason in my head*
> *Yet reasons I have without a doubt.*
>
> *Deep printed on the yielding land*
> *Each zig and zag makes perfect sense*
> *To those who recognize the hand*
> *Of nature's clerk experience.*
>
> *This tracks a chasm deep and wide,*
> *That skirts a bog, this finds a ford,*
> *And men have suffered, men have died,*
> *To learn this wisdom of my Word—*
>
> *—That seeming right is sometimes wrong*
> *And even on the clearest days*

The shortest way may still be long,
The straightest line may form a maze.

What am I?

Got it yet?

You were always a smart dog at a riddle!
I've been thinking a lot about paths lately, the paths of the living, the paths of the dead, how maybe there's only one path, and I have set my foot upon it.
I was pretty busy for a few days after my Great Adventure began, so I had little chance to mark its beginning by any kind of celebration. But as the weekend approached, I felt an urge to do something different, a little special. And I recalled my cheerful AA man telling me how chuffed he'd been on his return from Corfu to discover that a new Greek restaurant had just opened in town.
"In Cradle Street, the Taverna," he said. "Good nosh and there's a courtyard out back where they've got tables and parasols. Of course, it's not like sitting outside in Corfu, but on a fine evening with the sun shining and the waiters running around in costume, and this chap twanging away on one of them Greek banjos, you can close your eyes and imagine you're back in the Med."
It was really nice to hear someone being so enthusiastic about foreign travel and food and everything. Most Brits tend to go abroad just for the sake of confirming their superiority to everyone else in the world.

Down there too?
There's no changing human nature.
Anyway, I thought I'd give the Taverna a try.
The food wasn't bad and the wine was OK, though I abandoned my experiment with retsina after a single glass. It was just a little chilly at first, sitting outside in the courtyard under the artificial olive trees, but the food soon warmed me up, and with the table candles lit, the setting looked really picturesque. Inside the restaurant a young man was singing to his own accompaniment. I couldn't see the instrument but it gave a very authentic Greek sound and his playing was rather better than his voice. Eventually he came out into the courtyard and started a tour of the tables, serenading the diners. Some people made requests, most of them for British or at best Italian songs, but he tried to oblige everyone. As he reached my table, the PA system suddenly burst

into life and a voice said, "It's Zorba time!" and two of the waiters started doing that awful Greek dancing. I saw the young musician wince, then he caught my eye and grinned sheepishly.

I smiled back and pointed to his instrument, and asked him what its name was, interested to hear if his speaking voice was as "Greek" as his singing voice. It was a bazouki, he said in a broad Mid-Yorkshire accent. "Oh, you aren't Greek then?" I said, sounding disappointed to conceal the surge of exultation I was feeling. He laughed and admitted quite freely he was local, born, bred and still living out at Carker. He was a music student at the university, finding it impossible like so many of them to exist on the pittance they call a grant these days and plumping it out a bit by working in the Taverna most evenings. But while he wasn't Greek, his instrument he assured me certainly was, a genuine bazouki brought home from Crete by his grandfather who'd fought there during the Second World War, so its music had first been heard beneath real olive trees in a warm and richly perfumed Mediterranean night.

I could detect in his voice a longing for that distant reality he described just as I'd seen in his face a disgust with this fakery he was involved in. Yorkshire born and bred he might be, but his soul yearned for something that he had persuaded himself could still be found under other less chilly skies. Poor boy. He had the open hopeful look of one born to be disappointed. I yearned to save him from the shattering of his illusions.

The canned music was growing louder and the dancing waiters who'd been urging more and more customers to join their line were getting close to my table, so I tucked some coins into the leather pouch dangling from the boy's tunic, paid my bill and left.

It was after midnight when the restaurant closed but I didn't mind sitting in my car, waiting. There is a pleasure in observing and not being observed, in standing in the shadows watching the creatures of the night going about their business. I saw several cats pad purposefully down the alleyway alongside the Taverna where they kept their rubbish bins. An owl floated between the chimneys, remote and silent as a satellite. And I glimpsed what I'm sure was the bushy tail of an urban fox frisking round the corner of a house. But it was the human creatures I was most interested in, the last diners striding, staggering, drifting, driving off into the night, little patches of Stimmungsbild— voices calling, footsteps echoing, car doors banging, engines revving—which played for a moment against the great symphony of the night, then faded away, leaving its dark music untouched.

Then comes a long pause—not in time but of time—how long I don't know for clocks are blank-faced now—till finally I hear a motorbike revving up in the alleyway and my boy appears at its mouth, a musician making his entry into the music of the night. I know it's him despite the shielding helmet—would have known without the evidence of the bazouki case strapped behind him.

He pauses to check the road is empty. Then he pulls out and rides away.

I follow. It's easy to keep in touch. He stays well this side of the speed limit, probably knowing from experience how ready the police are to hassle young bikers, especially late at night. Once it becomes clear he's heading straight home to Carker, I overtake and pull away.

I have no plan but I know from the merriment bubbling up inside me that a plan exists, and when I pass the derestriction sign at the edge of town and find myself on the old Roman Way, that gently undulating road which runs arrow-straight down an avenue of beeches all the five miles south to Carker, I understand what I have to do.

I leave the lights of town behind me and accelerate away. After a couple of miles, I do a U-turn on the empty road, pull on to the verge, and switch off my lights but not my engine.

Darkness laps over me like black water. I don't mind. I am its denizen. This is my proper domain.

Now I see him. First a glow, then an effulgence, hurtling towards me. What young man, even one conditioned to carefulness by police persecution, could resist the temptation of such a stretch of road so clearly empty of traffic?

Ah, the rush of the wind in his face, the throb of the engine between his thighs, and in the corners of his vision the blur of trees lined up like an audience of old gods to applaud his passage!

I feel his joy, share in his mirth. Indeed, I'm so full of it I almost miss my cue.

But the old gods are talking to me also, and with no conscious command from my mind, my foot stamps down on the accelerator and my hand flicks on full headlights.

For a fraction of a second we are heading straight for each other. Then his muscles like mine obey commands too quick for his mind, and he swerves, skids, wrestles for control.

For a second I think he has it.

I am disappointed and relieved.

All right, I know, but I have to be honest. What a weight—and a wait— it would be off my soul if this turned out not to be my path after all.

But now the boy begins to feel it go. Yet still, even at this moment of ulti-mate danger, his heart must be singing with the thrill, the thrust, of it. Then the bike slides away from under him, they part company, and man and machine hurtle along the road in parallel, close but no longer touching.

I come to a halt and turn my head to watch. In time it takes probably a few seconds. In my no-time I can register every detail. I see that it is the bike which hits a tree first, disintegrating in a burst of flame, not much—his tank must have been low—but enough to throw a brief lurid light on his last moment.

He hits a broad-boled beech tree, seems to embrace it with his whole body, wrapping himself around it as if he longs to penetrate its smooth bark and flow into its rising sap. Then he slides off it and lies across its roots, like a root himself, face up, completely still.

I reverse back to him and get out of the car. The impact has shattered his visor but, wonderfully, done no damage to his gentle brown eyes. I notice that his bazouki case has been ripped off the pillion of the bike and lies quite close. The case itself has burst open but the instrument looks hardly damaged. I take it out and lay it close to his outstretched hand.

Now the musician is part of the night's dark music and I am out of place here. I drive slowly away, leaving him there with the trees and the foxes and owls, his eyes wide open, and seeing very soon, I hope, not the cold stars of our English night but the rich warm blue of a Mediterranean sky.

That's where he'd rather be. I know it. Ask him. I know it.

I'm too exhausted to talk any more now.
Soon.

V

On Thursday morning with only one day to go before the short story competition closed, Rye Pomona was beginning to hope there might be life after deathless prose.

This didn't stop her shovelling scripts into the reject bin with wild abandon, but halfway through the morning she went very still, sighed perplexedly, re-read the pages in front of her and said, "Oh hell."

"Yes?" said Dick Dee.

"We've got a Second Dialogue."

"Let me see."

He read through it quickly then said, "Oh dear. I wonder if this one too is related to a real incident."

"It is. That's what hit me straight off. I noticed it in yesterday's *Gazette*. Here, take a look."

She went to the Journal Rack and picked up the *Gazette*.

"Here it is. 'Police have released details of the fatal accident on Roman Way reported in our weekend edition. David Pitman, 19, a music student, of Pool Terrace, Carker, was returning home from his part-time job as an entertainer at the Taverna Restaurant in Cradle Street when he came off his motorbike in the early hours of Saturday morning. He sustained multiple injuries and was pronounced dead on arrival at hospital. No other vehicle was involved.' Poor sod."

Dee looked at the paragraph then read the Dialogue again.

"How very macabre," he said. "Still, it's not without some nice touches. If only our friend would attempt a more conventional story, he might do quite well."

"That's all you think it is, then?" said Rye rather aggressively. "Some plonker using news stories to fantasize upon?"

Dee raised his eyebrows high and smiled at her.

"We seem to have swapped lines," he said. "Last week it was me feeling uneasy and you pouring cold water. What's changed?"

"I could ask the same."

"Well, let me see," he said with that judicious solemnity she sometimes found irritating. "It could be I set my fanciful suspicions alongside the cool rational response of my smart young assistant and realized I was making a real ass of myself."

Then his face split in a decade-dumping grin and he added, "Or some such tosh. And you?"

She responded to the grin, then said, "There's something else I noticed in the *Gazette*. Hold on . . . here it is. It says that AA man's inquest was adjourned to allow the police to make further enquiries. That can only mean they're treating it as a suspicious death, can't it?"

"Yes, but there's suspicious and suspicious," said Dee. "Any sudden death has to be thoroughly investigated. If it's an accident, the causes have to be established to see whether there's any question of neglect. But even if there's a suspicion of criminality, for something like this to have any significance . . ."

He held up the Dialogue and paused expectantly.

A test, she thought. Dick Dee liked to give tests. At first when she came new to the job she'd felt herself patronized, then come to realize it was part of his teaching technique and much to be preferred to either being told something she already knew or not being told something she didn't.

"It doesn't really signify anything," she said. "Not if the guy's just feeding off news items. To be significant, or even to strain coincidence, he'd have to be writing before the event."

"Before the reporting of the event," corrected Dee.

She nodded. It was a small distinction but not nit-picking. That was another of Dee's qualities. The details he was fussy about were usually important rather than just ego-exercising.

"What about all this stuff about the student's grandfather and the bazouki?" she asked. "None of that's in the paper."

"No. But if it's true, which we don't know, all it might mean is that the story-teller did have a chat with David Pitman at some time. I dare say it's a story the young man told any number of customers at the restaurant."

"And if it turns out the AA man had been on holiday in Corfu?"

"I can devise possible explanations till the cows come home," he said dismissively. "But where's the point? The key question is, when did this last Dialogue actually turn up at the *Gazette*? I doubt if they're systematic enough to be able to pinpoint it, but someone might remember something. Why don't I have a word while you . . ."

". . . get on with reading these sodding stories," interrupted Rye. "Well, you're the boss."

"So I am. And what I was going to say was, while you might do worse than have a friendly word with your ornithological admirer."

He glanced towards the desk where a slim young man with an open boyish face and a sharp black suit was standing patiently.

His name was Bowler, initial E. Rye knew this because he'd flashed his library card the first time he appeared at the desk to ask for assistance in operating the CD-ROM drive of one of the Reference PCs. Both she and Dee had been on duty, but Rye had discovered early on that in matters of IT, she was the department's designated expert. Not that her boss wasn't technologically competent—in fact she suspected he was much more clued up than herself—but when she felt she knew him well enough to probe, he had smiled that sweetly sad smile of his and pointed to the computer, saying, "That is the grey squirrel," then to the book-lined shelves: "These are the red."

The disc Bowler E. wanted to use turned out to be an ornithological encyclopaedia, and when Rye had expressed a polite interest, he'd assumed she was a fellow enthusiast and nothing she'd been able to say during three or four subsequent visits had managed to disabuse him.

"Oh God," she said now. "Today I tell him the only way I want to see birds is nicely browned and covered with orange sauce."

"You disappoint me, Rye," said Dee. "I wondered from the start why such a smart young fellow should make himself out to be a mere tyro in computer technology. It's clearly not just birds that obsess him but you. Express your lack of enthusiasm in the brutal terms you suggest and all he'll do is seek another topic of common interest. Which indeed you yourself may now be able to suggest."

"Sorry?"

"Mr. Bowler is in fact Detective Constable Bowler of the Mid-Yorkshire

CID, so well worth cultivating. It's not every day us amateur detectives get a chance of planting a snout in the local constabulary. I'll leave him to your tender care, shall I?"

He headed for the office. Clever old Dick, thought Rye, watching him go. While I'm being a smart-ass, he's busy being smart.

Bowler was coming towards her. She looked at him with new interest. She knew it was one of her failings to make snap judgments from which she was hard to budge. Even now, she was thinking that him being a cop and possibly motivated in his visits to the library by pure lust didn't stop him being a bird nerd.

The suit and tie-less shirt were hopeful. Not Armani but pretty good clones. And the shy little-boy-lost smile seemed to her newly skinned eye to have something just a tad calculating in it which she approved too. The way to her heart wasn't through her motherly instincts, but it was nice to see a guy trying.

"Hello," he said hesitantly. "Sorry to bother you . . . if you're too busy . . ."

It would have been entertaining to play along for a while but she really was up to her eyes in work even without this short story crap.

She said briskly, "Yes, I'm pretty well snowed under. But if it's just a quickie you're after, Constable . . ."

The shy smile remained fixed but he blinked twice, the second one removing all traces of shyness from his eyes (which were a rather nice dove-grey) and replacing it with something very definitely like calculation.

He's wondering whether I've just invited him to swing straight from boy-next-door into saloon-bar-innuendo mode. If he does, he's on his way. Bird nerd was bad, coarse cop was worse.

He said, "No, look, I'm sorry, I just wanted to ask, this Sunday I was thinking about driving out to Stangdale—it's great country for birds even this time of year, you know, the moor, the crags and of course the tarn . . ."

He could see he wasn't gripping her and he changed tack with an ease she approved.

". . . and afterwards I thought maybe we could stop off for a meal . . ."

"This Sunday . . . I'm not sure what I've got on . . ." she said screwing up her face as if trying to work out what she was doing seventy-two weeks rather than seventy-two hours ahead. "And a *meal*, you said . . . ?"

"Yeah, there's the Dun Fox this end of the moor road. Not bad nosh. And now the law's changed, they've started having discos on Sunday nights as well as Saturdays . . ."

She knew it. An old-fashioned road-house on the edge of town, it had recently decided to target the local twenty-somethings who wanted to swing without being ankle-deep in teenies. It wasn't Stringfellows but it was certainly a lot better than a twitchers' barn dance. Question was, did she want a date with DC Bowler, E?

She studied his hopeful face. Why not? she thought. Then distantly behind him she glimpsed Charley Penn, who'd twisted round in his usual kiosk and was observing the scene with that smarl which suggested he could overhear not only their dialogue but their thoughts.

She said abruptly, "I'll think about it. Look, sit down if you can spare a moment from keeping the world safe from crime."

"Thought it was you who was up to your eyes in it," he said, sitting.

Touch of satire there.

"I am. And this is work. Your work, maybe."

She explained briefly as she could, which wasn't all that brief as awareness of how weird it all sounded made her veer towards longwindedness.

To do him credit, he didn't fall about laughing but asked if he could see the Dialogues. She showed him the Second which he read while she retrieved the First from the drawer where Dee had stored it.

He read this as well then said, "I'll hang on to these. Got a plastic folder or something?"

"For fingerprints?" she said, half mocking.

"For appearances," he said. "Don't think there's going to be much in the way of prints with you and your boss crawling all over them."

She got him a folder and said, "So you think there could be something in this?"

"Didn't say that, but we'll check."

Not a trace of shy smile here, just professional brusqueness.

"Like at the *Gazette*, you mean?" she said, slightly irritated. "I think you'll find Dick Dee, my boss, is taking care of that."

"Yeah? Fancies himself as a private dick, does he?" he said, smiling now.

"Ask him yourself," said Rye.

Dee had come back into the library and was approaching them.

His gaze took in the transparent folder and he said, "I see Rye has brought you up to speed, Mr. Bowler. I've just been talking to the *Gazette*. No joy, I'm afraid. No record of time or even date of receipt kept. Stuff marked Story Competition gets dumped straight into a bag for dispatch round here when it's full, plus anything else looking like fiction."

"Would have thought that covered half the stuff they print," said Bowler.

"An observation I resisted," said Dee.

"Probably right. They can be sensitive souls, these journalists. OK, I'll take these with me and check them out when I've got a spare moment."

His offhand manner got to Rye and she said, "Check them out? How? You said you doubted if there'd be any prints. So what are you going to do with them? Call in the police clairvoyant?"

"That's been tried too, but I don't think we'll be getting out the Ouija board for this one," grinned Bowler.

He's enjoying this, thought Rye. Thinks he's making a better impression on me as cocky cop than shy ornithologist. Time to disabuse him with a withering put-down.

But before the withering could commence, Dick Dee spoke.

"I think DC Bowler plans to check whether any information given in the Dialogues is (a) true and (b) not obtainable from newspaper reports," he said. "As for example the AA man's holiday habits or the origins of the bazouki."

"Right. Sharp thinking, Mr. Dee," said Bowler.

Meaning, you've thought along the same lines as me therefore maybe you're brighter than you look, parsed Rye.

"Thank you," said Dee. "I took the liberty of enquiring about that also when I talked to the *Gazette*. No, the reports which we have drawn your attention to were the only items touching on the two deaths. And, in case you're worried, I was careful not to alert them to a possible police interest. We have a local interest computer reference programme and they're used to such cross-checking."

He smiled at Bowler, not a smart-ass grin but a pleasant all-friends-together smile at which it was impossible to take offence, but offence was what the young DC felt like taking, except that he guessed it wouldn't be a smart move in his campaign to impress Rye Pomona.

In addition, a good cop didn't spurn help from any source, especially when that source was likely to be more clued up about something than the good cop's self.

"This funny drawing at the start of the First Dialogue. Any thoughts on that?" he asked.

"Yes, I have been wondering about that," said Dee. "And something did come to mind. I was going to tell you, Rye. Take a look at this."

He went to the office and returned with a large folio which he set on the table. He began turning the pages, revealing a series of, to Bowler's eyes, weird and wonderful designs, often in rich and vibrant colours.

"I need to be able to read Celtic scripts for some research I'm doing," he explained. "And that's made me aware of the huge range of illuminated initials their scribes used. This is what the Dialogue illustration reminded me of. Oh, here, look at this one. The Dialogue version has no colour of course and is greatly simplified, but basically they have much in common."

"You're right," said Rye. "It's obvious now you've pointed it out."

"Yeah," said Bowler. "Obvious. What is it, then?"

"It's the letters I N P. This particular illumination is taken from an Irish manuscript of the eighth century and it's the opening of the Gospel according to St. John. *In principio erat verbum et verbum erat apud deum et deus erat verbum.* All the letters of which seem to have tumbled into that little pile under the P."

"And what do they mean, exactly?" said Hat, adding the last word to suggest, falsely, that it was merely detail he wanted adding to his own rough translation.

"In the beginning was the Word and the Word was with God and God was the Word, or the Word was God, as the Authorized Version has it. An interesting way for our dialogist to introduce himself, don't you think? Words, words, words, much in love with words."

"Oh yes," said Rye taking the folder from Hat and staring hard from the ornate illumination to the black and white sketch. "But maybe it means something else. As well as the words."

"That struck me too. It's clearly illustrative. That could be the humpback bridge with the unfortunate AA man in the water . . ."

"And there's a bird, though it doesn't look much like a pheasant . . . and are those things with horns meant to be cows?"

Hat, feeling he was being sidelined, retrieved the folder from her hands and said, "Let's wait till we see if there's been a crime committed before we start looking for clues, shall we? And if there has been, don't worry, we'll soon have this word-lover banged up. Pity they've shut Alcatraz."

"Alcatraz?" they said in simultaneous puzzlement.

"Yes, then he could be the Wordman of Alcatraz."

If it had fallen any flatter it would have been a map.

He said, "It was a movie . . . on telly the other night . . . there was this guy, Burt Lancaster, who killed somebody and got locked up . . ."

"Yes, I recall the film," said Dee. "Well, well, the Wordman. Very droll, Mr. Bowler."

Again, it didn't sound like a put-down, but Hat felt put down.

"Yeah, well, thanks for your input, we'll bear it in mind," he said, trying to regain the professional high ground.

"My pleasure," said Dee. "Well, back to the grind."

He sat down at the table, picked up another story and started to read. Rye followed his example. Bowler remained standing, gradually deflating from cocky cop to would-be wooer.

There are more ways of withering than a blast of hot words, thought Rye gleefully.

Dee glanced up and said, "I'm sorry, Mr. Bowler, was there something else?"

"Just something I was asking Rye, Miss Pomona."

"About the . . . *Wordman?*"

Hat shook his head.

"Ah, a library enquiry then. Concerning your ornithological studies, I've no doubt. Rye, are you able to help?"

"Not straightaway," said Rye. "It's something I'll need to think about, Mr. Bowler . . ."

"Hat," he said.

"Sorry?"

"My friends call me Hat."

"How very paronomasiac of them," she said, glancing at Dee, who smiled and murmured, "One might even say paronomaniac."

"Yeah, well, what about it?" said Hat, his irritation at what felt like the intimacy of mockery making him abrupt.

"Tell you what," said Rye. "Leave it with me. Perhaps we can talk again when you come back to tell us what you've found out about the accuracy or otherwise of the Dialogues. That suit you, Mr. Bowler? *Hat?*"

He frowned for a moment then the smile broke through.

"OK. That's fine. I'll get back to you. Meanwhile I'd keep this to yourselves. Not that there's like to be anything in it, but better safe than sorry. See you."

He turned and walked away. He moved well, with a cat-like grace. Perhaps that explained his interest in birds.

She glanced at Dee. He gave her a conspiratorial smile. Then he dropped his gaze to the sheets before him and shook his head ruefully.

"Truth really is so much more interesting than fiction, isn't it?" he said.

She looked down at her next story.

The writing was familiar, large and spiky and purple.

It began *Last night I had another wet dream* . . .

"You could be right," she said.

VI

Detective Constable Bowler's considered professional opinion of the suspicions roused by the two Dialogues was that they were a load of crap, but if taking them seriously was a way to Rye Pomona's heart and/or bed, then it was pursed lip and furrowed brow time. But only in her sight. Once out of the library, he did a little jig of delight at his luck and the sight of a wavering line of greylags crossing the rectangle of sky between the police station and the coroner's court tuned up his spirits another notch.

He watched them out of sight then ran up the stairs to the CID floor whistling merrily.

"You sound happy," said Edgar Wield. "Found Lord Lucan, have you?"

"No, Sarge, but got something almost as odd."

He showed the sergeant the two Dialogues and told him the tale.

"It's certainly odd," said Wield, sounding like he meant daft. Bowler couldn't blame him.

"Thought we should check it out," he said. "Just a feeling."

"A feeling, eh?" said Wield, those dark eyes surveying him coldly from that fragmented face, as if well aware that the feeling in question had more to do with Rye Pomona and hormones than detective intuition. "You're a bit junior for feelings. Even sergeants are only allowed three or four a year, between consenting adults. You'd best try this out on someone with a bit more brass about him."

Bowler's spirits hit an air pocket and sank as he contemplated taking something as airy-fairy as this to Andy Dalziel. It had been made quite clear to him that his fast-track transfer from the Midlands had been effected without Dalziel's approval. "We'll see how you shape," had been the gist of his welcome six months earlier. In his own eyes, he had shaped pretty well, or at least not made any major mistakes. But far from wriggling his way into the Fat Man's affection, from time to time in the past few weeks he'd turned round as though prodded in the back to find those ice-pick eyes fixed on him with an expression somewhere between simple distrust and out-and-out loathing.

On the other hand, it was a comfort that only last week, the DCI hadn't hesitated to pick him out for a bit of delicate investigation, checking out some nutter he thought was harassing him.

"Yes, I thought maybe I'd mention it to Mr. Pascoe. Need to chat to him anyway," he said airily, trying to give the impression of a special relationship existing between graduate entrants.

Wield, noting the attempt, said, "When you next report to him about Franny Roote, you mean?"

It didn't do to let junior members of the team imagine they knew anything he didn't. Peter had probably stressed to young Bowler that his interest in the behaviour and habits of Roote was technically unofficial and should not be mentioned in the super's presence. In his present mood, the Fat Man seemed to believe that telling Bowler anything was like ringing up the tabloids.

"Found anything interesting, have you?" pursued Wield.

"Not yet," admitted Bowler.

"Keep trying. But keep out of sight. He's got an eye like a hawk by all accounts."

"Oh, don't worry about that, Sarge," said Bowler confidently. "I won't raise enough breeze to stir a feather. So what do you think about these Dialogues? Speak to Mr. Pascoe?"

"No," said Wield judiciously. "I think you'll find that Mr. Headingley's your man."

Detective Inspector George Headingley had a reputation for being a by-the-rules, straight-down-the-middle cop who treated hunches with embrocation and gut feelings with bismuth. "A safe pair of hands" Pascoe had once called him in Bowler's hearing, to which Dalziel had replied, "Nay, that were true once, but since he started counting the days to demob he's become a safe pair of buttocks. Give owt to George and his first thought now is to sit on it till it can't do him any harm. I blame all this new legislation. I'd hang bent cops by the bollocks till they twanged, but you can't do the job properly if you've got to be looking over your shoulder all the time."

This was a reference to the new climate of accountability. Gone, or at least going, were the good old days when a policeman who made a mistake could slip gratefully into a secure pension "on medical grounds." And even those who'd retired in the fullness of time were no longer secure from retrospective investigation and changed pensionable status.

So perhaps it wasn't surprising that someone as cautious as George Headingley entering the final straight of an honourable if not over-distinguished career, should have decided that the best way of not blotting his copybook was to write in it as little as possible.

Bowler's suspicion that Wield was saying indirectly that the best place for something as daft as the Dialogues was under the DI's ample buttocks was slightly allayed when he discovered that the case of the AA man's death was there already. When the coroner had adjourned the inquest for the police to make further enquiries, Uniformed had passed it upstairs for CID to take a look at. Headingley had taken a glance, yawned, and was on the point of tossing it back downstairs with the required annotation that CID found no evidence requiring further investigation.

"Now you come along with this," said the DI accusingly. "It's a load of nothing. Can't see why you think it's worth bothering with."

"There has to be some reason why the coroner adjourned," said Bowler evasively.

"Yeah, well, I suppose so. Silly old buffer's always been terrified of making a mistake so when the family started causing a fuss, he took the easy way out. Anything goes wrong, it'll be our fault."

Takes a one to know a one, thought Bowler as he studied the inquest report.

He soon saw there was a bit more to it than Headingley had implied, but not a lot. The question of why Ainstable had stopped in the first place hadn't been satisfactorily answered. Call of nature had been theorized, losing his balance as he relieved himself over the shallow parapet. But his wife had tearfully protested that her Andrew was not the kind of man to pee off a bridge situated on a public highway, the pathologist had pointed out that his bladder was still fairly full, and PC Dave Insole, first cop on the scene, had confirmed that his flies were fastened.

Perhaps then he'd had a dizzy turn before he got started and had fallen? The post mortem hadn't found evidence of any kind of "dizzy turn," though the pathologist could think of several versions of this syndrome which would have left no sign, and the police report mentioned rather tentatively some scuffs on the parapet of the bridge which might possibly indicate he'd been sitting down and gone over backwards.

But the really puzzling thing was his tool box, which had been found resting on the road by the parapet.

Headingley didn't think this was significant.

"Clear as daylight," he said. "Driving along, feels dizzy, stops to get some air, climbs out, automatically picks up his tool box en route, 'cos that's what he always does and, having a dizzy turn, he's not thinking straight, right? Sits down on the bridge, everything goes black, over he goes, bangs his head on a stone, unconscious, drowns. Pathologist found no signs of foul play, did he?"

"There wouldn't be, would there, guv?" said Hat respectfully. "Not when the crime's letting someone die without trying to save them."

"Murder by neglect? On the basis of this?" Headingley waved the Dialogues folder scornfully in the air. "Get real, son."

"And the other, guv? Driving straight at that kid on the bike? If the Wordman did that, well, that's not neglect, is it? That's pretty positive, wouldn't you say?"

"What did you call him?" said Headingley, postponing answering the question.

"The Wordman," said Hat. He explained about the *In principio*, then explained his joke, and if anything got an even dustier response than he had in the library. Clearly the DI felt that giving the author of the Dialogues a nickname gave him substance, making him harder to ignore, which was what he would have liked to do.

But Hat was determined to pursue him to a decision.

"So you think we should just drop it, guv?" he persisted.

He watched with hidden amusement as uncertainties chased each other like clouds across Headingley's broad open face.

"Well, I suppose you'd better take a look. Likes his t's crossed with a ruler, that coroner," said Headingley finally. "But don't waste too much time on it. I want a full report on my desk first thing tomorrow. That's the real test of a theory, son, how much of it you're willing to put in writing."

"Yes, guv. Thank you, guv," said Bowler, just staying this side of open mockery. Headingley might be a boring old fart, ambling towards retirement with little interest in anything other than protecting his ample back, but he still had rank, plus he had survived for many years under the unforgiving eye of Andy Dalziel, so there had to be something there.

He went to his desk, checked out the names and addresses he wanted, then set out on his quest. He had a double reason for being meticulous now—first, to impress Rye Pomona; second, to satisfy George Headingley. Not that he needed either part of the reason to motivate him. One thing he'd quickly learned as a young graduate cop was to be nit-pickingly thorough if you didn't want some antique plod who'd come up the hard way shaking his head and saying, "Nay, lad, just because tha's on the fast track don't mean tha's allowed to cut corners."

He started with Constable Dave Insole who'd been driving the first police car to arrive at the scene. Once Bowler's easy manner had dissolved his natural suspicion that CID was second guessing him, Insole was co-operative enough. In his view, the most likely explanation was that Ainstable had stopped for a pee, clambered down the bank, slipped and fell as he reached the bottom.

"You mentioned some scuffs on the parapet in your report," said Bowler.

"That was my partner, Maggie Laine," said Insole, grinning. "Got ambitions to join your lot, has Maggie. Always looking for clues. No, he got caught short, and was in such a hurry to get out of sight of the road, he slipped. If he'd wanted to sit on the parapet or piss over it or whatever, he'd have parked on the bridge itself, wouldn't he?"

"His tool box was by the parapet, wasn't it?"

"Yeah, but by the time we arrived there were half a dozen yokels gawking, any one of them could have moved it out of the way."

"But hardly have taken it out of his van," said Hat. "Which was parked where? Not actually on the bridge, I gather?"

"No. He stopped just before it, right where he could scramble down the side to the bank of the stream," said Insole triumphantly.

"Just about where he'd have stopped if there'd already been a car parked on the bridge then?" said Bowler.

"Yeah, I suppose, but what are you driving at?"

"Better ask Maggie," laughed Bowler, heading for the door.

The Ainstable house was a thirties semi on the northern fringe of town. The stout woman who answered the door turned out to be Mrs. Ainstable's sister from Bradford who'd come to stay. The first thing Bowler noticed as he was ushered into the living room was a tank of tropical fish standing on top of a sideboard. The second thing was a small pale-faced woman curled up on a large settee. Grief usually ages, but in Agnes Ainstable's case it had shrunk the mature woman into an ailing child who looked more like her sister's daughter than her sibling.

But when she spoke, Bowler began to understand why the coroner had opted to adjourn the inquest for further enquiries. Her attitude was simple. If something as slight as a slip of the foot had deprived her of her husband, she wanted the circumstances to be laid out before her in unambiguous detail. There was nothing rational in her demands, but they were made with an intensity that would have daunted the most insensitive of men.

The upside of this was that she answered all Bowler's questions without showing the slightest curiosity about his reasons for asking them. It was enough that they related to the further enquiries the coroner had promised her.

Yes, Andrew had once talked about his tropical fish on a local radio chat show; yes, they'd been to Corfu for their holiday this year; yes, they'd had a meal at the Taverna.

At the front door as he left, the sister said, half apologetically, "It's her way of hanging on to him. Once she admits she knows everything there is to know, he's gone completely, and that terrifies her. All these questions you're asking, they mean anything or are you just going through the motions?"

"Wish I knew," said Bowler.

He wasn't being disingenuous. There were many ways in which the writer of the First Dialogue could have got the details it contained. He could simply have known Ainstable, be a workmate or a member of the tropical fish fancy, have travelled to Corfu on the same package holiday . . . the possibilities if not endless were numerous enough to leave suspicion uselessly fluid. Facts were the only hardener that a good detective took any heed of. And he was a long way short of anything he'd like to hear himself explaining to a nit-picking coroner.

Now he drove south, leaving the town behind, and speeding along Roman Way as young David Pitman had sped on his way home to Carker.

The Pitman house was a spacious whitewashed cottage in a large garden, very different from the Ainstable semi, but the grief it contained was much the same. Bowler spent a heart-rending hour being taken through a family photograph album by Mrs. Pitman, David's mother. But he came away with confirmation that everything written in the Second Dialogue about the bazouki was accurate.

On his way back into town along Roman Way he stopped at the accident site. It was easy to identify. The tree which the bike had hit bore a scorched scar like a roughly cauterized wound. The impact of the boy's body against the neighbouring tree had left damage less visible, but close up the bruising of the smooth beech bark was unmistakable.

He didn't know why he'd stopped. Even Sherlock Holmes would have been hard put to glean anything significant from the scene. Without the Dialogues, there was little suspicious in either of the deaths and in both cases it was easy to think of ways the Wordman could have got hold of the information they contained.

So really he'd got nothing, which was precisely what George Headingley hoped he would get. But he hadn't joined CID to keep the likes of old George happy.

He raised his eyes to take in the long straight road down which the Roman legions had marched for the last time seventeen hundred years ago when the order came to abandon this chilly corner of the empire to its troublesome natives. The town boundary was only a mile away but the brow of the hill completely hid any sign of its encroaching sprawl. Only one building was visible among the fields bordering the road and that was an old grey farmhouse which looked like it had been there long enough to be naturalized as part of the landscape.

You'd have a perfect view of the road from its windows, thought Bowler.

He started the MG and drove up the long potholed driveway to the house which had the initials I.A.L. and the date 1679 engraved over the door.

A woman answered his ring. At first glance to Bowler's young eye she looked as old as the house. But the voice which demanded his business was strong, and now he saw that through a fringe of grey hairs he was being observed by a pair of bright blue eyes, and if her skin was beginning to wrinkle like an old apple's, she still had the flush of a sweet pippin in her cheeks.

He introduced himself and learned he was speaking to Mrs. Elizabeth Locksley. When he mentioned the accident, she said, "How many times do you need to be told?"

"Someone's been round?"

"Yes. Next morning. Lad in uniform."

So they had been thorough. No mention of the visit in the report, which meant it was subsumed under the terse comment, *No witnesses forthcoming or discovered.*

"And you told him?"

"Nothing. Which was all there was to tell. We go to bed early here and sleep sound."

"Speak for yourself," called a man's voice from within.

"Nowt wrong with your lugs then," she shouted back.

"Nor my eyes either. I told you what I saw."

Bowler looked at the woman enquiringly and she sighed and said, "If you want to waste your time . . ." then turned and vanished into the house.

He followed her into a long living room which, apart from the addition of a TV set on which *Mad Max* was playing, didn't look like much had been done to it since the seventeenth century. A man rose from a chair. He was a giant, at least six and a half feet, and there was very little clearance between his head and the exposed crossbeams. He shook Bowler's hand with a vigour that made him wince and said, "You've come to ask about the lights. Didn't I tell you, Betty?"

"Not more than fifty times, you daft old sod," she said, switching off the television. "So tell him, you'll not be satisfied till you do."

There was some exasperation in her voice but it got nowhere close to overpowering the strong affection in her gaze as she looked at the man.

"I will," he said. "I got up to have a pee—old man's trouble, it'll come to you, lad, if you live that long. I looked out the landing window and I saw this headlight going down the hill there, just the one. Bike, I thought. And the bugger's moving. Then I saw these other headlights, two on 'em, so, a car, coming this way. Out of nowhere they came. One moment dark, next there they were. Then the single light were all over the place. Till suddenly it went out. And then there were a puff of flame."

"And what happened then?"

"Don't know. If I'd stayed any longer I'd have pissed down the stairs and then I'd have been in trouble."

He roared with laughter and the woman said, "You're not wrong there, lad."

"And did you tell this story to the other policeman who came?" asked Bowler.

"No, I didn't."

"Why not?" he asked.

"Didn't recall it till later," said the man.

"Later?"

"Aye," said the woman. "Later. He usually recalls things later if he recalls them at all."

There was something going on here he didn't yet fully understand. He decided to concentrate on the woman.

"You didn't think it worthwhile ringing us when you heard Mr. er . . . ?"

"Locksley," she said.

"Your husband?" he said, looking for clarity where he could find it.

"Well, he's not my bloody tallyman!" she said, which seemed to amuse them both greatly.

"You didn't think to contact us?" persisted Bowler.

"What for? Sam, what night was it you saw the lights?"

"Nay, lass, that's not fair. It was this year, but, I'm certain of that."

"And what film would you have been watching that day whenever it was?"

He thought a moment then said, "Likely *Mad Max*, it's my favourite. Do you like it, mister? He was a cop, too."

"It takes all sorts," said Bowler. "Yes, I've seen it on the box. Bit too violent for my taste."

He was beginning to get the picture. In the interests of diplomacy he'd have liked to get the woman by herself, but he had a feeling that she wouldn't take kindly to any attempt to talk behind her husband's back.

He said, "So you think that Mr. Locksley might be confusing what the other policeman told you about the accident with images from the movies he watches?"

He kept his voice low but the man's sharp ears picked him up with ease.

"You could be right there, lad," he said cheerfully. "I do get things mixed up and as for recalling what happened when, I'm hopeless. Doesn't bother me mostly, but there's some things from the past it'd be nice to bring back now I'm getting old. For instance, I can't recall the last time I had a good jump, and that's sad."

"You silly old bugger," said his wife fondly. "It was just afore you had your breakfast this morning."

"Was it?" he said, regarding her with bright hopeful eyes. "And did I enjoy it?"

"Well, you asked for a second helping of porridge," she said.

Their laughter was infectious and Bowler was still chuckling as he let himself out. As he began to drive away, Mrs. Locksley came to the door and called, "Hey, just because his memory's going and he gets a bit confused, doesn't mean he's wrong, but."

"That," said Bowler, "is very much the trouble."

But it wasn't his trouble; it was or soon would be DI Headingley's. Something obliging him to make a decision would drop into Jolly George's broad lap like a mug of hot coffee. It was a prospect not altogether displeasing.

But the DI, when provoked to action, could be a nimble ducker and weaver, and it would be wise not to leave any gaps for him to slip through, saying accusingly, "But you forgot to do that, Constable."

Bowler scanned the possibilities and saw one he hadn't covered. The Greek restaurant where the Wordman claimed to have dined on the night he talked to David Pitman. He glanced at his watch. Five forty. Probably the Taverna didn't open till seven or half six at the earliest. He'd never eaten there—young detectives got used to eating on the hoof and became uneasy if they found themselves spending more than ten minutes on a meal—but he had followed Franny Roote there one night last week, watched him go inside, thought, *Sod this, it's unofficial and I'm not on overtime,* and headed home to a takeaway and a soccer match on the telly.

That was when? Suddenly he felt uneasy. Wednesday, Pascoe had given him the job, so it had to be . . . He pulled over and took out his pocketbook to check the date.

Shit! It was Friday, the same night that young Pitman had had his "accident."

Best not to mention it, he decided. It would just muddy the waters. He hadn't gone inside, he hadn't seen any other customers, he hadn't done anything except sit in his car for a minute watching Roote go into the building. If his own bad vibes about the two deaths were translated by the brass into a full-scale investigation—which he doubted, given George Headingley's determination not to let his boat be rocked with the harbour of retirement in sight—then he might speak. Or perhaps not. Somehow he suspected from the way Dalziel had been looking at him lately that the fat bastard would be glad to put a black mark against his name simply for being in the vague vicinity of a possible crime.

For a moment he even thought of scrubbing his plan to visit the Taverna, but only for a moment. Wanting to cover his back didn't stop him from being conscientious. Then, because he was a positive thinker, much happier looking on the upside of things than contemplating possible downsides, he suddenly grinned as he saw a way of getting something good out of the situation.

He took out his mobile and dialled the Central Library number. It rang for a long time before someone answered. He recognized the voice.

"Mr. Dee? Hi, it's DC Bowler. Listen, is Rye there?"

"I'm sorry, she's gone home, like all sensible people," said Dee. "The only reason you got me was that I often stay on after closing time to do some work."

"That's very noble of you," said Bowler.

"I fear you credit me with more virtue than I possess. I don't mean work for the public weal. This is private research for a book I'm writing."

"Oh yes. Detective story, is it?"

Dee laughed, picking up the irony.

"I wish. No, it's a history of semantic scholarship. A sort of dictionary of dictionaries, you might call it."

"Sounds fascinating," said Bowler unconvincingly.

Dee said, "I think I should work on your projection of sincerity if you fancy trying your hand at undercover work, Mr. Bowler. Now, is there any way that I can be of help to you?"

"Only if you've got a number I can reach Rye at," said Bowler.

There was a pause then Dee said, "Well, I do have her home number, but I'm afraid we're not allowed to give such things out to the public at large. But I could pass on a message, if you like."

Bastard! thought Bowler.

He said, "It was just about my enquiries. I'm going to the Taverna this evening to check out a few things and I thought as Rye was so interested she might care to join me. I'll be there at seven."

"Now that does sound fascinating. I'll pass your message on. I'm sure Rye will be as intrigued as I am."

But you're not invited, Dick-head Dee, thought Bowler.

Then, being both a fair and a self-analytical young man, he asked himself, Am I jealous? But quickly, because he was above all a *young* man, he went on to dismiss as absurd the idea that in matters of love a dotard of at least forty years could give him any cause for jealousy.

Showered, shaved, and arrayed in his sharpest gear, he was in the Taverna by six forty-five. He ordered a Campari soda because he loved the colour and it gave him a sense of sophistication. At seven ten he ordered another. A third at seven twenty. At seven thirty, tired of sophistication, he ordered a pint of lager. At seven forty-five he ordered a second pint and asked to see the manager.

This was Mr. Xenopoulos, short, fat and genuinely Greek though he spoke English with a disconcerting Liverpool accent. Suspicious at first that Bowler was an Environmental Health snoop, he became more helpful when he learned that his enquiries were to do with Dave Pitman, though he did wonder mildly whether it might not have been more sensible for the detective to have started interviewing his staff an hour earlier when he first arrived rather than now when the restaurant was getting busy. Both he and the waiters expressed what seemed like genuine sorrow at the dreadful accident which had overtaken their bazouki player, but were unable to recall anything pertinent about the patrons that night. Solitary diners were not unusual, attracted by the sense of communal jollity which often developed as the evening wore on and the dancing began.

"But why're you asking all these questions?" enquired Xenopoulos finally. "It was an accident, wasn't it?"

"So far as we know," said Bowler carefully. "But it's possible one of the diners that night could have been a witness. You keep a record of table bookings, I suppose?"

"Natch. Like a copy of that page in the reservation diary, would you?" said the manager, pre-empting Bowler's next request. "No sweat. Have a seat at the bar and a drink on the house, I'll be with you in a jiff."

Bowler had another pint of lager and was sitting staring into the empty glass like Frank Sinatra about to burst into "One More for the Road" when a hand tapped gently on his shoulder, a musky perfume rubbed seductively against his nose and a voice breathed in his ear, "Hi. Whatever you lost in that glass, I think you've swallowed it."

He spun round on his stool smiling, and found himself looking at a small, slim blonde in her mid-twenties, with piercing blue eyes and a generous mouth whose smile matched his, except that it did not fade as his now faded.

"Oh, hi," he said. "Jax. How're you doing?"

Jax Ripley considered the question for a moment then said, "Well. I'm doing well. And you, Hat. How are you? All by yourself?"

"Yeah. That's right. I am. You?"

"With friends, but when I saw you at the bar, I thought no one so good looking should be so sad so early in the evening and came across. So what are you here for, Hat? Business or pleasure?"

Discretion vied with ego. She was wearing a dress which didn't offer much hope of concealment to even the smallest of microphones, but with Jax the Ripper, you never could tell.

He said, "Pleasure. Or it would have been if I hadn't got stood up."

"My favourite policeman? Tell me her name and I'll let the world know what a stupid cow she is."

"Thanks, but maybe not. I'm a great forgiver," he said.

She regarded him quizzically for a moment then her gaze drifted over his shoulder.

"Mr. Bowler, here's that page you wanted. Hope it's useful, but a lot of our customers just come in off the street on the off chance."

He turned to find Xenopoulos proffering a photocopied sheet.

"Yes, thanks, that's great, thanks a lot," he said, folding it and shoving it into his jacket pocket.

He turned back to the woman to find her expression had shifted from quizzical to downright curious.

"Just improving the not so shining hour," he said.

"Yes? Anything that would improve mine?" she asked. "Over a friendly drink?"

"Don't think so," he said. "Really, Jax, it's nothing."

Her unblinking eyes made him feel like a guilty child, so he let his gaze drift over her shoulder. And found himself looking straight at Andy Dalziel who had just come into the restaurant with the well-rounded woman rumour had it he was getting it on with. But the expression on the Fat Man's face suggested he had slaughter rather than sex on his mind.

Bowler jerked his gaze back to Jax Ripley whose eyes by comparison were soft and kind.

"That drink," he said, "make it a tequila sunset."

"You mean sunrise?"

"I know what I mean," he said.

VII

Detective Inspector George Headingley was a stickler for punctuality. With the end of his career in sight, he might have decided he wasn't going to do anything he didn't want to do, but that didn't mean he wasn't going to be unpunctual not doing it. He was due at his desk at eight thirty the following morning and at eight twenty-nine he was approaching it with the measured tread which made his footsteps recognizable at fifty paces.

He could see that the cleared top which he prided himself on leaving at the end of every shift had been sullied by a document. At least the sullier had taken care to place it dead centre so that in many ways it enhanced rather than detracted from the effect of perfect order which Headingley was always at pains to achieve.

He hung his coat up, removed his jacket and draped it over the back of his chair, then sat down and pulled the document towards him. It was several pages thick and the first of these declared that its author was DC Bowler who, as requested, had gathered together all available information which might help DI Headingley to assess whether anything in the deaths of Andrew Ainstable or David Pitman required his, that is DI Headingley's, further investigation.

Why was it that something legalistic about this form of words made his heart sink?

He opened it and began to read. And soon his heart was sinking deeper, faster. He'd wanted firm no-no's so that he could consign these daft Dialogues to the waste bin, but all he was getting was a series of boggy maybe's.

When he finished he sat for a moment, then gathered all the papers together and set out in search of Bowler.

There was no sign of him. He encountered Wield and made enquiry after the young DC.

Wield said, "Saw him earlier. Think he went off to do something for Mr. Pascoe. Was it urgent?"

"Was what urgent?" said Andy Dalziel, whose approach was sometimes audible at twice the distance of the DI's but who could also exercise the option of materializing like the ghost of Christmas Yet To Come, moving silent as mist over the ground.

"The DI's looking for Bowler," said Wield.

"And the bugger's not in yet?"

"In and out," said Wield reprovingly.

"Aye, like Speedy Gonzales," said Dalziel with a lip curl like a shed tyre. "What do you want with him, George?"

"Well, nothing . . . just a query about a report he's done for me," said Headingley, turning away.

"About those deaths, was it?" said Wield. "The library thing."

Headingley shot him a glance which came as close to malevolence as a man of his amiable temperament could manage. He still had hopes of squashing this bit of awkwardness or, in the unlikely event of there being anything in it, at least shelving it till such time as he was long gone. To that end, the less Dalziel knew, the better.

"Library thing?" said Dalziel. "Not a body-in-the-library thing, I hope, George. I'm getting too old for bodies in libraries."

Headingley explained, playing it down. Dalziel listened then held out his hand for the file.

He scanned through it quickly, his nostrils flaring as he came to the end of Bowler's report.

"So that's what the bugger were doing at the Taverna," he muttered to himself.

"Sorry?"

"Nowt. So what do you reckon, George? Load of crap or a big one for you to go out on?"

"Don't know yet," said Headingley as judiciously as he could manage. "That's why I want to see Bowler. Check through a couple of points with him. What do you think, sir?"

Hopeful of dismissal.

"Me? Could be owt or nowt. I know I can rely on you to do the right thing. But while you're thinking about it, George, mum's the word, eh? Go off half-cocked on summat like this and we'll look right wankers. Don't want them blowflies from the media sniffing around till we know there's dead meat, and it's not us."

A mobile rang in Headingley's pocket. He took it out and said, "Yes?"

He listened then turned away from the other two men.

They heard him say, "No, not possible . . . of course . . . well, maybe . . . all right . . . twenty minutes."

He switched off, turned back and said, "Need to go out. Possible information."

"Oh aye. Anything I should know about?" said Dalziel.

"Don't know, sir," said Headingley. "Probably nowt, but he makes it sound urgent."

"They always do. Who'll you take? We're a bit short-handed with Novello still off sick and Seymour on leave."

"I can go," said Wield.

"No, it's OK. This one's not a registered snout," said Headingley firmly. Registered informants required two officers to work them for protection against disinformation and attempted set-ups. "I'm still working on him. He's a bit timid, and I reckon that seeing me turn up mob-handed might put him off for ever."

He turned and began to move away.

Dalziel said, "Hey, George, aren't you forgetting something?"

"Eh?"

"This," said the Fat Man, proffering the Dialogues file. "You don't get shut of it that easy."

The bugger's a mind reader, thought Headingley, not for the first time. He took the file, tucked it under his arm and headed out of the office.

Dalziel watched him go and said, "Know what I think, Wieldy?"

"Wouldn't presume, sir."

"I think it was his missus reminding him to pick up her dry-cleaning. One thing you've got to say about George, he's been real conscientious helping us break in his replacement."

"Thought we weren't getting a replacement, sir."

"That's what I mean," said Andy Dalziel.

He returned to his office, sat looking at the phone for a minute, then picked it up and dialled.

"Hello," said a woman's voice which even on the phone was filled with a husky warmth which communicated itself straight to his thighs.

"Hi, luv. It's me."

"Andy," said Cap Marvell. "How nice."

She made it sound like she meant it too.

"Just rang to say how're you doing. And sorry you didn't enjoy that place last night."

She laughed and said, "As you well know, it wasn't the place I didn't enjoy, it was you going on about that handsome young officer and the very pretty TV girl. I thought we had an agreement. No shop till after sex when you can unburden yourself to your heart's content and I can go to sleep."

"Chance would have been a fine thing," he grumbled.

"Chance went out of the window with my pleasant night out. I'm game to experiment with most kinds of foreplay, but police politics I find a real turn-off. But I accept your apology for an apology."

"Grand. Then let's fix summat else up. Your choice. Anything you say and I promise you'll think I'm a civilian."

"You say so. OK, couple of invitations I've got this morning. One is to my son's regimental ball. It's being held a fortnight on Saturday out at Haysgarth, that's Budgie Partridge's country seat. He's the regiment's Colonel-in-Chief . . ."

Cap's son by her dissolved marriage was Lieutenant-Colonel Piers Pitt-Evenlode MC of the Yorkshire Fusiliers, known to Dalziel as The Hero.

"Budgie? That's Lord Partridge to us commoners, is it?"

"Sorry. I knew him in another life."

This other life had been the period of marriage into the landed gentry which had led to the Hero, self-knowledge, disillusionment, rebellion, divorce, and ultimately Dalziel.

"Met him once myself in this life," said the Fat Man, "but I doubt he'd remember me. What's the other invite?"

"That's to the preview of the art and craft exhibition in the Centre Gallery. A week on Saturday."

"That it? No one want you to open a new brewery or summat?"

"Choose," she said unrelentingly. "It's either tin soldiers and champagne cocktails or nude paintings and cheap white wine."

He thought then said, "Don't know much about art but I know what I like. I'll pick the mucky pictures."

❖   ❖   ❖

Hat Bowler yawned widely.

He'd had a restless night, his bed afloat on a turbulent ocean of lager and Campari and the sky full of dull red stars each glowing down upon him with the accusing intensity of Andy Dalziel's gaze. He'd risen very early and made his way to work where he ordered his notes into the report which, not without malice aforethought, had so upset George Headingley. Franny Roote's name hadn't been on the Taverna reservation list. He examined his reasons for not mentioning him, decided albeit uneasily they were as good this morning as they'd appeared last night—better maybe after that encounter with Dalziel's glowering glare—then, partly to avoid being present when the DI read his report, and partly to reassure himself that Pascoe was getting his knickers in a twist over nothing, he'd driven out to the suburb where Franny Roote had his flat and resumed surveillance.

There was, he was glad to confirm, nothing here to wake a young DC up. In fact, for a convicted felon and a suspected stalker, Roote really led an incredibly boring life. The guy got up in the morning, got into his old banger (correction: it looked like an old banger but the engine sounded remarkably sweet), drove to work, and worked hard all day. Most evenings he spent reading and taking notes in the university library. His social life seemed to consist of attendance at a St. John Ambulance class and occasional visits to a restaurant (like the Taverna, bugger it!) or a cinema, always alone. No, this was one very dull character. And Wield had said he'd got an eye like a hawk! The sergeant was a man to admire and listen to, but he didn't know much about birds, thought Bowler complacently as he watched Roote pruning a rosebush with such methodical concentration that he'd probably not have noticed if a full-scale film crew had turned up to take pictures.

Time to move before he fell asleep.

As he drove away from the university, Bowler let his thoughts drift to Rye Pomona. Now that he'd reported on his investigations to the DI, he felt obligated to bring her up to speed too. He had convinced himself that she hadn't got his message last night. Probably Dee, through indolence or inadvertence, or, more likely, simple indisposition, hadn't made contact with her. He pulled over and dialled the library and asked for Reference.

He recognized her voice at once. She on the other hand didn't recognize his and seemed to require an effort of memory even to register his name.

"Oh yes. Constable Bowler. Message last night? Yes, I believe I did get a message, but I had other plans. So how can I help you now?"

"Well, I thought you might like to hear how I got on."

"Got on? With what?"

"With looking into these Dialogues you gave me."

"Oh yes. The Wordman of Alcatraz."

She sounded more amused at the memory of his attempted joke than she'd been at the attempt.

He decided this was a positive sign.

"That's right. The Wordman."

"All right. Tell me. How did you get on?"

"Actually it's quite complicated," he said cunningly. "I'm a bit rushed now. I wondered if you could spare a few minutes at lunchtime, say?"

A pause.

"I don't have long. One of us has to be here. And I usually eat a sandwich in the staffroom."

A staffroom was not what he had in mind.

"I thought perhaps a pub . . ."

"A pub?" As if he'd suggested a House of Assignation. "I don't get long enough to spend time in pubs. I suppose I could meet you in Hal's."

"Hal's?"

"The café–bar on the Centre mezzanine. Don't policemen get asked the way any more?"

"Yes, yes, I'll find it."

"I won't hold my breath. Twelve fifteen."

"Yes, twelve fifteen would be fine. Maybe we can . . ."

But he wasn't talking to anyone but himself.

At twelve thirty Dick Dee was perched behind the Reference enquiry desk, peering pensively at a computer screen when he heard a sexy cough.

It is not everyone who can cough sexily and he looked up with interest to see a young woman with blonde hair and sparkling blue eyes smiling at him. She was small and slightly built, but exuded the kind of energy a man could imagine being put to very good use.

"Hello," he said. "Can I help you?"

"I hope so," she said. "I'm Jax Ripley."

"And I'm Dick Dee, Miss . . . Ripley, was it?"

Jax thought, the bastard's pretending not to remember me!

Or, worse, she emended, looking into those guileless eyes, he really doesn't remember me!

She said, "We met the other week. On the council tour . . . when the shelf collapsed . . . I did want to interview you but wherever we pointed the camera, dear old Percy seemed to be in shot, talking about the way he'd like to see the Centre develop . . ."

She raised her eyebrows, inviting him to join in her amusement at Percy Follows' well-known appetite for publicity, especially with the council considering the appointment of an overall Centre Director.

Dee let his gaze run up and down her body, assessingly but without lubricity, and said, "Of course. Miss Ripley. Nice to see you again. How may I help?"

"It's about the short story competition. I gather you're in charge of the judging panel."

"Far from it," he said. "I'm merely one of the preliminary sorters."

"I'm sure you're more than that," she said turning her charm on full blast. She knew men and thought she'd detected beneath his politely neutral examination a definite effervescence of interest along the arteries. "When do entries close?"

"Tonight," he said. "So you'll have to hurry."

"I'm not thinking of entering," she said sharply, then saw from his faint smile that he was taking the piss.

Come to think of it, he wasn't a bad-looking guy, a long way from a hunk but the kind who might grow on you.

She laughed out loud and said, "But tell me, if I did want to enter, is the standard high?"

"There's a great deal of promise," he said carefully.

"Promise as in politicians, marriage or the Bank of England?" she asked.

"You'll need to wait till the result is announced to decide that," he said.

"Which is when?" she said. "I'd be interested in doing a piece on *Out and About,* maybe interviewing the short-listed authors. Or perhaps we could even have the result announced live on air."

"Nice idea," he said. "But I suspect Mary Agnew will want the news of the winner to be announced in the *Gazette.* Sell more newspapers that way, you see."

"Oh, I know Mary well. I used to work for her. In fact I was just talking to her earlier this morning and I'm sure we can come to some arrangement," said Jax with the confidence of one who takes as read the superiority of television over newsprint. "What I was after was a bit of preliminary information. I might even do a trail on tonight's show. Do you have a few moments? Or maybe I could buy you lunch?"

Dee was beginning to refuse politely when the library door burst open and a tall willowy man with a mane of golden hair framing a face as small as a monkey's came in and approached them with arms outstretched.

"Jax, my dear. They told me you were loose in the building. Your face is too famous to pass my sentinels unremarked. I hope you were going to come and see me, but I couldn't take the risk."

He rested his arms on Jax's shoulders and they exchanged a three-kiss salute.

Jax at her very first meeting with Percy Follows had marked him down as a prancing prat. But in the world of men, being a prancing prat didn't necessarily mean he was either stupid or incapable of rising to heights from which he might be able to extend a helping hand to an ambitious woman, so she said sweetly, "I assumed you'd be far too busy at some important working lunch, Percy, which incidentally is where I'm trying to take Mr. Dee here, but he was just telling me you work him far too hard for such frivolities."

"Do we?" said Follows, slightly nonplussed.

"It seems so. He doesn't even seem to have time for a working fast. And I'm desperate to pick his brain for a series of pieces I'm planning to do on this short story competition you thought up. It's the kind of cultural initiative we really need in Mid-Yorkshire. I'll want to interview you later on, of course, but I always like to start at factory-floor level . . ."

She's very good, thought Dee as she flashed him a smile and the hint of a wink from the eye furthest from Follows.

"Is that so?" said Follows. "Then of course you must go, Dick. I hereby unlock your chains."

"I'm by myself," said Dee. "Rye is on her lunch break."

"No problem," said Follows expansively. "I'll mind the shop myself. We're a true democracy here, Jax, everyone ready and able to do everyone else's work. Go, Dick, go, while the giving mood is on me."

Dee, Harold Lloyd to his boss's Olivier, cleared the computer screen, put on his leather-patched tweed jacket and with an old-fashioned courtesy took Jax's arm and ushered her through the door.

"So where are you taking me?" he enquired as they walked down the stairs.

Her mind printed out the alternatives. Pub? Too crowded. Hotel dining room? Too formal.

His hand still rested lightly on her arm. To her surprise she found herself thinking, rest it anywhere you like, darling.

This was quite the wrong way round, this feeling that he would be easy to like, easy to talk to. That was how he was supposed to be feeling!

She recalled the wise words of Mary Agnew when she'd worked for her.

You'll recognize a good story by what you're willing to do to get it. One thing though . . . lay yourself on the table by all means, darling, but never lay your cards. Knowing more than other people know is the only virginity in our game. Keep it.

Still, nothing wrong with enjoying yourself along the way.

"You call it," she said. "My treat. But I make a lovely open sandwich if I can find the right topping."

"This is nice," said Bowler. "Why's it called Hal's?"

They were sitting opposite each other at a table on the balcony of the café–bar which gave a view down the length of the main shopping precinct. On a clear day you could see as far as Boots the Chemist. The disadvantage of the situation was that the prurient youth of the town had discovered that a seat on the edge of the fountain in the atrium below gave them with luck an excellent view up the short skirts of those sitting above. But on entering Hal's, she had discovered Bowler at an inside table next to one occupied by Charley Penn. Had to be coincidence, but preferring the prying eyes of youth to the flapping ears of age, she'd suggested they move outside.

"Think about it," said Rye. "Heritage, Arts and Library complex? H. A. L."

"Disappointing," said Bowler. "I thought it might be named after an artificial intelligence which had gone wrong and was trying to control our lives."

She laughed and said, "You could be right."

Encouraged, he said, "You know what I thought the first time I saw you?"

"No, and I'm not sure I want to know," said Rye.

"I thought *redwing*."

"As in Indian Maid?"

"You know that song? Odd company you keep, or do you play rugby? Don't answer. No, as in *turdus iliacus*, the smallest of the common thrushes."

"I hope, for your sake, this is an extremely attractive, highly intelligent bird."

"Naturally. Also known as Wind Thrush or Swine Pipe from its sharp voice."

"And *iliacus* because it comes from Troy? The resemblances to the way I see myself don't seem to be multiplying."

"Helen came from Troy."

"No she didn't. She got abducted and ended up there. So forget the soft soap and tell me, where's the connection, Constable?"

"Simple really and entirely soap-free," he murmured. "The redwing is a bird with lovely chestnut colouring and a prominent pale strip over the eye. So when I saw this, I thought *redwing*."

He reached over and brushed his index finger against the tongue of silvery grey running through her hair.

That's enough, buster, thought Rye. Verbal jousting is one thing, but stroking my hair's a familiarity too far.

"So you really are a bird nerd," she said. "And here's me thinking it was just a cover story. Ah well, each to his own anorak."

She saw she'd scored a palpable hit and should have felt gleeful but didn't.

"Anyway, it's a better come-on than the guy who said it reminded him of Silver Blaze," she went on.

"Sorry?"

"Silver Blaze. The racehorse in the Sherlock Holmes story? Don't you all get issued those at Hendon, or is being a detective a cover story too?"

"No, that's for real too, I'm afraid."

"Oh yes? So prove it."

"OK," he said. "First off, this Wordman stuff is confidential, OK?"

"Confidential? It's me who brought you these Dialogues, remember? And now you're telling me just because you've invented a nickname for him, it's confidential."

"What I've found out in the course of my investigation is police business and I can't share it with you unless you accept its confidentiality," he said, deliberately ponderous.

She thought, nodded, said, "OK. So let's hear it."

"First, all that stuff about Ainstable—the tropical fish and the Greek holiday—is true. As is the story about where the bazouki came from. Plus there's a witness who might have seen a car's headlights just before the motorbike crash. And there could have been a car on the humpback bridge in front of where the AA van was parked."

"Oh, shit. So this lunatic really did kill them!" exclaimed Rye, horrified.

"Not necessarily. There are other ways the Wordman could have got the information and there's no way of knowing for certain if Ainstable stopped to help someone. And my witness who saw the lights is going senile and isn't a hundred per cent sure what he had for breakfast."

"Great! And this is what I've been sworn to secrecy over?"

Bowler said seriously, "It's important either way. If there's nothing in it, then we don't want to be spreading alarm and despondency about a possible serial killer on the loose, do we? And if there is something in it . . ."

"Yeah, yeah," she said. "So you're right, which could be an irritating habit. All right, Sherlock, what's your professional opinion?"

"Me? I'm far too junior to have opinions," said Bowler. "I just pass things up to my superiors and they've got to decide what to do next."

He smiled as he spoke and Rye said coldly, "You think it's something to joke about?"

"Hell, no. I'm not laughing at that. I'm just thinking about my DI who's only interested in sailing into retirement peacefully and just hates the idea of having to make a decision about something as difficult as this."

"I'm glad to know the public weal's in such safe hands."

"Don't worry. He's not typical. You should see the guy at the top."

His expression turned sombre at the thought of Andy Dalziel. Why did the guy dislike him so much? Couldn't just be because of his degree. Pascoe was a graduate too and he and the Fat Man seemed to be able to work together without too much blood on the carpet.

"Hello?" said Rye. "You still with me or are you getting messages from Planet Zog?"

"Yes. Sorry. Just the thought of our super does that to me. Look, I'll keep you posted about any further developments on the Wordman front, I promise. I assume there's been nothing more at your end?"

"Any more Dialogues, you mean? No, of course not, or we'd have called you. And the closing date for entries is tonight so there's not much time left."

He regarded her gravely and said, "Maybe if our Wordman really is killing people, he won't be much bothered by a closing date for a short story competition."

She looked irritated but with herself not him and said, "Thanks for making me feel stupid. That part of your job?"

"No. Is it part of yours?"

"When did I do it?"

"When you and Dee started using long words you assumed, rightly, I wouldn't understand."

"Such as?"

"When I told you what people called me, you said something about that being very *paranoidistic* or something."

"*Paronomasiac,*" she said. "Sorry. You're right. It's just the adjective from paronomasia which means any form of word-play, like a pun."

"And what Dee said?"

"*Paronomaniac.*" She smiled and said, "From *paronomania,* meaning an obsessive interest in word games. It's also the name of a board game Dick's very fond of. Bit like Scrabble, only harder."

He didn't really want to hear about Dee's cleverness or anything which hinted at intimacy between Rye and her boss, but couldn't help saying, "You've played this *para* whatsit, then?"

She gave him a cool smile which seemed to say she understood precisely the direction of his thoughts and said, "No. It seems only two can play and those two are Dick and Charley Penn."

"The writer?"

"Is there another?"

He decided this was leading nowhere and said, "So now we've both made each other feel stupid, what about this Sunday?"

She didn't pretend not to understand but said, "I don't know if I'm that stupid. What's the E stand for?"

"What E?"

"E. Bowler. On your library card. That E. Come on. What are you hiding under your hat, Hat?"

He looked at her doubtfully then took a deep breath and said, "Ethelbert."

"Ethelbert," she repeated, savouring the name like a jam doughnut, then running her tongue round her lips as if to pick up the residual sugar. "I like it."

"Really?" He examined her closely in search of ambush. "You'll be the first. Most people fall about laughing."

"When you've got a name that makes you sound like an alcopop, you don't laugh at other people's names," she said.

"Rye Pomona," he said. "I see what you mean. But it's nice. Isn't Pomona a place in Italy?"

"No," she said. "But it is Italian. Pomona was the Roman goddess of fruit trees."

She watched to see if he would lumber into a joke or ooze into a compliment.

He nodded and said, "And Rye, is that a nickname, or what?"

"Short for Raina," she said.

"Sorry? Never heard that one."

She spelt it for him, and pronounced it carefully, stressing the three syllables, *Rye-ee-na*.

"Raina," he echoed. "Raina Pomona. Now that's really nice. OK, it's unusual, but it's not naff, like Ethelbert Bowler."

She found herself pleased that he didn't make a big deal of asking where the name came from but just took it in his stride.

"Don't undersell yourself," she said. "Think positive. Ethelbert Bowler . . . it has an artistic ring . . . makes you sound like a minor Victorian watercolourist. Are you interested in art, Ethelbert? Under any of your hats?"

"I could probably dig out an old French beret," he said cautiously. "Why?"

"The Centre's new gallery opens week after next with a local arts and crafts exhibition. There's a preview the Saturday before, lunchtime. Care to come?"

He said, "Are you going by choice or because you're on the payroll?"

She said, "Does it matter? OK, it's sort of semi-duty. Centre politics, you wouldn't be interested."

"Try me till I yawn," he said.

"OK. The Centre's tri-partite, right? Heritage, Arts, Library. Library was easy, Percy Follows was Head of Library Services already, so he just slid into the new position. And it looked like Philomel Carcanet who ran the old municipal museum/art gallery on Shuttleworth Hill would likewise take over the new Heritage and Arts strands in the Centre. Except it's all proving a bit much for her. You yawning yet?"

"No, just breathing deeply with excitement."

"Fine. Dead things Philomel is really good with, living things in any quantity scare her stiff. She was delirious with excitement when the builders' digging unearthed that mosaic pavement. Then they decided to incorporate it into this Roman Experience thing—you must have read about it, a Mid-Yorkshire marketplace at the height of the Roman occupation?"

Hat nodded, he hoped convincingly.

"I believe you," she said, not bothering to sound convinced. "Anyway, that meant Phil had to start thinking about catering for live punters, live people again and it all got on top of her. So she's on sick leave. Meanwhile, someone's had to sort out the new gallery. Normally our Percy would run a mile rather than get involved with extra work, but there's a new factor. Word is that the council, Stuffer Steel apart, are contemplating appointing an overall director of the Centre. And our Percy imagines he's at the front of the queue for the job. But a trumpet sounds upstage left. Enter Ambrose Bird, the Last of the Actor–Managers."

"Who?"

"Where do you live? Ambrose Bird, who ran the old municipal theatre till it was closed last month, mainly as a result of Councillor Steel's opposition to the large grant needed to refurbish it up to health and safety standards. This has left the Last of the Actor–Managers (that's his own preferred title) with nothing to act in or manage but the Centre's much smaller studio theatre. That was definitely a yawn!"

"No, it was the beginning of an interjection. I was going to guess that this Bird guy has decided he'd like to put in for the Centre Director's job too."

"Have you ever thought of becoming a detective?" asked Rye. "Spot on. So Bird and Follows are locked in deadly combat. It's quite fun to watch them, actually. They don't try very hard to conceal the way they feel about each other. Anything in the Centre they can lay claim to, the pair of them are there, like dogs after a bone. The Roman Experience is drama, says Ambrose, so he takes responsibility for sound effects and training the people playing the market stallholders. Poor old Perce is left with language and smells."

"Smells?"

"Oh yes. The authentic smells of Roman Britain. Cross between a rugby changing room and an abattoir, as far as I can make out. Look, I'm beginning to yawn myself. The upshot of this is that Percy has countered by grabbing the lion's share of the preview arrangements and, with typical sexist insensitivity, has volunteered all his female staff to run around with the chardonnay and nibbles. End of story. You did pretty well, unless like a horse you can sleep with your eyes open."

"So why is a bright, lively, independent, modern woman like yourself putting up with this crap?" said Hat with what he hoped was convincing indignation.

She said defensively, "It's no big deal. I'd have gone anyway. Dick will have a couple of paintings in. He's a bit of an artist."

She saw him toy with a crack, but was glad to see he was bright enough to drop the idea.

"In that case," he said, "and as I too am on the public payroll, why not? Dress casual, is it?"

"Dress artistically," she murmured. "Which brings me to a very important question. What does the well-dressed twitcher wear in Stangdale, Hat?"

He studied her seriously to hide his delight at having guessed rightly that he was being offered a trade-off, then said, "Well, starting from the inside out, have you got any thermal underwear?"

VIII

Jax Ripley's colleagues had noticed that she was in vacant or pensive mood all that Friday afternoon. Normally as she put together the items for her early evening show, she was incisive and openly impatient with anyone who wasn't moving at her speed. But today she didn't seem to be able to make up her mind about things. *Out and About* was usually made up of several pre-recorded pieces linked by Jax, concluding with a live studio piece on some topic of particular local interest. All that she had pencilled in for this today was *short story comp trail?*

"Who are the guests?" asked John Wingate, the station manager. He was a middling aged plump man with a lean and hungry face, as if his chronic anxiety about everything had done a deal with his body and drawn a demarcation line around his neck. Below this, the soft folds of pink flesh glowed with health, and, warmed by sun or sex, gave off an odour which reminded Jax of her childhood bed beneath which her provident mother laid out rows of apples to see them through the North Yorkshire winter. Screwing Wingate had been a pleasure as well as a career move.

"No guests . . . Just me."

"So, couple of minutes," he said doubtfully. "That leaves us well short, Jax."

"No, I need the time."

"Why? How the hell can you spin something as boring as a short story competition trail out beyond ninety seconds?"

"Trust me," she said.

"You up to something, Jax?" he said suspiciously. "I hate it when you say 'trust me.' "

She finally made up her mind, reached out a hand to rest on his thigh and smiled.

"It'll be all right, John," she said.

In a life of bad career moves, John Wingate wasn't certain where he placed screwing Jax Ripley. She'd been a journalist on the *Gazette* when they first met and the chance of a one-night stand after a media party which Moira, his wife, hadn't attended because she was over in Belfast visiting her sick mother had seemed too good to pass by. And it had been good. He grew warm now just recalling it and the other encounters that followed, one in particular which had taken place in his office a couple of weeks later when she presented herself for interview. "I've come about the position," she said, climbing on to his desk and spreading herself before him. "How about this one for starters?"

And under the doubtless approving gaze of the members of Unthank College old boys rugby fifteen whose photo, holding the Mid-Yorkshire Cup which they'd won some years ago under his captaincy, hung on the wall behind his chair, he accepted the invitation, after which she accepted the job.

She'd learned quick and her rapid advancement was easily justifiable in terms of sheer talent, or so he reassured himself whenever, as now, he gave way to her wishes. There'd never been any hint of menace from Jax and she'd always behaved with the utmost discretion, but this didn't stop him from feeling that he had less control over his life, both professional and personal, than before her arrival. At least, thank God, he knew he didn't have to worry she was after his job. She had set her sights over the hills and faraway, in the greener pastures of Wood Lane, and if golden opinions from himself could speed her on her way, all the better.

Maybe that was the explanation of her distraction today.

He said, "Big day next Monday, then. Getting nervous? No need. You'll piss it."

She said, "What? Oh, the interview. No, I'll wait till I'm on the train before I get nervous."

He believed her. She was, he reckoned, that controlled. She might let herself get nervous as she drew near to her interview for the job with the national news service because taut nerves made you sharper, pitched you higher. But she'd know exactly how far to go.

Yet, though Wingate didn't know it, he'd hit pretty close to the mark.

Jax Ripley had a decision to make. Wingate's assurances that with her record and his recommendation she'd walk into the job were very comforting and she had no false modesty about her abilities. Sex she might use as a shortcut but only to get where she felt she deserved to be. Yet though she rated her talents high, she was not so arrogant as to rate them unique. It hadn't been difficult to come to the fore in the small show ring of Mid-Yorkshire, but the provinces are full of thrusting talents and it would take something extra to stand out among the ranks of competing clones nation-wide, all desperate to march on the Big Time.

And now she felt she might have the something extra.

But there were risks.

It would be burning boats, that's for sure. She was sworn to secrecy. Her revelations would this time be tracked unrelentingly to their source, and such a public act of betrayal would ensure that no one in Mid-Yorkshire would ever again open their mouths to her, not even with the promise that she would open her legs to them.

Plus, if it all went wrong and just came out as a bit of journalistic scaremongering, then she could even end up being dumped by BBC MY.

On the other hand, it was a good story. A couple of phone calls would alert some friends in London. National air coverage over the weekend plus the Sunday tabloids descending on Mid-Yorkshire to dig up—or make up—something really sensational could raise a news tsunami to sweep her into her interview on Monday. Once she got that job, it didn't matter what happened back here in Sleepy Hollow. In the real world down there, no one minded if today's scoop was tomorrow's poop. It happened all the time. It wasn't the apologies and retractions that stayed in people's minds, it was the banner headlines.

So why was she pussy-footing around? In this life you were either a player or a stayer. And I'm a player! she told herself as she headed into her office to make the necessary wake-up calls. No point jumping off a sky-scraper unless you had the audience you wanted.

It was, viewers opined later, by Jax Ripley's usual standards a rather slow show. In her intro and her link passages she seemed somewhat muted, a little lacking in her usual sparkle. Usually she almost came out of the screen at you. But not tonight. Tonight she clearly had something on her mind.

The last of the filmed items was an interview with Charley Penn about the new Harry Hacker series starting on television the following week. It was a good interview, with Jax at her seductive and Penn at his saturnine best. It ended with her asking him about the *doppelgänger* effect which he often used in his books, with Hacker finding himself being warned or otherwise aided by glimpses of a mysterious shadowy figure which seemed to bear a close resemblance to himself.

"Charley, tell me, do you really think it's possible for a person to be in two places at the same time, or are you going to surprise us one day by revealing that Harry's got a twin?"

Penn smiled at her, then looked straight into the camera.

"I don't know about being in two places at the same time, but I have no problem with a character being in two times at the same place."

She'd laughed at that. She was one of those few people whose mouth wide open in close-up was an on-turning rather than an off-putting experience.

"Too deep for me, Charley. But I love the new book. And though I say it as shouldn't, reading it's much better than watching the telly."

End of film. Cut to Jax live in the studio, no longer relaxing, bare legs folded beneath her, on the white leatherette sofa she shared with her interview guests, but sitting on a hard upright chair, knees locked tight together, fingers closely clasped, face set and serious, looking like a young schoolteacher about to administer a stern rebuke.

"*Doppelgängers* apart," she said, "it's usually agreed that truth is stranger than fiction, but I did not realize just how much stranger it could be until a little earlier this week.

"The fiction in the case is contained in most of the entries submitted to the *Gazette*'s short story competition. Entries close tonight, so those of you still scribbling had better get your skates on. I hope to announce the short list and perhaps interview some of the hopeful authors on the show next week.

"But there is one person submitting material who probably won't be rushing forward to be interviewed, the person the police are calling the Wordman . . ."

As she went on, around the county most listeners carried on with what they were doing, only gradually increasing their focus on what she was saying as its import struck home. But some there were who at the first mention of the short story competition had raised their heads, or reached forward to turn up the volume, or risen out of their seats, and a couple there were who as she went on began to swear violently, and there was one who sat back and laughed aloud and gave thanks.

After she'd finished and the brass band had played the show out, Jax sat still for a moment. Then John Wingate came bursting in.

"Jesus, Jax! What the hell was that all about? Is it true? It can't be true! Where'd it come from? What evidence have you got? You should have cleared this with me first, you know that. Shit! What's going to happen now?"

"Let's wait and see," she said, smiling, back to her old self now that the die was cast.

They didn't have long to wait.

Even Jax was taken aback by the sheer weight of the reaction.

It came in a confusion of telephone calls, faxes, e-mails and personal visits, but it was divisible into four clear categories.

First came her employers, at levels stretching up from Wingate himself to top management in London and their legal oracles. As soon as these had pronounced, with all the usual caveats and qualifications, that there did not on the face of it seem to be anything actionable in what she had said, she passed rapidly from potential liability to embryonic star. This was a hot news scoop in the old style, something rarely seen on national let alone provincial television. Hence the interest from category two, the rest of the media.

Once she'd made up her mind to go ahead, Jax had seeded word of her intention in several potentially fruitful areas. Long hardened against hype, no one had fallen over with excitement, but now the smell of blood was in the air and jackals everywhere were raising their snouts and sniffing. If this turned out to be a story that ran, then it was crazy not to be in at the beginning and by the end of the evening Jax had signed up for a national radio spot, a TV chat show and a Sunday tabloid article, while a broadsheet had opened negotiations for a profile. Mary Agnew of the *Gazette* had rung too. A pragmatist, she didn't waste time reproaching her former employee for scooping the story out of her lap.

"Well done, dearie," she said. "You got a head start, but you're going to need my help now."

"Why's that, Mary?"

"Because now you've done the dirty, your police source is going to dry up like a mummy's crotch," said Mary. "And because it's the *Gazette* that this nut—if there is a nut which I'm not yet convinced—is sending his material to. So when the next one comes . . ."

"What makes you think there'll be a next one, seeing you're such a sceptic?" interrupted Jax.

"You do, dearie. You've practically guaranteed it. Even if it was a joke before, you've made sure every nut in the county will want to get in on the act, and God knows how far some of them will be willing to go. I'll keep in touch. Sleep well."

Bitch, thought Jax. Sick as a parrot and trying to get her own back by getting inside my skull. Do I need her? Probably not. On the other hand, pointless telling her to piss off till I'm sure.

But category three, calls from the public, made her think that maybe Agnew had called it right after all. Some were concerned, some abusive, some plain dotty, a couple positively threatening, but none obviously useful. All were recorded and copies of the tapes made ready for the police. One tape definitely wasn't for the police, however. This was the call she had from Councillor Cyril Steel eager for any further ammunition she could supply him to aid his anti-cop crusade. Like Agnew, he was insignificant nationally but locally a big-hitter in his crusade against inefficiency and corruption. He'd given her a lot of good leads and what was more his omnivorous gut was the only appetite she was expected to satisfy in return. Now he was delighted at what he saw as a win-win situation. Either the police had failed in their duty by not telling the council about a possible serial killer in the town, or the ruling party had failed in theirs by keeping it to themselves. Minus her police ally, Jax was delighted to have whatever high-level support she could hang on to in Mid-Yorkshire and she let the halitotic councillor rabbit on for ten minutes or so before cutting him off with a promise to keep him up to speed.

Now she settled back to await the final category of calls.

This was the constabulary. The one she expected from her furious Deep-throat didn't come, but an hour after the programme ended, Mid-Yorkshire's press officer, a user-friendly inspector with a pleasant homely manner which disguised a very sharp mind, rang to wonder if the best interests of both the BBC and the Force might not be served by a bit of mutual co-operation. For example, if he promised to keep her in the picture, maybe she could tell him where she'd got her information? She'd laughed out loud and he'd laughed with her then said, "Please yourself, luv. But don't be surprised if you hear a loud barking just now. It'll be them upstairs coming round with the Rottweilers."

In the event the Deputy Chief Constable who turned up was dogless, but did his best with his own teeth. He asked her to reveal her sources. She refused on the grounds of journalistic privilege. He spelled out the obligations the law placed upon anyone with information relevant to a crime, whether already or still to be committed. He then wished her all the best in her future career, hoped for her sake it would be in an area far removed from Mid-Yorkshire, smiled caninely, and left.

You'd better get this London job, girl, she told herself. I think things could get pretty uncomfortable for you round here.

But the pluses were too many for the negativisms of Mary Agnew and the DCC to depress her spirits for long and when she finally decided to call it a night, she was bubbling inside like a bottle of champagne about to pop. John Wingate was still around, looking slightly less anxious now that it seemed likely her revelations on air were going to attract plaudits rather than brickbats. Sex seemed a good way to uncork her energies and she said, "Fancy coming back with me for a celebratory drink, John?"

He looked at her, looked at his watch, all the anxiety back on his face. He's recalling what it was like, she thought. He's thinking that with a bit of luck I'll be out of his hair and his life in a very short while, so why not one for the road? If I reached out and touched him and said, "Let's do it here," he'd be on me like a flash. But she didn't want a quickie on a dusty office floor.

She said, "You're right, John. Family first, eh?" kissed him lightly on the cheek and walked away, aware that the sway of her end in retreat was probably making him ache with regret. But she didn't want a man who'd be thinking of going even as he was coming. Tonight was an all or nothing night, and as she ran through a list of possibles in her head, it began to seem more and more like nothing. No one seemed to fit the bill perfectly . . . except maybe . . . but no, she couldn't ring him!

She let herself into her flat and kicked off the murderously high heels she wore to work. Despite or perhaps because of coming at people like Penthesilia on the charge, she was desperately self-conscious about her height, particularly on camera. Her clothes followed. She let them lie where they fell and slid her arms into her fine silk robe and her feet into a pair of unbecoming but supremely comfortable soft leather mules. Too wound up to think of sleep, she went to her computer and rattled off an e-mail to the one person she could talk to with (almost!) complete freedom: her sister, Angie in America. It wasn't sex, but it was a form of relief after a day spent weighing her words as closely as she'd been doing for the past several hours.

As she finished, the phone rang.

She picked it up and said, "Hi."

A voice started speaking immediately.

She listened then said incredulously, "And you've actually got this third Dialogue with you?"

"Yes. But it will have to be handed in tomorrow. If you want to see it . . ."

"Of course I want to see it. Could you come round to my place?"

"Now?"

"Yes."

"OK. Five minutes."

The phone went dead.

She put down the receiver and punched the air, a gesture she'd always thought rather naff when she saw footballers and gameshow contestants using it. But now she knew what it was expressing.

"Ripley," she said. "Someone up there really likes you."

the third dialogue

Ave!

Why not?
In the beginning was the Word, but what language was the Word in?
Spirits always speak in English at séances. Except probably in France. And Germany. And anywhere else.
So what language do the dead really speak if, as I presume, all the dead are capable of conversing with each other? A kind of Infernal Esperanto?

No, I reckon the dead must understand everything or else they understand nothing.
So how are things going? Comment ça va? Wie geht's?

With me? Well, things are picking up speed. Yes, it's harder. Don't think I'm not glad to be getting more responsibility, but I won't disguise, it's harder.
I knew she would be back late after the broadcast, but I didn't mind waiting. What's a couple of hours in a journey as long as mine? And part of the pleasure lies in the anticipation of that moment when time will stop completely and everything will happen in an infinitely savourable present.
She'd been a possibility ever since the bazouki player, of course, but there'd been others with equal claim. I had to listen to them all to make sure.

Nation shall speak unto nation, but it was that individual speaking to this individual that I wanted to hear. Then she made her broadcast and though her words were measured, with one eye fixed firmly on the Law, I could hear her underlying message aimed at one person only. Write me another Dialogue, she was saying. Please, I beg you, write me another Dialogue.

How could I resist such a clear invitation? How would I dare resist it when in this, as with the others, I feel myself your chosen instrument?

But being chosen does not exempt me from responsibility. Help I would be given, I knew that, but, after last time, only in the same measure as I showed myself able to help myself.

That is why I sat in the car and waited to make sure she came home by herself. A woman with her appetites might easily bring back a companion for her bed. I waited a little while longer after I'd rung. I could have been with her in thirty seconds but I didn't want her thinking I was so close.

When I pressed her bell she answered immediately through the intercom.

"Is that you?"

"Yes."

The front door opened. I went in and started climbing the stairs.

Already I could feel time slowing till it flowed no faster than oil paint squeezed on to an artist's palette. I was the artist and I was ready to set my new mark on this canvas which, complete, will place me in that dimension outside of time where all great art exists.

The door to her flat is open. But the chain is still on. I applaud such carefulness. I see her face in the interstice. I raise my left hand which is clutching a brown foolscap envelope.

And the chain comes off, the door opens fully. She stands there, smiling welcomingly. I smile back and move towards her, putting my hand inside the envelope. I see her bright eyes glisten with anticipation. She is in that moment of expectancy truly beautiful.

But like Apollonius looking at Lamia, I see through that fair-seeming to what she really is, the corrupter, the distorter, the self-pleasurer—and the self-destroyer too, for there is at the heart of the worst of us a nugget of that innocence and beauty we all bring with us into this world, and though I purpose to cut the depraved part out, that nugget will, I hope, remain, sending her out of the world as beautiful and innocent as she came into it.

I seize the haft of the knife inside the envelope and slide the long thin blade into her body.

I've read about the blow—under the ribs then drive upwards—but naturally I've had no chance to practise on living flesh. It's the kind of thing people notice. But for all the trouble it causes me, you might imagine I came from a long line of Mafiosi.

Oh, how good it is when the word so surely conveys the deed and theory blends so smoothly into practice. The current runs along the wire and the bulb begins to glow; the spaceship balances on its tail of flame then begins to climb into the sky. Just so the blade slices under the ribs and almost of its own volition angles up through the lung to the beating heart.

For a moment I hold her there, all the sphere of her life balanced on a point of steel. The fulcrum of the planets is here, the still centre of the Milky Way and all the unthinkable intervacancies of infinite space. Silence spreads from us like ripples on a mountain tarn, rolling over the night music of distant traffic noises borne on a gusting wind, deadening all of humanity's living, loving, sleeping, waking, dying, birthing gasps and groans, snores and sniggers, tattle and tears.

Nothing else is. Only we are.

Then she is gone.

I raise her in my arms and carry her into the bedroom and lay her down reverently, for this is a solemn and holy step in both our journeys.

The parents still watch anxiously, but now the child, with wandering step and slow, begins to move alone.

I pray you, do not let me stumble. Be the strength of my life; of whom then shall I be afraid?

Speak soon, I beg you, speak soon.

X

On Saturday morning Rye Pomona had to field so many questions about Ripley's TV programme from her colleagues en route to the reference library that she arrived ten minutes late and found that she'd missed the beginning of a half-furious row in the office.

The furious half was Percy Follows whose angry tirade bounced off the placid surface of Dick Dee, leaving no trace but a faint puzzlement.

"I'm sorry, Percy, but I got the distinct impression you didn't want to be troubled with anything to do with the short story competition. In fact I recall your exact words—you always put things so memorably. You said that this was such an inconsiderable task, you could see little reason why it should disturb any of the essential routines of the department and none whatsoever why you yourself should be troubled with it beyond news of its successful completion."

Rye took a positive pride in her boss's performance. That attention to and memory for detail which made him such an efficient Head of Reference also gave him a forensic precision in an argument. Not wanting to interrupt such good entertainment, she didn't go into the office but sat down at the enquiry desk. The department's morning mail had been placed there plus the all too familiar plastic bag containing the latest and (her spirits rose) presumably the last batch of short stories from the *Gazette*.

Lying at the top of the bag, half in, half out, was a single sheet with only a few lines typed on it. Still listening to the row, she picked it up and read.

> *I see thee as a flower,*
> *so fair and pure and fine.*
> *I gaze on thee and sadness*
> *steals in this heart of mine*

"But this wasn't about the competition, was it?" Follows was bluster-ing. "These Dialogues, so far as I can make out, must have got mixed up with that by accident. Ripley said they were probably meant for the news desk of the *Gazette*."

Trying to put distance between the library and any bad fall-out from the Dialogues, thought Rye as her eyes continued to scan the verses.

> *It is as though my fingers*
> *should linger in your hair,*
> *praying that God preserve thee*
> *so fine and pure and fair.*

In the office Dee was enquiring courteously, "Are you saying I should have known this and returned them to the *Gazette*?"

"That's what Mary Agnew thinks," said Follows. "She was on to me as soon as that Ripley woman finished last night. I don't think she believed me when I protested total ignorance."

"I'm sure on mature reflection she won't have any difficulty with that concept," said Dee.

This was good stuff, uttered so politely that Follows could only do him-self damage by acknowledging the insult, thought Rye. The poem was pretty good stuff too. It would be nice to think that Hat Bowler had broad-ened his chat-up technique to include this old-fashioned approach, but somehow she couldn't see him as a lovelorn poet. In any case, she didn't need to be Miss Marple to detect the true source of the stanzas. Slowly she raised her eyes and found herself, without surprise, looking across the li-brary at Charley Penn, twisted round in his usual chair, regarding her with undisguised pleasure.

She let the sheet slip to the floor, wiped her hand as if to remove some sticky substance, then ostentatiously applied herself to the task of opening the mail. There wasn't much and what there was didn't require her special attention, so finally with reluctance she turned her attention to the story bag. This might be the last consignment, but its bulk suggested there'd been a last-minute rush.

The row was still going on though clearly not going anywhere.

Dee was saying, "If I'd any idea this was going to blow up the way it has, of course I would have filled you in, Percy. But the police urged absolute discretion upon us, no exceptions."

"No exceptions? Don't you think you ought to have consulted me before involving the police in the first place?"

At last Follows had laid a glove on Dee, thought Rye. But the Library Chief didn't have enough sense to jab at this weak point but kept flailing away in search of a knockout blow.

"And how the hell did Ripley get to know about this anyway? She took you to lunch yesterday. What did you talk about, Dick?"

Not a bad question, thought Rye, easing the stories out on to the counter.

"The short story competition, of course. It was clear she was on a fishing expedition, asking about strange and unusual entries. Without direct reference to the Dialogues, she gave me the impression she somehow knew a great deal about them, but I certainly didn't add to her knowledge."

True or false?

She certainly couldn't imagine Dick Dee being indiscreet unless he wanted to be. On the other hand, he would probably be scrupulous in a deal, even if the terms were unspoken. And just because he'd never used the opportunities offered by their working proximity to make even the most casual of physical contacts, let alone cop a feel, why should she be surprised, and even a little jealous, to find that Jax Ripley with her blue eyes, blonde hair and wide mouth had proved the type to ring his bell? As for the journalist herself, she thought with less generosity, her burning passion for a good story would probably have made her very willing to waggle Dee's clapper.

She almost laughed aloud at the way her metaphor had developed, and close by heard an answering chuckle. Penn had left his seat and come to the desk.

"Good, isn't it?" he murmured. "I'm so glad I got here early. Ah, there it is. I should hate it to get mixed up with these . . . effusions."

He stooped and picked up the poem from the floor.

"I stopped at the desk with a bunch of stuff I wanted to talk over with Dick, but the fun was just starting and I didn't want to interrupt. This must have slipped out. A version of *"Du bist wie eine Blume."* I quite like it. What did you think?"

"Me? Didn't really take it in. Now, if you'll excuse me, I'm busy. Unless you'd like to help me sort out your fellow writers?"

He grinned at the attempted gibe and moved away, saying, "I fear not. How could my little light bear the glare of all that talent?"

But she wasn't paying attention. As was her usual practice, she'd been dividing the stories into handwritten and typewritten, following which she would dump all those in the former group which didn't reach her increasingly exacting standards of legibility. But it was a typewritten sheet she had in her hands and was studying with growing agitation.

"Oh shit," she said.

"In any case," Dick Dee was saying, "I dare say that despite Miss Ripley's efforts to stir it up, this will after all turn out to be nothing more than a storm in a tea-cup, leaving her (to re-direct the image) with egg on her face, and your good self without so much as a breadcrumb on the snow-white lace doyley of your reputation."

It was, Rye had come to know, a habit of Dee's to coat his more acerbic ironies with garishly colourful layers of language, but the assurance seemed enough to mollify Percy Follows, a process signified physically as he came out of the office by an attempted smoothing down of his mane of golden hair which at times of stress exploded electrically like the tail feathers of a randy bird of paradise.

I shouldn't bother, Perce, thought Rye.

Dee followed, smiled at Rye and said, "Good morning."

"Morning. Sorry I was late," she said, watching Follows and hoping he would leave the Reference.

"Were you? I'm not in a position to notice. I seem to have mislaid my watch again. You haven't seen it?"

Dee's watch was a running joke. He didn't like working at a keyboard with it on, claiming it unbalanced his prose, but once removed it seemed to have what Penn called *Fernweh*, a longing to be somewhere distant.

"Try the middle shelf. It seems very fond of there."

He ducked down behind the reception desk, came up smiling.

"How clever of you. I'm back in time's ever rolling stream which means I suppose we should get down to some work. Percy, are we finished?"

Follows said, "I hope so, Dick. I hope we've heard the last of this silly business, but if there are any further developments, I want to be the first to know. I hope you and your staff understand that."

He looked accusingly at Rye who smiled at him, thought, *OK, Perce, if that's what you want, let me make your day,* and said to Dee, "Dick, I'm afraid we've got another one."

She held up the sheets of paper carefully by one corner.

She could see Dee understood her instantly but Follows was a little slower to catch on.

"Another . . . ? Oh God, you don't mean another of these Dialogue things? Let me see."

He attempted to snatch it from her fingers but she moved away.

"I don't think it would be too clever for anyone else to handle it," she said. "I think we ought to get it round to the police straightaway."

"That's what you think, is it?" said Follows, his hair sun-bursting once again.

She thought for a moment he was going to try ordering her to hand the Dialogue over. The library staff, he liked to claim, were one big happy family, but, as Dick Dee had once remarked, democracy was not a form of organization much practised in family life.

But on this occasion Follows had enough sense not to push things to confrontation.

"Very well," he said. "And perhaps we should make a copy for Miss sodding Ripley while we're at it. Though it wouldn't surprise me if she didn't have one already."

"No," said Rye. "I don't think so. Though she may be privy to the gist."

She shook the sheets of paper gently.

"I hope it's all a sick fantasy, but if I read this aright, I think the Wordman is telling us that he's just murdered Jax Ripley."

XI

Hat Bowler stared down at Jax Ripley's body and felt a pang of grief which
for a second almost took the strength out of his legs.

He had seen bodies before during his short service and had learned
some of the tricks of dealing with the sight—the controlled breathing, the
mental distancing, the deliberate defocusing. But this was the first time
he'd seen the corpse of someone he knew. Someone he liked. Someone as
young as he was.

It's yourself you're grieving for, he told himself savagely, hoping to
regain control via cynicism. But it didn't work and he turned away un-
steadily, though careful not to grasp at anything in an effort to control his
unsteadiness.

George Headingley was moved too, he could see that. In fact the portly
DI had turned away and left the bedroom before Bowler and was now sit-
ting in an armchair in the living room of the flat, looking distinctly un-
well. He hadn't looked too good when he arrived at work that morning.
Indeed he'd been five minutes late, inconsequential in the routine of most
CID officers over the rank of constable, but a seismic disturbance of the
Headingley behaviour pattern.

When Bowler had burst into his office with the news that Rye had just
given him over the telephone, he seemed to have difficulty taking it in.
Finally, after Bowler had tried to contact the TV presenter at the studios,

then by phone at home, Headingley had allowed himself to be persuaded that they ought to go round to Ripley's flat.

Now, sitting in the armchair, staring into space, instead of a healthy fifty-year-old sailing serenely into a chosen retirement, he looked more like a superannuated senior citizen who'd hung on till decrepitude forced him out.

"Sir, I'll get things under way, shall I?" said Bowler.

He took silence for an answer and rang back to the station to get a scene-of-crime team organized, adding, *sotto voce*, "And make sure the DCI knows, will you? I don't think Mr. Headingley's up to it this morning."

He'd managed to persuade the DI that an armchair in a murder victim's flat was not the cleverest place to let a senior officer find you in and got him outside into the damp morning air before Peter Pascoe appeared.

"George, you OK?" he asked.

"Yeah. Well, no, not really. Touch of flu coming on. Could hardly get out of bed this morning," said Headingley in a shaky voice.

"Then if I were you I'd go and get back into it," said Pascoe crisply.

"No, I'll be OK. Got to get back inside and take a look round while the trail's still hot . . ."

"George, you know no one's going inside there till everything's been done that needs to be done. Go home. That's an order."

And to take the sting out of pulling rank on an old colleague who'd been a DI ever since Pascoe first arrived in the Mid-Yorkshire force as a DC, Pascoe said in a low voice as he ushered Headingley to his car, "George, with days to do, you don't want this, do you? I mean, who knows, it could roll on forever. Grab the money and run for the sun, eh? And don't worry, I'll see you get credit for what you've done so far. Love to Beryl."

He watched the DI's car drive slowly away then with a shake of the head he turned back to the apartment building.

"Right," he said to Bowler. "Better bring me up to speed on this."

"Yes, sir. Hope you didn't mind me asking for you to be brought in. The DI really didn't look well . . ."

"No, you were quite right," said Pascoe. "You don't look too clever yourself. Hope that there isn't something going around."

"No, sir, I'm fine. Just a bit of a shock seeing Jax . . . Miss Ripley . . . I knew her a bit, you see . . ."

"Yes," said Pascoe regarding him thoughtfully. "See her show last night, did you?"

"Yes. Bit of a turn up, I thought. You saw it, did you, sir?"

"No, as a matter of fact."

But he'd heard about it when Dalziel had rung him up, uttering dreadful threats about what he was going to do to Ripley and Bowler, together and separately, when he got his hands on them.

Pascoe had calmed him down, pointing out that it wasn't good policy to publicly assault a TV personality, and as for Bowler, if it could be proved he'd passed on the information, he'd be dealt with by a Board of Enquiry which at the very least would get him out of the Fat Man's thinning hair.

The thought occurred to the DCI that maybe Dalziel had ignored his advice and that the DC's pallor and maybe even the woman's death were down to his direct intervention.

But when the scene-of-crime team had finished their preliminary examinations and he finally got to look at the body, he crossed the Fat Man off his list of suspects. The stiletto wasn't his weapon. He'd have torn her head off.

Such frivolous thoughts were his usual technique for distracting himself from the close encounters with the dead kind which were his most unfavourite occupational hazard. A greater distraction was imminent. He heard it first like a distant mighty rushing wind entering the building and he checked his head for cloven tongues of fire in the long mirror above the bed. But of course it was only the most unholy spirit of Andrew Dalziel that burst into the room.

"Fuck me," he said, coming to a halt at the foot of the bed. "Fuck me rigid. Last night I wished her dead, I really did. You should never wish things, lad, less'n you're sure you can thole it if they come true. How long?"

"Eight to ten hours estimate from body temp and the degree of cyanosis, but we'll need to wait . . ."

". . . for the PM. Aye, I know. Always the sodding same, these medics. More scared of commitment than a randy Iti. That's a handy mirror."

Long used to such sudden changes of direction, Pascoe studied the reflection in the long wall glass above the bed-head. Ripley looked very peaceful. The silk robe she was wearing had been parted to permit the medical examiner to check the fatal wound but Pascoe had drawn the garment together again to cover her torso.

"For sex, you mean?" he said.

"Nay, wash tha mind out with carbolic! You've been reading them mucky books again. Has she been moved?"

"Only as much as was necessary for the ME to do his job. I said you'd want to see her in situ."

"Oh aye? That one of them Japanese beds? This one's old-fashioned Yorkshire by the look of it. Nice strong bed-end to give a man something to push against. No, lad, take a look at her in the mirror. What do you see?"

Pascoe looked.

"Roots?" he hazarded. "She dyed her hair blonde?"

"Yes," said the Fat Man impatiently. "But we'd have spotted that on the slab, wouldn't we? No, I mean the other end."

Pascoe looked at the woman's feet up against the bed-end which Dalziel so favoured. She was wearing a pair of comfortable-looking leather mules. From the bottom of the bed they were invisible. From the side, they were unremarkable. But viewed in the mirror, there was something . . . hard to tell, they were so shapeless, but . . .

"They're on the wrong feet?" he said tentatively.

"Right. And how'd they get on the wrong feet?"

"Presumably they dropped off as the Wordman carried her through . . ."

"The Wordman? Aye, where did that bloody name come from anyway?"

"Seems it was DC Bowler's nickname for the lunatic who's writing these Dialogues."

"Boghead's name, you say? And Ripley were bandying it about on her programme?" Dalziel scowled. "I want a word with that young man. Where's he at?"

"I sent him to the library to pick up this new Dialogue, the one that put us on to . . . this."

"You sent *him*? Nay, come to think of it, doesn't matter, does it? Who's he going to leak it to with the Ripper dead? This Wordman bang her, front or back, before or after the event, did he?"

Dalziel's apparent callosity in face of murder was, Pascoe hoped, his preferred way of dealing with distress. Or maybe he was just callous.

"We'll need to wait for the PM results, but the preliminary exam didn't turn up signs of sexual interference in any quarter. Sir, these shoes . . ."

"Mules, lad. Wordman must have put 'em back on. Ergo, he touched them. And they've not been dusted for prints, have they?"

He was right. Every other likely surface in the flat bore a light scattering of powder.

"I'll see they get done," said Pascoe. "Here's Bowler now."

The young DC came hurrying into the flat but stopped short when he saw Dalziel.

"You look like you've just remembered somewhere else you ought to be, lad," said the Fat Man. "That this Dialogue thing drooping in your hand or are you just sorry to see me?"

"Yes, sir. The Dialogue, sir," stuttered Bowler.

He handed it over in its transparent plastic folder.

Dalziel scanned through it then passed it to Pascoe.

"Right, young Bowels," he said. "Let's you and I have a look around, to see if she kept a notebook or a diary."

He observed the DC closely for signs of a guilty start as he said this but got nothing, or maybe the youngster's expression was already too unhappy for anything else to show.

When the Fat Man found a small appointments book, he tossed it to Pascoe as if afraid that Hat would snatch it from his hand and try to eat it, then said, "Right, lad. Why don't you pop downstairs and tell those grave robbers out there that the late Ms. Ripley is ready for removal to the mortuary?"

When he'd gone, Dalziel turned to Pascoe, who'd been rifling through the pages of the book, and said, "Anything?"

"Relevant to the murder? Not that I can see, sir."

"Relevant to who's been leaking this stuff," snarled the Fat Man.

"Looking back, there's a significant number of appointments with someone or something designated as GP," said Pascoe.

"GP? What's that? Her sodding doctor?"

"Whatever it is, I can't see how you could turn it into DC Bowler. Initial E. Nickname Hat."

"Code, mebbe," said Dalziel, disgruntled.

He turned away and Pascoe rolled his eyes upward.

"Don't roll your eyes at me, lad," said Dalziel without even looking.

"I'm just thinking, shouldn't we concentrate a little harder on solving this case, sir, rather than finding out who the mole is?"

"Nay, that's down to you, Pete. This is one of them clever-cuts cases. Old-fashioned bugger like me's right out of his depth. I'll fade into the background and let you call the shots on this one."

Oh yes? thought Pascoe sceptically. Previous experience had taught him that having the Fat Man in the background tended to block out the light.

He continued his examination of the appointments book and said, "That solves one mystery."

"What one's that?"

"Why she went public last night. She must have known that she was going to have us down on her like a ton of bricks and probably scare off her police contact forever. But it was a risk worth taking. She's got . . . she would have had an interview with BBC News in London on Monday. And a big story like this a couple of days before wouldn't have done her chances any harm, I reckon. That's probably why she tried to sensationalize it."

"Well, she's certainly succeeded now," said Dalziel as the mortuary men came in accompanied by Bowler and started preparing the corpse for removal.

The three policemen watched in silence, not broken till the men bore their sad burden out of the apartment.

"Lesson to us all there," said Dalziel.

"What's that, sir?" said Pascoe.

"Ambition," said the Fat Man. "It can be a killer. Right, I'm off. Keep me posted."

Hat watched him go with unconcealed relief.

Pascoe said, "Hat, I looked at the report you did for Mr. Headingley. It was good. Really gave the indicators there was something nasty going off. Tragic it had to be confirmed like this, but no one's going to be able to say we weren't on the ball. Well done."

"Yes, sir, thank you," said Hat, recognizing the DCI's kindness in so reassuring him and feeling all the worse for it. "Sir, there's something else, just occurred to me now really . . . that guy Roote you've had me watching . . ."

He had Pascoe's full attention.

"I think he was . . . I mean, he certainly was eating at the Taverna the night David Pitman was killed . . ."

And now Peter Pascoe was looking at him with no kindness whatsoever in his eyes.

XII

The good thing about Pascoe was that he didn't nurse grudges, or at least didn't seem to, which might of course be the bad thing about Pascoe.

Hat had volunteered to go and interview Roote about his visit to the Taverna but the DCI had said no, and then, as was usual with him though unusual in most senior officers, gone on to explain his reasoning.

"Roote doesn't know your face—unless you've alerted him?"

"No way, sir," said Hat confidently.

"Let's keep it that way then. I'll send Sergeant Wield to do the interview. He is, of us all, the most . . . how shall I put it? . . . unreadable. If anyone can convince Roote he's just a possible witness like everyone else who dined at the Taverna, then it's Wield. Of course, that's all that Roote probably really is. A possible witness."

Oh yes, thought Hat. But you're hoping like mad he's a lot more than that!

"Meanwhile," said Pascoe, "you get yourself round to the *Gazette*. Ripley was killed late last night. Unless the Dialogue was written in advance, and it certainly doesn't read like that, it must have got into the bag some time in the ten hours before nine this morning when it was found. I want to know how. I'll double check the library end. Meet me there when you're done. And, Hat, play it cool, eh? All hell's going to break loose when the press get on to this story. Let's stretch out the calm before as long as we can!"

◆   ◆   ◆

Hat's visit to the *Gazette* office didn't last long. Pascoe's hopes for a breathing space proved vain. News of the latest Dialogue had already reached here, and Mary Agnew was more interested in trying to get information than in giving it. Eager to be out of her reach, Hat stonewalled stubbornly till he got what he'd come for. It wasn't very helpful. Friday night was always hectic with preparation for the Saturday edition, and Jax Ripley's broadcast had made it even more so, giving Mary Agnew a last-minute lead story she couldn't ignore. This meant that no one had noticed a secondary effect of Ripley's revelations which was that for some reason they seemed to have reinforced her reminder of the closing date for entries to the story competition. Early next morning the post-boy who, having better things to do than watch television on a Friday night, remained blissfully ignorant of all the excitements, discovered the dozen or more late entries, shoved them into the sack with all the others which had turned up during the day on Friday and, glad to see the end of what he found a very tedious task, delivered them post haste to the Centre. Mary Agnew, who'd naturally checked everything in the sack after watching Ripley's show, was furious when she now realized for the first time that more had been added later and Hat sneaked away under cover of the fire and fury she was raining on the post-boy's bewildered head.

As he reached the Centre, which was only a couple of minutes' walk away, he saw the DCI's lean and rangy figure pushing through the glass doors and hurried to catch up with him.

"You've been quick," said Pascoe accusingly.

Hat, who'd been expecting compliments for his speed, gave what he thought was a very professional almost Wield-like summation of his findings, but found insult added to injury when Pascoe seemed inclined to believe he must have let the cat out of the bag about the Dialogue. He defended himself vigorously but it turned out unnecessarily, for when they entered the Reference, evidence that Agnew already knew everything was there in the shape of the spare, stooping nicotine-impregnated figure of Sammy Ruddlesdin, the *Gazette*'s senior reporter.

He was in the middle of what seemed a heated exchange with Percy Follows and a short stocky man wearing a check suit bright enough to embarrass a bookie and a ponytail like a donkey's pizzle. Standing to one side like adjudicators at a livestock show were Dick Dee and Rye.

Dee, noting their arrival first, said, "Visitors, Percy," in a quiet voice which somehow had sufficient force to cut through the debate. The three men looked towards the newcomers. Follows' mouth stretched into a smile almost too broad for his small face and with an equine toss of his luxuriant mane he made a bee-line for Pascoe, thwarting the attempts of ponytail to interpose his own body, but unable to prevent the man from interposing his own voice which was astonishingly deep and resonant, as if issuing from the depths of a cavern.

"DCI Pascoe, isn't it? I have the pleasure of your wife's acquaintance, sir. Ambrose Bird. This is a dreadful business. Dreadful."

So this was Ambrose Bird, the Last of the Actor–Managers. Hat recalled what Rye had said about the rivalry between Bird and Follows for the proposed overall directorship of the Centre. This, it became clear, was the reason for his presence. As news of the murder and the Dialogue had run round the building (no prizes for guessing its source, thought Hat, looking at the still vainly chirruping librarian), Bird had decided that his self-assumed status as Director Apparent if not yet Elect would be enhanced by appearing as the Centre spokesperson to the media. He was probably the one who'd picked up the phone and tipped off the *Gazette*.

Pascoe, with a diplomatic ease that Hat could only admire and hope to learn, quickly relegated the trio to the public area of the reference library while Hat ushered Rye Pomona and Dick Dee into the office.

Pascoe closed the door, checked on the trio of men through the glass panel, then murmured to Hat, "Keep your eye on that lot. Any of them come close, especially Sammy, get out there and break their legs."

The office had a lived-in feel about it. Coffee machine, tin of biscuits, one old armchair that didn't look like municipal issue, a square of Oriental carpet the same, and the walls crowded with pictures, some prints, some photos, all of men. Maybe Dee was gay, thought Hat hopefully. But he didn't feel gay, though this was a dangerous touchstone to be applied by anyone who worked with Edgar Wield. Looking for evidence that the librarian was a family man, he spotted on the desk a silver-framed photo of three schoolboys. The one on the right looked like it might be Dee junior. Or perhaps, indeed, Dee senior when junior. Also on the desk was a box containing small plastic tiles with letters and numbers on, plus three wooden tile racks, standing on a large folded board. Presumably this was *Paro*-whatsit, the crazy word game Rye had told him about.

He caught her eye and risked a smile.

She didn't smile back.

Pascoe took her and Dee through the events of the morning with clinical precision while Hat took notes, glancing through the panel from time to time to make sure the journalist was keeping a safe distance.

When she said that the first thing she picked out of the open sack had been Charley Penn's translation of one of Heine's poems, Hat felt yet another pang of this silly jealousy.

"So Mr. Penn was in the library already when you arrived?"

"Oh yes."

"And saw everything?"

"Mr. Penn doesn't miss much," said Rye carefully.

"I didn't notice him when we arrived just now," said Pascoe.

"No," intervened Dee. "Charley said that there would probably be so much fuss in the library that he'd be better off working at home."

From the faint smile that accompanied this, Hat guessed it was a paraphrase of what Penn had actually said.

"And home is where?"

Dee stumbled over the address and Rye came in and recited it correctly. Did this mean she'd actually been there? wondered Hat, jealousy once more bubbling up, without, he hoped, showing on his face. She'd already picked up he was jealous of her fondness for Dee. Let her get the impression he was some kind of possessive nut and that could really fuck up his prospects.

Finally Pascoe was satisfied.

Leaving the two librarians in the office, he moved out with Hat. Near the library door, Bird and Follows were continuing their running row while Ruddlesdin, chewing on an unlit cigarette, spectated with world-weary indifference. The dispute stopped when Pascoe called, "Gentlemen!" and all three moved to join him.

He stepped aside to usher them into the office.

"I'm finished here," he said. "Thank you for waiting so patiently."

Then, to Hat's delight and admiration, he gently closed the door behind them and moved towards the exit at a pace which stopped just short of running.

Ruddlesdin caught up with them just before the door of the car-park lift closed.

"Quote, Pete," he gasped. "Give us a quote."

"Smoking can seriously damage your health," said Pascoe.

"Where are we going, sir?" asked Hat as they got into the car.

"To talk to Charley Penn, of course," said Pascoe.

Penn's flat was on the top floor of a converted Edwardian townhouse which was corralled in scaffolding and resonant with the shouts, crashes, clangs and radio music which proclaim to the world that the British work-man is earning his pay.

They found Penn on his way out. With a resentful glower, he turned round and led them back into his apartment, saying, "Would you bloody believe it, I fled the library, thinking it was soon going to be echoing to the heavy plod of constabulary feet, making it impossible to work, and came back to this hell?"

"But you must have known that work was going on," said Pascoe.

"They hadn't started when I left and I thought, Saturday morning, maybe the buggers refuse to get out of their pits unless they get quadruple time."

"So what are they doing?"

"My landlord's tarting the building up, reckons he can get five times what he paid for it a couple of years back if he sells it as a single dwelling." The writer showed his uneven teeth in a canine grin. "But he's got to get shut of me first, hasn't he?"

While these pleasantries were being exchanged, Hat took a look around.

The flat, so far as he could work out without being too obvious, con-sisted of a bedroom, bathroom, kitchen, and the room they were in. High-ceilinged and with a deep bay window which gave a good view (even framed in scaffolding) over the interesting roofscape of the older part of town, it had a sense of spaciousness which not even the detritus of a deter-mined bookman could disguise. There was a huge desk in the bay, its sur-face completely hidden by papers and books which overflowed on to the floor a couple of metres in all directions. At the other side of the room stood a green-baized antique card table with a rotatable top on which very neatly laid out was a large board in the shape of a five-pointed star, marked in squares, some coloured, some bearing strange symbols, flanked by a dish full of letter tiles and three wooden tile racks.

They really must enjoy this game, him and Dee, thought Hat. A board each! Maybe there were more. Presumably there'd be one in Dee's home too, and God knows where else.

Then his attention was diverted to the wall directly behind the table on which hung a framed photograph. It showed three boys standing close together, arms round each other. It was the same picture he'd seen on Dick Dee's desk, except that this print was much larger. The enlarging had exaggerated the fuzziness caused by the poor focus to produce a strange otherworldly effect, so that the boys appeared like figures seen in a dream. They were standing on grass and in the background were trees and a tall castellated building, like a castle in a misty forest. The two outer boys were almost of a height, one perhaps two or three inches taller than the other, but they were both a good six inches taller than the boy in the centre. He had a mop of curly blond hair and a round cherubic face which was smiling with undisguised delight at the camera. The shorter of the other two, the one who looked like Dee, was smiling also, but a more inward-looking, secretively amused kind of smile, while the third wore an unambiguous scowl which Hat saw again as a voice snarled, "Having a good poke around, are you?" and he turned to look at Charley Penn.

"Sorry, it was just the game," he said, indicating the board. "Rye—Miss Pomona, mentioned it . . . some funny name . . . para something . . ."

"Paronomania," said Penn, regarding him closely. "So Ms. Pomona mentioned it, did she? Yes, I recall her taking an interest when she saw me and Dick playing one day. But I told her that like all the best games, only two could play."

He smiled salaciously, his gaze fixed on Hat, who felt his face flush.

"Some kind of Scrabble, is it?" said Pascoe.

"Oh yes. Like chess is some kind of draughts," sneered Penn.

"Fascinating. My young daughter loves board games," murmured Pascoe. "But we mustn't detain you any longer than necessary, Mr. Penn. Just a couple of questions . . ."

But before he could begin there was a loud knock at the outer door.

Penn left them and a moment later they heard the outbreak of a loud and increasingly acrimonious discussion between the writer and the foreman of the renovators, who required access to the windows of Penn's flat and seemed to think some written instruction from his employer gave him a legal right to this.

Pascoe moved across to a tall bureau and examined the books on the shelves. All of Penn's Harry Hacker series were there.

"Read any of these, Hat?" enquired Pascoe.

"No, sir. Better things to do."

Pascoe regarded him curiously then said, "Maybe you should. You can learn a lot about a writer from his books."

He reached up and took from a shelf not a book but one of two leather-cased files marked SKULKER. Opening it, he found bound inside copies of a magazine with that name. It was clearly an amateur production, though well organized and laid out. He opened a page at random.

A Riddle

My first is in Dog House, though not in demand:
My second's incrassate until it's in hand:
My whole is in Simpson when it isn't in Bland.

(Answer on p.13)

Hat was looking over his shoulder.

"A riddle," he said excitedly. "Like in the Second Dialogue."

"Don't get excited," said Pascoe. "This is a different kind of riddle, though it is not the kind of riddle it at first appears to be. It sounds as if it should be one of those simple spelling conundrums. But in fact it isn't."

"So what is it?"

"Let's look at the answer and see, shall we?"

He turned to page thirteen.

Answer: Lonesome's loblance.

"What the hell does that mean?" said Hat.

"I would guess it's a schoolboy joke," said Pascoe.

But before he could speculate further, Penn came back in.

"Make yourselves at home, do," he snarled. "I keep my private correspondence in the filing cabinet."

"Naturally, which is why I did not anticipate finding anything private on your bookshelves," said Pascoe urbanely. "But I apologize."

He replaced the volume and said, "Now, those few questions . . ."

Penn quickly recovered his equilibrium and readily confirmed Rye's account of the sequence of events. He explained in unnecessary detail that on his arrival in the reference library, he'd approached the desk in search of Mr. Dee but, seeing he was busy in his office, he'd returned to his seat, inadvertently leaving some of his work on the counter where Ms. Pomona had found it. He even produced the translated poem for them to read.

"I got the impression," he added, eyes fixed sardonically on Hat, "that she might have mistook it for a billy-doo. Kind of billy-doo lots of lasses would like to get, I reckon. Not enough old-style romance around these days, is there?"

Hat's hardly suppressed indignation came out as a plosive grunt and he might have got down to some really hostile interrogation if Pascoe hadn't said, "That's been very helpful, Mr. Penn. I don't imagine we'll need a written statement. We can see ourselves out."

In the street he said, "Hat, it's not a good idea to let your personal animosity towards a witness shine through quite so clearly," adding, to soften the reproof, "I speak from experience."

"Yes, sir. Sorry. But he really rubs me up the wrong way. I know it's not evidence, but I can't help feeling there's something weird about that guy. Maybe it's part of his job description, being a writer."

"I see. Writers have to be weird, do they?" said Pascoe, faintly amused.

Suddenly Hat remembered Ellie Pascoe.

"Oh, shit. Sorry, I didn't mean . . ."

"Of course you didn't. It's only elderly male writers who leave romantic poems lying around for impressionable young women to find who are weird, I understand that."

Laughing, he got into their car.

Well, so long as I'm keeping the brass amused, I must be doing something right, thought Hat.

The first few days of a murder enquiry, particularly one which promised to be as complex as the hunt for the Wordman, are always incredibly busy. At this stage it's impossible to say what will prove productive busy-ness and what will turn out to be a complete waste of energy, so everything is done with a time-consuming attention to detail. The one positive thing that had come up was a partial thumbprint, not Ripley's, on her left mule. Dalziel to his credit didn't even look smug, but maybe this was because the experts said that even if they found a possible match, it was likely to be well short of the sixteen points of comparison necessary for a print to be admissible in evidence. Computerization permitted much quicker checks than in the old days, but so far nothing had come up.

The post mortem had confirmed cause of death as a single stab wound from a long thin knife. The ME's on-site opinion that he could see no external evidence of sexual assault was also confirmed. She may have had protected intercourse some time on the day of her death, but if it had been against her will, she'd been too frightened to resist.

So the initial PM report had not been very helpful, but later the pathologist had rung up to say that a second examination had produced evidence of a bite mark on her left buttock, difficult to spot because it was right in the area of maximum hypostasis or post mortem lividity. The implication was that it might have been missed had it not been for the pathologist's devotion to duty. "More likely it was the mortuary assistant or the cleaning lady," said Dalziel cynically. Photographs were taken and shown to Professor Henry Muller, Mid-Yorkshire's forensic dental expert, known to his students and the police alike as Mr. Molar. The professor's diagnosis was as vague as the fingerprint expert's. Yes, he'd be able to say definitely which teeth had definitely *not* made these marks, but doubted if he would be able to go beyond a strong possibility if presented with teeth that seemed to fit.

"Experts," said Dalziel. "I've shat 'em. It's blood, sweat, and good honest grind that'll catch this bugger."

From the start Hat Bowler was one of the grinders. On the first Saturday he found he hardly had a minute to spare to ring Rye and confirm what he'd known from the moment he saw Jax's body, that his free Sunday was free no longer, and their trip to Stangdale had to be cancelled.

To his delight she said, "No sweat. The birds won't have all migrated by next week, will they?"

"Hell, no," he laughed. "Anyway, I'll drop them a line to tell them to hang on."

"Do that."

They'd then talked about the case till Hat became aware of Dalziel's bulk looming in the doorway of the CID room and hastily brought the conversation to a close.

"Witness?" said the Fat Man.

"Yes, sir," said Hat.

"Things have changed. Talking to witnesses didn't used to be a laughing matter. I were looking for Sergeant Wield."

"He's talking to a witness too, sir."

"Hope he's not laughing," said Dalziel. "Not that any bugger would notice."

Edgar Wield certainly wasn't laughing.

The witness he was talking to was Franny Roote and Wield was playing this completely deadpan. He didn't want to give the slightest hint that they'd had Roote under surveillance. Wield thought his friend Peter Pascoe was treading a very narrow line with Roote. There'd been no official complaint against Pascoe after the events which had led to the young man's so-called suicide attempt, but hints of undue pressure had been made in certain quarters of the press, and notes would have been taken in the Force's press monitoring division. Another "incident" would probably get a more direct response from both bodies. So Wield had been meticulous in his approach to the Taverna. He needed a reason for knowing Roote had been there on the night in question and it had come as a relief to discover that his bill had been paid by credit card. Sight of the bill also confirmed that he'd been there alone but even with the help of a photo, none of the waiters remembered him particularly.

Wield had then set out to interview everybody else known to have dined there that night, putting Roote well down the list.

Yet, for all this, he found himself greeted by a very faint, very knowing smile, as if the man recognized every inch of the path that had been trodden to his door.

He answered the questions courteously.

Yes, he'd been to the Taverna, just the once, not his kind of food. Yes, he remembered the young bazouki player. No, he couldn't recollect noticing anyone in particular chatting to him.

"And you, sir, did you talk to the lad?" asked Wield. "Give a request, mebbe?"

"No, not my kind of music."

"Not your kind of music. Not your kind of food. If you don't mind me asking, sir, why did you choose to visit that restaurant in the first place?"

This got the Roote open shy smile.

"Don't know, really. I think someone may have recommended it. Yes, that's it. A recommendation."

"Oh yes. Someone you can remember?"

"Not really," said Roote. "Just somebody I met in passing, I think."

And that was it. He reported back to Pascoe who brought Hat in to listen.

"And none of the other diners we've talked to recall seeing David Pitman talking to a single diner?" said Pascoe.

"No. Sorry," said Wield. "Dead end. Any word yet on that partial they found on Ripley's mule?"

"No match in the records, Sarge," said Hat.

Which meant, thought Wield, that it wasn't Roote's; as a convicted felon, his prints would be on record.

But he didn't rub the point in.

As the weekend approached, things slowed down a little, which wasn't good for the atmosphere in CID but gave Hat hope that he might be able to keep his rearranged date. Also he was determined to make it to the lunchtime preview on Saturday, fearful that if he didn't show there, Rye might back off from their rearranged Sunday afternoon trip to Stangdale.

On Friday morning he presented his weekly report on Roote to Pascoe. Any hope he'd had that the Ripley murder enquiry would get him off this deadly dull surveillance had vanished when the DCI had used Roote's visit to the Taverna to make the job official. Dalziel hadn't looked happy, however, and Wield's report plus the negative fingerprint evidence gave Hat hope the job wouldn't last forever.

"And you're sure he didn't clock you?" asked Pascoe, still seeking a reason for Roote's innocent behaviour.

"Stake my life on it, sir," said Hat confidently. "If I'd been any discreeter, I'd have lost sight of myself in my shaving mirror."

This had made Pascoe smile. Then he said resignedly, "OK. I think we'd better call it a day. Thanks for all your hard work. You did well." Which Hat took to mean the Fat Man had finally sat heavily on the surveillance job.

But he was careful not to let his interpretation show, especially as, emboldened by the praise, he seized the chance to ask, with explanation, if he could have time off to attend the preview.

"Why not?" said the DCI. "Everyone else seems to be going. And who am I to stand in the way of true love?"

"Thank you, sir," said Hat. And not wanting to appear too young and frivolous, he'd added, "Sir, it did strike me, with the Wordman using the library to get his Dialogues noticed, and this preview taking place in the Centre, do you think there's any chance he could turn up there?"

And Pascoe had laughed and said, "You mean, if the two of us keep our eyes skinned and stay ready to pounce on anyone who looks like they're about to commit murder, we might pull off a real coup! Seriously, Hat, you don't get much free time in our job. My advice is, forget work, relax. No reason why our Wordman should be there, and, even if he is, he's not going to be doing anything different from the rest of us, which is to say, looking at what's on display and enjoying it. Right?"

"Absolutely right, sir," said Hat. "I'm sorry. It was a daft thing to say."

"Not daft, just above and beyond the call of duty. Forget the Wordman. Like I say, just relax and enjoy the preview."

the fourth dialogue

Preview.
Now there's a word to make a ghost laugh!

It amused me too. First thing I noticed as I wandered round the gallery was that nobody actually seemed to be viewing anything other than the wine glasses in their hands and the people they were talking to over them.

And as the crowded gathering seemed to comprise all the great and the good of Mid-Yorkshire who presumably had viewed each other many times before, it was hard to see where the actual previewing came in.

The only exhibit which attracted instant attention was a sort of priapic totem pole, six foot high, carved in oak with a chainsaw. But even that, after an initial lewd comment or two, was generally ignored except by those who used its rough-hewed ledges to rest their glasses on, though I did hear as I passed the art critic from the Gazette *saying to his epicene companion, "Yes, it does have a certain, how shall I put it? a certain aura."*

Aura.
Now there's another word.
From the Greek αυρα meaning breath or breeze.
But in medicine it is used to describe the symptoms which presage the onset of an epileptic fit.
Remember old Aggie who suffered from epilepsy?

◆　　◆　　◆

That's the one. Her aura consisted not of the usual facial twitchings or muscular spasms, but a sudden euphoria. Knowing what it presaged, she would cry, "Oh God, I feel so happy!" in a tone of such despair that strangers would be thrown into greater confusion by the oxymoronic clash of manner and meaning than by the subsequent fit.

Later when my burgeoning interest in the arcana of our existence made me aware that the old medicines interpreted fits as the reaction of weak human flesh to the invasion of divine energy when used as a channel for prophetic utterance, I thought of Aggie but I couldn't bring to mind anything of significance in the sounds she made during her attacks. Might be worth asking her if you see her.

Please yourself. Anyway, now I've got personal experience to confirm what the old priest-doctors diagnosed.

For I too experience an aura, a divine breath blowing through me, though my aura might as easily be cognate with Latin aurum, *meaning gold, as with the Greek. For the beginning of a new Dialogue is like a summer day's dawning in me. I feel my whole being suffused in an aureole of joy and certainty which spreads further and further, stilling time for all who are included in its golden limits.*

I felt its onset as I moved around the gallery but I confess to my shame that at first I tried to deny it. For though I knew that in the light of that aura, I had no one to fear, yet my Thomas of a mind kept asking, how could such a thing be, here, among all these people?

How could it be?

When Hat arrived at the preview, it was already fairly crowded, but to his surprise Percy Follows, gold mane freshly permed, and Ambrose Bird, ponytail freshly curried, broke off in mid-altercation and, like a quarrelling couple surprised by the vicar, made a bee-line towards him, their faces split by welcoming smiles.

It was only when they both passed him by that he realized with some relief that he was not their obscure object of desire.

Behind him, the Lord and Lady Mayor had arrived. He was Joe Blossom, a stout middle-aged man known in the local business community as Lord of the Flies as he'd made his money out of breeding maggots for the fishing fancy. She was Margot Blossom, the second wife for whom he'd abandoned his first, a one-time cabaret wrestler, ten years his junior, over whom he watched with possessive jealousy and on whom he lavished whatever gifts he felt would make her happy, or at least keep her honest, which included expensive foreign holidays, emerald nipple-studs, capped teeth and silicone implants. Of late she had developed a range of cultural pretensions which included passions for the classical ballet, fine wines, and the works of Charley Penn. Despite, or perhaps because of, these new and spiritually uplifting preoccupations, she was still capable of reverting to the habits of her youth and body-smashing anyone foolish enough to make a reference in her presence to the source of her husband's wealth. Risk takers used the local pronunciation of her name which voiced the **t**, and behind her back they dropped the **r** too, but only those in love with death did this to her face.

Bird and Follows were competing wildly to be my host. For a moment it looked as if things might turn nasty, but in the event only verbal blows were struck and they divided the spoils, Bird making off with the maggots and Follows with the silicone.

Watching the bright check suit recede, Hat, who'd agonized over his own choice of burgundy chinos and a leather jerkin over a pale blue T-shirt inviting you to Save the Skylark, felt better already.

Now, like a good policeman, before progressing further into the gallery he paused and scanned the crowd. The casual observer might have thought he was checking faces against a mental mug-book, but in fact he paid scant attention to individuals till he'd spotted what he was looking for, that head of rich brown hair with a silver-grey flash.

She was moving around offering a trayful of drinks and nibbles to the guests. As if attracted by the intensity of his gaze, she glanced his way, nodded a welcome and resumed her duties.

Helping himself to a glass of wine from another young woman who gave him a smile he might have responded to if Rye hadn't been within clocking distance, Bowler now began to register the crowded room in detail.

There was a police presence significant enough to make him wonder if he couldn't perhaps claim overtime. The DCI was there and his wife whom Bowler liked. On their previous meetings Ellie Pascoe had run her bold and friendly gaze over him in a manner which was assessing and approving but in no wise inviting, and called him Hat, and not pulled any vicarious rank, confirming her reputation of being all right. She was standing next to Charley Penn on the edge of a group into which Follows had just insinuated his mayoral prize, who looked as if she were already favouring them with her considered judgment of the exhibits. As Hat watched, Ellie Pascoe turned her head away to yawn behind her hand, glimpsed him, and smiled. He smiled back and continued his scan and found himself smiling at the super, who didn't smile back. Was there no escaping the man? By his side was the woman who'd been with him at the Taverna, a well-made lady but very much cruiser-weight to Dalziel's super-heavy. Still, not a mismatch, by all accounts.

He broke away from the Fat Man's basilisk gaze, but his sense of being back at work still continued, for now, perhaps even more surprisingly, Sergeant Wield's unmissable features gloomed out at him like a goblin who'd strayed into an elfin rout. But why should this be a surprise? A man didn't need to be a work of art to appreciate art, and in any case, as Bowler knew himself, there were reasons other than aesthetic to urge attendance.

Rye was still moving, but not in his direction, so he let his gaze keep drifting.

He encountered the quiet reflective gaze of Dick Dee who gave him a friendly nod which he returned. OK, so he felt jealous of the guy, but no need to give him the satisfaction of knowing he felt jealous. Lots of others he recognized. He was good at faces and he'd made it his business on arrival in his new patch not only to study the mug-shot albums but also to get acquainted with the features of anyone else likely to prove important in an ambitious young copper's life. Journalists, for instance . . . there was Sammy Ruddlesdin, the *Gazette* reporter, lean and cadaverous and clearly bored out of his skull, into which from time to time he inserted a cigarette until memory of the prohibitive age into which he'd survived made him take it out again. . . . At least his suffering seemed less than that of his editor, Mary Agnew, who was talking with head averted to a bald man shovelling canapés into his mouth from a piled-up plate like he'd just escaped from a health farm. He reached for a name . . . found it . . . Councillor Steel a.k.a. Stuffer . . . a man to avoid, by all accounts, not only because of his lethal breath but because it was frequently expended bad-mouthing the police and all other alleged abusers of the public purse. Still, the way he was gobbling that grub, he wouldn't be long for this world!

Rye had disappeared now. Perhaps she'd gone to replenish her tray. Would need to if there were many appetites like Stuffer's. Or perhaps she was secretly observing him to see if he took an intelligent interest in the exhibits. He certainly felt observed. He turned his head suddenly and caught the source of the feeling. Not that it was hard to catch, as the man viewing him from behind what looked like a huge wooden phallus didn't turn away guiltily but gave him a friendly nod.

It was Franny Roote. Whose discreet surveillance he'd been boasting about to the DCI only yesterday.

But if he'd been so sodding discreet, how come Roote was smiling at him like an old buddy and heading his way?

"Hello," he said. "DC Bowler, isn't it? Are you into art?"

"Not really," said Bowler, seriously hassled and trying for sang-froid. "You?"

"As an extension of the word, perhaps. Words are my thing, but sometimes the word is a seed which needs to flower into something non-verbal. It's a circular thing, really. Pictures came first, of course. Nice cave paintings, a lot of them done, recent research suggests, while the artist was high on grass or whatever they used in prehistoric times. It's easy to see how their pictures might have some sort of religious significance. Also they could have been of practical use, such as saying, *If you go out of the cave and turn left down the valley you'll find a nice herd of antelope for supper.* But when it came to saying, *Run like hell, boys. Here comes a Tyrannosaurus,* pictures left something to be desired. So language, to start with, was no doubt born out of necessity. Yet soon it must have flowered into song, into poetry, into narrative, into the exchange of ideas, and out of these developed new and subtler forms of art, which in turn . . . well, you take my point, I'm sure. It's a circle, or perhaps a wheel as it makes forward progress as it turns, and we are all bound upon it at some point or other, though for some it is a Ferris wheel, and for others it is a wheel of fire."

He paused and looked at Bowler as if he'd just said something like, "Is it still raining outside?"

Bowler, slightly punch-drunk, said, "Have we met? I don't remember you . . ."

"No, you're right. In fact we haven't actually met, though I think we may have come close to an encounter recently. Roote. Francis Roote. Franny to my friends."

"So how do you know me, Mr. Roote?"

"I'm not really sure. A mutual friend could have pointed you out, I suppose. Sergeant Wield, perhaps. Or Mr. Pascoe. There he is now."

He gave a little wave. Bowler followed its direction and found himself looking straight into DCI Pascoe's accusing eyes. He couldn't blame him for not looking happy. To come to something like this and find the guy you suspected was stalking you chatting merrily to the DC instructed to check him out with maximum discretion was enough to give anyone a touch of the Dalziels.

Roote said, "Excuse me. Time to get down to business, I think. Jude Illingworth the engraver's here demonstrating her techniques and I don't want to miss that."

He moved away towards an alcove in which Bowler could see a tall woman with no hair talking to a knot of people. At the same time out of the corner of his eye he saw Pascoe heading in his direction and prepared to be defensive.

"Sir," he said pre-emptively as the DCI arrived, "I've no idea what he's doing here. Shall I check the invite list? Or maybe he came with a friend . . ."

"Relax," said Pascoe. "I've a good idea how he got in. What I'd like to know though is how come you're so friendly with him?"

Bowler explained what had happened.

"I've no idea how he got on to me, sir," he concluded unhappily. "I really did tiptoe around . . ."

"The man's a spider," said Pascoe. "Not the kind that builds a web but one of those who leaves trailing threads drifting in the breeze. Slightest touch and he knows you're there."

This was almost as airy-fairy as Roote's spiel, thought Bowler.

"Anyway, glad you've made it, Hat. I won't keep you any longer. You'll be keen to look at what's on offer. And if you see something you fancy, grab it, that's my advice. Don't waste time."

Jesus, why did the sight of young love provoke even sensible cops like Peter Pascoe into the jocularity of maiden aunts? Hat asked himself resentfully.

Then he glimpsed what he'd been looking for: Rye, appearing with a newly laden tray of nibbles.

"No, sir," he said, moving away from Pascoe. "I'll not waste any time."

Time was still here and I was still in it, but as I moved around and regarded those who are its unwitting servants, my aura was coming in waves, or rather pulses, as if its source were a great beating heart like the sun. Twice, three times, its heat and brightness grew almost unbearable as I encountered first this face, then that. Could they all be marked down? Perhaps . . . but their time, or rather their time-out, was not yet . . . and in any case could surely not be here . . .

And then you brought us face to face.

◆   ◆   ◆

"Councillor Steel, I'd like a word with you," said Charley Penn.

"Oh yes? Normally I'd say words come cheap, but not from you writers, eh? I saw the price of one of your books in Smith's the other day. Feed a family for a week, you could, on that money."

"Not your family, I shouldn't have thought," said Penn, glancing at the nibble-loaded plate in the councillor's hand.

"Me?" Steel snorted contemptuously. "Don't have no family except meself, Mr. Penn."

"That's what I mean."

Steel laughed. One of his political strengths was that he was uninsultable.

He said, "You mean I like my grub? Fill up while you can, that's what growing up rough taught me. Mebbe if I'd gone to a posh school like you, I'd eat more dainty. Not that a man's going to get fat on this bird-seed they feed you here. And who's paying for it, eh? And the vino, too. The ratepayers, that's who."

"Well, they can afford it, can't they? Out of those millions they'll be saving once you get my literature group grant axed. Feeling pleased with yourself now you've kicked that bunch of sheep on your committee into recommending it, are you?"

"Nowt personal, Mr. Penn. You've got to treat the symptoms till you can cure the disease."

"And what would that disease be?"

"Civic melogamania," said Steel, mispronouncing the word carefully.

"That would be, what? An over-enthusiasm for music?" said Penn.

"Got it wrong, did I?" said Steel indifferently. "Doesn't matter, you know what I mean. Building Fancy Dan centres like this when they've cut the council house budget by sixty per cent in ten years. That's melogamania, however you say it. You want to complain about a few trendy trollops not getting paid to read mucky books, you should speak to the mayor. Or his missus. She's a big fan of yours, I hear. Not big enough to save your class, but, not even rationing his oats. Not to worry, more to go round the rest, eh? Talk of the devil, there he is. How do, Your Lordship! Who's looking after the maggots?"

The mayor was passing by. He gave Steel a nasty look, while across the room his wife turned her head to send Steel a promissory glare which turned to a lionizing smile when she saw Charley Penn.

Steel appropriated the smile to himself, and called, "How do, Margott? Looking well. Hey, luv, don't pass a starving man without throwing a crumb."

This change of direction was caused by Rye Pomona's approaching within hailing distance with her tray which the councillor proceeded to lighten with more speed than discrimination.

"Shall I get you some more, Mr. Steel?" enquired Rye sweetly.

"No, lass. Not unless you can lay your hands on something a bit more substantial."

"Such as?"

"A few slices of rib beef and a couple of roast spuds wouldn't come amiss."

"Rib beef and roast spuds. I'll mention it in the kitchen," said Rye seriously.

"I bet you will," said Steel, laughing splutteringly. "You work in the library, don't you, luv?"

"That's right."

"So tell me, this waitressing job you're doing, you getting paid library rates plus overtime, or skivvy rates plus tips?"

"Watch it, Steel," grated Penn. "That's offensive even by your low standards."

Rye looked at him coldly and said, "I think I can speak for myself, Mr. Penn. In fact I'm doing it on a purely voluntary basis, so there's no charge to the public purse. But of course, if you care to leave a tip . . ."

"Nay, lass," laughed Steel. "Only tip I'll give you is, I like my spuds roasted almost black. But I don't suppose I'll be getting any here, so I'll just have another handful of these to put me on till me lunch."

He reached towards a plateful of cocktail sausages but Rye pushed the whole tray towards him so that he had to grasp hold of it to keep it off his chest.

"Tell you what, Councillor," she said. "Why don't you take the lot, then you can pick through them at your leisure. And I can take a look at the art."

She let go of the tray, nodded at Steel, ignored Penn's congratulatory smile and turned to meet Hat Bowler.

"So you made it, then?" she said. "Come on, there's something I want you to see."

❖   ❖   ❖

There are some revelations which are certain without being clear.

For a fraction of a second—though I knew without doubt that this was the one—I didn't understand why, and I could not foresee how.

But even before I could commit the blasphemy of asking why and how, my averted head let my eyes see the single answer, and all that remained was when.

Though whether when? *is appropriate for an event which takes place outside of time is a question to scotch a Scotist.*

Perhaps, the fancy came to me, time suspended would permit me to perform my duty, and when time resumed, all these people, policemen and journalists included, would find to their uncomprehending horror that one of their number lay dead among them, and no one had noticed a thing!

But it was not to be. My aura still burned bright but the flow of time was not yet slowing. I was still here and now.

But soon . . .

Oh yes, I knew it must be soon . . .

XIV

As Pascoe watched Bowler move away, making a bee-line for the girl from the library, he found he was smiling.

Who was it said that middle age began when you started looking fondly on the young, and old age when you started really resenting the bastards?

Probably Dalziel.

Time to check out the art.

He'd been checking for several minutes without much enthusiasm when someone touched his shoulder and said, "Peter, how're the muscles? Recovered enough for another go?"

He turned to see Sam Johnson grinning at him.

"You've got to be joking," he said. "Nice to see you, though. I wanted a word. I spotted Franny Roote earlier. He with you?"

It was hardly a subtle approach but Johnson was too sharp for obliquities, as Pascoe had discovered when he'd checked out Roote's story with him. Now the lecturer emptied his wine glass, seized another off a passing tray, and said, "Yes, I got Franny an invite. Is that a problem?"

"No problem. Just an occupational reflex," said Pascoe lightly. "You see him as a bright student, I see him as an old customer."

"I also see him as a friend," said Johnson. "Not a close friend maybe, but getting that way. I like him very much."

"Well, that's all right then," said Pascoe. "Can't be much wrong with a bright student whose supervisor likes him very much."

It came out a bit sharper than he intended. Something about Johnson acted on him as a mild irritant, the same thing probably which had provoked him into that farcical non-game of squash from which his shoulder was still aching. Not that there was anything obviously irritating about the young academic. Boyish without being childish, good-looking this side of matinee idol, bright but not in-your-face smart ass, entertaining in a self-mocking rather than self-congratulating style, totally non-menacing, he had somehow contrived to ripple the Pascoe pond. The DCI had thought about it long and hard. Jealousy? A man might be forgiven for feeling a little jealous of someone who could make his wife laugh so much. But Ellie Pascoe had been through experiences in recent months which might have crushed a lesser woman and to Pascoe the sound of her laughter was a blessed affirmation that all was well. He heard it now and over Johnson's shoulder glimpsed her with a trio consisting of Charley Penn, Percy Follows and Mary Agnew. Which of them had made Ellie laugh wasn't clear, but Pascoe felt nothing but gratitude. Not that either of these men looked possible candidates for jealousy. Penn with his cavernous eyes and sunken cheeks was hardly a romantic threat, while Follows was of the type Ellie unkindly categorized as prancers, with his mane of honey gold hair, his flamboyant gestures, his flowery language, his bow ties and garish waistcoats. "I don't mind if he's really gay," Ellie had said, "but I can't be doing with it as a fashion statement."

So, no jealousy there, and not even in the case of the much more desirable young lecturer. Then what was it in Johnson that stirred him up?

Eventually and reluctantly he'd come to the conclusion that he felt Johnson as a challenge to, or more accurately perhaps, a comment on his way of life.

There'd been a point years back at the end of university when he'd stood uncertainly at a fork in the track; then, with a deep breath and many a half-regretful backward glance, he'd set his foot on the road that had brought him to his present state.

The other path, he guessed, might well have led him to some condition not unlike that of Johnson. They were, roughly speaking, of the same generation, but Sam looked younger, dressed younger, talked younger. On campus, the casual observer would probably find it hard to distinguish him from the students he taught. Yet he could take his place among his seniors at conferences or in the senate as a respected equal, even a potential superior, with a bright beginning behind him and the promise of glittering prizes ahead. At the very least he had the prospect of spending the years of his maturity in comfortable old rooms looking out on a smooth razed lawn running down to a river gay with punts in term time and serene with swans through the long vacations. . . .

OK, that was probably a pie-in-the-sky picture of academic life which didn't exist or, if it did, had no appeal to Johnson. But in his own career, not even his most way-out fantasies could devise any comparable pastoral idyll.

Toil and trouble, trial and tribulation, till he was put out to grass, which was the only version of pastoral his future seemed to offer.

On the other hand, he didn't have a drink problem, and his heart, so he'd been told on his annual medical check-up, was in perfect condition.

Johnson was looking at him as if expecting a response.

"Sorry," said Pascoe. "Hard to hear with all this noise."

Enunciating very clearly as if in a large lecture hall with a bad acoustic, Johnson said, "I was saying, we all make mistakes, Peter. Happily, most of us come to terms with them and get on with our lives."

For a moment Pascoe felt like he'd been thought-read, then the lecturer went on, "And it can't be pleasant for Franny, feeling he's under constant observation."

How about not being pleasant for me either? wondered Pascoe. But it was a blind alley of a conversation so he said lightly, "Depends on who's doing the observing. I think one of us is being summoned."

Ellie was beckoning. He gave a little wave and she replied by pointing her finger towards Johnson.

"You, I think," said Pascoe.

He followed in Johnson's wake. Charley Penn gave them both a nod and Ellie smiled a welcome and said, "Sam, do you know Percy Follows who runs the library service? And Mary Agnew, editor of the *Gazette*?"

"Hi," said Johnson.

"Percy was just telling me about this short story competition the library and the *Gazette* are running together. It seems they're having a bit of bother with the judging."

"Yes," said Follows. "To be quite honest, I don't think that Mary or myself realized the degree of interest there was going to be. My staff are doing the preliminary sorting and it's turned into quite a task for us, I can tell you. We've had well over seven hundred entries, a very high standard, and we want to be sure that our winners really are *la crème de la crème*."

"To cut a long story short," said Ellie brutally, "Mary and Percy were looking for an expert panel. They naturally turned to Charley here as our most distinguished local lion who was kind enough to mention my own imminent elevation to the pride, then naturally your name came up."

"Yes," said Agnew. "This writing course of yours, seems to me that many of the entrants to the competition must be potential customers. You could almost look upon it as a recruitment campaign."

Sam Johnson, if he'd had a quiz-glass, looked as if he'd have used it. Pascoe didn't blame him. Ever since MYU's creative writing course had been started, the *Gazette* had debated whether this was a sensible use of educational time, staff and money when the country was full of young people desperate for qualifications in subjects with some relevance to the real world.

It wasn't hard to work out what had changed.

Agnew and Follows had initially taken the short story competition so unseriously that the librarian had wished the initial sorting out on Dick Dee, while Agnew had dumped the final judging into the lap of the Hon. Geoffrey Pyke-Strengler. Two things had happened. First, they'd probably been genuinely surprised by the number of entries. And secondly, after Jax Ripley's final broadcast and subsequent death at the hands of the Wordman, the short story competition had entered the public consciousness in a big way. OK, it had little real connection with the investigation, but the national media, as always greedy for any crumb falling from such a richly set table, would be focusing in on the result. There'd already been a feature on Pyke-Strengler in one of the colour supplements. He was just the kind of anachronistic, sub-Wodehousian aristocrat the British love. His answers to his interviewer's questions had been tinged with a vague bafflement at all the fuss, a quality which also informed his photographed face. One thing, though, had shone quite clearly through the vagueness—this was a man singularly unqualified to judge of literary merit.

So old pro Agnew was suddenly keen to have a judging team whose literary credentials wouldn't make her paper look totally stupid. Charley Penn was an obvious choice. He'd passed the parcel to Ellie who in turn had involved Sam Johnson, who now said, "But surely you already have a judge in place: Mr. Pyke-Strengler. He's here, isn't he? I was admiring some of his wildlife watercolours earlier, painted I presume before he shot the creatures. Has he been consulted about the proposed changes?"

"If he hasn't," said Ellie, "now's your chance. There he is talking to Mr. Dee. Perhaps they're discussing the competition."

Dick Dee and his companion were certainly deep in discussion of something and that's how, or so it seemed to Pascoe, Agnew would have liked to leave them, but Ellie in mischief-making mood was not to be denied and she called loudly, "Hello! Mr. Pyke-Strengler! Do you have a moment?"

She winked at Johnson who grinned back. Then all gazes turned to watch the Honourable Geoffrey Pyke-Strengler come shambling towards them.

In the Great Outdoors, remote from human habitation, on mountain, moor or riverbank, the Hon. was by most accounts, certainly his own, a creature at one with the environment, soft of foot, sharp of ear and eye, endlessly ingenious in devising methods of getting close enough to the fur, fish and fowl he so loved to make easy the task of slaughtering them. He had been the kind of child who, if his parents had opted for the once popular upper class alternative to an expensive boarding school of staking him out on a cold mountain, would probably have dispatched the first wolf or bear that came marauding with his bare hands, then eaten it. In fact, as the supplement article had informed Pascoe, by the time he was ten his parents had abandoned him even more completely than by exposure to the elements. His father, Baron Pyke-Strengler of the Stang, a famous defender of animal rights in the Upper Chamber, had run off to Tahiti with an Australian anthropologist, as a consequence of which his deeply if idiosyncratically religious mother had entered a vegan cult's Californian commune from which she had not emerged for twenty-five years, leaving the Hon. Geoffrey to grow up watching most of his inheritance steadily eroding under the very different but uniformly large financial demands of his absent parents. By the time he reached his majority, only the unassailable entail remained, consisting of the ancestral house (let as a corporate rest home), plus large chunks of Stangdale containing a few tumbledown farms.

Little wonder perhaps in view of his parents' predilections that the Hon. Geoffrey should have declared war on the natural world, and in the Great Outdoors developed those predatory skills for which he was justly famed.

Indoors, however, though still as destructive, his depredations tended to be accidental. As he approached he kicked over a table bearing a display of wooden bowls, moved sharply to his left to avoid treading on them, jostled a girl bearing a trayful of wine glasses, ducked away from the resultant shower of chardonnay and caused a nasty friction burn down the arm of the Lady Mayor with his ancient hacking jacket which was cut from the most spikily horrent tweed known to man.

Finally he made it and smiled benevolently on the group. He had a rather attractive doggily-trusting sort of expression. In fact he gave the impression that with the slightest encouragement, he'd have placed his paws on your shoulders and licked your face.

Mary Agnew introduced him. When she mentioned the short story competition, he nodded knowingly and said, "Stories, eh? Picture's worth a thousand words, isn't that what they say? And a pair of Purdys are worth a thousand pictures, that's what I say. But could be worse. Could have been a novel competition instead of stories. God, now that would have been really hard."

"Wasn't it Chekhov who said that people only write novels because they don't have time to write short stories?" said Johnson.

"Think you may have got that the wrong way round, old boy," said the Hon. helpfully.

"Geoffrey," said Mary Agnew, "I was thinking, maybe you could use a bit of help judging these stories . . ."

"No need. Just talking to Dick about it. He says he'll steer me right. Good man, Dick," said the Hon., beaming confidence. "Anyway, man who can judge a good terrier shouldn't have any problems with a few scribbles."

Pascoe noted with mild interest this apparent familiarity with Dee who, from his own limited knowledge, didn't appear the huntin' shootin' fishin' type.

"Nevertheless," said Agnew with the firmness of one who is certain of her absolute authority, "I've decided that you shouldn't have to cope alone and I've just been asking Dr. Johnson here, and his colleagues, if they would form a judging committee. With you, of course."

"No, count me out," said the Hon. "Would have done it myself, noblesse oblige, honoured my commitment sort of thing, but this is different. Can't abide committees. Good luck with it, old boy." (This to Johnson.) "Make sure she pays you the going rate."

Johnson looked surprised at the mention of money, but Penn's eyes lit up and he said, "Just what is the going rate then?"

"No idea," said the Hon. "Didn't apply to me. I'm sort of staff, you see. Was, anyway."

"Was?" echoed Agnew, looking at him as if she didn't object to the idea.

"Yes. Going to tell you. Heard this morning. The old man's dead. Boat accident. Sad, but haven't seen him for twenty-five years, so . . . well there it goes. Anyway, means the bits and bobs he couldn't get his hands on come to me, so I shan't need to do the column any more. And now you've got yourself a committee, don't need to do the judging any more, do I?"

Still the benevolent smile, but Pascoe had a sense he was enjoying this.

Ellie said, "So that means you're Lord Pyke-Strengler now?"

"Of the Stang. Yes. But normally don't use the title till the previous holder's been buried."

"Which is when?"

"Well, could be a bit of a problem there, actually," said the Hon. reflectively. "Seems the sharks were a bit faster getting to him than the rescue boats, you see."

Oh, what fun it is to look at their faces and see that they are seeing what you want them to see but completely missing the many-splendour'd thing. They think we are all moving forward along the same broad highway, all crowded together, all jostling for the best position, some congratulating themselves on having outdistanced those they started with, others feeling themselves pushed to the edges, even trampled into the gutter, but none of them denying that the choice lies between striving forward along that road or stepping off it into annihilation. And all the time I am following the twist and turns of my own path whose existence they are only just beginning to believe in, and whose route they cannot hope to track because its purpose is so far beyond their comprehension. I look at them looking at these so-called works of art and laugh because I know that the true artists in this life use brush strokes too delicate and colours too bright for the ordinary eye to detect or to tolerate . . .

"So what do you think of this?" asked Rye. "Rather good, wouldn't you say?"

She had come to a halt before a watercolour of a rather tumbledown house on the bank of a lake with the evening sun turning the water into wine. Or blood.

"It's OK, but I'd rather look at you," said Hat.

"Watch a lot of old Cary Grant movies, do you?" said Rye, eyes firmly on the picture.

"Not if I can help it. OK, let the dog see the rabbit."

He moved her gently to one side, enjoying the excuse for contact.

"Oh yes," he said. "Stangcreek Cottage."

Now she looked at him then down at her catalogue.

"You've seen it already," she said accusingly.

"No. I've seen the cottage and you'll see it tomorrow. That's Stang Tarn, which, unsurprisingly, like Stang Creek and Stangcreek Cottage, is in Stangdale. As close with their words as they are with their money, these Yorkshiremen. If you like the look of it so much, we'll take a photo, save you the bother of buying the painting."

If she wanted to play the connoisseur, he was quite happy to play the philistine.

"Is that all paintings are to you? Just some form of record?"

"Nothing wrong with records, is there? Here's a place I liked the look of on such and such a date at such and such a time?"

"Is that all it says? Doesn't the light and the colouring and the time of day tell you anything?"

"Sure. It's getting dark, and maybe the painter's run out of blue and green but he's got lots of red. Or maybe he's just better at blood than water. Yes, I'd say he should stick to blood."

"OK, so let's stick to blood. Any leads yet on the Wordman?"

This pulled him up short and he said, "Hey, I'm off duty here, remember?"

"Are you? Clearly you don't want to talk about Dick's painting, so I thought you must be one of those sad bastards who can't relate to anything outside his job."

"Dick's painting? You mean, Dick Dee painted this?"

"Didn't you realize? I thought that maybe that was why you were being so resistant."

Clever clogs. She'd picked up on his antipathy to her boss even though he'd scarcely acknowledged it to himself.

He said, "No, I didn't realize . . . sorry. I just thought we were playing a game. Actually, I think it's very striking, you know . . . atmospheric. . . ."

"You like playing games, do you?"

"Oh yes," he said. "Anything but solitaire."

Let her twist and turn as much as she liked, she wasn't going to shake him off.

"So what about the Wordman? What game is he playing?"

"What makes you think he's playing a game?"

"Those Dialogues. No reason to write them except to involve someone else."

"They could just simply be a record."

"Like this painting?"

"You've persuaded me it's more than that."

"Then look at the Dialogues . . . surely they've got a subtext, too . . . an atmosphere. . . ."

"Like blood on the tarn, you mean?" said Hat, staring at the painting of Stangcreek Cottage.

"Blood on the tarn? Why didn't I think of that for a title?" said Dick Dee.

He had come up behind them.

"Hello, Dick," said Rye with the welcoming smile Hat had not received. "We're just deconstructing your opus."

"I'm flattered. You remember Ambrose Bird?"

"Who could forget the Last of the Actor–Managers?" said Rye fluttering her eyelashes in a manner which Hat, not without relief, identified as ironical.

"Yes, of course, we met in Dick's office. Alas, with the dreadful news of Miss Ripley's death weighing on us, the normal courtesies went out of the window, but distracted though I was, I recall making a mental note to improve our acquaintance," said Bird, matching her mock admiration with his own histrionic gallantry. "Let's start afresh. Dick, a formal introduction, if you please."

"This is Rye Pomona, who works with me in Reference," said Dee.

With not *for,* acknowledged Bowler grudgingly.

"Pomona . . . you're not related by any chance to Freddie Pomona?"

"He was my father."

"Good lord. He must have had you late, I think. Dear old Freddie. He was Titinius when I carried my first spear in *Caesar*. I recall how well he died, too well indeed for the director who had to get him to tone it down a bit. Can't have the support out-Brutusing Brutus."

"He was a ham, you mean?" said Rye.

Bird laughed and said, "I mean he belonged to an older school of acting than that which now prevails. In any case, a well-cured *jambon* is the tastiest of meats. Who knows better than I? But dear Freddie is sadly missed. And your mother too . . . Melanie, wasn't it? Of course it was. I recall dear Sir Ralph at a cast lunch given by some unusually generous management saying, 'I think I shall start with a slice of Melanie accompanied by the merest morsel of Pomona Ham.' Such a wag, dear Ralph."

Dick Dee, who had been regarding Rye with some concern, said sharply, "I think, to persuade us of that, you might have found a better example of his wit."

"I'm sorry," said Bird, acting being taken aback. "Perhaps it wasn't dear Ralph. Sir John, perhaps? G, of course, not M. Not his style at all."

"I was commenting on the matter rather than the manner," said Dee, glancing significantly at Rye.

"What? Oh, I see. My dear, I'm so sorry. No offence intended. I recall dear Freddie laughed like a drain."

"No offence taken," said Rye, smiling.

"There, you see, Dick. You're far too sensitive. Now is no one going to introduce me to this fine-looking young man whose face also looks strangely familiar?"

"That's because he is Detective Constable Bowler, who was so ably assisting DCI Pascoe on that same day you met Rye," said Dee.

"Well, well. DiCaprio eat your heart out," said the actor–manager, taking Bowler's hand and squeezing it hard.

"Nice to meet you," said Hat, pulling his hand away.

"I hope we may improve our acquaintance also," murmured Bird. Then, like a grand duchess signalling an audience was over, he turned abruptly to the painting and said, "So, Dick, this is one of your masterpieces, is it? Hmmm."

The *hmmm* was the first thing that Hat had liked about the man. It spoke a whole hiveful of reservations.

The two men stepped closer to the painting and Hat took Rye by the arm and steered her away, saying, "Why don't we take a look at that engraver woman?"

"Because it sounds like metalwork?" said Rye. "I bet at school you were hot on metalwork."

"You bet. Straight A's. Talking of which, that asshole Ambrose is a bit over the top, isn't he?"

"Bird? He's harmless. Just an act."

"Acting being a great actor, you mean?"

"It happens all the time. Of course, if you can't hack it on the stage, you soon get found out. But Bird's acting being an old-fashioned actor–manager which is a much meatier role. To give him his due, he does a pretty good job. Have you seen any of his productions?"

"Not yet," said Bowler, wondering if he was going to have to brush up his Shakespeare as well as his art to get near this girl. He was full of curiosity over the revelation that she came from a theatrical family, but a close study of the psychology of interrogation had taught him the supreme importance of rhythm and timing in getting a result. So another place, another time . . .

"Is he acting being gay as well?" he said.

"Think he fancies you? Now that's really vain," she said.

"The way he shook my hand, either he fancies me or he's a member of some Lodge I don't know about."

"So it's true. You do have to be a homophobic mason to get on in the Filth," she said.

But she said it with an affectionate smile and he smiled back as he replied, "I thought everyone knew that. Now why don't we go and look at some etchings?"

XV

All good things come to an end. Provincial previews take a little longer but even they have their natural term. The guests had their various reasons for coming—some to see, some to be seen; some out of obligation, some out of love; some out of interest, some out of boredom—but they needed only one of two reasons for going—they had either got what they came for, or it wasn't there for the getting.

Getting the weapon was so easy I hardly noticed that I'd taken it and certainly no one else did. Then I bided my time, in every sense of the phrase. Eventually people began to drift away, and when I saw my particular piece of flotsam join the drift, I followed close behind, but not so close as to draw attention. My aura was strong now, so strong I felt myself borne along on its brightness like a piece of debris on the wind which follows a nuclear blast. Breathe on me breath of God, I sang inside, for this surely must be what His breath feels like. I was aglow with its gloriole, but still time flowed strongly around me. Then I saw him turn away from the main drift and at the same moment I felt time begin to ebb.

"Well, it's time we were off," said Andy Dalziel. "*Ars longa*"—he gave the ess its full sibilance—"and if I stay here much longer, me belly'll think me throat's cut."

Cap Marvell let her gaze linger on the quercine throat in question and said, "You must have a very imaginative belly."

But the Lord Mayor who felt he had stayed far beyond the requirements of duty was on Dalziel's side.

"You're right, Andy," he said. "If we show the way, then all these other good folk can be off to their lunches, eh?"

His touching belief that, as with royalty, nobody ate till he ate or left before he left, was contradicted by the steady flow of exiting guests as one o'clock approached. But his eagerness to join them was not shared by his wife, who had recovered from her brush with the Hon.'s jacket and was now displaying the oenological expertise recently acquired on a *Sunday Times* Wine Society weekend. Having expressed the opinion that overoaked chardonnay had had its day, she had been brought a newly opened bottle of red by Percy Follows.

"Don't tell me what it is," she cried, sniffing deeply at the glass cradled in her hands. "Ah, this is good, this is interesting. I'm getting exotic fruit, I'm getting mangrove swamps, I'm getting coriander, I'm getting cumin, I'm getting jaggery."

"Shouldn't let it bother you, luv," said Dalziel. "After fifteen pints of best, I sometimes get a bit jaggery meself. Now are we going, or what?"

"It's a Shiraz Merlot blend, I'd say. Western Australia? About '97?" said Margot.

All eyes turned on Follows who, keeping his hand clamped firmly over the bottle's label, said, "Spot on, my dear. What a nose you have there."

It was indeed a nose to be proud of. If you were a macaw, thought Cap.

She saw a similar thought form on Dalziel's lips, got him in a restraint-lock disguised as an affectionate linking of arms, and said, "You're right, dear. Time to be on our way."

They moved off, closely followed by the mayor and his triumphing wife.

Ambrose Bird approached Follows, prised the bottle from his fingers, examined the label which read *St-Émilion,* and said magnificently, "Creep!"

And now the gallery really did begin to empty fast. Soon, of the hundred or so guests who'd attended, only a couple of dozen remained. Among them was Edgar Wield, the glass of chilled white wine he'd received on arrival now warm in his hand. He had little interest in art but his partner, Edwin Digweed, had wanted to come. Sensing Wield's reluctance he had said acidly, "Very well. I shall remember this next time you want me to attend an autopsy." Any more realistic argument might have made Wield dig his heels in, but this made him smile and give in with a good grace, neither of which would have been detectable to a stranger but both of which Digweed spotted and appreciated.

Now he waited with ironic patience for Digweed, who couldn't sharpen a pencil without cutting his finger, to finish a deep discussion he was having with a hunky young wood-turner about the relative merits of elm and yew, and looked forward to the rest of the day which, with luck, would give him the pleasure of his partner's company away from any disruptive crowd.

He saw Pascoe and Ellie by the exit talking to Ambrose Bird, or rather Ellie and the Last of the Actor–Managers were talking. Wield knew that if Ellie had a weakness, it was a tendency to be star-struck by fully paid-up luvvies. Pascoe, who wore the sweet smile with which he masked impatience, caught Wield's eye, made a wry face, then moved towards him.

Wield watched him approach, noting with approval the grace of movement, the pleasant manner with which he greeted acquaintance, the general sense of ease and rightness which emanated from that slim figure. The boy was good, would have still been good if this had been a top-level diplomatic reception rather than a provincial arty-farty piss-up. Others must have noticed too. He'd done well, but not too well, or rather not too quickly. Others had flown to DCI and beyond a lot quicker than Pascoe, but those who hit the top too soon always posed the question, Did you hang around anywhere long enough to get your hands dirty? You've made the climb but have you done the time? Looking ahead when he was a sprog, setting out on the steep ascent laid out before a graduate entrant, if Pascoe had been able to foresee his long sojourn in Mid-Yorkshire CID, he'd probably have felt his career must have stalled. But not now. He didn't wear his heart on his sleeve, not even with his closest friends, but he had said enough for Wield to know he was aware of his true worth. And aware even more that there were things in his life more important far than ambition. If he had pushed, gone hunting for the glittering prizes, he could probably have been up and away long since. But now he had other agendas. Hostages to fortune, that's what some clever bugger had called wife and family, probably meaning it cynically. Well, Pascoe had come close to losing both his child and his missus in the past few years, and now he knew beyond any doubt what ransom he was willing to pay to keep them safe, which was everything he had or could expect to have. So nothing was going to happen without the imprimatur of their happiness.

Young Rosie's move to secondary school a few years ahead was going to be the testing time, Wield guessed. The old days of bully-boy tactics from above—*Take the job or you're off to Traffic!*—were, if not passed, at least passing. Others would be aware of this window too and poised to haul the lad up through it as soon as it was fully open.

Of course they'd need to get King Dalziel's approval.

"Wieldy, you've been standing here so long, I'm amazed someone hasn't bought you."

"You know me, Pete. Always find people more interesting than pictures."

Behind them, they heard an uprising of voices which seemed to emanate from the alcove in which the engraver had been displaying her craft. Then it was drowned by the more distant but to their sensitized ears more disturbing sound of sirens.

"The meat wagon?" said Pascoe.

"Yes. And our boys too," said Wield.

"You switched on?"

"No. I'm off-call," said the sergeant firmly.

"Me too."

"Sounds close, but."

"Probably some poor old girl in the precinct's shopped till she dropped," said Pascoe, knowing that Ellie, alert to the dangers signalled by police alarums, was watching him keenly for sign of any inclination to get involved.

"Excuse me," said a broad Yorkshire voice behind him. "Somebody said you were a copper, is that right?"

He turned to see a lanky woman in a red smock and black tights, with a razored haircut that gave her a look of Sigourney Weaver in *Alien 3*. He recognized her as Jude Illingworth, the engraver.

"Yes," he admitted reluctantly. "Is there something wrong?"

"Aye, is there. You expect it out of doors at a craft fair, mebbe, somewhere open to everybody. If it's not nailed down, it'll go. But at a posh do like this . . ."

I am in no hurry, for where there is no time, haste has no meaning. I follow with my eyes only and wait. The door opens, a man comes out. I watch him out of sight and then go in.

And there he is as I know he must be, alone, stooped over a washbasin, laving his face.

As I approach from behind he looks up and sees me in the mirror.

Oh, this is fine. This is my reward for faithfulness. I have no choice in these matters, but if I had a choice, this I might have chosen, for this allows me to be both player and audience.

I can see his face in the mirror and mine too, my lips curved in a smile, his eyes rounded in surprise but not in fear. I am not night's dark agent but a bringer of light, and fear is no part of my message. This man with his lust to glut his own body as he starves the souls of others of their natural nourishment is driven not by evil but by a warped good which is worse. It is his own pain as much as that he causes others that I am sent to release him from.

So I speak to him reassuringly, uttering a few soft words sweetly. Then I drive the weapon into the base of his skull and up through I know not what layers of matter, certain that another hand than mine is guiding the point to its appointed destination.

He spasms, but I hold him there with ease. If a million angels can dance on the head of a pin, then a single man twisting and turning on my much broader point is a piece of cake.

And now he goes slack. I withdraw my weapon and let him slide to the floor, face down, his bald head gleaming like metal under the striplight.

Before Pascoe could ask Jude Illingworth what the hell she was talking about, there was another interruption. Hat Bowler, who'd left some time earlier, came back into the gallery, pushing between Ellie and Bird with scant ceremony, and making straight for Pascoe.

"Sir," he said breathlessly, "can I have a word?"

His face was pale.

Pascoe said, "What's happened?"

Jude Illingworth said, "Hang about, I was first."

Pascoe said, "Sorry. Wieldy, could you deal?"

"Sure. Now, Miss . . ."

"You a cop, too?" she said regarding his cragged and potholed face doubtfully.

"Aye. Sergeant. So . . . ?"

"So some sod's pinched one of my burins."

"Oh aye? Happens a lot when you're wearing tights, does it?" said Wield.

Pascoe heard the exchange as he moved aside with Bowler and stifled a smile. Live with Andy Dalziel long enough, something was bound to rub off.

"So tell me," he invited the DC.

"I found him, sir," said Hat. "I went into the Gents and he was on the floor. He wasn't quite dead, he was trying to say something and I leaned down close to try and hear what it was but it didn't make sense and then it just turned into a death rattle. I checked his pulse and there was none, and I went through all the resuss procedures, just in case, but nothing, so I called HQ for assistance and told them to send an ambulance too, though he looked beyond help to me, then I got a Centre security man to stand by the door and keep everyone else out, and I thought I'd better get up here and let you know, sir . . ."

He ran out of breath.

Pascoe said, "That's good, Hat. You've called up assistance and you've secured the scene. Now perhaps we could just slow down and get a bit of necessary detail. Like, how about telling me who it is you've found?"

"Councillor Steel, sir. You know, the one they call Stuffer."

"Good God," said Pascoe. "And he's definitely dead, you say? What was it, you reckon? Stroke?"

"No, sir. I'm sorry. It's daft but it shook me up a bit. He's been murdered. I should have said, he's got a hole in the base of his skull. And I found what could be the weapon on the floor. I marked the spot and bagged it. Didn't want anyone else to see it, it's a bit unusual and I thought that it was best to keep it to ourselves for a bit. I've got it here."

He pulled a transparent plastic bag out of the inside pocket of his jerkin and held it up. It contained what looked like some sort of small chisel.

"Did I do right, sir?" said the young DC anxiously.

But before Pascoe could reply, Jude Illingworth edged him aside.

"Now that's what I call service," she said. "I don't care what your customers say about you, I think our police are bloody wonderful. Where did you find it?"

"Sorry?" said Pascoe.

"My burin," said the woman, her eyes fixed on Bowler's evidence bag. "Where did you find my burin?"

I stoop and make my necessary mark.

So there he lies, brought by a burin to his buriness, that breath that sank a thousand friendships stilled forever, that appetite which seemed ambitious to devour the earth soon to be engorged by it. I look down upon him and I share his peace.

But then like the Illyrian merchant who sees the Adriatic's silken skin wrinkle at the first touch of the bora, I suddenly feel uneasy. In here all is peace, but outside in the corridor I sense movement, as if the bora were indeed beginning to blow . . .

Surely the Power that guides my fate cannot permit anything to go wrong?

Yes, I know I could have asked, but just then there seemed only one way to find out.

I move swiftly to the door and pull it open.

And I laugh out loud as I realize all I have felt is the return of time, exploding along the corridor as the dam breaks.

I compose my face and step out into its rushing current, happy to let it bear me where it will, certain that it will set me ashore safe on whatever spit or island is appointed for our next thrilling Dialogue.

Talk again soon!

"He was trying to speak, you said," said Pascoe as he hurried down the stairs with Bowler. "Could you make out anything at all? Think hard while it's still fresh in your mind."

"Yes, sir. I've been trying. And . . . well, it's a bit daft . . . but what he was trying to say sounded like . . ."

"Yes?" prompted Pascoe.

"*Rosebud.* It sounded like *rosebud.*"

XVI

"Rosebud?" said Andy Dalziel. "Go to the pictures a lot, young Boiler, does he?"

"No, sir," said Pascoe, relieved not to have to make the decision whether to explain to Dalziel that *rosebud* was the mysterious last utterance of the dying millionaire in *Citizen Kane*. The Fat Man could be brutally sarcastic if he felt his underlings were patronizing him. "Bowler's never seen the movie so it meant nothing to him. More important, of course, is whether it meant anything to the councillor."

"Mebbe. But I can't see Stuffer going to the flicks unless there was free popcorn. You say young Bowler gave him the kiss of life?"

"So I understand," said Pascoe.

"Braver man than me," declared Dalziel. "I've had me doubts about the lad, but I reckon anyone who can give Stuffer Steel the kiss of life ought to be put up for the Queen's Medal!"

Pascoe glanced nervously around in case there was anyone in earshot ready to be offended, but the mezzanine floor which included Hal's café–bar and a book and souvenir shop was deserted except for a couple of uniforms. He'd been reluctant to close the Centre completely, but Dalziel had had no such qualms on his return.

The Fat Man was staring up at a security camera as if contemplating ripping it off the wall.

It wouldn't have made any difference if he had.

One of the first things Pascoe had done was send Wield up to the security office on the top floor in the hope that there'd be something on video. His own expert eye had told him that the system was far from the state-of-the-art set-up you might have expected in such a new complex. Old-fashioned fixed cameras, and not a lot of them. But he hadn't been prepared for the news that Wield returned with.

"You won't credit this," he said to Pascoe. "System's not on during the day."

"What?"

"No. Theory is that the sight of the cameras is deterrent enough. Wouldn't have been on at night either if Stuffer had had his way."

"Stuffer?"

"Aye, ironic, isn't it? Every penny they spent on building this place, they got a battle from Stuffer over it. They had to let him win a few small victories else they'd never have got it finished. Security was one of them. He got the budget for installation, use and maintenance cut by eighty per cent. It was either that or lose a couple of staff."

"Shit," said Pascoe. "But it does mean that whoever did this probably knew he wasn't on Candid Camera. That's something."

"Not much consolation to Stuffer, wherever he is, knowing if he'd not been so penny-pinching, he might still be here," Wield had mused.

"How long's yon sodding quack going to take?" demanded the Fat Man, turning his attention from the useless camera to the side corridor where the Gents was situated. "What's he doing in there, for God's sake? Going through Stuffer's pockets for change?"

Yon sodding quack was the police medical examiner who was presently examining the councillor's body. When Bowler's judgment that Steel was definitely dead was confirmed by the paramedics, Pascoe had made them leave the body where it was, both to prevent further contamination of the scene and to please the imminent superintendent who had been heard to aver that looking at a murder site without a corpse was like eating an egg without a waxed moustache.

"I'm sure he'll be out shortly," said Pascoe.

"Talking of bogs, where's our Boghead at now?"

"Up in the gallery with Wieldy, taking statements."

There'd been some muttering when he'd told the remaining preview guests that they could not leave till they'd been interviewed, but he'd been adamant. The near certainty that the murder weapon was Jude Illingworth's lost burin made everyone in the gallery a potential witness. Pursuing the departed guests was going to soak up a lot of man hours, so it made good sense to hang on to those still in the gallery.

"Not that bright when he's a key witness himself, Pete. It's his statement I want to hear. Get him down here, will you?"

Pascoe had learned not to defend himself against Dalziel's reproofs. No way you could win even when you were entirely in the right. Also there was a trade-off, which was that if anyone else dared reprove you, the Fat Man was usually ready to interpose his own body, even if you were entirely in the wrong.

In this case, Pascoe, seeing how shook up the young detective had been by his discovery of the body, had thought it best to keep him fully occupied. Now he went personally to fetch him. It was an act both kind and professional. Bowler must know he wasn't the Fat Man's favourite son at the moment and could easily be intimidated into stupidity. So a bit of tender loving reassurance would be timely, both to cheer him up and to make him a better witness.

In the gallery he found the previewers had adopted a defensive huddle round the priapic totem pole, like a herd of antelope scenting a marauding lion. An exception to this was Edwin Digweed who was patrolling round the group with a look of repressed rage on his face, more leonine than cervine. Bowler and DC Dennis Seymour had set up tables by the doorway, presumably to prevent flight, and were busy taking down details. Bowler's witness was a man so nervously prolix that Pascoe stood around for several minutes before finally intervening by placing one hand under the man's elbow, easing him out of the chair, and guiding him through the exit, the whiles murmuring the platitudes of gratitude.

"Thanks," said Hat with a smile that faded when Pascoe told him the superintendent would like a word.

"Just tell him what you told me," said Pascoe. "You know Mr. Dalziel, he likes to hear things from the horse's mouth. I've already told him that in my opinion you acted with good sense and dispatch and did everything by the book."

The youngster looked a little reassured and Pascoe asked, "Where's Sergeant Wield, by the way?"

"He's through there," said Bowler, indicating one of the small side-galleries running off the main exhibition area. "There were a few people who'd left the preview but we managed to catch them before they got out of the Centre and he thought it best to keep them separate from this lot as they might be able to tell us something about the councillor's movements downstairs."

Plus, having left the gallery, as well as possible witnesses they were potential suspects, thought Pascoe. He strolled across the gallery and peered into the side-room. Among those gathered there he spotted Sam Johnson and Franny Roote, engaged in close conversation; also Dick Dee and Rye Pomona, similarly occupied. He thought of wandering in and suggesting to Wield that he took a specially close look at Roote, then cancelled the idea, partly because it felt neurotic, but mainly because he was sure Wield wouldn't need any prompting.

"You OK on your own here for a while, Dennis?" he said to Seymour.

"No problem," said the redheaded DC cheerfully. "Oh, by the way, I processed Mrs. Pascoe first and she said to tell you she'd see you at home later."

"Very thoughtful of you," said Pascoe sincerely, knowing that in Seymour's case the thought would not have included the possibility of ingratiating himself by doing the DCI's wife a favour. "I would suggest you take Mr. Digweed's statement soon otherwise I think he'll explode."

"Right," he said as he left the gallery with Bowler, "you might as well take me through the sequence en route."

"Fine. Well, we came out and down the stairs like we're doing now . . ."

"We being . . . ?"

"Me and Rye, that's Miss Pomona who works in the reference library."

"Good. And were there others coming down the stairs at the same time?"

"Oh yes. Quite a lot, in front and behind."

"Did you notice anyone in particular? I know I asked you before, but as we're actually on the stairs now . . ."

Bowler shook his head.

"Not really. Like I said earlier, we were pretty deep in conversation, me and Rye—Miss Pomona, I mean . . ."

"For heaven's sake, call her one or the other. I'm not interested in your romantic life," said Pascoe.

"Sorry," said Bowler. "Well, when we got here, people started going off different ways."

They were approaching the mezzanine level which had the huge disadvantage from an investigative point of view of being the hub of the Centre. From here you could get to anywhere else within, or head for either the underground car park or main shopping precinct without. Even the fatal loo itself was situated in a corridor running between the mezzanine and a landing from which stairs ran up and down to the rest of the Centre. Dalziel had put his finger on the problem straight off. "Place is a fucking maze," he'd said. "You'd need to be a trained rat to find your way to the cheese round here."

Talking of Dalziel, there was no sign of him. Probably got impatient and went in to hurry the sodding quack along.

"Did you see Councillor Steel at all?" said Pascoe.

"I think I might have noticed him, his bald head, I mean, going down the stairs a bit in front of us, but I couldn't swear to it," said Bowler. "I was, you know . . ."

"Yes, deep in conversation with Miss Pomona," said Pascoe. "How long was it before your own call of nature grew strong enough to drag you away from her?"

"Couple of minutes, no, probably a bit more. Sorry," said Bowler, clearly irritated at his own vagueness. "Rye went off to pick up her coat and things that she'd left in the reference library . . ."

"Ah. Did she go down the corridor with the toilet in it, by any chance?"

"No, she went that way," said Bowler, pointing to a door inscribed STAFF ONLY. "It would be quicker, I suppose."

"And you . . . ?"

"Like I say, I pootered around the book shop for a couple of minutes . . ."

"Or maybe a bit more?"

"Or maybe a bit more. Then I thought I'd take the chance to have a leak and I went to the toilet. . . ."

"Why that one?" said Pascoe. "If you were down there by the book shop, there's another Gents, very clearly signed, just outside."

"Well," said Bowler uncomfortably, "to tell the truth, I'd just seen Mr. Dalziel going in there. . . ."

Pascoe laughed out loud. He could recall a time shortly after his arrival in Mid-Yorkshire when he'd found himself standing alongside the terrifying figure of the Fat Man in a urinal, quite unable—despite a very full bladder and the usually mimetically encouraging sound of a vigorous flow hitting the next basin—of producing a drop. It wasn't displeasing to see that today's laid-back youngsters weren't entirely free of such hang-ups.

"So you went down the corridor," said Pascoe. "Anyone else in sight, either end?"

"Definitely not, sir," said Bowler, pleased to be on firm ground at last.

"And you went inside and saw Councillor Steel," said Pascoe. "Well, that's twice you've told me. You should be word perfect for Mr. Dalziel. Anything else you'd like to add?"

"Don't think so. Except, well, you don't think this could have anything to do with these Wordman killings, do you, sir?"

"At the moment there's nothing to suggest it has," said Pascoe. "Why do you ask?"

"No reason really. Just, well, when you've had three deaths and there comes a fourth . . ."

"That's the kind of mistake it's easy to make," said Pascoe. "The Wordman murders are one case, this is another. Try to put them together without evidence and all you do is risk buggering up both investigations. OK?"

"Yes, sir. Sorry."

"Good lad. One more thing just in case the super asks. You said you'd noticed him going into the other loo. When you found the body, didn't you think of getting hold of him? He must have still been in the vicinity."

"It did cross my mind, sir," said Bowler. "But by the time I'd tried resuscitation and called up assistance and alerted the Centre security staff, he was probably long gone, whereas I knew you and the sarge were still up here and I just thought it would be best to be sure."

Meaning that, uncertain he'd done everything by the book and aware that he was a little shook up, he didn't fancy running breathless down the street to put himself at the judgment of Fat Andy.

"I think perhaps it might be simpler to say nothing about seeing the super going into the other Gents," said Pascoe. "So far as you knew, he was long gone. Ah, that sounds like him now."

The Gents' door opened and a short ochrous-complexioned man who looked as if he'd rather be playing golf, for which he was indeed dressed, emerged, followed by Dalziel.

"And that's it, Doc, he's dead? Well, I'm sorry I interrupted your game. How'd it go, by the way?"

"As a matter of fact I was dormy three against my revolting brother-in-law whom I haven't beaten for five years and he was in a bunker and I was on the green when my pager went."

"Moral victory then."

"In dealings with my brother-in-law, there is no moral dimension. The game is void. As to the unfortunate councillor, I'm sorry, I cannot tell you what I do not know. He was killed, certainly within the past hour and probably as a result of a blow at the base of his skull from a narrow sharp weapon. The wounds to the top of his head are slight and appear more likely to have been inflicted after rather than before the fatal wound, though for what purpose I cannot even speculate. You must await the post mortem for a more considered view. Now, I bid you good day."

"Well, thank you, Dr. Caligari," said Dalziel to his retreating back. "DC Bowler, nice of you to drop by. Step in here and show me what things looked like afore you and every other bugger who came near him started chucking poor Stuffer around."

Bowler went through the toilet door. He avoided looking down at the figure on the floor, uncomfortably aware that Dalziel was watching him closely in the mirror which ran along the facing wall.

"He was slumped down in front of the washbasins, slightly over to his right side. I got the impression he must have been washing himself when he was attacked."

"Oh aye? That a wild guess or do you hear voices?"

"No, sir. I noticed his hands were wet and his face too, I noticed that when I tried to give him the kiss of life."

"Aye, I heard about that. So, he'd had a pee, washed his hands and was splashing a bit of water on his face. What do you reckon happened next?"

"The door opened, the assailant came in. It's only two or three paces across the floor, and with the councillor washing his face, the assailant could have been right up behind him before he looked up and saw him in the mirror. Then it would be too late."

"Might have made no difference anyway," said Pascoe. "You see someone come into a public toilet, you don't think, *That guy's going to attack me,* not unless he's foaming at the mouth and carrying a bloodstained axe. Something the size of that burin, you wouldn't even notice he had it in his hand."

"Yes, sir," said Bowler. "That was something I've been thinking about. A weapon like that directed against the head, from what I recall of anatomy, you'd have to be very expert or very lucky to kill somebody or even incapacitate them with a single blow."

He paused and Dalziel said impatiently, "Come on, lad, don't arse about like Sir Peter Quimsby, make your point."

"Well, it might make sense if we assume this was unpremeditated, I mean, like someone wandered in here who just happened to have a burin in his hand and he saw Steel stooping down and thought, *Hello, I think I'll have a stab at him.* But our perp didn't just happen to have a burin, he had to steal it. That was risky in itself. I mean, who knows, by the time we interview everybody who was in the gallery, we might find somebody who saw something suspicious around Jude Illingworth's display, not suspicious enough to cry, Stop thief! but something they recall when we start asking questions."

"Perhaps he didn't steal it as a weapon but for some other reason," said Pascoe. "And it just came in handy when he suddenly decided to attack Councillor Steel."

"Yes, sir, possibly, though on a scale of improbabilities, I'd say . . . not that I mean it's not possible, only . . ."

"Nay, we don't stand on ceremony in murder investigations," interrupted Dalziel. "If you think the DCI's talking crap, just spit it out."

"I wouldn't quite say that . . ."

"Well, I would. I think you've got the right of it, lad. Chummy made up his mind to stiff old Stuffer, he wanted a weapon and the burin was the best he could come up with in a hurry."

"Which would mean it was premeditated, but not all that much pre," said Bowler. "Something must have happened at the preview to make it necessary to kill the councillor."

"You mean like someone saw him eating for the first time and got to worrying about kids starving in Ethiopia?" said Dalziel.

"Or maybe it was something he said," interposed Pascoe, feeling sidelined by this unexpected rapprochement between the Fat Man and Bowler. "The councillor was a great one for stirring things up, as we know to our cost."

"Aye, happen it's a good job we're investigating this," said Dalziel. "I mean, with Jax the Ripper and Stuffer being shuffled off in quick succession, if you start looking for someone with a motive for shutting them up, I reckon we'd come high up the list."

Pascoe glanced at Bowler, recalling his recent lecture on making illogical connections and said, "You're not really suggesting there could be a connection with the Wordman here?"

"Wash your mouth out, lad!" exploded Dalziel. "Yon daft business is the kind of thing that gets CID a bad name. No, with a bit of luck, what we've got here is a good old straightforward killing, and once we've interviewed all the preview guests, we'll have it all tied up, neat and tidy, afore *Match of the Day*."

◆   ◆   ◆

But for once Dalziel's prognostication was wrong. By mid-evening all the guests had been tracked down and interviewed. None of them had noticed anything suspicious in regard to the theft of the burin. Councillor Steel's conversation, though as full as ever of complaint and accusation, did not seem to have broken any new ground. The nearest thing to an altercation was Charley Penn's annoyance at Steel's efforts to shut down his literature group. But, as the novelist pointed out, if you took that as a motive, then everyone employed in the HAL Centre must be suspect as the councillor proposed to make half of them redundant and slash the salaries of the rest. Mary Agnew recalled descending the stairs from the gallery with him, during which short interlude she got a quick-fire summary of her newspaper's major failings. On reaching the mezzanine, he'd said, "Got to spend a penny," and turned away, presumably towards the men's toilet. She hadn't noticed anyone else going after him.

Pressure applied by Dalziel to the Chief Constable had been passed on and a preliminary post mortem report was available by early evening. It stated that Steel had died as a result of a single blow from the burin (now confirmed as the murder weapon by Forensic), which had cut right through to the medulla and pons of the brainstem, and had been, as Bowler had said, either very lucky or very expert. The burin had been wiped clean of prints.

Andy Dalziel read the report, said, "Sod it," and went home.

He checked his phone for messages. There was just one, from Cap Marvell. She regretted again the ruining of their planned afternoon by Steel's untimely death and would have been happy to sit around like Marianna of the moated grange had she not received an invite from some old radical chums to go out on the bevvy and maybe check out the latest Full Monty act at Jock the Cock's Nite Spot.

Dalziel sighed. He could not fault the wisdom of her choice, but he missed her. On the other hand, left to his own devices, there were certain refined pleasures a man could enjoy without fear of comment or complaint.

He went into the kitchen, emerging a few moments later equipped with what he thought of as The Four Last Things, viz a fork, a jar of pickled herring, a half-pint mug and a bottle of Highland Park. He poured the fourth into the third, plunged the first into the second and settled back to enjoy *Match of the Day* which was a poor substitute for a real game like rugby football, but Manchester United were playing Leeds, so the violence factor ought to come close.

Two yellow cards later the phone rang.

"Yes!" he bellowed.

"It's me," said Pascoe.

"Oh shit."

"That's a pretty fair description," said Pascoe. "Security man at the Centre doing a sweep heard the main letter box rattle and when he checked he found an envelope marked 'Reference Library.' Normally he'd have left it, but because of the murder, they're very much on the qui vive, and he reported to his Control and they got on to the factory."

"And you were still there?" said Dalziel. "What's up? Ellie locked you out?"

"No, sir. I was at home. Seymour rang me. I think he didn't want to disturb you . . ."

"Glad there's someone who's got some consideration. All right, lad, the music's stopped, the parcel's in my lap. Tell me I'm guessing wrong."

"Doubt it," said Pascoe. "You know you were hoping the Steel case would turn out a nice straightforward murder? Forget it. The envelope contained a Fourth Dialogue. Looks like the Wordman has uttered again."

There was silence, then a great anguished cry.

"Sir? You there? You OK, sir?"

"No, I'm bloody well not," said Dalziel. "First you tell me my unfavourite loony's still at it, then, to cap it all, Man, United have just scored!"

XVII

Murder investigation is the conventional peak of detective work, but Hat Bowler was beginning to discover how much it could snarl up your social life. Any vague hope he had of being able to keep his Sunday date vanished with the discovery of the Fourth Dialogue. He'd seen Rye briefly the previous afternoon after she'd made her statement and had tried to sound optimistic, but she'd looked at him sceptically and given him her home number in case there were problems and on Sunday morning, for the second week in succession he rang her to cancel.

She listened to his apologies for a while then cut in, "Hey, no big deal. Another time maybe."

"You don't sound very disappointed," he said accusingly.

"Disappointed? If you listen hard, you can probably hear the rain lashing against my bedroom window, and you want me to be disappointed I'm not getting up to spend most of the day dripping wet looking for so-called dumb creatures who have probably got sense enough to stay cosily tucked up in their burrows?"

"Nests. Are you saying you're still in bed?"

"Certainly. It's my day off even if it's not yours. Hello? You still there? You're not fantasizing about me, I hope?"

"Of course not. I'm a cop. We have our imaginations surgically removed. But we get issued with surveillance equipment instead, so no need for fantasies."

"You mean you've got me under observation? OK, what am I doing now?"

He thought for a while. This was fun, but he didn't want to ruin things by going too far too fast, even verbally.

"Scratching your nose?" he said cautiously.

She giggled and said huskily, "Nearly right. So how's the case going? Are we all still suspects?"

It had been Rye who had pointed out the obvious to him on Saturday afternoon when he'd apologized for the time she'd spent being questioned as a possible witness. "And suspect," she'd added. "Don't sell us short. Everyone who was at the preview and left before or at the same time as Councillor Steel is a potential suspect. My money's on Percy Follows."

"Why's that?"

"Because I understand he's used to assaulting men with a very small weapon."

He'd regarded her gravely and said, "You should have joined the police too."

"Because of my insights?"

"No. Because you know how to avoid letting the nastiness of things get to you by making bad jokes."

Even as he spoke he thought, You pompous twit! She's going to love you for coming over all righteous on her.

But her reaction was worse than indignation. Her eyes filled with tears and she said, "I'm sorry . . . I was only trying not to . . ."

Which was when he'd put his arms around her and pulled her close and was prevented, or perhaps saved, from discovering whether this was their first embrace or just a comforting hug by Sergeant Wield's dry cough and drier voice, saying, "When you've quite finished with that witness, Detective Constable Bowler . . ."

Now he said, "Of course you're all still suspects. Which is why I intend to keep you under close personal surveillance. Listen, I'll be in touch. Let's forget the Stangdale trip, maybe we can do a movie or something . . ."

"Like *The Birds*, you mean? Sorry. Yes, that would be nice too, but I'm a woman of my word. I said I'd twitch with you and twitch I will. Next week OK?"

"Yes, if you're sure. I mean, that's great. And we'll go back to making it a whole day, OK? I'll provide a picnic."

"Don't get carried away. Fine, that's fixed. Ring me. Now you get on with keeping society safe for decent folk and I'll get back to scratching my nose. Bye."

He switched off his phone, scratched his nose, and smiled. He'd always found the idea of telephone sex a turn-off, but the way he felt now, maybe there was something in it. His relationship with Rye had certainly taken a step forward; though he could see it being knocked a couple of long steps back when she realized he'd kept stumm about the Fourth Dialogue. The temptation to tell her had been strong but, over the phone at least, not as strong as Sergeant Wield's prohibition on spreading the news.

"Keep this to yourself," Wield had said. "As far as the world's concerned, Councillor Steel's death is an isolated incident until the super decides different. And you want the super to feel you're reliable, don't you? Especially around young women."

Hat had thought of arguing that as Rye Pomona had been instrumental in bringing them into contact with the Wordman, she had a right to know, but it wasn't an argument he felt he could sustain in face of those louring features.

So instead he said, "Any reason why the super shouldn't think I'm reliable, Sarge?"

"I think," said Wield carefully, "he felt you might have got a bit close to Jax Ripley."

He watched the youngster's face closely, saw puzzlement bubble to understanding then boil into indignation.

"You mean all that stuff she did about us falling down on the job, Mr. Dalziel thought she was getting inside info from me? Jesus, Sarge, nearly every time I saw her, we got in a row about those programmes. OK, so we stayed friends, sort of, but we both knew we were just using each other. I might have done the odd trade-off with her—I'll show you mine if you show me yours—but if she had a real Deep-throat in the Force, it certainly wasn't me!"

Wield noted but did not comment on the sexual imagery used in the denial. Though unsusceptible to such things himself, he was perfectly aware when a woman was turning up the heat in his direction, and he'd got a good warm blast on the couple of occasions he'd met the TV reporter. If, and he tended to believe him, Bowler hadn't succumbed beyond the point of professional discretion, then it said much for the young man's self-control.

"Do you think I should say something to the super?" Bowler had asked in some agitation.

"I shouldn't," said Wield. "Denial afore you're asked is as good as an admission in our game. He seemed quite pleased with the way you handled yourself yesterday. So forget it. The future's what matters, not the past. But be warned. You see a reporter, you run a mile."

That would mean taking up the marathon, thought Hat. The media interest in Ripley's murder had been vast and though there was as yet no official acknowledgement of a link with Steel's death, they were close enough in time and location for the bloodhounds to be sniffing the air once more and sending up their howls of speculation. Privately Hat thought Dalziel's notion of keeping quiet about the Fourth Dialogue was stupid, but not as stupid as giving any hint of what he thought.

"Yes, Sarge. So what's the state of play at the moment? Any other developments?"

"Well, there's a meeting in the super's office at ten. It's the DCI's idea. The Great Consult, he calls it."

"What's that mean?"

"Something about all the devils getting together to decide how to get out of hell. Mr. Pascoe sometimes lets himself go a bit poetic when things get tough," said Wield indulgently. "Any road, he's persuaded the super that it's time to call on some outside expertise, like Dr. Pottle, the shrink, and some language expert from the university."

"Jesus, things must be bad!" exclaimed Hat, who knew how the Fat Man felt about what he usually referred to as *arty-farty crap-merchants.*

"You're right. We're really scraping the barrel. You're invited."

"Me?"

Exhilaration fought with apprehension at the news.

"Aye. So get yourself right up to speed. But first you'd best go and ring that lass from the library and tell her you'll definitely not be coming out to play today."

As he began to dial Rye's number, Hat had wondered how the hell Wield knew he had a date with Rye. But by the time he'd pressed the final digit, he'd worked out that the sergeant must have overheard all of the conversation before the hug which might have turned into an embrace.

That sod misses nothing, he thought, half admiringly, half resentfully. But I'm a lot prettier!

Half seemed a good measure and he decided he'd take only half of Wield's advice. He wouldn't say anything to the Fat Man about his unjust suspicions but he wouldn't forget them either. He knew he was innocent, which meant some other bugger wasn't and he didn't see why he should go through his career with this question mark against his name in Dalziel's book of remembrance.

Meanwhile, he was determined to build on the good impression he seemed to have made on the super yesterday. Being invited to join the Holy Trinity at this Great Consult was a large step. He recalled the pangs of envy he'd felt on earlier occasions when he'd seen DC Shirley Novello, who wasn't that much senior, being admitted more and more to the inner triangle. Novello was still on sick leave after taking a bullet in the course of duty a couple of months before. Any hopes Bowler had had of filling the gap had soon been squashed, leaving him disappointed and puzzled till Wield had made things clear. Now he had his chance to shine and he wasn't going to miss out.

He spent the hour's grace he had going through witness statements. As every guest at the preview had been interviewed, there wasn't time to read them all. Fortunately, with typical efficiency Sergeant Wield had already collated these under several headings with cross-references. The largest group was those who left the preview and the Centre more than ten minutes before the councillor's departure and also gave negative responses to the key questions—*Did you talk to Councillor Steel or overhear him talking to anyone else? Did you observe anyone behaving oddly in the vicinity of Jude Illingworth's engraving demonstration?*

A note had been added in Pascoe's boyish scrawl. *I don't think the killer would risk lying about the time of his departure though it is of course possible that he left earlier then waited for the councillor's departure. As for answering the two questions, I think it unlikely the killer would give a negative response to both, partly because I reckon that he probably did talk to Steel, but mainly because I doubt that someone as wordy as the Wordman could bear to say nothing.*

Clever sod, thought Hat. Though it was well to remember that the Wordman was a clever sod too. But it helped him choose what to look at and what to shove aside for later examination.

He turned his attention to those who had something to report about the councillor and/or thought they'd noticed something at the demonstration.

He rapidly came to the conclusion that most of the reports of odd behaviour were motivated either by an over-eagerness to help or by a simple longing for importance. None of the professional observers there, i.e. himself, Wield, Pascoe, and the super, contributed anything, which might or might not be significant. Five witnesses recalled that when they were watching the engraver at work, a nearby table had been jostled and a couple of glasses had fallen to the floor, which could have been a deliberate diversion. Unfortunately, none of them had a distinct memory of who was in the vicinity at the time; indeed only one of them could recall the presence of any of the others.

Stuffer Steel had made rather more impression, though much of the recollection centred on the amount of food he managed to put away. Reports of his actual conversation suggested a preoccupation with two themes. The first was that most of the art on display was a load of crap and spending public money on displaying it was a scandal and he'd be proposing a motion of censure on the Finance Committee at the next council meeting. The second was that Jax Ripley's death had fallen very fortuitously for the Mid-Yorkshire police whose extravagances and inefficiencies she was, with his assistance, in the midst of exposing.

Mary Agnew in particular had got an earful, as had Sammy Ruddlesdin, and John Wingate from BBC MY. Several witnesses reported that Wingate had interrupted Steel after a while and there had been a heated exchange, ending with the TV man walking away. Wingate himself gave a full account of this, saying that he'd got pissed off with listening to the councillor rattle on as if the only important thing about Jax Ripley's death had been its effect on Steel's campaigning. This was an understandable reaction from a colleague of the dead woman, but Bowler recalled his own speculation when getting a statement from Wingate after the murder that there might have been a more than professional relationship between the two of them.

He made a note and read on, concentrating on those who'd left round about the same time as the councillor. Wield had already done the groundwork here also, producing a neat graph showing who was where at what time. A copy of Hat's own statement was here, of course, and he read through it with as much detachment as he could muster. It was a good policeman's statement, precise and detailed. It said nothing of that feeling he'd had when he entered the toilet of stepping into a new dimension in which nothing existed but himself and the body on the floor, curled in a foetal question mark. How long he'd simply stood and looked at it he did not know. In fact, *How long?* did not seem a question that applied, not when it seemed possible to step back into the corridor, wait a second, then re-open the door and find that the image had been erased. Of course he'd done no such thing. Of course the training had snapped in and he'd gone into the sequence of checking pulse, calling help, attempting resuscitation, making the scene secure, and by the time he went to bed that night, the sense of disassociation had faded to a memory of natural shock at such a grisly discovery.

But when he read the copy of the Fourth Dialogue Wield handed him that morning and realized he had been only a few heartbeats behind the Wordman, it all came back to him so strongly that he found himself grasping at the hardness of a table and staring fixedly at the second hand on his watch to assure himself of the continuance of corporeality.

Now he reconsidered his statement in view of the new information that this wasn't merely a one-off killing but part of the Wordman's sequence. Perhaps his feelings were now relevant . . . But how? And his heart sank at the thought of trying to explain them to Dalziel. He might be able to retrieve his reputation from the false accusation of being Deep-throat, but Air-brain was probably beyond recovery.

He put his statement aside and went on with the others.

It would of course be nice to be able to go to the meeting and perform a piece of mental gymnastics which took him leaping from one small overlooked item to another, ending with a triple somersault before landing firmly on the Wordman's back. In his mind's eye he saw the Trinity looking on with wonder and admiration before holding up their score-cards awarding maximum points for both style and content.

But such flights of inspiration, though the commonplace of fiction, were very rarely spotted in the world of a humble detective constable. Close attention to detail, no matter how dull and repetitive, was what solved cases. And as he read, Hat cross-checked with Wield's graph, not in expectation of finding an omission but in the not very strong hope of spotting a discrepancy. The closest he came was in Rye's statement (direct and detailed enough to be a policeman's) in which she said that when she collected her coat from the reference library she saw a few members of the public working, but no one she knew. Yet according to the graph, two people who'd been at the preview should have been there—Dick Dee and Charley Penn. He started shuffling through the statements.

"You got something?" said Wield, who'd come up behind him soft-footed.

"Not really . . . maybe . . ."

He found Dee's statement. He'd left the preview a couple of minutes before Hat and Rye and gone straight to the library. On his arrival, the woman on duty had taken the opportunity to head off to the toilet. Dee had been at the far end of the library, checking a reference in some tome, when he glimpsed Rye collecting her coat from the office.

So he saw her, she didn't see him.

Penn in his statement said he'd gone straight to the library and taken his place in his usual cubicle. *Facing the wall,* he'd written, *you tend not to see many people.* But later when he'd gone to the lavatory *(not the* locus in quo *but the staff loo adjacent to the reference library, access to which I enjoy as a kind of "favoured nation" privilege),* he had noticed Dee. So, a general cancelling out.

"No, sorry. Nothing. Look, I'm not trying to second-guess you, Sarge . . ."

"Aren't you? That's a pity. DC who's not trying to second-guess his sergeant is no use to anyone. But don't get so absorbed you miss the time. Ten more minutes. Be late for Mr. Dalziel and you could be late forever."

Hat abandoned the statements and spent the remaining time processing a selection of people through the computer. It was like panning for gold in a worked-out claim. Dross, dross, nothing but dross.

Then at last, like a buttercup growing through a cow-pat, he glimpsed one tiny nugget of gold.

He drew it out, weighed it, recognized it wasn't going to make him rich. But properly worked, it might make an elegant link in a chain. He glanced at his watch. Five minutes to go.

Probably more. Academics were notoriously bad timekeepers.

He reached for the telephone.

XVIII

"**Well, look who's** here," said Andy Dalziel. "Come in, lad. Find a chair. Make yourself comfortable. Good of you to spare the time."

The academics, unreliable as ever, must have been punctual.

Spouting apologies, Hat concentrated on the guests, to blot out Dalziel's threatening glower and Pascoe's reproachful pout. Even Wield's blankness spelt out well-I-did-warn-you.

Dr. Pottle, the psychiatrist, was a small man in late middle age who had deliberately cultivated a natural resemblance to Einstein. "Patients find it very reassuring," he'd once told Peter Pascoe who was, unofficially and intermittently, one of those patients. "Also I like to tell the really dotty ones that I've built a time machine and travelled into the future and everything's going to be all right for them."

"And how does it look for me, Professor?" Pascoe had replied.

Pottle's other idiosyncrasy was that despite all the social, medical and political pressure, he still chain-smoked. Dalziel, who was an off-on smoker currently going through a pretty extensive *off* patch, bowed to the inevitable, helped himself to a handful of Pottle's fags, and was drawing on the first like a drowning sailor come up for the third time.

The other expert was introduced as Dr. Drew Urquhart. Not very old, as far as Bowler could make out through a wilderness of beard. Fortunately he kept his upper lip bare. Had he worn the kind of Einsteinian moustache Pottle favoured, his features would have been beyond even a mother's recognition. Dressed in non-matching trainers, threadbare jeans and a T-shirt which had rotted under the armpits to provide what seemed like very necessary ventilation holes, he looked more like a resident of cardboard-box country in the shopping centre than the Groves of Academe.

"Fuck this," he growled in a Scots accent, unidentifiable to Bowler except that it wasn't Glaswegian. "If I'm going to be choked dead then I might as well do it on my own weed."

He produced a cigarette paper and began to fill it with something he took from a small leather pouch.

Dalziel said, "You light that, sunshine, and I'll kick you all the way back to the Kingdom of Fife."

"You check up on all your visitors, do you, Superintendent?" sneered Urquhart.

"Don't need to check. Should have thought being a linguist you'd know you give yourself away every time you open your gob."

"I'm impressed. Deeply offended but impressed," said Urquhart.

He put away the pouch with the offending substance and said, "Can we start? I've got places to be."

"Oh aye? Going ratting, are you?" asked Dalziel, letting his gaze run up and down the linguist's dress.

Pottle said, "Now that we have got these necessary pecking-order rituals out of the way, I too should like to put in an appeal for expedition."

"I'll not argue with that. Quicker the better, in my view," said Dalziel. "Pete, this is your circus, so you'd better crack the whip."

"Thank you," said Pascoe. "May I say first of all how grateful we are to Dr. Pottle and Dr. Urquhart for coming along this morning at such short notice. It seemed to me that as we must now admit without any prevarication that we have a serial killer on our hands, the wider we cast our net in search of expert assistance, and the sooner we set about casting it, the better. I realize you have had what is in analytical terms a ludicrously short time in which to study the Wordman documents, but what first impressions may lack in depth they can make up in freshness, Dr. Pottle."

"Let me first apologize to my esteemed colleague, Dr. Urquhart, in case anything I say should seem to trespass on his mystery, for of course my only route to understanding the writer of these pieces is via the words the writer uses."

"Dinna fash yersel', Pozzo," said the Scot. "I'll not be backward in dishing out the psychobabble."

"Thank you. *First Dialogue.* The very use of the word Dialogue is significant. A dialogue is an exchange of ideas and information between two or more people. For these to be true dialogues our Wordman—I use the term for convenience—must be listening as well as speaking. And I think we can see that he is doing this in two ways. Firstly there are gaps in the text, blank lines, and it is not difficult to fill these in with unrecorded replies to the Wordman's comments or questions. For the most part these would be conversational trivia rather than matter of deep import such as you might expect to find in a dialogue proper. For example, in this first one, between *How're you doing?* and *Me, I'm fine, I think*, we might interpolate *OK. How about yourself?* Then between *Me, I'm fine I think* and *It's hard to tell sometimes*, we might put *What do you mean, 'think'?* It should be noted that the tone here, as throughout the Dialogues in these small exchanges, is friendly and familiar, as between people who are very close and on a fairly equal footing."

"I think we just about got there by ourselves," said Pascoe apologetically, aware of steatopygous squeakings from Dalziel's chair. "You said there were two forms of dialogue. . . ."

"Indeed. The other is the more formal and mysterious one in which the Wordman believes he is receiving advice, aid, and instruction from some otherworldly power who may or may not be or may be in part only the familiar communicant of the first form. Finally of course the Wordman is indulging in a dialogue with us. That is, with you the investigators of these crimes, with Mr. Urquhart and myself as your associates, and with the world at large who form as it were his wider audience."

"Can I say something here?" said Urquhart. "You may have missed it, Pozzo, and me I only picked it up through a reference in a dictionary, but then I got a friend to check it out . . ."

"Friend?" said Pascoe, again pre-empting the Fat Man. "You haven't been showing the Dialogues to anyone unauthorized, I hope."

"Don't get your Y-fronts in a tangle," said Urquhart. "It was just a wee hairie in the Eng. Lit. Department that I bang from time to time and she disna ken any more than she needs to ken. What she told me was that there's this thing in literature called a 'Dialogue of the Dead.' Started way back with Lucian . . ."

"That'd be Lord Lucian?" said Dalziel.

"Ha ha. Second-century Syrian rhetorician who wrote in Greek. There was a big revival of interest in England in the eighteenth century, the Augustans and what followed, all that classical crap. Biggest success was Lord Lyttelton's *Dialogues of the Dead* in 1760. Twenty-eight dialogues including three by some bluestocking called Mrs. Montagu—the best three my wee friend assures me, but she may be partial. There were a few more written right through the nineteenth century but the form had pretty well died the death before Queen Vicky snuffed it."

"And what did this form consist of?" enquired Pascoe.

"Debates in the Nether Regions between the shades of real historical characters and imagined characters, sometimes with supernatural beings from mythology holding the ring. I checked a few out. There's one with Mercury and an English Duellist and a North-American Savage, another with Sir Thomas More and the Vicar of Bray. Purpose usually, though not always, satirical. Written out like drama, name of character then what he or she says, but no stage directions or settings described. Meant to be read, not performed."

"But we don't get names given here," said Pascoe, looking down at his copy of the Dialogues.

"You wouldn't expect them, would you? That would give the game away from the start. May be a blind alley, but seems to me the Wordman's dialogue is with someone dead and he's certainly bent on increasing the population of the underworld. Seemed worth a mention. Anyway, in your business, leave no stone unturned if you want to see the wriggly wee insects run, eh?"

"We're much obliged, Doctor," murmured Pascoe, who'd been making notes.

"Oh God," groaned Dalziel. "Not past the first word yet, and already me brain's hurting."

"Perhaps if we could move on," said Pascoe, glancing at his watch. "I know your time is precious, gentlemen."

"Very well," said Pottle, lighting another cigarette from the butt-end in his hand. "After the title, the illustration—or should I say illumination? I gather that you have already received expert advice about the stylistic source . . ."

"In a manner of speaking," said Pascoe carefully. "DC Bowler, perhaps you would like to fill us in?"

Taken by surprise, Hat swallowed nervously before replying, "Well, Mr. Dee at the library said he thought it was based on some medieval Celtic script. He showed me something that was a bit like it in, I think it was some eighth-century Irish gospel . . ."

He was aware that the Fat Man's eyes had closed and his mouth opened in a hippopotamic yawn, and he cursed Pascoe for making his first contribution to the Great Consult something which was almost bound to get up those huge nostrils. But now the DCI, perhaps feeling guilty, took up the running and went on, ". . . and it would seem that the design represents the *In P* of the opening line of St. John's Gospel: *In principio erat verbum . . ."*

"In the beginning was the word and the word was with God and the word was God," intoned Dalziel, opening his eyes. "Yeah yeah, we all did Bible Studies, except maybe young Bowler here who probably had to learn the Kama Sutra or something. Doctor Pottle, can we mebbe just cut to a few conclusions and save all the fancy stuff for an article?"

"The first thing that struck me about the drawing was the way all the continuation letters were piled up together. I was reminded of a virus which once got into the hospital computer system and sent all the letters you typed tumbling to the foot of the screen. I wondered if perhaps this meant our Wordman felt of himself that he had some kind of virus affecting his brain."

"You mean he knows he's off his chump?" said Dalziel. "Great!"

"It fits in with other indications that he is not yet completely at ease with the idea of killing people," continued Pottle serenely. "The drawing is only one of many attempts to fit his behaviour into a quasi-religious context which has two main functions. The first is, of course, justification. It is God, or his agent in the Other World, who points the finger in some sequential way still to be fathomed. The Wordman is to some extent an instrument of divine purpose, or of divine requirement if the Wordman is to achieve some purpose of his own, which is not altogether clear. Yet despite this pretence to supernatural necessity, the Wordman's unease shows in the need he feels to suggest that the victims are better off dead, either for their own sakes or for the sake of society at large, or sometimes both. You have probably noticed that the drowned man in the water under the bridge also resembles a figure crucified, like St. Andrew, on an X-shaped cross."

"Know how he felt," muttered Andy Dalziel.

Pascoe gave him a glower and urged, "You said the religious context had two functions, Doctor. Justification and . . . ?"

"Yes. And invulnerability. This suspension of time thing. It seems to be literal, not a metaphor. God or his agent is masterminding events and, being all-powerful, he is not about to let his instrument get caught. Herein perhaps lies your best hope of catching the writer. The risks taken in respect of Councillor Steel's murder were enormous and could only be countenanced by someone who felt completely invulnerable. The longer this goes on, the greater the risks taken are likely to be."

"You're saying that with a bit of luck, and if he goes on long enough, we'll catch him in the act?" said the Fat Man incredulously. "If that's the best you can do, don't it make all this palaver a bit pointless, *Doctor*?"

The degree of scorn Dalziel could infuse into a form of address could probably provide a linguist with material for a thesis, thought Pascoe.

"Maybe I can give a wee bit of practical help here," said Urquhart. "See this bit of the illumination here . . ."

He pointed to the bottom of the twin stems of the **I.**

"Aye, the cows," said Dalziel.

Urquhart laughed and said, "They'd need to be Highland cattle with horns like these. No, not cows. Oxen, I think."

"Oxen. Great. Now we're really getting somewhere. Make a note of that, Chief Inspector."

"What are you getting at?" asked Pascoe.

"Aleph," said Urquhart significantly.

"Is that Aleph in Wonderland or Aleph Through the Looking Glass?" enquired Dalziel.

"Aleph is the first letter of the Hebrew alphabet," said Urquhart. "It is also the Old Hebrew and Phoenician word meaning ox, and it seems likely that the form the letter takes is based on a hieroglyph of an ox's head. Greek *alpha* is derived from this, and ultimately Roman and our own *a* which, in some versions of its capital form can still be seen to contain those original hieroglyphic elements. As thus in the *Book of Kells* . . ."

He took out a pen and drew a letter: 𐤀

Dalziel looked at it in silence for a moment then said, "If they served me that as an ox's head, I'd send it back. Is there any point to all this, lad?"

"*A* of course is also a word, the first word as it is the first letter of our alphabet. *In the beginning was the word* . . . And note the references in the Dialogue to the indefinite beginnings of the path. *A* is the indefinite article. You will be wondering perhaps why there are two oxen, two *alephs* . . ."

"The AA man," said Pascoe. "Whose initials are also AA. Which the Wordman took for a sign. So what are you saying, Dr. Urquhart? That there could be some alphabetical sequence here?"

"No, sorry. I can see how that might be useful, but there's nothing obvious in the others. You might get a *b* from *boy* or even *bazouki* in the Pitman case, but that would be stretching, and all the *c*'s in the Ripley case and the *d*'s in the Steel case seem completely out of reach. So I doubt if what you've got here is a straightforward alphabetical progression. Your Wordman might, of course, be simply spelling a word. In which case let us hope it's a short one, but it's just as likely it could be several words which form a message."

"*Am having a good time, wish you were here,*" suggested Dalziel, scratching his crotch like a man refuting Bishop Berkeley. "Look, gents, as the actress said to the bishop, can you make this a quickie as I've got work to do? Any long-term stuff, or general theorizing, mebbe you could set it down in writing when you've had more chance to study the Dialogues, and I'll hang it up in the CID bog so we all get a chance to use it."

Bowler, who'd been puzzled by the academics' apparent indifference to the Fat Man's sceptical rudeness, caught a glance passing between Pascoe and Pottle, and it came to him that the DCI had forewarned them of Dalziel's likely reaction, which previous acquaintance had probably prepared them for anyway.

Urquhart said, "I'd certainly like more time to check out this illumination. It wouldn't surprise me to find a lot more stuff hidden there. But for the time being I think I can say that what you've got here is someone obsessed with language, not just at a linguistic level, but at a philosophical level, maybe even a magical level. Words originally were simply the names of things and human transactions, both practical and abstract, couldn't have functioned without them. I mean, if you don't know the names, you have to produce the things themselves, and you end up like the academicians in Swift's Lagado, dragging around a bagful of articles you may possibly want to refer to. In primitive societies the belief still exists that knowledge of the real names of individuals or even certain objects gives you power over them which is why they are at such pains to keep them secret. Spells are words arranged in a significant order and often coupled with the secret names of deities or devils—"

"So we're looking for a nut who probably likes doing riddles and crosswords?" Dalziel crashed in brutally. "Dr. Pottle?"

"I think your Wordman is a seriously disturbed personality who will show very little sign of this on the surface, in fact may appear a particularly laid-back and unflappable individual. But this will have been acquired behaviour and if you look back far enough in their lives, such individuals will almost inevitably have done something or experienced something which gives a hint that dangerous currents and tangling weeds may lie beneath that placid surface."

"Well, that really narrows things down," said Dalziel. "That it, then?"

His tone didn't invite further discourse but Pascoe said, "Before you go, I wonder if this means anything to either of you?"

He showed them a piece of paper on which was drawn P⋌П.

Pottle examined it, turned it round, shrugged and said, "I'd need to know much more about its context to even hazard a guess."

Pascoe said, "There was a wound on Councillor Steel's head. It may be, and certainly we can find no other candidate, the *necessary mark* referred to in the Dialogue. When the blood was washed away, these are the marks left by the burin. They could of course be accidental, but their resemblance to letters, a **P** certainly, and a badly formed **M** perhaps. The squiggle between could be simply an incidental ripping of the skin or it may be another less well-defined but nonetheless deliberate mark."

Dalziel looked sceptical but his left hand was scratching his stubble pate as if impelled by some irresistible sympathy.

Urquhart suddenly snickered a laugh.

"Share the joke, sunshine?" suggested Dalziel.

"The councillor was called Cyril, wasn't he?" said the linguist. "In the Russian Cyrillic alphabet, what looks like our **P** is in fact an **R**, while that thing that you called a badly formed **M** could be a Cyrillic **P**. And if the scratch in between is just a shorthand **I** which is rather a complex letter in Russian and not easy to do in a hurry on a head with an engraving tool, this could simply be **RIP** in the Cyrillic alphabet. Gerrit?"

Dalziel shook his head as if to clear it of the after-effects of long slumber and rose slowly to his feet.

"Gorrit," he said in a mild, long-suffering voice. "Right joker, this Wordman, ain't he? What's it they say? Laugh and the world laughs with you. Thanks, gents. That's definitely it. Sergeant Wield will show you out."

Pascoe, clearly feeling that this expression of appreciation fell some way short of warm, said, "It's been really useful. Many thanks for giving us your time this morning. We'll look forward to hearing from you again as soon as you've had time for mature reflection, won't we, sir?"

"Can't wait," said Dalziel. "And Sergeant Wield, be sure to arrest Dr. Urquhart if he starts smoking that stuff afore he leaves the building."

The linguist, who had once more taken his leather pouch from his pocket, paused in the doorway, smiled at Dalziel and said, "Away play wi' yersel', Hamish."

It wasn't often his underlings had the pleasure of seeing their Great Master nonplussed but for a moment after the door closed behind

Pottle, Urquhart and Wield, this was an experience Pascoe and Bowler enjoyed.

Then he turned his gaze on them and they both smoothed away all signs of anything but alert intelligence from their faces.

"So, Peter, you happy now?" demanded Dalziel.

"I think it was a very useful meeting, sir, and with luck we'll get a great deal more help from the pair of them."

"You reckon? And mebbe I'll join the Women's Institute. Jesus, you'd think on the Sabbath, we could get just a little bit of real help in taking things forward. Owt 'ud do. Just a name with enough justification for me to go and kick shit out of it."

"There's always Roote."

"Still whistling that tune, Pete? Thought your dog here had sniffed him out and found nowt."

First Wield, now the Fat Man. Not forgetting, of course, Roote himself. Did the whole world know about his so-called secret surveillance? wondered Hat.

"And there weren't owt in his statement nor anyone else's to put him in the frame for the councillor, were there?"

"He's a clever fellow," said Pascoe.

"Ah, I see. That means the cleaner he looks, the guiltier he obviously is, does it? Tell you what, minute you see him walking on water with an angelic choir singing 'Jerusalem,' you pull your wellies on and put him under arrest. Bowler, how about you? Are you good for owt more than kissing strange men in public lavatories?"

It wasn't a very inviting invitation, but Hat guessed it was the only one he was likely to get.

He said, "I checked out one or two people, and something came up, probably nothing . . ."

"You'd best not be wasting my time with it if it's probably nothing, lad," growled Dalziel.

"No, sir. It's this writer fellow, Charley Penn. He was at the preview, and it's reported that he had a bit of a set-to with Councillor Steel, so that's why I ran him through the computer. And it turns out he has a record."

"For writing crap?" said Dalziel.

"No, sir. For assault. Five years ago he got bound over in Leeds for assaulting a journalist."

"Oh aye? Should have given him the George Cross. Pete, you know owt about this bugger's homicidal tendencies?"

"Yes, sir," said Pascoe almost apologetically, not wanting to sound like he was putting Hat down. "I mean, I've heard a story, though I wasn't sure how apocryphal it was. Version I heard, Penn got pissed off with a review and crowned said journalist with a slice of gateau, so not exactly a deadly weapon."

"Way my missus baked, it was," said Dalziel. "That it then, Bowler? You reckon we should pull Penn in and wire his bollocks to a table lamp just because he shampooed some miserable reporter with a cream cake?"

"No, sir. Not exactly . . . what I mean is, I thought he might be worth a chat . . ."

"Oh aye? Give me half a good reason."

"The journalist's name was Jacqueline Ripley, sir."

Dalziel's jaw dropped in exaggerated amazement.

"Jax the Ripper? By God! Pete, why'd you not tell me it was Jax the Ripper?"

"Didn't know, sir. Sorry. Well done, Hat."

"Thank you, sir," said Bowler, blushing faintly. "I even managed to get a copy of the article."

"How on earth did you manage that?" said Pascoe.

"Well, I rang the *Yorkshire Life* office. Chances of finding anyone there on a Sunday didn't seem good, but I hit lucky and got the editor, Mr. Macready, and he was very helpful and dug out the piece and faxed me a copy . . ."

"You mean you've alerted a journalist to the fact that we're trying to make connections between Charley Penn and a murder victim?" snapped Pascoe. "For God's sake, man, what were you thinking of?"

Hat Bowler, who had produced the fax sheet with the flourish of a Chamberlain announcing peace in our time, looked aghast at the speed with which war had been declared.

But help came from an unexpected source.

"Nay, never fear," said Dalziel, plucking the fax from his nervous fingers. "I know Alec Macready, big church man, big swordsman too. He'll be no bother, not if he wants to stay on the Bishop's Christmas card list. Well done, young Bowler. It's good to know there's still someone round here willing to do a bit of old-fashioned police work. Charley Penn, eh? Now, if I recall aright, his chosen place of worship on a Sunday morning is The Dog and Duck. Let's go and find him."

"Sir, wouldn't it be better to ask him to come here perhaps . . . I mean, it's a bit public . . ."

"Aye, that's why they call them pubs, lad. For God's sake, I'm not going to arrest him. Hit Jax the Ripper with a slice of cake, did he? Good old Charley! I'll mebbe buy the bugger a drink."

"I think," said Pascoe, "in view of the fact that Ripley has just been murdered it would be undiplomatic to take that line in the pub, sir."

"Bad taste, tha means? Likely you're right. I'll not buy him a drink then. Bowler, got your wallet? You can buy us both one!"

XIX

Charley Penn said, "Aye," into his mobile phone for the second time, switched it off and replaced it in his pocket.

"Interesting," said Sam Johnson.

"What?"

"You answer your mobile without that expression, or at least grimace, of apology with which most civilized men of a certain age usually preface its use, then you have a conversation, or should I say transaction, to which your sole contribution is the word *Aye*, used once as an exordial interrogative and once as a valedictory affirmative."

"And that's interesting? You lecturers must lead very quiet lives. Cheers, lad."

Franny Roote, just returned from the bar, placed a pint of bitter in front of Penn and a large Scotch in front of Johnson, then pulled a bottle of Pils out of his duffel-coat pocket, twisted off the top, and drank directly from the bottle.

"Why do you buggers do that?" asked Penn.

"Hygiene," said Roote. "You never know where a glass has been."

"Well, I know where it's not been," said Penn through the froth on his pint. "It's not got the shape."

Roote and Johnson exchanged smiles. They'd discussed Penn's self-projection as a hard-nosed northerner and come to the conclusion it was a protective front behind which he could write his historical romances and pursue his poetical researches with minimum interference from the patronizing worlds of either the literary or the academic establishments.

"On the other hand," Johnson had said, "it may be he's gone on too long. That's the danger with concealment. In the end we may become what we pretend to be."

Which was the kind of clever-sounding thing university teachers were good at saying, thought Roote. He himself had got the patois off pat and didn't doubt that when the time came to move from the economically challenged freedom of student life to the comfortable confines of an academic job, he would be accepted as a native son.

Meanwhile there were worse things to be doing on a Sunday morning than sitting having a drink with this pair of, in their different ways, extremely entertaining and potentially useful men, and worse places to be doing them than in the saloon bar of The Dog and Duck.

"So Charley, did you settle on a satisfactory honorarium with the dreaded Agnew?" asked Johnson.

"Nothing's settled with a journalist till it's down on paper and witnessed by a notary public," said Penn. "But it will be. Not that I was helped in my negotiations by the evident willingness of you and Ellie Pascoe to offer freebies."

"Strictly speaking, it can be viewed as part of my work," said Johnson. "And of course Ellie is still in that happy state of feeling so flattered to be treated as a real writer, she'd probably pay for the privilege. I believe we're being landed with fifty possibles. You're content with the preliminary sorting, I hope? I'm not well enough acquainted with Mr. Dee and his amiable assistant to comment on their judgment, but I get the impression the task was thrust upon them, not because they were qualified but because they were *there*."

"I've known Dick Dee since he were a lad, and he's probably forgotten more about the use of language than most of you buggers in English Departments ever learnt," retorted Penn.

"Which I take it means you're definitely not inclined to read any of the submissions he's rejected," laughed Johnson.

"Can't say I'm looking forward to reading them he hasn't," said Penn. "You pick the best of crap, it's still crap, isn't it?"

"Careful," murmured Johnson. "Never speak ill of a man whose drink you are drinking."

"Eh?" Penn's gaze turned on Roote. "You've not entered a story, have you?"

Franny Roote sucked on his bottle again, smiled his secretive smile, and said, "I refuse to comment on the grounds I may be disqualifying myself."

"Sorry?"

"Well, suppose I had entered and suppose I won, then it came out I had been seen buying prominent members of the judging panel a drink, how would that look?"

"I don't think they'd hold the front page on the *Sun*. Or even the *London Review of Books*."

"Nonetheless." Roote turned his gaze on Johnson. "And what makes you think I may have entered anyway?"

"Just that I recall seeing the page from the *Gazette* announcing the competition lying around your flat when I had coffee there a couple of weeks back," said Johnson. "It's an occupational hazard of literary research, as Charley and I well know, and you yourself must be finding out, that your eyes are irresistibly drawn to anything with print on it."

"Aye, like the sign on that pump over there which says *Best Bitter*," said Penn, setting down his empty glass with a significant crash.

Johnson tossed back the rest of his Scotch, picked up the pint-pot, and headed to the bar.

"So you've got literary ambitions, have you, Franny?" said Penn.

"Perhaps. And if I had, what advice would you offer?"

"Only advice I ever offer young hopefuls," said Penn. "Unless you can pass for under sixteen and an infant prodigy, forget it. Go off and be a politician, fail miserably or at least turn into a grotesque, *then* write your book. That way, publishers will fall over themselves to buy you and newspapers to review you and chat shows to interview you. The alternative, unless you're bloody lucky, is a long haul up a steep hill with nowt much to see when you get up there."

"What's this? Philosophy?" said Johnson, returning with the drinks.

"Just advising young Fran here that the shortest way to literary fame is to become notorious for something else first," said Penn. "I need a slash."

He rose and headed to the Gents.

"Sorry about that," said Johnson.

"Sorry that I've achieved a happy anonymity?" said Roote with a smile. "That was always my hope. Mind you, I was tempted to draw myself up and say *not to know me argues yourself unknown,* but he might have taken that the wrong way."

"Not unknown. Half-known, which is probably worse. Neither owt nor nowt, as Charley would say, suffering equally from the gross familiarity of complete strangers when your name is recognized and their blank look of incomprehension when it isn't. So you prepare yourself to meet either by pretending that neither matters."

Roote sucked at his new bottle and said, "We are still talking about Charley Penn, aren't we? Not some minor poet whose name I forget?"

"What a sharp little mouse it is," said Johnson with a grin. "Like the man said, misery still delights to trace its semblance in another's face."

"You saying that the placid waters of academia are a rougher sea than real life?" said Roote.

"My God, yes. The indignities Charley may have to suffer are on the whole accidental whereas the ivory towers are crowded at every level with bastards plotting to pour boiling oil on those below. Often it's just a little splash. Like wondering at High Table if I've ever thought of doing any creative writing myself. But sometimes it's a whole barrelful. That shit Albacore at Cambridge, the one who paid me back for helping him with his Romantics book by ripping off my idea for Beddoes' bicentennial biography, well, I heard on Friday that he's brought forward his target publication date by six months to pre-empt me."

"It's a hard life," said Roote. "You ought to take up gardening."

"What? Oh yeah, sorry. Me with my worries and you've got all that winter pruning. Seriously, it's working out OK, is it?"

"Fine. Healthy outdoor life. Lots of time to think. Talking of thinking, I've got a few ideas I'd like to try out on you. Can we fix a time?"

"Sure. None like the present. Why don't we head back to my place when we're done drinking? We can pick up a couple of sandwiches en route. What's up, Charley? Been propositioned in the loo?"

Penn had resumed his seat, shaking his head sadly.

"No such luck. Did you know there's a machine in there that will sell you crispy-bacon-flavoured condoms?"

"The modern pub has to cater for all tastes," said Johnson.

"Aye, and this one must specialize in pork. How're your consciences? I think one of us may be about to be arrested."

Dalziel and Bowler had just entered the bar and were standing looking towards their table. The Fat Man spoke to the young DC, then began making his way across the crowded room. It looked as if a man of his bulk would have to plough his way through the tables and chairs and drinkers, but somehow people melted aside at his approach and he slipped between the furniture as easily as a champion skier negotiating a beginner's slalom course.

"Well, here we are," he said genially. "Mr. Penn, and Dr. Johnson, and Mr. Roote. No wonder the churches are empty when the leading lights of literature and learning prefer a pub chair to a pew."

"Morning, Andy," said Penn. "I'd offer you a drink but I see your minder's well trained."

Bowler was coming from the bar, bearing a pint of bitter and a bottle of lager.

"Aye, he's an off-comer, but you can do a lot with 'em if you catch 'em young."

"So, Superintendent," said Johnson. "Are you here professionally?"

"Any reason I should be?"

"I thought perhaps something to do with that sad business yesterday . . ."

"Poor Cyril, you mean? Aye, like you say, a sad business. These muggers, they don't care how far they go these days, specially when they're on drugs."

"That's what you think it was?" said Johnson. "A mugging that went wrong?"

"What else?" said Dalziel, his gaze running over them like a shaft of sunlight from a stormy sky. "Thanks, lad."

He took his pint from Bowler and reduced it by a third.

"Can't ask you to sit down, Andy. Bit full in here today," said Penn.

"So I see. Pity, 'cos I'd have liked a crack with you, Charley."

Quick on his cue, Johnson said, "Have our chairs, Superintendent. We're leaving."

"Nay, don't rush off on my account."

"No, we've got a tutorial arranged, and the atmosphere in here is hardly conducive to rational dialogue."

"Tutorial? Oh aye. You're Mr. Roote's dominie, I hear."

For the first time he turned his gaze full on Franny Roote who returned it equably.

"An old-fashioned word," laughed Johnson.

"Best kind for old-fashioned things," said Dalziel.

"Like study, education, literature, you mean?" said Johnson.

"Aye, them too. But I was thinking more of murder, assault, betrayal of friends, that sort of thing."

Roote stood up so suddenly, the table rocked and Penn had to grab his glass.

"Careful, Fran," he said. "You nearly had it over."

"Oh, Mr. Roote's always been very free and easy with other people's booze," said Dalziel. "He may have paid his debt to society, but he still owes me a bottle of Scotch."

"A debt I look forward to repaying, Superintendent," said Roote, back in control. "Ready, Sam?"

He set off towards the door.

Johnson looked at Dalziel for a moment then said quietly, "Another old-fashioned thing is called harassment, Superintendent. I suggest you refresh your memory about the law in that area. See you, Charley."

He followed Roote out of the pub.

Dalziel finished his pint, handed the glass to Bowler and sat down.

"Same again, sir?" said Hat.

"Or you could fetch me a Babycham wi' a cherry in it," said Dalziel.

Bowler headed back to the bar and Charley Penn said, "Well, that were like a Japanese porno movie, entertaining even though I didn't understand a word of it."

"No? Thought you bloody scribblers took notes on everything. Don't you recall a few years back when there was all that bother at the old teachers' training college?"

"Vaguely. Principal got knocked off, didn't she?"

"Aye, and some others. Well, yon lad Roote were the one mainly responsible."

"Was he, by God?"

Penn began to laugh.

"What?"

"I was just advising him that the best way to sell books isn't to write well but to get yourself headlined for something else first."

"Is that right? Ever the diplomat, eh, Charley? He got literary ambitions, has he?"

"Don't know. We were just talking about this short story competition which me and Sam Johnson and your Ellie Pascoe have been dragooned in to judge and it seems young Roote may have entered."

Bowler, who'd returned with a second pint (having discovered as many before that being Andy Dalziel's bheesty might be expensive but it didn't half get you good service), caught the end of this and opened his mouth excitedly, but on receiving a glance like a blow from the Fat Man changed his mind about letting words out and instead thrust the neck of his bottle of lager in.

"So what was all that about a bottle of whisky?" continued Penn.

"Bugger cracked one belonging to me over my head," said Dalziel.

"And he's still living? What's up, Andy? You got religion?"

"You know me, Charley. Strictly non-violent, except by way of self-defence. Which brings me to Jax Ripley. You were defending yourself when you assaulted her across in Leeds, were you?"

Penn yawned and said, "Oh, *that.*"

"You don't sound surprised, Charley."

"Supposed to leap up, wild-eyed, and make a run for the street where your sharp-shooters will gun me down, am I? No, I'm not surprised. Disappointed, maybe. When my front door wasn't knocked down by your wild bunch the day after the poor lass was murdered, I thought either it had got forgotten or maybe the case was being run by someone with half an ounce of sense."

"That's a bit subtle for me, Charley."

"It means, what the hell can me crowning her with a cream cake five years back have to do with some maniac sticking a knife into her last week? I bet if you went just a few more years back, you'd find some lad at school got detention for pulling her hair. Are you going to have him in for questioning?"

"Meaning your behaviour were infantile? Aye, that's how it looks to me too. But infantile behaviour in the middle-aged can have another name too, Charley."

"Which is?"

"Nay, you're the word man, you tell me."

Penn finished his drink and said, "OK, it was a stupid thing to do, I should have just ignored what she'd written, but I was across in Leeds having lunch with a publisher's rep, and I'd had a couple of drinks and when the sweet trolley came round and I saw this gateau, well, it seemed like a good idea at the time."

"And afterwards? I don't imagine you became best friends."

A sly smile tweaked at Penn's mouth.

"Funny you should say that. I realized what a prat I'd made of myself so after the case I sent her a big bottle of champagne with a note saying, *Sorry, hope we can kiss and make up.* Next day she turned up at my place with the bottle. At first I thought she'd come to tell me to stuff it, but she smiled sweetly and said, 'Hello, Mr. Penn. I've come to kiss and make up.' "

"And?"

"We kissed, and then we opened the bottle and drank it, and after that, well, we made up."

Dalziel looked at him in disbelief.

"You mean you and her were at it?"

"Only the once," said Penn regretfully. "But it cements a relationship, and we were OK after that. Which was, I came to realize later, probably the sole aim of the exercise. She was always heading onwards and upwards, our Jax. I saw a bit of her after she moved on from yon glossy magazine to the *Gazette* and she once said to me, 'Making friends is more important to an ambitious girl than making enemies. You mustn't be afraid of making enemies, but you shouldn't make them unnecessarily, else you never know when you're going to end up with crumbs and cream in your hair.' "

"Or a knife in your heart," said Dalziel.

"Aye, that too. No, we mended all our fences and she even started being nice about my books. If you saw her last show, you must have seen that interview she did with me."

"Aye, all sweetness and light. All that stuff about being in two times at the same place were a bit above my head, but."

"Still playing the thick yokel, Andy? I'll send you a copy of my book on Heine when it's done. There's a whole chapter on his *doppelgänger* poems. I thought it would add a bit of mystery to use the theme in my novels."

"I know more about doppel-whiskies myself," said Dalziel, "but I thought if you met one of them things, you died."

"We all die," said Penn. "Me, I think we meet our *doppelgänger* all the time. It's recognizing them that's the trick. To get back to Jax, I really liked her, Andy, and I was choked when I heard what happened. I hope you've got better leads than the one that led you to me, 'cos if you haven't, you're knackered, and I want to see you get the bastard who killed her. Here, lad. Do me a favour, trot up to the bar and get another round in."

He pushed a fifty-pound note toward Bowler who looked questioningly at Dalziel.

"Mr. Bowler here is my detective constable, not your pot-boy," said the Fat Man sternly.

Then he plucked the note from Penn's hand and added, "But we're here to serve the public, so off you go, lad. Same again, and mebbe I'll let Mr. Penn's publishers treat me to a chaser. HP."

"Sauce?" said Bowler, puzzled.

"Highland Park," said Dalziel long-sufferingly.

"New, is he?" said Penn as the DC once more made his way to the bar.

"Newish. Still on probation. So, Charley, flashing the monkeys around and a new telly series starting next week. You're doing well."

"Aye. Bloody marvellous," grunted Penn.

"If you'll excuse me saying, monkeys or no monkeys, you don't sound like a man who's all that happy in his work."

"Don't I? Tell me, Andy, you set out to be a cop?"

Dalziel considered then nodded.

"Aye," he said. "Didn't want to be a baker like me dad and end up with flour in my hair. So I opted for the Law. Mind you, I had to toss a coin to work out which side!"

Penn said, "Lucky us. Well, I didn't set out to be part of the production line for a big tits and funny hats telly series."

"Hold on, you hit Ripley with a cake for more or less saying that's what you were."

"It's one thing for me to say it, another for a nineteen-year-old dolly bird," said Penn.

"Fair enough. But it makes no odds, does it? I mean, you know one day you're going to amaze the world by producing this great tome about yon Kraut fellow you mentioned. Heinz, was it? Any relation to the fifty-seven varieties?"

"Keep it up, Andy. You've got the face for it. Heine."

"Aye, him. Ripley mentioned him in that article that pissed you off. I've got it here, as it happens."

He pulled the fax out of his pocket.

"Writes well . . . sorry, wrote well, the lass," he said with the air of one who'd spent several hours in stylistic analysis rather than thirty seconds in a cursory glance in the car as Bowler had driven him to the pub. "Yes, here it is. You're right. Heine not Heinz. She seemed to reckon you had as much chance of finishing your Great Work as England did of winning the next World Cup. Was it that maybe that got her the cream shampoo, not the cracks about your novels? Made you wonder if she might be right. And she was writing how long ago? Five years? Close to writing *The End,* are you, Charley?"

"Close enough," said Penn. "Five years ago, yeah, maybe I had doubts. But not now, Andy. Not now."

He caught and held the Fat Man's questioning gaze and it was Dalziel who broke off contact first.

Bowler had returned unnoticed at some point and the two men now looked down at their fresh drinks as if they were a manifestation of divine grace and raised the pint-pots with balletic synchrony.

"Let's forget Ripley," said Dalziel. "How'd you feel about Councillor Steel, Charley?"

"Stuffer? Anyone who stopped his breath was doing the environment a favour," said Penn.

"That's a bit strong. Jesus, what's this?"

Dalziel had turned his attention to his Scotch.

"They didn't have any Highland Park, sir," explained Bowler. "It's Glen something . . ."

"Glenfiddich. I know it's Glenfiddich, that's how I know it's not Highland Park."

"Yes, sir. The barman said you'd probably not notice the difference," said Bowler, eager to divert the Fat Man's anger.

"Did he now?" said Dalziel, scowling barwards. "Standards, eh, Charley? Man like that 'ud not get employed over the border. So you didn't care for the councillor?"

"He was a man for causes, was Cyril, mainly saving public money."

"Don't tell me," said Dalziel. "He thought owt spent on the police was a waste of cash. Cars, for instance. 'Get the buggers back on the beat. Shoe leather comes cheaper than petrol and at least the public have got someone who can tell them the time.' "

"That sounds like Cyril. The Arts too. Library spending. The theatre subsidy. And the few bob they give my literature group, you'd have thought that was enough to cancel the Third World debt."

"So you had a motive, then?"

"Well spotted, Sherlock. Aye, you and me both, Andy. A motive to kick him up the arse, but not to kill the silly old bugger."

"Well, let's not speak ill of the dead, eh?" said Dalziel, a little late in Hat's eye. "One thing you had to say about him, he practised what he preached. He never wasted any of his own cash on daft things like buying a round of drinks or paying for his own grub. But his heart was in the right place."

"It is now," said Penn. "I liked the subtle way you moved from Ripley to Stuffer. You reckon there's a connection between their deaths?"

Dalziel downed the offending whisky with no sign of distaste and said, "Only connection I'm looking at at the moment seems to be you, Charley."

Penn grinned and said, "The old techniques are still best, eh? When you've not got the faintest idea which way to go, prod every bugger with your stick, then follow the one who runs off quickest."

"We could have made a cop of you, Charley, if we'd got a hold of you afore you started ripping bodices. Seriously, but, and just for the record, we've got a nice statement from you about the preview yesterday, but I don't think anyone ever asked you where you were and what you were doing the night Ripley got killed."

"No reason why anyone should have asked, was there?"

"Not then."

"And now?"

Dalziel waved the fax of Ripley's article.

"Scraping the barrel, Charley. But you know what Mr. Trimble's like. Comes from the southwest, and they live off barrel scrapings down there. So . . . ?"

"Tell you what, Andy," said Penn. "I'll go off now and have a long think, and if I can remember anything about that night, I'll scribble it down on a bit of paper and let you have it."

"Nay, don't rush off for me," said Dalziel. "Stay still, young Bowler here 'ull buy you another. In fact, I'm thinking of having a spot of lunch here. They do a lovely sticky toffee pudding. My treat."

"Yuck. Don't know what the opposite of a sweet tooth is, but that's what I've got. Too much force-feeding with sugary goo when I were a kid. Which reminds me, Andy. I'd love to stay, but Sunday's family visiting day, at least for us who've got families to visit, it is."

That sounded like a dig, thought Hat.

"Oh aye. Your mam well, is she?" said Dalziel. "Still taking care of the three K's out in the sticks?"

And that, though incomprehensible, sounded like a riposte.

Penn for a moment looked like he'd have enjoyed tipping the rest of his ale over the Fat Man's huge head, but he reduced his reaction to a snarling smile and said, "Yes, Andy, my old mam's still alive and kicking, and it's me she'll be kicking if I don't turn up to see her on a Sunday. So I'll have to postpone that drink you've so kindly if vicariously offered me, Constable. Cheers. See you both tomorrow, I expect."

"Tomorrow?" said Dalziel.

"You've not forgotten? What is it? Alzheimer's or just so many bodies in your business, you lose track? Let me remind you. Now the inquest's over, and the ghouls have done chopping her up, they're going to let poor Jax be buried. Don't the books tell us murderers always like to attend their victims funerals? See you."

He downed his drink, swept up his change which Bowler had put on the table, stood up and strode towards the door.

"Sir?" said Hat, looking after him. "Do we just let him go?"

"What do you want to do?" said Dalziel. "Rugby tackle him then slap the cuffs on?"

"I suppose not. Sir, what was that about the three K's?"

"*Kinder, Küche, Kirche.* Children, kitchen and church. What German women are supposed to occupy themselves with, don't they learn you owt these days?"

Hat digested this.

"But Mr. Penn's local, isn't he? He sounds real Yorkshire."

"Sounds it, aye. Bred, but not born. Mam and dad got out of East Berlin a couple of steps ahead of the *Stasi* when the Wall went up. You remember the Wall, do you, lad?"

"I remember it coming down. There was a lot of fuss."

"Aye, there always is," said the Fat Man. "Number of times in my life I've joined in singing 'Happy Days Are Here Again' . . . but they never are, mebbe because they never were . . ."

He looked into his glass with what might have been melancholia or was perhaps just a hint that it was almost empty.

"So his parents came to Yorkshire to settle, did they?"

"Got brought to Yorkshire. Lord Partridge, big Tory politician way back, he sponsored them. Bit of a gesture to show he was doing his bit to fight the red peril, I expect. Fair do's but, he took care of 'em. She worked around the house, he helped with the horses. And Charley got a good education. Unthank College. Better'n me. Mebbe I should have been a refugee."

"Unthank College? But isn't that a public, I mean a private school? Boarders and all that?"

"So what? You're not one of them trendy Trots, are you?"

"No. What I meant was, he doesn't sound like he went to one of those places. He sounds more like . . ."

He tailed off, fearful of giving offence, but Dalziel said complacently, "More like me, you mean? Aye, you're right, whatever else they did to Charley there, they didn't get him speaking like he'd got a silver spoon up his arse. Interesting, that."

Encouraged, Hat said, "Are both his parents still alive?"

"Don't know much about 'em apart from what I've told you. In fact, come to think of it, I'd not heard Charley mention either of them till he started on about rushing off to see his mam just now."

"She must be a good age. Penn's no spring chicken," said Hat.

"Nay, Charley's not as old as he looks," said Dalziel. "Continental skin tone, you see. Doesn't age half as well as us home-grown stock. Likes to think he passes for a native, but you can always tell. But that's no reason to be racially prejudiced, lad. He might look like an old-time axe-murderer, but I can't see anything here that looks like a motive, not even in the dusk with the light behind it. You heard what he said about Ripley. They'd kissed and made out."

"Yes, sir. But, well, even if, or especially if he'd killed her, he would say that, wouldn't he?"

Dalziel laughed and said, "Now you're thinking like a cop, lad. No, even if he were lying about that, he'd still need a better reason than her badmouthing his books five years back. Not that I think that were his real reason for assaulting her. Like I told him, I think what really pissed him off were her suggesting he'd never finish this thing he's writing about Heinz."

"Heine," said Bowler.

"Both on 'em," said Dalziel. "Any road, he tells me now it's coming on nicely, so bang goes that motive if it ever was one."

"Don't quite follow . . ."

"Someone takes the piss saying you're not up to finishing something you've started, you sock it to 'em by finishing it, not by killing 'em. It's only if you think they may be right that you turn violent, which was why Charley reached for the pudding trolley in the first place. But now he reckons he's cracked it, and in any case a peace treaty's been sealed with a loving bang, where's the point?"

"But surely the thing about the Wordman is he doesn't need a motive, not in the strict sense. He's got some other agenda," argued Hat, reluctant to give up on Penn.

"Oh aye? I should never have let you listen to yon pair of academic mutton-tuggers," said Dalziel. "You'll be talking profiles next. How do you think Charley Penn fits in here, then?"

The Fat Man's tone was sceptical and mocking, yet Bowler felt that there was a real and testing purpose in his question.

He recalled what Rye had told him about Penn and said, "He's a man who feels he's been diverted for the last twenty years or so from his real purpose by having to make a living out of some historical fantasy world."

"And that makes him doolally? That would mean all novelists are a bit dippy, wouldn't it? You could have something there."

"Yes, sir. But the real purpose Penn has been diverted from isn't getting to grips with the real world but writing about what another writer was writing about back in the historical world these novels of his are set in. I mean, I know he comes over as very direct and down to earth, a bit cynical even, the typical blunt Yorkshire tyke . . ."

He realized Dalziel was regarding him leerily and hastened on.

". . . but even that's an act, isn't it? He's not a tyke, he went to public school, he's not even English. And when you look at where he spends his inner life, he's a long way detached from reality, it seems to me. That's what our job's about, isn't it, sir? Some of the time, anyway. Working out what's actually going on inside people who are trying to hide it. We all do that, I reckon, all try to hide it a lot of the time, and it's hard to know what anyone's really feeling or thinking. But a writer, an artist, has to give his inner life away much more than most people, 'cos that's what he's trying to sell us."

He halted, breathless, feeling he'd let his tongue run away with him and probably undone what little progress he'd made in his rehabilitation with the Fat Man, whose bloodshot eyes were regarding him like he'd just materialized out of a space capsule.

"You been spending a lot of time with Mr. Pascoe, have you, lad?" he said finally. "Me, I can't get to grips with my Inner Life on an empty stomach, and from the way you're rambling, I reckon you've not been eating properly either. All right, don't look like I've just sat on your hamster. There's definitely something weird about Charley Penn, I'll give you that. But then I think there's definitely something weird about Charley Windsor too, and I'm not going after him. Now let's get serious. I recall that once upon a time they did a decent Scotch pie and mushy peas in this place. But I'll tell you something . . ."

"What, sir?" said Bowler.

"If yon barman gives me a Cornish pasty and says I won't notice the difference, I'll shake the bugger till he spews his Inner Life all over the bar!"

XX

Jax Ripley had been born and brought up in a large village with aspirations to be a small town on the southern fringe of the North Yorkshire moors, and it was here that her widowed mother brought her back to be buried.

If Charley Penn was right and Jax Ripley's killer was at her funeral, then the police were spoilt for choice, thought Hat Bowler, looking at the teeming graveyard from the vantage point of the church porch. Family, friends, and professional colleagues would probably have formed a large congregation, but add to these those who imagined they knew her because of her TV show and those who were merely and vulgarly curious, and you were into celebrity proportions.

John Wingate was there, of course, plus his cameraman filming from a discreet distance. A similar duality was visible in the *Gazette* presence, with Mary Agnew in mourning black, very much the grieving friend and colleague, while Sammy Ruddlesdin made sure that local decorum didn't prevent the *Gazette* photographer from sharing the photo-opportunities so ruthlessly seized by the unconscienced nationals whose hyenas were there in packs. Percy Follows and Dick Dee were there from the library. Hat had rung Rye to check if she was going but been told fairly brusquely that (a) she hardly knew the woman and (b) someone had to stay and do the work. Unmissable was Ambrose Bird, the Last of the Actor–Managers. Hat wondered what his relationship with the dead woman had been. Perhaps he simply did not feel able to deprive such a theatrical scene of his strikingly melancholy presence, though there were some who felt that a calf-length purple cloak was more ham than Hamlet. He had overtaken Follows up the aisle and managed to get the last seat in the second row of pews, turning to smile triumphantly at his rival.

Franny Roote was there too. Why he had come might be interesting to find out, but in his inevitable black garb, standing to one side, quietly observing the others, he looked like death's footman waiting for a signal to come forward and be of service. He made a strong contrast with Charley Penn, who had been moved by the occasion to change his usual cracked leather jerkin and balding corduroys for a wide-lapelled jacket and slightly flared trousers in a pale almost luminous grey with a faint pink pin-stripe, so that he looked better suited for a seventies wedding than a contemporary funeral. Dalziel, on the other hand, was wearing a jacket so black it made the undertaker's look like Day-Glo. Pascoe, by his side, was elegantly slim in a suit of Italian cut which Hat guessed had been chosen by his wife, not because he doubted Pascoe's taste but because he suspected, left to his own device, the DCI would have opted for something more conservative. To look smart and have the social graces was a definite plus in the upper reaches of today's police force, but to look expensively flash still raised eyebrows. In reverse of civvy practice, the wise cop with the gold Rolex always claimed it was a Hong Kong clone.

The day was still and the mourners were so quiet despite their number that the words and sounds coming from the graveside carried quite clearly even to those like Hat at some distance from the dull centre of these exequies.

. . . earth to earth, ashes to ashes, dust to dust . . .

. . . the throb of a woman sobbing . . .

. . . and that most final of sounds, the slat of earth on the coffin lid . . .

Then it was over, and the crowd, unified for a space in the presence of the great mystery of death, returned with an almost audible sigh of relief to the even greater mystery of life and decoalesced rapidly into the small groups and diurnal concerns by which we avoid contemplating either.

Hat watched the dispersal from the porch. Some moved swiftly to their cars, guessing that a traffic jam awaited them half a mile down the narrow country road where it joined the arterial. Others strolled in the opposite direction towards the village centre. There were two pubs, The Baker's Arms and The Bellman. Mrs. Ripley's cottage was too small for large numbers and the family had booked a room at The Bellman for the funeral meats, which were by invitation only, a wise precaution, thought Hat, who had observed in the past the ravenous appetites of media men. As far as he knew, none of the police present had been invited either, though he doubted if this would inhibit Dalziel.

He saw the family party moving past now in company with the vicar, led by Mrs. Ripley, pale as moonlight, between a young man and woman who, Hat guessed, must be her son, a schoolteacher in Newcastle, and her other daughter who was a nurse in Washington, DC. From time to time he had opted for an interchange of information and anecdotes about families as a way of resisting Jax's efforts to get him to be indiscreet about his work. He'd never slept with her despite her assurance on one occasion that she wanted him as a groin, not a grass, but it had been a close-run thing. Now he felt a huge pang of regret. He'd really liked her and he would never see her again.

Also, of course, with Andy Dalziel convinced he'd been spilling the inner secrets of CID in pillow talk, his self-denial hadn't done anyone much good.

As the family group passed, the young woman glanced towards Hat, said something to her mother, slipped her arm free and came towards him.

She had just enough resemblance to her sister for Hat to be glad it was bright sunshine with lots of people around.

"Excuse me, you're Detective Bowler, aren't you?"

She probably still sounded very English in the States but her six years over there had laced her speech with a definite American edge.

"That's right."

"I'm Angie, Jax's sister."

"Yes, I guessed. I'm so very very sorry . . ."

He felt his voice break, to his surprise and his irritation too, fearful that it might sound deliberately contrived. But her face only showed understanding and she laid a hand on his arm and said, "Yeah, me too. Jax said you were nice."

"She told you about me?" he said, flattered.

"Yes, we'd always been really close, and we stayed that way even when I started working over there, e-mails, letters, we told each other everything. I was talking to two other cops just now when they came to pay their respects to Mum, and I got them to point you out."

Two other cops. Could only be Dalziel and Pascoe. His heart sank at the construction Dalziel was likely to have put on Angie's knowledge of his name.

"I'll miss her," he said. "We were friends . . . at least, I felt like her friend, I don't know if . . . I mean, what . . ."

She helped him out.

"That's what she said. You started off as a possible contact and you became a friend. And you didn't try to take advantage as a possible contact. And she wouldn't have minded if you had as a friend. Hey, don't blush. We tell . . . told each other everything. Have done since kids. Which is why I wanted to talk to you. Jax was very ambitious, well, you must have spotted that, and she liked to get the inside track on anything that might help her in her job, and she reckoned that glass ceilings didn't need bother a career girl so long as they were mirrors she was looking at some useful man's bottom in. You're blushing again. I told you we were frank."

"Sorry. I'm more used to people trying to hide things when they talk to me."

"Some job, eh? Listen, I was away on holiday, touring round Mexico when the news came about Jax, so I didn't get to know about it till I got back a couple of days ago. It was eerie. I checked my computer and found a lot of mail from Jax and right alongside them this message from my brother asking me to contact him straightaway, and I didn't want to because somehow I knew he was going to tell me Jax was dead."

"I'm sorry," said Hat helplessly. "It's truly terrible. I found her . . . I can't tell you how it felt . . . look, we'll get the bastard . . . I know that's what cops always say, but this time I mean it. We'll get the bastard."

"That's why I wanted to talk to you," said Angie. "Listen, walk with me. You're coming to the pub?"

"Well, no, I mean, I haven't been invited. . . ."

"I'm inviting you. Come on. We stand much longer in this porch, people will think I'm propositioning you."

She took his arm and gently urged him after the other mourners. He glanced back and saw Dalziel and Pascoe watching him. The Fat Man's face was blank but Bowler needed no special art to read the construction he was putting on this new alliance.

"So what is it you want to tell me?" he said.

She said, "Look, I don't want to sound like some crazy person with ambitions to be a gumshoe, but there was something in that last e-mail from Jax which I felt you guys ought to know, though it could be you know about it already."

Hat didn't try to puzzle this out but just waited.

"She sent it the same night she got killed. She told me she'd just broken this big news story about a possible serial killer, and she hoped like hell it would help her get this job she was after in London. Then she went on to say that, whatever happened, she'd better get out of Yorkshire soon as there was this guy who was going to be so pissed off that she'd broken the story, he'd probably feel like killing her. I think she meant it as a joke. I mean, cops in England don't go around killing people, do they? But I knew I had to talk to someone. . . ."

"Hang on," said Hat. "You said cops . . . you're talking about a policeman?"

"Of course I am," she said impatiently. "Aren't you listening? I'm talking about her inside man, the one who fed her all the stuff on what you guys were up to, including this serial killer stuff. You didn't think you were the only one she set her sights on? Difference was, this guy was really happy to play. And I got to thinking as I flew over, he must have been really pissed off that she'd gone public."

"Not much of a motive for murdering someone," said Hat. "Being pissed off, I mean."

"It's enough for some people. But suppose he got to thinking that now she'd let him down, it was only a matter of time before, either by accident or design, she named her inside source, and where would that leave his career? And if he was going to shut her up, this must have seemed a great time to do it, straight after she'd been on telly, sounding off about this madman. Where else were you guys going to look, especially as he'd be in a good position to help push things in that direction?"

"You're saying you know who this man is?" demanded Hat.

"No," said Angie. "At least I didn't. She never gave his actual name, only said he was pretty high up."

"Listen, Angie," said Hat, "it's not me you should be talking to. I'm going to have to take this to my bosses, Mr. Dalziel and Pascoe, that's them you were talking to before, so you might as well see them now. They're coming along behind us, I think . . ."

He glanced over his shoulder to confirm this and felt her gentle grip on his arm become a savage elbow-lock.

"Don't be stupid!" she hissed. "That was what I was going to do earlier when I met them and realized they were top cops."

"Oh," said Hat, feeling inappropriately miffed to realize he hadn't been her first choice of confidant. "So what did they say?"

"Nothing. I said nothing. Jax never gave me his name. Whatever they say about e-mail security, if you're a journalist, you don't trust it that much.

But over the past few months, she'd given me a description, a pretty detailed intimate description, I mean. Like I say, we let it all hang out. So I think I could be dead sure if I saw him in the skin, but even with his clothes on, the description fitted well enough to make me think it might not be such a good idea to talk to this guy, which is why I came looking for you."

"Hold on," said Hat. "You're saying you think that one of them . . ."

He glanced back again to where Dalziel and Pascoe were tracking their path.

"Which one, for God's sake?"

"She described him as middle-aged, what hair he had going grey, always nicely turned out in an old-fashioned kind of way, and so well padded that being on top of him was like bouncing on sponge rubber but having him on top of you was like wrestling with a large gorilla. Not just his weight, he was also very hairy, and there was other stuff about his sports tackle that means I could pick him out pretty definitely in a sauna, but even with his clothes on, that guy Dalziel came close enough for me not to take any risks."

"Dalziel? For God's sake, he's my boss, he's head of CID!"

"And that means he doesn't enjoy sex with a woman half his age? If that's a condition of promotion, I'd get out as soon as you can. No, listen, I can't be definite, but everything fits. And I think he suspects something. When I asked if you were here, because Jax had mentioned you to me, I thought his eyes were going to start smoking. You want to watch out for him."

"No, I think that's something else . . . I think you're wrong . . ."

But part of him, not a big part but large enough to make itself felt, was speculating with something close to glee on the possibility that the Fat Man himself had been Jax's mole, which meant his aggressive attitude to Hat might be based on . . . jealousy?

"You mean you're going to let some silly sense of loyalty stop you from following this up?" she said fiercely. "Maybe I should do what Jax did and go public."

"No, please. I'll check it out, I promise. Was there anything else she said? We found a diary, more of an appointments book, and she jotted down the letters GP from time to time, but there didn't seem to be anything medically wrong . . ."

"No," said Angie excitedly. "No, that was him. Georgie Porgie. You know, pudd'n and pie, kissed the girls and made them cry. That was what she called him because he was so fat. Hey, your Dalziel's not called George, is he?"

And suddenly Hat saw the truth, almost as unbelievable as discovering Dalziel was Deep-throat, and infinitely sadder.

"No," he said unhappily. "No, he's not."

But he knew somebody who was.

XXI

"**So what are** you going to do about it?" asked Rye.

"If I knew that I wouldn't be sitting here spoiling your coffee break," said Hat.

He should have gone to Dalziel straightaway, or Pascoe at least, or even Wield. Off-loaded his suspicions, let them earn the extra money they got for being in positions of authority and responsibility. In fact he wouldn't even have needed to point the finger himself, merely handed over the copies of Jax Ripley's e-mail which her sister had given him and let them draw their own conclusions. Instead he'd gone back to the station, found that George Headingley was still off sick, and persuaded himself that it could do no harm to sleep on it.

It hadn't done any good either. The first person he'd seen when he entered the CID office the following morning was Headingley. He was a very different man from the relaxed, rather genial figure who'd been navigating his way serenely into the imminent harbour of retirement, and unrecognizable as the sexual athlete described in the e-mails. Jax had told her sister that she first detected her GP's interest at a media briefing when she'd caught him eyeing her, not with the calculation of a sexual predator but with the yearning of a small boy outside a sweet shop whose only calculation is that he can't afford to go in. She'd stayed behind and when he asked, "And what can I do for you, Miss Ripley? Something you want to chew over?" she'd replied, "Yes, as a matter of fact. I was wondering about chewing over your dick and my pussy," and watched his face turn such a vein-bulging puce that she feared their relationship might be about to end before it had begun. But these symptoms, she soon discovered to her amusement and also to her pleasure, were merely the facial expression of a sexual arousal which turned the whole of his body into an erogenous zone. Now his portly figure seemed to have collapsed in on itself, his clothes hung baggily on his sagging frame and he looked a good ten years older than before.

It was easy to trace the earth-slide of emotions which had been carrying him along for the past ten days. First the shock of Ripley's TV revelations and the fear that his own involvement might soon come out. Then her death, a second shock, accompanied by an initial great surge of relief followed almost immediately by a still greater surge of self-disgust that he could find comfort in the death of someone he'd been so intimate with. After that he'd headed for home, to the security of the undemanding domestic comfort which he probably expected to be ripped from him at any moment. It must have seemed impossible that the close and detailed investigation of Jax's affairs following her murder plus Dalziel's natural desire to find out who'd been leaking CID secrets to her, wouldn't rapidly bring the Fat Man to his door. And then everything would go. Pension . . . marriage . . . reputation . . . character . . . the rest of his life as he had planned it . . .

And now with Jax Ripley buried, he was perhaps beginning to allow himself to hope that, despite his sins, all manner of things could still be well. At the very least it must have seemed better to come into work and check for himself what was going on.

He'd greeted Hat like a prodigal son and then questioned him about the course of the investigation in a manner which was both probing and hesitant, like a man who fears he may have cancer but does not dare ask his doctor direct.

In the end, Hat had pleaded an urgent appointment and left the office. He had to talk to someone and almost without conscious decision he found himself ringing the library number. At first Rye had sounded rushed and faintly irritated, and, fearful she might be about to ring off, he said, "Sorry to trouble you, but you did say you would like to be kept in the picture about the Wordman."

"The Wordman? Has he . . . ? You mean . . . ? Look, if you fancy a coffee, I'll take my break early at Hal's."

Which was where they were now, at the same balcony table as before.

News of the Fourth Dialogue hadn't been made public yet, but it couldn't be long before it was. At least so Hat assured himself as he heard himself whispering the details to Rye. Her interest and the fact that whispering meant they had to have their heads very close together made the risk of Dalziel's wrath if he ever found out seem almost inconsequential. Rye prodded him with questions then when she'd finally got all she wanted, she put her hand over his, squeezed, and said, "Thanks."

"For what?"

"For trusting me."

"No problem," he said. "In fact, if you can spare a couple of minutes more, there's something else I'd like to trust you with."

He'd explained his dilemma without any exordium of confidentiality. She'd listened without interruption, asked if she could see the e-mails, read them, raised her eyebrows at, presumably, the raunchier parts, then asked her question, "So what are you going to do about it?"

And in reply to his answer she smiled and said, "I wouldn't have come if I'd thought you were going to spoil anything. Look, I don't want to teach my grandmother to suck eggs, but isn't your first priority to check if he could have done it?"

"Sorry?"

"Killed Jax Ripley to shut her up. Isn't that why her sister came to you with this in the first place?" She sat back and observed his expression then said, "Ah, I get it. You've automatically discarded that possibility. This colleague of yours might be an adulterous untrustworthy snake, but being a cop means he couldn't possibly be a killer."

"Now hold on, I know him, you don't. Honestly, there's no way . . ."

"There's no way," she mimicked. "Should have thought you heard that all the time from wives, mothers, fathers, brothers, husbands, friends."

"Yeah, but . . ." He paused, collected his thoughts, then resumed, "OK, you're right. I still think there's no way the DI could be involved in her death—no, wait, not just because I know him, but because there definitely isn't any way he's the Wordman and that's who killed Jax. OK, you're probably going to say he's seen the Dialogues and he could have faked one, but the next one refers back to the Ripley murder and surely you're not going to say he killed Councillor Steel as well?"

Rye, who had been eating a buttery croissant, swallowed and said, "A girl could get fat talking to you. I mean, I don't need to open my mouth except to put food in, with you telling me all the time what I'm going or not going to say."

"Sorry," he said. "But you see what I mean."

"Maybe. All right, it doesn't seem very likely, though Steel was in cahoots with Ripley, wasn't he? And maybe your DI thought Jax had let him in on their little secret. But it doesn't matter. What I'm saying is you need to get that possibility entirely out of the way so that all you're left with is the big decision, do you drop this guy in it or not? He's not a friend, is he?"

"No way."

"And he didn't mind letting that Yorkshire yeti you call your boss go on thinking you were the departmental leak, did he?"

"I don't know if he knew about that," said Hat.

"There you go, defensive again. Why do you give a toss what happens to this guy? He's cheated on his wife and he's cheated on his colleagues. Sounds like just the sort of scumbag who ought to get his comeuppance."

She looked at him challengingly.

He shook his head and said, "No, he's not a scumbag. He's been in the job for thirty years and by all accounts he's been a good cop. Fat Andy would have seen him down the road a long time back if he hadn't been that. So he's coming to the end of his career and probably wondering what it was all about when this good-looking bird half his age makes herself available . . ."

"Her fault then?"

"No one's fault, but you read the e-mail. Mid-life crisis, last-chance saloon, call it what you like, but he was a sitting duck. As for the stuff he seems to have told her, well, it wasn't exactly earth-shaking stuff . . ."

"It shook Jax Ripley into the earth."

"She took a risk. And she really egged the mix! All we had then were two doubtful deaths and she made it sound like Hannibal the Cannibal was roaming the streets! Not his fault, though I reckon he blames himself. Anyway, one life gone. Is it worth another, I ask myself."

"And how do you answer yourself?"

He grinned at her and said, "Well, you'll be pleased to hear I'm going to take some excellent advice I just received. I'll check out his alibi for the night of Jax's death and once I've got that sorted, then I'll make up my mind."

She grinned back and said, "You know, we might make something of you yet. Is that it? Because I'm running on library time already."

"Tell them you were dealing with a ratepayer's research problem. That should ease your conscience. And to ease mine, a little bit of official business—when you were waiting to be interviewed by Sergeant Wield in the gallery, did you chat with anybody?"

"I expect so. There wasn't a rule of silence, was there? Why are you asking?"

"Well, it was just that when you went back to the library for your things, you didn't specify anyone you saw, and I wondered if you mentioned that's where you'd gone to anyone else while you were waiting."

She was lightning quick.

"So they could give themselves some kind of alibi by mentioning they'd seen me, you mean?"

"That kind of thing."

And now she was angry and he could see all his good approach work going for nothing.

"Is this about Dick? It is, isn't it?"

"No," he protested. "OK, he did say he saw you and you didn't say you saw him . . ."

"And that means he's lying? That he wasn't there when I was because he was in the lavatory killing Councillor Steel? For God's sake, when you lot take against someone, you really go all the way, don't you? No wonder the jails seem to be full of innocent people fitted up by the fuzz!"

She stood up, knocking her coffee mug over, and he jumped up to avoid the flood.

He said quickly, "Right idea, wrong guy. It's that novelist fellow, Penn, I'm curious about. He mentions seeing both you and Dee. Neither of you mention him."

He watched as the anger drained from her face and thought, but had the wisdom not to say, that it was fascinating the way her indignation at a possible encroachment on civil liberties didn't extend to include Charley Penn.

"No," she said slowly, "I definitely didn't notice him. And yes, when I chatted to Dick while we were waiting to make our statements Penn was hanging around like he usually does. But you're not really suggesting . . ."

"I'm not suggesting anything," he said. "But we've got to cover every angle and we are looking for someone highly educated with a devious mind who gets a kick out of playing around with words."

"Then maybe you should be raiding all the senior common rooms in the county," she said, but without heat. "Look, I've got to go or Dick will kill me . . . sorry, I mean . . . oh shit, I'm getting as neurotic as you. I'll see you on Sunday."

"Yeah, sure. Listen, maybe we could meet up before that, do a movie or something . . ."

"From what I've seen of your job a girl would be crazy to arrange to meet you anywhere but in her own warm flat," she replied. "You can give me a ring when you're definitely and unrecallably free. See you."

He watched her walk away, lovely carriage, head held high, with just a touch of sinuosity around the waist producing the merest hint of a sway of the buttocks.

Oh, you're the girl for me, he told himself as she passed out of sight.

He turned to lean over the balustrade, feeling able at will to share the warm joy flooding through his body with all the hurrying people in the shopping centre below.

And found himself looking straight into the accusing eyes of Peter Pascoe, standing among the shoppers, peering up at the balcony, with his right hand pressing his mobile phone to his ear and his left waving an angry summons to descend.

XXII

Ripeness is all, as every spin doctor knows, and what the seer beholds is usually what the beholder is ready to see.

In fact Peter Pascoe's gaze was relieved not accusing, and his summons was imperative rather than angry.

He'd been on his way to the Heritage, Arts and Library Centre when the phone rang and it had been the voice he heard that had stopped him in his tracks.

"Roote? How the hell did you get this number?"

"I don't really recall, Chief Inspector. I'm sorry to trouble you, but I didn't know who else to try. I mean, I could have rung 999 but by the time I explained, especially as I'm not sure what I'm explaining . . . but I thought you would know what to do for the best."

He sounded uncharacteristically agitated. In all their acquaintance, even at moments of great crisis, Pascoe could never recall the man being anything but controlled.

"What are you talking about?" he demanded.

"It's Sam. Dr. Johnson. I went round to his room in the Uni yesterday after the funeral to pick up a book he'd promised to lend me, but he wasn't there. I thought he'd just forgotten. I tried again later, but still no sign. So I rang his flat last night but didn't get any reply. I've just been up to his room again during my morning break and it's still locked and there were some students hanging around, waiting for a seminar, and they said he had missed a lecture yesterday too, so I tried ringing his flat again, but still no reply. So now I was really worried and thought I ought to tell someone in authority, and I thought you would be best as you're a friend, of his I mean, and would know what to do."

"Where are you now?" asked Pascoe.

"At the university. English Department."

Pascoe's mind was racing. He knew it was stupid, but around Roote, he never felt fully in control. He tried to see the angle here but couldn't.

But it was at this point he saw Bowler.

"Stay there. I'll come round," he ordered as he waved at the DC.

Hat hurried down, rehearsing his explanation for being discovered lounging on the balcony at Hal's like a gentleman of leisure taking his ease in the middle of the morning.

"You got your car here?" said Pascoe.

"Yes, in the multi."

"Good. You can give me a lift. I walked from the station."

"And you want a lift back?" said Hat.

"No. To the university. It will save me a bit of time."

It was a weak excuse, but he didn't feel like explaining he preferred to have a witness in any encounter arranged by Roote.

They didn't talk as they strode to the car park.

"Oh God," said Pascoe. "I'd forgotten the MG."

Bowler's ancient two-seater lay between a Discovery and a Jeep like a whippet between a pair of St. Bernards.

"Takes you back, does it, sir?" said Bowler proudly.

"*Back* is not so far that I need to be *taken* there," said Pascoe acidly, slipping with what he hoped was athletic ease into the passenger seat. "Don't give many lifts to the super, I presume."

"No, sir. Don't have the insurance," laughed Bowler. "Any particular reason we're going to the Uni?"

Pascoe explained, making light of Johnson's alleged disappearance with the anticipatable result that the DC was even more puzzled than he might have been.

"So why the rush, sir? Most likely this Johnson guy's taken a long weekend. I mean, when I was a student, it sometimes seemed like you had more chance of getting hold of Madonna than getting hold of your tutor. Is it Roote ringing you that makes the difference?"

Smart ass, thought Pascoe. He reminds me of me.

He said, "What the devil were you doing in that gallery anyway?"

The form of the question might have puzzled Bowler a little if the content hadn't disconcerted him a lot.

"I was having a coffee, sir." It occurred to Hat that he'd no idea at what point Pascoe had first observed him and he went on, "In fact, I'd been having a coffee with Miss Pomona. There was something I wanted to ask her and she suggested we met outside the library."

"Oh?" said Pascoe, smiling. "Discretion in this case being the better part of *amour*, eh?"

Hat's French was up to this and he shook his head vigorously.

"No, sir. Strictly business."

"In that case, presumably it's my business too. So do tell."

For a second Hat thought of coming clean about George Headingley, but off-loading his problem felt pretty naff and certainly wasn't going to win him any Brownie points, so instead he told the DI about his unease in re Charley Penn.

"You seem to have it in for Charley," said Pascoe. "First Jax Ripley, now Cyril Steel. Nothing personal, I hope?"

"No, sir. Just that he keeps popping up." Then, batting the ball firmly back he added, "Like Roote."

Pascoe glanced at him sharply but detected nothing but proper subordinate deference.

Oh you do remind me of me, you cocky sod, he thought.

The rest of the journey passed in silence.

The plate-glass windows of the Ivory Tower which housed the English Department were flashing what might have been an SOS as the scudding clouds intermittently masked the autumn sun. They found Roote in the foyer talking to a maintenance man who was protesting that he couldn't open up a member of staff's room just because a student asked him.

"Now I'm asking," said Pascoe, showing his warrant card.

Ascent was via a paternoster lift, so called in Pascoe's opinion because even a practising atheist (and especially a practising atheist with claustrophobic tendencies) was ill-advised to use such a contraption without resort to prayer.

The maintenance man stepped in and was translated. The next platform rose and Pascoe motioned Bowler in while he summoned up all his aplomb. Two more platforms passed and there was still no sign that his aplomb had heard the summons. He took a deep breath, felt a gentle pressure on his elbow, then he and Franny Roote stepped forward in perfect unison. The pressure vanished instantly. He glanced sharply at the young man in search of signs of amusement or, worse, sympathy. But Roote's eyes were blank, his expression introspective, and Pascoe began to wonder if he'd imagined the helping hand. Bowler's legs suddenly came into view.

"Here we are," said Roote, and Pascoe, determined not to be assisted again, exited with an unnecessarily athletic leap.

It took only a few seconds to establish that Johnson's room was empty and, from the evidence of a series of notes pushed under the door in which students recorded their vain attempts to keep appointments, had been empty since the weekend.

"You say you've been round to his flat?" said Pascoe.

"Yes," said Roote. "I rang the bell. No reply. And no reply on the phone, either. His answering machine's not on. He always left his answering machine on when he went out."

"Always?" said Hat. "That's a bit precise."

"In my experience," emended Roote, frowning.

"So let's go and see," said Pascoe.

Back at the paternoster, he hurled himself on to the first platform. That way at least he was able to make his flustered exit unobserved.

Outside a problem arose because there was no way they could get three into Bowler's MG without breaking the law.

Roote said, "I'll go in my own car. Care to join me, Mr. Pascoe? Could be more comfortable."

Pascoe hesitated then said, "Why not?"

The car turned out to be a Cortina of some antiquity. But it was certainly easier to get into than the MG and the engine sounded sweet enough.

"Thought you said it was an old banger?" said Pascoe.

Roote glanced at him and smiled his secret smile.

"I had the engine tuned," he said.

He drove with the exaggerated care of a man undergoing a driving test. Pascoe could almost feel Bowler's exasperation as he trailed behind them. But he also felt that there was more than just mockery in Roote's mode of driving. He was going slow because he was reluctant to arrive.

The flat was on the top floor of a converted townhouse in a Victorian terrace which had gone down and was now on its way up again. They gained entry by ringing all the bells till a man responded. Pascoe identified himself and they went in. There was no lift and the stairs were steep enough to make him almost nostalgic for the paternoster. At Johnson's door, he rang the bell and could hear it echoing inside. Then he tried knocking, registering that the door was pretty solid and didn't feel like it would yield easily to even a young man's shoulder.

He called down to the elderly man who had let them in and was lurking curiously a little way down the stairway, and asked who the flat agents were. It was a well-known firm with their office only a mile or so away. He dialled the number on his mobile, got a girl who seemed disinclined to be helpful, advised her then to call a carpenter and a locksmith to make good the damage that usually resulted from opening a door with a sledgehammer and rapidly found himself talking to the firm's general manager who assured him he'd be there within ten minutes.

He made it in five.

Pascoe took the key from him and turned it in the lock.

He opened the door a fraction, sniffed the air, and closed it again.

"I'm going to go in now," he said. "Bowler, you make sure nobody else comes in."

"Yes, sir," said Bowler.

He opened the door just enough to let his slim frame slip through, then closed it behind him.

There was death here, he'd known that as soon as he first opened the door. The blast of warm air that hit him carried its odour, not yet unbearably pungent but still unmistakable to anyone who'd had cause to be around corpses as often as Peter Pascoe.

If it hadn't been for this, he might have thought Sam Johnson was simply asleep. He sat in an old wing chair, his feet stretched out on to the fender of a fireplace tiled in the high Victorian style, like a scholar made drowsy by draughts from the whisky bottle standing by his arm and the lulling rhythms of the volume which lay open on his lap.

Pascoe paused to take in the room. First impressions were important. The old grate had been replaced by a modern gas fire which was the source of the heat. On the mantelshelf an ormolu clock had stopped at twelve. Beside the clock lay what for an unpleasant moment Pascoe thought was a turd but on closer examination proved to be some blocks of melted chocolate. Alongside the whisky bottle and empty glass on the low table next to the chair stood a cafetière and a coffee mug. On the other side of the fireplace was a small sofa with a broken leg "repaired" by a hefty tome and another low table with an empty tumbler on it.

He turned his attention to the body and confirmed by touch what he knew already.

There was nothing to show how Johnson had died. Perhaps after all it would turn out to be a simple heart attack.

He looked at the open book without touching it.

It was open at a poem called "Dream-Pedlary." He read the first verse.

> *If there were dreams to sell*
> *What would you buy?*
> *Some cost a passing bell;*
> *Some a light sigh,*
> *That shakes from Life's fresh crown*
> *Only a rose-leaf down.*
> *If there were dreams to sell,*
> *Merry and sad to tell,*
> *And the crier rang the bell,*
> *What would you buy?*

Dreams to sell. His eyes prickled. Detectives don't cry, he told himself. They do their jobs.

He retreated to the door as carefully as he'd advanced. There was a lot of noise outside on the landing, Roote's voice raised angrily, Bowler's at first reassuring, then stern. Better to get the machine rolling before he went out there to restore order. He took out his mobile and dialled.

He was halfway through issuing his precise instructions when the voices outside suddenly reached a climax of screaming and the door burst open, catching him in the back and throwing him forward into the room.

"Sam! Sam!" screamed Franny Roote. "Oh, Jesus. Sam!"

He rushed forward and would have flung himself on top of the corpse if Pascoe hadn't grappled one of his legs, then Hat Bowler arrived in a flying tackle which ended with all three sprawling on the carpet in a heaving, swearing tangle of bodies.

It took another couple of minutes for the two of them to drag the distraught man out of the room, but once the door was closed, all strength of muscle and emotion seemed to drain out of Roote and he slid down the wall and sat there with his head bowed between his legs, still as an imp carved on a cathedral tower.

"Sorry about that, sir," whispered Bowler to Pascoe. "He just exploded. And he's a damn sight stronger than he looks."

"I know it," said Pascoe.

He stared unblinkingly at Roote's bowed head.

The man's eyes were invisible; if open they could only see the landing floor.

So why do I feel the bastard's watching me? thought Pascoe.

XXIII

From the start it was Franny Roote who cried murder. Which, as Dalziel pointed out, was odd, as at the moment if they wanted a suspect, he was the only one on offer.

"Then we'd be silly not to take him," said Pascoe, too eagerly.

"Nay, lad. First thing you do with a gift horse is kick it in the teeth," said Dalziel. "Four possibilities. Natural causes, accident, suicide, murder. Post mortem report will give us a line mebbe, but at the moment what we've got is a guy with a heart condition looking like he died peaceably by his own fireside. God send us all such a nice exit."

This pious sentiment was offered with the unctuous smile of a TV evangelist looking forward to getting out of the studio back to his hotel bedroom where a trinity of booted ladies stood ready to mortify his sinful flesh.

"Look, sir, I know we're under pressure with this Wordman business . . ."

"Wordman? What the hell has this got to do with the Wordman?" demanded Dalziel, moving from unction to abrasion with no perceptible interval. "That's why I'm sitting on the Stuffer Dialogue. Once that gets out, they'll all be like you. Every little old lady falling downstairs will have been shoved by the sodding Wordman!"

This was so manifestly unjust that Pascoe untypically allowed himself to be provoked.

"Well, I think you're making a big mistake there, sir. OK, there's nothing to suggest Sam's death has anything to do with the Wordman, but if there is another Wordman killing, you're going to have a lot of explaining to do."

"Nay, lad, that's why I keep clever sods like you, to do my explaining."

"Then perhaps you should listen when I say that Roote's not crying murder without a reason."

"Double bluff, you mean? Because he did it? Nay, I'll give you he may be feeling guilty, but there's all kinds of guilt. What if him and Johnson had got a thing going . . ."

"A thing?"

"Aye. A thing. Buggering around with each other. I were trying to save your blushes. That Sunday they go to the flat for a quick bang then have a tiff. Roote flounces out. Johnson thinks he'll be back any minute and settles down with his book and a coffee, then this dicky ticker you told me about reacts to all the excitement of the row and whatever else they'd been getting up to, and he snuffs it."

The preliminary medical examination hadn't got any further than suggesting heart failure as the cause of death. The examiner reckoned that Johnson had been dead at least two days which took them back to Sunday when Roote was the last person to admit to seeing him alive. The full post mortem examination would take place the following morning. Roote's prints were on the glass by the other armchair but not on the coffee mug or whisky bottle which had been sent to the police lab for further examination and analysis.

"Meanwhile Roote's really taken the huff," continued Dalziel. "He doesn't go back, reckoning that Johnson will come running after him some time in the next couple of days. When he doesn't, Roote starts to get worried, and naturally when he sees him dead, he doesn't want to blame himself so he cries murder. What do you think?"

I think, thought Pascoe, you're feeling the pressure, Andy, and you'd kill someone if it meant not having another murder on your patch.

"I think if there was much more assumption in what you're saying, they'd make this a feast day," he said forcefully. "For a start, Sam's heart problem wasn't life-threatening. And what makes you think either of them's gay?"

"Well, blind man on a galloping horse can see there's summat very odd about Roote. Bit of a swordsman back in yon college, by all accounts, but it didn't stop him getting tangled up with that lecturer who died, the one who topped himself. Funny, now I think back, weren't he called Sam too? Which brings us to this Johnson, I only met him the once at yon pre-view, but he's another of your arty-farty intellectuals, isn't he?"

"For God's sake!" exclaimed Pascoe. "Is that the full menu, then? Big slice of guesswork topped up with prejudice?"

"I'll let you be the judge of that, Pete," said Dalziel. "I mean, I'm no lover of Franny Roote, but it seems to me you can't look at the guy without wanting to blame him for everything in sight. That's what I call prejudice."

Feeling he had been set up, Pascoe said stubbornly, "All right, I've got no evidence that Roote's directly involved in this. But one thing I know for certain, Roote's not crying murder because he feels guilty. That bastard never felt guilty about anything in his life!"

"First time for everything, lad," said Dalziel genially. "I might start putting Ribena in my whisky. Who the hell's that?"

The phone had rung. He picked it up and bellowed, "What?"

As he listened, he looked increasing less genial.

"Fucking champion," he said banging the receiver down. "They've traced Johnson's next of kin."

Following usual procedure in suspicious deaths, the police had checked to see if anyone profited. They found Sam Johnson had died intestate, which meant his next of kin got what little he had to leave. Pascoe recalled Ellie asking the lecturer about his family when he came to dinner. He had replied tipsily, "Like Cinderella, I am an orphan, but I am fortunate in hav-ing only one ugly step-sister to avoid," then refused, with a pantomimic shudder, to be drawn further.

"The step-sister, is it?" said Pascoe. "So?"

"So you know who she turns out to be? Only Linda Lupin, MEP. Loopy bloody Linda!"

"You're kidding? No wonder he didn't want to talk about her!"

Linda Lupin was to the European Parliament what Stuffer Steel had been to Mid-Yorkshire Council, a thorn in the flesh and a pain in the ass. So right wing she occasionally even managed to embarrass William Hague, she never missed a chance to trumpet financial mismanagement or creeping socialism. A lousy linguist, she could nevertheless cry I accuse! in twelve languages. Deeply religious in an alternative Anglican kind of way, and passionately opposed to women priests, Loopy Linda, as even the Tory tabloids called her, was not the kind of relative a trendy left-wing aca-demic would care to admit to. And she was certainly not the kind of crime victim's next of kin an investigator under pressure wanted knocking at his door.

"As if things weren't bad enough with Desperate Dan and all the tabloids on my back," groaned Dalziel, "now I'm going to have Loopy Linda sitting on my face."

Pascoe tried turning the words into a picture but its grotesqueries required a Cruikshank or a Scarfe.

But at least the entrance of Loopy Linda on the scene had the good effect of ending the Fat Man's brief flirtation with the role of Wise Old Sensible Cop.

"Right, Pete, I'm converted," he declared, pushing himself to his feet. "Whatever that bastard Roote's guilty of, let's start pulling out his fingernails till he confesses!"

But this pleasant prospect had to be postponed till the following day as, whatever Roote's real state of mind, he had convinced the medics that he was too distraught to be questioned.

There was no doubt about the genuineness of Ellie Pascoe's distraction when she heard the news of Johnson's death.

She went out into the garden where, despite the chill evening air, she stood unmoving under the skeletal ornamental cherry tree for almost half an hour. Her rangily athletic frame seemed somehow to have lost its old elasticity and Pascoe, watching through the French window was shocked to find himself for the first time thinking of that lithe body he knew so well as frail. Rosie, his young daughter, came to his side and asked, "What's Mum doing?"

"Nothing. She just wants to be alone for a bit," said Pascoe lightly, concerned not to let adult distress spill over into the child's world, but Rosie seemed to take this desire for solitude as entirely natural and said, "I expect she'll come in if it starts raining," then went off in search of her beloved dog.

"Sorry," said Ellie when she returned. "I just had to get my head round it. Not that I have. Oh God, poor Sam. Coming here to make a new start, then this . . ."

"New start?" said Pascoe.

"Yes. It was pretty much a sideways move, you know. He'd had . . . a loss back in Sheffield, it seems, and just wanted to get away, and this job came up unexpectedly, so he applied, got it, then took off abroad for the summer. That's how they landed him with this creative writing thing. That should really have been a separate post but he wasn't in a state to argue and naturally the bastards took advantage . . ."

"Hang on," said Pascoe. "This loss . . . you never said anything about this and I never heard Sam mention it."

"Me neither," admitted Ellie. "It was just gossip, you know what they're like at the Uni, bunch of old women . . ."

On another occasion this combination of ageism and sexism from such a doughty defender of human rights might have cued mock-outrage, but not now.

"In other words, your old SCR chums filled you in on Sam's background? Or at least the gossip," said Pascoe.

"That's right. Gossip. Which was why I never said anything to you. I mean, it was Sam's business. It seems that in Sheffield there was some student Sam got very close to, and he had some kind of accident, and he died . . ."

"He?"

"Yes. So I understand."

"Sam Johnson was gay?"

"I doubt it. Bisexual maybe. Worried about playing squash with him? Sorry, love, that was a stupid thing to say."

"It was a stupid thing to do, certainly," said Pascoe. "This accident, what do the old women say about it, was it something Sam could have blamed himself for?"

"I've no idea," said Ellie. "I didn't encourage anybody to go into detail. Peter, you said you weren't sure yet exactly how Sam died, so what are you getting at?"

"Nothing. There's a lot of possibilities . . . and with Roote being involved . . ."

Ellie shook her head angrily.

"Look, I know it's your job, but I'm not ready yet to start thinking of Sam's death as a case. He's gone, he's gone, it doesn't matter how. But just one thing, Pete, every time Franny Roote comes up, you start twitching like a dog that's seen a rabbit. Remember what happened last time. Maybe you ought to tread very carefully."

"Good advice," said Pascoe.

But he was thinking, not a rabbit. A stoat.

◆   ◆   ◆

Next morning Roote came in voluntarily, as insistent as ever that Johnson must have been murdered and demanding to know what they were doing about it. Pascoe took him into an interview room to calm him down, but while he was waiting for Dalziel to join them, Bowler appeared to tell him the super wanted a word.

"Sit with him," said Pascoe. "And be careful. If he wants to talk, fine. But you keep your mouth shut."

He could see he'd offended the young DC but he didn't care.

Upstairs he found the Fat Man perusing copies of the post mortem report and the lab analysis.

"Case is altered," he said. "Take a look at these."

Pascoe read the reports quickly and felt both sick and triumphant.

Johnson had died of heart failure. Not long before death he had eaten a chicken sandwich and a chocolate bar and drunk coffee and substantial quantities of whisky. But most significant from the police point of view was the discovery in his system of traces of a sedative drug called Midazolam used as an anaesthetic in minor surgery, especially of children. Combined with alcohol, it became life-threatening, and this combination taken by someone with Johnson's heart condition was likely to prove fatal unless antidotal measures were taken quickly.

The drug was present in large quantities in the whisky bottle and there were traces in the coffee cup, but none in the glass with Roote's prints nor in the cafetière.

"We've got the bastard!" exulted Pascoe.

But far from confirming the Fat Man's conversion to the DCI's side of the argument, the news seemed to have reawakened all his doubts.

"Give it a rest, Pete. It means we've got nowt."

"What do you mean? Now we know it's murder. At the very least, it puts the kibosh on your theory. See, no evidence of recent sexual activity."

"So they never got round to it. But nowt to say that the rest doesn't hold, except that Johnson expected Roote to come back a lot sooner, within the hour, say, and he took a dose of this drug so he'd be passed out, just to give his boyfriend a fright."

"Oh yes? And what's Johnson doing with Midazolam in his medicine cabinet? You don't get that on prescription."

"What's Roote doing with it then?"

"He worked in a hospital in Sheffield, remember?" said Pascoe. "And he's just the kind of creepy bastard who'd help himself to something like that just in case it came in useful one day."

"Hardly evidence," said Dalziel. "Right, let's go talk to the lad. But we'll go easy."

"Thought we were going to pull his nails out?" said Pascoe sulkily.

"We're going to take a witness statement, that's all," said the Fat Man seriously. "Remember that or stay away."

Pascoe took a deep breath, then nodded.

"You're right. OK. But give us a minute. I need a word with Wieldy."

The sergeant listened to what he had to say in silence. Trying to read reaction on that face was like seeking a lost stone on a scree slope, but Pascoe sensed unease.

"Look," he said slightly exasperated. "It's really simple. We've got a guy who the super thinks may have topped himself and I've heard that he might have suffered a distressing personal loss some few months ago. Won't the coroner want to hear anything we can give him which might throw light on Sam Johnson's state of mind?"

"So why don't you ring Sheffield yourself?"

"Because as you well know, Wieldy, the last time I asked them for help, things went a bit pear-shaped. Roote ended up in hospital with his wrists slashed and there were mutterings about police harassment. So the name Pascoe might raise a few hackles."

"Only if it was linked again with the name Roote," said Wield. "Which this isn't?"

"Of course not. It's apropos a suicide enquiry. No need to mention Roote's name. Though while you're at it, you might as well check with that hospital Roote worked at whether any Midazolam ever went missing while he was there."

"Still without mentioning his name?" said Wield.

"I don't care what you mention," said Pascoe, growing angry. "All I know is I smell a rat and it's name's Roote. You going to do this or shall I do it myself?"

"Sounds like an order to me, *sir*," said Wield.

It was the first time in a long while Wield had called him sir other than on formal public occasions.

But as he turned away, the sergeant's voice said, "Pete, you be careful in there, eh?"

In the interview room, Dalziel laid out the facts about the poisoning rather more baldly than Pascoe would have done. When he mentioned that the

Midazolam had been placed first in the whisky bottle then transferred to the coffee mug, Roote interrupted.

"We didn't drink coffee. This proves it. Someone else must have been there."

Dalziel nodded and made a note, as if grateful for the suggestion. Pascoe came in.

"What did you drink?"

"Whisky. And we had sandwiches."

"What kind?"

"I don't know. Mine was cheese, his was chicken, I think. He stopped at a garage on the way back from the pub and bought them, so they all tasted much the same, I dare say. Is this relevant to anything?"

"Just necessary detail, Mr. Roote," said Pascoe, who knew the value of grinding away at matters that irritated a suspect. "You eat anything else? Either of you?"

"No. Yes, Sam bought a couple of chocolate bars, Yorkies. He ate his. I don't eat chocolate."

"Why's that?"

"It brings on migraine. What the hell is going on here? What's this got to do with Sam's death?"

"Please bear with me, Mr. Roote. This Yorkie bar you didn't eat, did you take it out of its wrapper?"

"Of course I didn't! Why the hell should I?"

"Maybe you miss chocolate and even though you can't eat it, you like to look at it, smell it, perhaps?"

"No! For God's sake, Mr. Dalziel, I've lost a dear friend here and all I'm hearing is waffle about my diet!"

Anyone in his seat appealing to the Fat Man for assistance was really in trouble, thought Pascoe gleefully.

Dalziel said, "Mr. Pascoe's just trying to get things straight, Mr. Roote. Let's get back to this coffee. You say you didn't drink any, so he must have made it after you left, right?"

"Right. Someone else must have come, someone he knew."

"You're very keen on this other visitor," said Dalziel doubtfully. "But we only found one mug, and our lab has established that Johnson definitely drank from it."

"What's that prove? It's easy to wash a mug. Which cafetière did he use?"

"How do you know he used a cafetière?"

"He always made real coffee. He despised instant. And he had a small one cup cafetière he used if he was by himself and a large one if he had company. It was the large one, wasn't it?"

"You got into the room, Mr. Roote. You probably saw for yourself. On the table by his chair."

"I wasn't looking at the fucking furniture, you moron!" shouted Roote, leaping up with a violence that knocked his chair backwards and shifted the table towards his two interrogators.

"Interview suspended while the witness gets a hold of himself," said Dalziel equably.

Outside, he said, "The lad seems upset. You weren't making faces at him behind my back, were you?"

"No," said Pascoe. "It's Roote who's making faces at us. We've got to get behind them."

"Bit of plastic surgery with a truncheon, you mean? Nay, don't take on so. I just can't see if he's involved why he's so keen to cry murder."

"He's clever and he's devious," said Pascoe. "Just because we can't see where he's heading, doesn't mean he's lost."

"Wish I could say the same for us. So, this bloody cafetière, which were Johnson using, the big 'un or the little 'un?"

"The large one. And yes, it looks as if several cups had been poured from it, always presuming he'd filled it to the top in the first place. Path. report suggests Johnson had downed a fair amount of coffee shortly before he died, but exact measures aren't on the menu."

"Never are when you want 'em. Useless sods, doctors," said Dalziel. "What's all this about a Yorkie bar?"

"Just winding him up. The other one had been taken out of its wrapper and put down on the mantelshelf. Probably Johnson was going to eat it but didn't get round to it."

"Wouldn't mind one myself," said Dalziel, rubbing his belly. "So what do you think, lad? I mean, if Roote weren't mixed up in this, would you be doing owt other than tell the coroner it looks like he topped himself?"

Pascoe thought then said, "I'd still want to know where Johnson got the Midazolam. And why he put it in the whisky first rather than straight into his coffee."

"Good questions," said Dalziel. "Let's get back in there, shall we? See if he's settled down, then we'll wind him up some more."

They went back inside. Roote was, outwardly at least, back to his usual fully controlled self.

Dalziel took up the questioning as if nothing had happened.

"This tutorial you were having with Dr. Johnson, bit of an odd time for it, Sunday lunch? I mean, most folk are sitting down to roast beef and Yorkshire pud with their nearest and dearest."

"I seem to recall we left you in The Dog and Duck, Superintendent," said Roote.

"Aye, well, pubs is where I meet my nearest and dearest," said the Fat Man. "So what were this tutorial about?"

"What has this got to do with anything?"

"It might help us understand Dr. Johnson's state of mind when you left him," murmured Pascoe.

"His state of mind is immaterial," insisted Roote. "You're not still trying to brush this aside as suicide, are you? Sam just wasn't the suicidal type."

"Takes a one to know a one, does it?" said Dalziel.

"Sorry?"

"You did slash your wrists a few months back, I seem to recall."

"Yes, but that was . . ."

"More a gesture? Aye, well mebbe the good doctor was making a gesture too. Mebbe he planned to be found sitting with his book in plenty of time to have his stomach pumped and then spend a happy convalescence been cosseted by his loving friends. You see yourself as a loving friend, do you, Mr. Roote?"

For a second it looked like there might be another outburst, but it came to nothing.

Instead he smiled and said, "Let me prevent you, Superintendent, in the archaic as well as the modern sense of the word. You think perhaps Sam and I were a gay couple who had a tiff that lunchtime, and I flounced out, and Sam decided to teach me a lesson by drinking a carefully measured non-fatal draught in the expectation that I would soon return in plenty of time to oversee his resuscitation, after which it would be all reconciliation and contrition, not to mention coition, for the rest of the day. But when I didn't come, he didn't stop drinking. And now I, filled with guilt, am trying to ease my agitated conscience by insisting it was murder."

Pascoe felt an unworthy pang of pleasure at hearing what he thought of as Dalziel's absurd theory so precisely anatomized.

The Fat Man, however, showed no sign of discomfiture.

"By gum, Chief Inspector," he said to Pascoe, "didst tha hear that? Knowing the questions afore they're asked! Get a few more doing that, and we'd only need to teach them to beat themselves up, and you and me 'ud be out of a job."

"No, sir. We'd still need someone to hear the answer," said Pascoe. "Which is, Mr. Roote?"

"The answer is no. Sam and I were friends, good friends, I believe. But above all he was my teacher, a man I respected more than any other I ever knew, a man who would have made a huge contribution to the world of learning and whose loss to me, both personally and intellectually, is almost more than I can bear. But bear it I must, if only to ensure that you bumbling incompetents don't make as big a cock-up of this investigation as you've made of others in the past."

"Nobody's perfect," said Dalziel. "But we got you, sunshine."

Roote smiled and said, "So you did. But you didn't get to keep me, did you?"

And Dalziel smiled back.

"We just catch them, lad. It's the lawyers as decide which are going to be kept and stuffed, which chucked back as tiddlers till they're big enough to be worth the keeping. You think you're big enough yet, Mr. Roote? Or are you still a growing boy?"

Pascoe would have been interested to see how this verbal tennis played but the door of the interview room opened at that moment and Hat Bowler, who'd looked very relieved to be rid of his Roote-sitting duty, reappeared.

"Sir," he said to Dalziel with some urgency. "Can I have a word?"

"Aye. Make a change to talk to a grown-up," said Dalziel.

He rose and went out. Pascoe recorded this on the tape but didn't switch it off.

Roote shook his head and said ruefully, "Knows how to get them in, doesn't he? You've got to give it to Mr. Dalziel. He's a lot brighter than he looks. Which perhaps explains why he chooses to look like he does."

"What's wrong with the way he looks?" asked Pascoe. "You're not being sizeist, I hope?"

"I don't think so, but every size has its limitations, doesn't it?"

"Such as?"

Roote thought for a moment then gave a conspiratorial grin.

"Well, fat men can't write sonnets," he said.

He's taking control, thought Pascoe. He wants me to ask why not. Or something. Change direction.

He said, "Tell me about 'Dream-Pedlary.' "

The change seemed to work. For a second Roote looked nonplussed.

"It's a poem," said Pascoe. "By Beddoes."

"Gee, thanks," said Roote. "What's it got to do with anything?"

"Dr. Johnson—Sam—was reading it. At least, that's where the book on his lap was open."

Roote closed his eyes as if in an effort of recollection.

"*Complete Works,* edited by Gosse, 1928 Fanfrolico Press edition," he said.

"That's right," said Pascoe looking at his, as always, comprehensive notes. "Decorated with Holbein's *Dance of Death.* How did you know it was this edition, Mr. Roote? There were several collections of Beddoes' poems on Sam's shelves."

"It was one of his favourites. He liked the woodcuts. And he'd been using it earlier."

"During your *tutorial,* you mean?"

Roote ignored the sceptical stress and said, "That's right. But it was the first volume he was using, the one with the letters and *Death's Jest-Book.* 'Dream-Pedlary' is in the Second Part. Whoever killed him must have put it there."

"Indeed," murmured Pascoe. "Any notion why?"

Roote closed his eyes and Pascoe saw his lips move silently. Despite his pallor and the dark hollows under his eyes, he looked for a moment like a child trying to recall its lesson. And Pascoe who had read and re-read the poem was able to follow the verses on those pale lips and observe the hesitation when they came to the fourth.

> *If there are ghosts to raise,*
> *What shall I call,*
> *Out of hell's murky haze,*
> *Heaven's blue pall?*
> *Raise my loved long-lost boy*
> *To lead me to his joy.*
> *There are no ghosts to raise;*
> *Out of death lead no ways;*
> *Vain is the call.*

"No," said Roote. "Can't see any special reason, except that it's about death."

"It would seem to me on a cursory glance through the volume," said

Pascoe, "that you could do a dozen *sortes* and ten of them would be guaranteed to be about death."

"As few as that?" said Roote with a savage grin. "I think I'll go now, Mr. Pascoe. Clearly we're getting nowhere. Mr. Dalziel is persuaded Sam killed himself. You, on the other hand, have a notion, or shall we call it a preference, that I killed him. Well, like Mr. and Mrs. Sprat, I hope you can come to an accord. Meanwhile . . ."

He began to rise.

Pascoe said, "You see, what I was wondering was whether in view of Dr. Johnson's reasons for wanting to leave Sheffield, the reference in the poem to his *loved long-lost boy* might not have been significant. Any view on that, Mr. Roote?"

The black-clad pale-faced figure froze like a mime artist in mid-movement.

Then the door opened.

Dalziel said, "Peter, a word. Best close the interview if you've not done it already."

Angrily, Pascoe switched off the tape and went outside.

"Lousy timing, sir," he said. "I was just getting to him."

"I doubt it. Either he knows a hell of a lot more than he's letting on or he's a very good guesser. Either way we need to call time-out and look at our tactics."

"Why? What's happened?" demanded Pascoe.

"You know we told the library staff to keep their eyes peeled? Well, they spotted another suspicious envelope this morning and sent it over. I've just been having a read."

"And?" said Pascoe, knowing the answer.

"Someone up there's had a big crap and pulled the plug on us," said Dalziel gloomily. "It looks like your mate Johnson was the Wordman's number five."

XXIV

the fifth dialogue

Oh, the bells bells bells.

Yes, I remember, like bagpipes, they make a fine noise—between consent-ing adults and a guid Scots mile away!

But close by, when you've got a hangover . . .

Who but a sadist would programme an alarm call on the one scheduled day of rest?

Sorry. Blasphemous. No sadist, but my light and salvation; which is why I don't have to fear any sod.

But the sound does get on my nerves.

Noisy bells, be dumb. I hear you, I will come.

And come I did eventually to that stately old terrace, led not by fore-thought but the convolutions of that serpent path which after the Feydeau farce of the events at the Centre I know now I can follow in utter inviolability.

Yes, I know I shouldn't need convincing but I was always a very good doubter.

He was just going into the building as I approached. As soon as I saw him I knew why I was there. But it wasn't yet, not yet a while, for clocks still ticked, and bells still rang, and all the chronometrical corsetry of everyday existence still clasped me in its shaping grip. Also, he was not alone and though two might be as easy as one, the purity of my course must not be sullied by an insignificant death.

In any case, I was not ready. There were preparations necessary to make, for each step along my path is an advancement of learning, taking me from eager pupillage to equal partnership.

Two hours later I returned. Two hours because that was the time my pace along my path required for my preparations, and it was no surprise in time to find my timing perfect, for the visitor was just leaving, slipping out of the street door like the shadow he resembles, with the result that the door didn't swing back with enough momentum to engage the lock and I was able to enter without having to ring any bell but that to his apartment.

He was surprised to see me though he hid it well and courteously invited me in and offered me a drink.

I said coffee to get him into the kitchen.

And as he turned and left me I felt my aura breathe through my flesh, as time began to slow like a goshawk soaring till it attains its motionless apogee.

Through the half-open door I see he is making filter coffee. In my book, casual and probably unwanted visitors merit no more than a spoonful of instant at best. I am flattered and touched by this courtesy.

And in return, I take just as much care with his drink, pouring a carefully judged measure from my little vial into the open whisky bottle standing by the open book and empty glass on his chairside table. No chance of interruption. I am examining his bookshelf when he comes in with the cafetière.

I see he has brought two mugs. If I were in time, I might have been disconcerted, fearful that by joining me in coffee, he will not take any more whisky till he is in another's company who might observe his symptoms and make efforts to save him. But out of time, I sit and smile, secure in my certainty that what is written is written, and nothing can change its course.

He pours the coffee, then picks up the bottle, offers to add some to my mug. I hesitate then shake my head. I have work to do, I tell him, work that requires a clear head.

He smiles the smile of a man who does not believe that liquor affects his judgment and, to make his point, adds a good inch of Scotch to his coffee.

Poor doctor. He is right, of course. Drink no longer affects his judgment because it is his affected judgment that makes him drink. Does he yet know where his unhappiness has brought him? Does he realize how unhappy he is? I doubt it, else he might have already sought without my help the quietus I am about to give him.

He drinks his doubly laced coffee with every sign of pleasure. This is well arranged. Two strong tastes to conceal one weak, though strong in everything else.

We talk and drink. He is enjoying himself. He pours more coffee, more Scotch. We drink and talk . . . and talk . . . though soon the words that he imagines pearls come rolling misshaped to his lips and stick there, hard to dislodge, yet because all is still so clear in his mind, he thinks this mere inadvertence, too dry a mouth perhaps, easily cured by yet more drink.

He yawns, tries to apologize, looks slightly surprised to find he can't, clutches his chest, begins to gasp. In time, I would have been surprised. I had looked to see him fall asleep, then I would have taken the cushion his head rests on and used it to send him to a still softer rest. But now I see that I am not called on to do any more, and I am not surprised. He stops gasping, closes his eyes and slumps back in his chair. Soon his breath is so light that it would hardly shake a rose-leaf down. Soon I cannot detect it at all. I place a hair over his lips then pass a few minutes washing my coffee mug and making sure no traces of my presence remain. Finished, I check that the hair has not moved. He has gone. Would that all our goings were so easy. Now I arrange him to be found as he would have wished, at his ease, with his book and his bottle, and steal away softly as if fearful of awaking him. Softly and sadly too.

Yes, this time I am surprised to detect so much of sadness in my joy, a sense of melancholy which remains with me even as I step out into the empty street and feel the tremor of time beneath the pavement once more.

Why so?

Perhaps because he smiled so welcomingly and made me real coffee instead of instant.

Perhaps because here was a man who should have been happy but for whom, as he might have said himself, life became too great a bore. . . .

No, not doubts, not second thoughts.

Just a sense that, no matter how desirable my ultimate destination, this journey might yet take me to places I would rather not visit.

Yes, to be sure, no one said it would be roses all the way. Yes, to be sure, death's fine, just another turn on the path. But maybe not being born is the very best option, eh?

Talk soon.

XXV

The Dialogue had been found in its usual buff envelope, once more addressed *Reference Library*, tucked away behind a pile of books reserved for collection on the reception counter close by where the morning mail basket was placed.

Whether it had fallen there by accident or been placed there by design was impossible to say as no one on the staff could assert with absolute certainty that it hadn't lain there unnoticed since Monday. Even worse, from Dalziel's point of view, was the fact that the young female librarian who'd found the envelope had excitedly shared her suspicion of its contents with her nearest colleagues and a couple of eavesdropping members of the public before calling the police. Keeping the Fourth Dialogue out of the public domain had been easy with only the Centre security firm who'd handed over the unopened envelope to threaten into silence. But with rumours of the Fifth already starting to circulate, sitting on the Fourth could rapidly turn into a public relations disaster, and Dalziel found himself ordered from above to get his revelation in first. So a statement was put out and a press conference promised for a later date.

Pascoe, after digesting the new Dialogue, saw no reason to change his tack.

"This alters nothing," he said. "Except maybe now we know why Roote's been sitting there crying murder. Why pretend it's anything else when you know the Dialogue admitting all is on its way? Or maybe he thought we'd seen the Dialogue already and were trying to do a bluff on him by ignoring it, and that really got up his nose."

"But, sir," said Bowler, "the Wordman describes seeing Roote go in with Dr. Johnson, then he had to wait till Roote came out."

"Jesus," said Pascoe in exasperation. "If Roote wrote the Dialogue, that's exactly what he would say, isn't it? I mean, he knows we know he was there. You two saw him going off with Johnson on Sunday, we've got witnesses who recall seeing them going into the block of flats—but none, incidentally, who recall noticing anyone else unaccounted for hanging around the place—and forensic have picked up traces of him all over the apartment."

"That it?" said Dalziel.

"And there's the poem Sam was reading. It took someone pretty familiar with both Beddoes and Sam's Sheffield background to make sure the book was open at something so appropriate."

He had told Dalziel about the alleged reasons for Johnson's move. The Fat Man had yawned. Now Pascoe concentrated his arguments on the potentially more sympathetic ear of Bowler.

"And if we look at the Dialogue, see here, there's a reference to the poem, this bit about his breath being so light it wouldn't have shaken a rose-leaf down. That's almost a direct quote from the first stanza, don't you see?"

"Yes, sir, I see, sir," said Bowler. "But . . ."

"But what?" Doubt from Dalziel was one thing, but from a DC it came close to mutiny!

"But it's all a bit . . . convoluted, isn't it, sir?"

"Convoluted?" echoed Dalziel. "It's fucking contortuplicated!"

That sounded like a Dalziel original, but Pascoe had been caught out before and made a note to look it up before making comment.

Dalziel went on, "It's bad enough having this bugger sitting out there, laughing at us, without going looking for trouble. You've had Hawkeye here give Roote the once-over already, and I dare say you're so obsessed with the nasty little sod that you've checked him out against every bit of nastiness that's gone on since he arrived in town. And you've not come up with owt, else you'd have him banged up, preferably underground and in shackles. Any other ideas? Anyone?"

Hat took a deep breath and said, "If we're looking for someone with a strong connection to all the victims, except the first two who seem to be random, well, there's Charley Penn. And he drives an old banger which would fit in with the First Dialogue."

"Oh God," said Dalziel. "Do I smell another obsession? I know Charley is mooning around after your bit in the library, but sooner or later, lad, you've got to start thinking with your head not your dick."

Hat flushed and said, "You said yourself, sir, he's something else!"

"Aye, he is, but that doesn't make him a killer," said Dalziel, rifling through his case file. "Here we are. Charley Penn. Asked as a matter of routine where he was Sunday afternoon. Said he went as usual to visit his mother who has a cottage on Lord Partridge's estate at Haysgarth . . . that checked out, did it?"

Pascoe said, "More or less."

Dalziel gave him a long look and said, "If I ask a lass, 'Did you enjoy that, luv?' and she answers, 'More or less,' I get worried."

Pascoe said carefully, "It was Hat here who checked."

"Bowler?" He looked at Hat with a predatory speculation. "You thought it worth a couple of hours of valuable CID time sending the lad out to Haysgarth rather than using the local woodentop? This one of your hunches, Pete?"

"I sort of volunteered, sir," said Hat nobly.

"I see. One of your hunches then. So what did the old lady say?"

"Not much, at least not much I could understand," said Hat ruefully. "Seemed to think I was a member of the Stasi, rattled away in German, and when I finally got her to speak English, her accent was so thick it was almost as hard to understand. All I got out of her was that her Karl was a good boy and loved his old *mutti* and the lovely cakes she makes so much he was hardly ever away from her. I asked about that Sunday and she said that he was with her every Sunday and every other day he could manage. And then she started in German again."

"Said he likes her cakes, did she?" said Dalziel thoughtfully. "So, no written statement then?"

"It didn't seem an option, sir," said Hat uneasily.

"Nor indeed a necessity," said Pascoe. "I think we've wasted enough time on Penn unless anyone knows of any *real* reason for putting Penn in the frame?"

"If you can fit Roote in, there's lots of room for any bugger," said Dalziel. "How about you, Wieldy? You got anyone you'd like to fit up? No? Good. Then let's all start pulling in the same direction and see if we can't plough this murdering bastard into the ground. Bowler, I reckon soon as I take my eye off you, you'll go swanning round to that library you're so fond of, so why don't you go there officially and don't come back till you've found out how and when this envelope was delivered, right? Even if it means stamping some of them dozy buggers overdue."

"Yes, sir. I'm on my way."

He vanished.

Dalziel said, "Nice to see someone so happy when I give 'em a job. Let's see if I can't do the same for you two miserable sods!"

Hat was indeed happy to have an excuse to visit the library. He'd thought of ringing Rye last night but decided it would be a wrong move. Progress was steady but a wise strategist knew when to press, when to hold back. That was the way the Jack-the-lad part of him analysed the situation. But there was another more shadowy area of thought and feeling which acknowledged that the more he saw of Rye, the more important it became to keep on seeing her. This wasn't just another skirmish in that unremitting sexual campaign which all Jack-the-lad young men enter upon at puberty— approach, lay siege, negotiate terms, occupy, move on. This was . . . well, he didn't quite know what it was because he belonged to a generation conditioned to mock the idioms of romantic love, and what we don't have words for, we find it hard to think about. But he knew that to lose her by crowding her would be a folly he'd never forgive himself for.

But now, with new secret information to share, he anticipated being made very welcome. Jesuitically, he had worked out that the decision to go public about the existence of the two latest Dialogues permitted him to use his own best judgment about who he passed on the details to. And of course he'd swear her to secrecy. This too was a kind of intimacy, the Jack-the-lad strategist pointed out gleefully; and each such move was a move in the right direction. Which was, of course, bed. But more than bed. Breakfast and beyond. Even the bed bit was different. He'd always looked forward to sex with a healthy young appetite, but never before like this, for imagining it with Rye Pomona made the marrow bubble along his bones and pushed him into a languorous swoon which almost made him drive up the exit lane of the Centre car park.

Retreating under a chorus of protesting horns conducted by a flurry of abusive fingers, he found the correct entrance, parked and made his way to the main library.

With the image of a roused Dalziel fresh in his mind, his investigation was painstakingly thorough to a degree which brought the two women and one man involved to a state of mutiny. But by dint of forcing them to recall which of the reserved books had been collected earlier in the week, he managed to establish that the weight of probability lay on the side of the envelope not having been there on Monday morning. Tuesday, which was yesterday, the day that Johnson's body had been found, was less certain. And today, Wednesday, it had of course been found.

Satisfied he could get no more out of them, he left and headed upstairs to the reference library. By now it was lunchtime, and he peered into the staffroom as he passed in case Rye was eating her sandwich there. No sign of her, nor at first glance in the deserted reference library.

He went up to the desk and through the partially opened door of the office behind the counter, he glimpsed Dick Dee, his head bent over something on the desk which absorbed him so much that he was oblivious to Hat's silent approach.

He was playing Scrabble . . . no, not Scrabble, it must be that funny game, Paronomania. Hat felt pleased with himself for recalling the word, but his pleasure was quenched almost instantly by a jealous certainty that Dee's opponent was Rye.

There was a click of tiles being moved and Dee shook his head, smiling in admiration at some adept move, and said, "Oh, thou crafty Kraut, well done indeed."

And Bowler just had time to feel puzzled as to why Dee should be addressing Rye as Kraut, when a most unfeminine voice replied, "Thank 'ee kindly, whoreson," and his tentative knock at the well-oiled door pushed it open sufficiently for him to see the distinctive profile of Charley Penn.

"Mr. Bowler, do step inside," said Dee politely.

He went into the office. The men on the wall all seemed to be examining him critically like a candidate for a job they didn't think he was going to get. On the other hand, the teenage trio in the photo on the desk seemed to look straight through him at a world which, united, they did not doubt their capacity to deal with.

"Is your errand avian, amoristic or authoritarian?" said Dee.

"Sorry?" said Hat.

Penn was grinning at him. Hat felt, unusually for one not naturally violent, like wiping his clock.

"Do you require information about birds? Or do you wish to ask after Rye? Or have you come to quiz us about the latest Dialogue?"

Hat forgot about Penn and said, he hoped neutrally, "What do you mean by that, Mr. Dee?"

"I'm sorry," said Dee. "Is it confidential? Of course it is. Forget I spoke. It was crass of me, and certainly not a subject to be flippant about."

The apology came across as sincere rather than an empty formality.

"Mr. Dee, I'm not saying there has been another, but if there was, I'd like to know what you know about it," insisted Hat.

"All I know is what all the library staff know, that a suspicious envelope was found this morning and handed over to the police and as it hasn't been returned since—though of course that too might be the purpose of your visit—then it seems likely it contained matter of interest to you. But please, forget and forgive my curiosity. I have no desire to embarrass you professionally."

"Doesn't bother me, though," said Penn in his grating voice. "My guess 'ud be that you've heard from yon loony again and it's something to do with Sam Johnson. Right?"

"That just a lucky guess, Mr. Penn?" said Hat.

His gaze engaged the writer's and locked for a while, then fell. Never get into a fight it's not worth winning. He found himself looking down at the Paronomania board. It was the same star shape as the one he'd seen in Penn's flat, but the designs on it were different. These seemed to have been taken from an old map, with wind-puffing cherubs, spouting whales, towering ice-cliffs, disporting mermaids. The game was well advanced with numerous tiles laid out, going in all directions, but none of the letter combinations made any sense to Hat. And there were three tile racks in use, one before each of the two facing players, the third between them. Only two can play, he recalled Rye telling him. Why should she lie? Unless she was the third player, involved in some weird *ménage à trois* with these two?

It was a thought as disgusting as silverfish in a salad bowl, but before he rinsed it from his mind, he found himself looking to see if there were anywhere Rye could have retreated to at his approach.

There wasn't. There wasn't even a window to climb out of.

Jesus, Bowler! What kind of nutty creep are you turning into? he asked himself angrily.

Charley Penn was answering his spoken question.

"Not lucky, by any standards, and hardly a guess, Constable. First thing we all thought when we heard about poor Sam yesterday was, it has to be this Wordman. Then folk started whispering suicide. Well, it seemed possible. Too much Beddoes could drive anyone down that road. But the more I thought, the less likely it seemed. I'd not known him long, but I'd have put him stronger than that. I'm right, aren't I? If this envelope Dick mentioned does contain another Dialogue, it has to be about Sam Johnson, right?"

"No comment," said Hat. "Mr. Dee, is Rye here?"

"Sorry, you're out of luck," said Dee. "She's got a touch of this flu-bug that's around. She looked so ill yesterday, I sent her home and told her not to come back till she was better and our readers were safe."

"Right. Thank you."

As he turned away, Dee said, "Would you like her phone number? I'm sure she would be comforted to know you were asking after her."

This was kind, thought Hat, recalling that not so long back, the librarian had felt unable to pass Rye's number on. She must have said something to suggest their relationship had taken a step forward.

Before he could respond, Penn sneered, "Not got her number yet, lad? You're not making much progress, are you?"

Hat resisted the urge to reply that he'd made a lot more progress than some geriatrics not a million miles away and she'd given him her number unasked. Instead he took out his notebook, said, "That would be kind, Mr. Dee. I seem to have mislaid my pen. May I borrow a pencil?"

He stepped forward to the desk, picked up a pencil, and stood with it poised.

From this angle he could see the tiles in the third rack.

There were six of them. J O H N N Y.

Dee, with a faintly conspiratorial smile as if he recognized a charade when he saw one, gave him the number. Carefully Hat wrote down *Johnny*.

"Thank you, Mr. Dee," he said. "I'll certainly be enquiring after Rye's health. Good day."

He left without looking at Penn. He could see, though he rather resented being able to, why Rye got so defensive of Dick Dee. There was something almost naively amiable about the man. However, any slight revision of his feeling towards the librarian was more than balanced by the steady augmentation of his antipathy for the novelist. Puffed-up prick!

And he found himself imagining how nice it would be to prove that Penn was the Wordman and have the fingering of his collar.

Such feelings were dangerous, he admonished himself sternly. Having got back to something like an even keel with the super, it would be foolish to risk rocking the boat by letting personal dislike cloud his judgment.

As he left the library he took out his mobile, intending to dial Rye's number, but before he could start, it rang.

"Bowler," he said.

"Pascoe. Where are you?"

"Just leaving the library, guv."

"You get anything?"

"Not really."

"You've been there a long time for nothing," said Pascoe accusingly. "You've not been in the Reference chatting up that girl again?"

"No, sir," said Hat indignantly. "She's off sick."

"Oh yes? And how do you know that? Never mind. Listen, someone's ringing wanting to speak to you urgently. Name of Angie. I wondered, is she some snout you haven't bothered to register? Or just one of your other conquests that you've got into trouble?"

Angie? For a moment his mind was blank, then he remembered. Jax Ripley's sister.

"No, sir. But it's personal."

"Is that so? Wasn't that sister we met at Ripley's funeral called Angie?"

"Yes, sir," said Bowler, thinking *shit!* "I told her if ever she wanted to chat about Jax, just to give me a ring."

"Maybe you should have been a social worker," said Pascoe. "But if she says anything you feel might be relevant to the case, you won't forget you're drawing your pay as a cop, will you? Back here soon as you can, OK?"

"Yes, sir," said Bowler.

He switched off thinking Pascoe sounded in an untypically sour mood.

He thumbed through his wallet till he found the piece of paper he'd scribbled Mrs. Ripley's phone number on. Angie answered on the first ring.

"Look," she said, "I've got to head back to the States at the weekend and I just wanted to check what you've done with that stuff I gave you."

"I'm still working on it," he prevaricated. "It's a delicate business . . ."

"The bastard who stuck a knife in my sister wasn't being delicate," she snapped. "This Georgie Porgie guy, is he being questioned?"

"Well, no . . . I mean, we don't know who he is for sure, do we?"

"How many cops have you got that fit that description?"

"More than you'd think," said Hat. "Believe me, Angie, if there's anything here that helps us find Jax's killer, I'll leave no stone unturned."

He spoke with all the vibrant sincerity he could put into his voice but she still sounded less than persuaded as she replied, "Well, OK. You'll get in touch? I'm relying on you, Hat."

"You can do. Take care," he said and switched off.

He stood outside the Centre, trying to work up a head of indignation because there was nothing he could do except help deprive a middle-aged detective of his dignity and perhaps even his pension, but all he felt was a rat.

He felt a strong need to talk to Rye about the affair again, but not on the phone. Anyway, it didn't seem such a good idea to ring her any more. If, as seemed likely, she was deep beneath the bedclothes feeling lousy, she wasn't going to be very well disposed to the idiot who got her out to ask how she was. Better to go round later with a bunch of grapes and a box of chocolates. That way if he got her out of bed . . .

He had a sudden vision of the door opening and Rye standing there, all bed-tousled in a loosely tied robe which permitted tantalizing glimpses of firm round flesh, like sun-warmed fruit seen through shifting leaves . . .

A yearning groan slipped through his lips and an old bag-lady passing by looked at him anxiously and said, "Are you feeling all right, son?"

"I hope so," he said. "Just hunger pangs, ma. But thanks for your concern."

And dropping a handful of change into her nearest bag, he walked briskly on.

XXVI

Pascoe was indeed in a sour mood.

Wield had contacted Sheffield as requested and got the bare bones of the dead student business.

"Seems this lad wasn't doing too well. Johnson was his main tutor and it fell to him to warn the boy that if his work didn't improve, he was out. There was a vital piece of work, some kind of dissertation, due in early in the summer term but the lad didn't show up with it and a couple of days later he was found dead in his room. Drug overdose. No suicide note. In fact his dissertation papers were all over the floor and it looked like he'd been trying to keep himself sharp in order to get the thing finished and he'd overdone it. The inquest jury brought in accident. But Johnson seemed convinced it was suicide and took it very personally, so much so he wanted a change of scene at any price, and in the end, got a special dispensation to take up this job at MYU even though he couldn't give the required amount of notice."

"And that's it?" said Pascoe. "No mention of Roote?"

"They didn't mention him and I wasn't going to, was I?"

"You could have dug a bit deeper," suggested Pascoe ungraciously. "Still could."

"Look, Pete, I got what they had to give me. This was supposed to be about possible state of mind in a possible suicide case, right? That was just about plausible. But now we know that Johnson's death was definitely a

Wordman killing, state of mind doesn't come into it. If you find something to tie Roote into all these killings, the super will give you a medal. But you've got to keep an open mind. No joy at the hospital either. If they lost any Midazolam, they've covered it up and are keeping it covered. So my advice is, forget Sheffield."

There had risen to Pascoe's lips a sharp reproof based on their difference of rank but fortunately he had caught it before it slipped out. Wield's friendship was important to him and he knew how punctilious the sergeant was never to overstep police hierarchical lines in public. His part of this unspoken accord must be never to insist upon them in private, else something would go forever.

But his mood stayed sour and when Bowler returned, he said, "Get your private business with Ripley's sister sorted, then?"

"Yes, sir. She was just ringing to tell me she had to get back to the States at the weekend and wanted to say goodbye."

"You must have made a strong impression on her, considering you'd never met till the funeral," said Pascoe.

"It was just me knowing Jax so . . . quite well," emended Hat, thinking, Jesus, this is just confirming all their suspicions that I was Deep-throat.

Perhaps it was time to speak.

The door opened and George Headingley came in. He was looking a lot more at ease than he'd done for some time. With just a few more days to do, he's beginning to think there's a light at the end of the tunnel, that he's got away with it after all, thought Hat. Well, he may get a shock yet!

But observing those naturally jovial features starting to regain something of their old colour and form, he knew he couldn't be the one to pull the plug.

"I've been thinking about these Dialogues," said Headingley.

"Kind of you to take the time, George," said Pascoe on whose crowded desk had spilled most of the extra work caused by the DI's absence, whether bodily or mental. "And?"

"They keep turning up at the library even now the story comp's finished. Could be not even the first one was really among the stories sent to the *Gazette*. Maybe they always got put into the bag after it arrived at the library, by someone who works there or uses the place a lot. I mean, what better place to find a Wordman?"

A sound like the crack of canvas in a typhoon made them all turn to the door where Dalziel stood applauding.

"Bravo, George. Glad to see you're not sending your mind into retirement ahead of your body. Let that be a lesson to you, lad . . ." (addressing Hat) ". . . good detective never takes time off, it's either in the blood or it's nowhere."

It wasn't altogether clear to Hat whether there was an element of satire in this or not, but as the others seemed to be taking it at face value, he nodded and tried to look grateful.

"So, George, all set for the big send-off? Next Tuesday, isn't it? With a bit of luck we'll see to it that you spend the first twenty-four hours of your retirement unconscious!"

"No change there then," muttered Pascoe as Headingley, looking a little flushed at all this attention, left the room.

"Now then, Chief Inspector," said Dalziel sternly. "Who's been rattling thy cage? Lot of sense in what George said. Wordman, library, the two things go together."

"Like needle and haystack," said Pascoe.

"Your boy, Roote, must use libraries a lot," said Dalziel.

"More the university than the Centre," said Pascoe with reluctant honesty.

"Same difference," said the Fat Man. "Man likes to be whipped, you don't worry which knocking shop. Charley Penn's another, never away, so I hear. From libraries, I mean. Then there's the staff. Mebbe we should take a closer look at them. Could be a cushy job there for you, young Bowler. Fancy taking a closer look at the staff, do you?"

The Fat Man smacked his lips salaciously and Hat felt himself flushing, out of both embarrassment and anger.

"All right, lad?" said Dalziel. "You're looking a bit fevered. Not getting this flu-bug, I hope."

"I'm fine, sir," said Hat. "You were saying about the library staff . . . anyone in particular?"

"Aye, yon Follows. Man who spends so much time crimping his hair must have something wrong with him. Check the Offenders' List. Then there's yon guy Dee. His name rings a bell."

"Perhaps you're thinking of that Dr. Dee who got done for necromancy," said Pascoe.

"Very like," said Dalziel. "Check him out too, Bowler, see if there's a connection. And if you can manage deep thought and mashing tea at the same time, I'd love a cup."

"Sir . . ." said Hat hesitantly.

He looked at each of the trio of faces in turn. Curiously it was Wield's, normally the most unreadable, which by some slight contraction of the left eyebrow confirmed that he was being sent up. Which felt much the same as being put down.

If a riposte that was smart as well as being angry had risen to his lips, he would probably have uttered it. But to exit on, "I'm not your bloody tea-boy, fatso. Make your own!" didn't seem wise, so he muttered, "I'll get right on to it," and went out.

"Hat."

He turned. Wield had followed him.

"Just because they're taking the piss doesn't mean they don't take you seriously."

"No, Sarge."

"And just because you're pissed doesn't mean you shouldn't take them seriously either."

"No, Sarge," he repeated, feeling for some reason slightly cheered up.

There were several *Follows* in the computer, but none called Percy and none bearing any resemblance to the librarian. A few *Dees*, but no Richard, no librarian. And no doctor either. That had been a Pascoe crack, which meant it was likely to be what Dalziel would call arty-farty clever. Worth finding out what it meant just to show that the DCI wasn't the only one here who'd got past his O-levels.

But first things first.

It was time to impress the Fat Man with his tea-making abilities.

By the time he left work that evening, Hat had fully recovered his normal cheerful spirits and persuaded himself that on the whole the signs were good. In the first months after his arrival, as his star rapidly sank, he had watched rather enviously as that of Detective Constable Shirley Novello steadily rose. But part of that rising he seemed to recollect had involved a deal of fetching and carrying and gentle mockery, so why should he now resent treatment which, doled out to her, he had once envied?

Plus he was going to see Rye and that was a prospect that automatically raised his spirits.

It's not often in this existence that a man's fantasies move, precise in every detail, out of his mind's eye into plain view, and the shock is often counter-productive.

So it was when the door of Rye's flat opened to reveal her standing before him in a loosely tied robe through whose interstices shone tracts of smooth flesh, both soft and firm, and all as richly golden as barley ripe for harvest.

He stood there, motionless and speechless, more like a man confronted by Medusa than his heart's desire, till she said, "Do words come out of your mouth or does it just hang open to give the flies somewhere to shelter from the rain?"

"Sorry . . . I just didn't . . . they said you were ill and I thought . . . I'm sorry to have got you out of bed . . ."

"You haven't. I'm feeling a bit better and I'd just got up to have a shower, which I thought a man in your line of business might have worked out for himself."

She pulled the towelling robe firmly shut as she spoke, and now he raised his eyes he saw that her hair was dripping water down her face. Sodden wet, the rich brown had darkened almost to blackness against which the streak of silvery grey shone as if composed of electric filaments.

"Those for me or are they evidence in your latest big case?"

He'd forgotten he was holding a bunch of carnations in one hand and a box of Belgian chocolates in the other.

"Sorry, yes. Here."

He proffered them but she didn't take them, only grinned and said, "If you think you're getting me to leave go of this robe, you're sadly mistaken. Come in and put them down somewhere while I get myself decent."

"Hey, don't let decent trouble you," Hat called after her as she went out of sight. "I'm a cop. We're trained to cope with anything."

He set his gifts on a coffee table and looked around the room. It wasn't large, but it was so neat and uncluttered that it felt more spacious than it was. Two small armchairs, a well-ordered bookcase, a standard lamp, and the coffee table, that was it.

He went to the bookcase. You could find out a lot about people from their books, or so he'd read somewhere. But only if you knew a lot about books in the first place, which he didn't. One thing he could see was that there were a lot of plays here, reminding him that Rye came from a theatrical family. He plucked out a complete Shakespeare and opened it at the flyleaf. There was a date, *1.5.91*, and an inscription, *To Raina, Happy fifteenth to the Queen from the Clown Prince, with love from Serge xxxxxxxxxxxxxxxx*

Fifteen kisses. Was that a pang of jealousy he felt? Of someone he didn't know who could be any age giving a prezzie to Rye years ago when she was still a child? You'd better watch it, my boy, he admonished himself. As he'd worked out before, any sign of his interest becoming obsessively possessive was going to be a real turn-off to Rye.

"Improving yourself?" she said behind him.

He turned. She'd put on a T-shirt and jeans and was still towelling her hair.

He said, "*To Raina.* I'd forgotten your full name."

"Rye-eena," she corrected his pronunciation. "Otherwise I'd be called Ray."

"Rye's better."

"Whisky rather than sunshine?"

"Loaves rather than fishes," he said with a grin.

She considered this then nodded approvingly.

"Not bad for a plod," she said.

"Thank you kindly. Where's it come from anyway, you never told me."

"I don't recall you asking. It's a play."

"Shakespeare?" he said, hefting the anthology.

"Next along," she said.

She went to the bookshelf and plucked out a volume.

He replaced the Shakespeare and took it from her hands.

"*Arms and the Man* by G. B. Shaw," he read.

"You know Shaw?"

"Nicked his brother once. GBH Shaw," he said.

"Sorry."

"Police-type joke. Funny title. Why'd he call it that?"

"Because he lived in an age when he could assume that most of his audience wouldn't need to ask why he called it that."

"Ah. And that was because . . . ?"

"Because a classical education was still regarded as the pedagogic *summum bonum* by the moneyed classes. And if you hadn't read at least the first line of Virgil's *Aeneid,* you'd clearly wasted your youth. 'Arma virumque cano,' which Dryden renders as 'Arms and the man I sing.' Good title way back then. But a man would have to be very sure he had a highly cultured, intelligent and alert audience to try anything like that now."

"You sound nostalgic. You reckon they were better times?"

"Certainly. For a start, we weren't born. Sleep's good, death's better, but best of all is never to be born at all."

"Jesus!" he exclaimed. "That's really morbid. Another of Virgil's little quips?"

"No. Heine."

"As in Heine, that Kraut poet Charley Penn, is working on?"

Something was ringing a very faint bell.

"In civilized circles I believe they're known as Germans," she said seriously. "You don't have to like them, but that's no reason to be beastly to them."

"Sorry. Same applies to Penn, does it?"

"Certainly. In fact there's a great deal to like about him. Even his apparent obsession with my person might by some be considered not altogether reprehensible. That was one of his translations I just quoted which he brought to my attention when my refusal to let him cop a feel was rendering him particularly despondent."

Hat was beginning to understand the subtle stratagems of Rye's mockery. She left doors invitingly ajar through which a prat might step to find himself showered with cold water or plunging down an open lift-shaft.

He said, "So what's it mean precisely, that stuff about sleep and so on?"

"It means that once upon a time we were all enjoying the best of possible states, i.e. not being born. But then our parents got stuck into each other in a hay field, or on the back seat of a car, or between acts during a performance of a Shaw play at Oldham, and they blew it for us, forced us without a by-your-leave to make an entrance, kicking and screaming, on to this draughty old stage. Fancy a coffee?"

"Why not?" he said, following her into a tiny kitchen which was as well ordered as the living room. "Hey, is that why they called you Raina? Because they were acting in this play when they . . . ? Now that's what I call really romantic."

"You do?"

"Yes. Can't see why you're so cynical about it. Nice story, nice name. Just think, you could have been called . . ." He flipped open the play to the cast list: ". . . Sergius! Just imagine. Sergius Pomona! Then you'd really have had something to complain about!"

"My twin brother didn't seem to mind," she said.

"You've got a twin?"

"Had. He died," she said, spooning coffee into a cafetière.

"Oh shit, I'm sorry, I didn't know . . ."

"How could you? He gave me the Shakespeare you were looking at."

Serge. He recalled the inscription and blushed at the thought of his infantile jealousy.

To cover his confusion he gabbled, "Yes, of course, that explains the inscription, the Queen, May the first, Queen of the May, and he was the Clown Prince . . ."

"He was full of laughter," she said quietly. "Whenever I was down he could always cheer me up. It didn't seem too bad being called Raina while he was around."

"I think it's a lovely name," said Hat staunchly. "And Sergius too. And I'm sure they were given to you with the best of intentions. Being called after characters in a play, you didn't get that kind of romantic idea in my family!"

"Sweet of you," she murmured. "Yes, there was a time when I too used to think it romantic to hear my mother and father explaining that we were named after Raina and Sergius, who are the two supremely romantic characters in the play, because these were the parts my parents were playing when they conceived us. Then one day when I was sorting out some of their stuff, I came across a collection of old theatre programmes. And there it was. *Arms and the Man* at Oldham. The date fitted perfectly. The only thing was when I checked the cast list, it wasn't Freddie Pomona and Melanie Mackillop who were playing Sergius and Raina, it was two other people. My parents were playing Nicola, the head serving man, and Catherine, Raina's middle-aged mother. How's that for romantic, and do you take sugar?"

"A spoonful. Well, it's not really so terrible, is it? Improving on the past isn't exactly a capital crime."

"I suppose not. Shaw would probably have liked it. The play's all about exploding inflated notions of romance and sacrifice and honour."

"Then why so cynical?"

She looked at him thoughtfully then said, "Another time, eh? Wetting my hair always loosens my tongue. Let's see if those chocs you brought are any good."

They went back into the sitting room. Rye opened the chocolate box, bit into one and nodded approvingly.

"Excellent," she said. "So how did you know I was ill?"

"Well, I was at the library today . . ."

"Why?" she demanded. "Has something happened?"

"Yes," he admitted. "Strict confidence, OK?"

"Guide's honour," she said.

He told her about the new Dialogue.

"Oh God," she said. "I wondered when I heard about Johnson's death . . ."

"What made you wonder?" he asked.

"I don't know. Just a feeling. And maybe because . . ."

"What?"

"This connection with the library. I don't just mean the Dialogues turning up there, but these last three killings, there's been a kind of link. OK, it's tenuous, but it does create a sort of illogical sensitivity. . . ."

Suddenly she looked very vulnerable.

"Come on," he said with an attempt at avuncular jocularity. "Cheer up. No need for you to worry."

"Really?" His reassurance worked insomuch as her evident vulnerability was instantly replaced by an air of nepotal admiration and trust. "Oh, do tell why I shouldn't worry."

"Well, because this guy, the Wordman, isn't one of your normal sexual psychos going around topping young women. So far there's only been one woman, Jax Ripley, and no sex. We don't know yet precisely what drum this lunatic's marching to, but there's nothing to suggest that someone like you is more likely to be in the firing line than, say, someone like me. As for the library thing, my notion is that the short story competition gave him the kind of way of slipping his Dialogues into the public consciousness which appealed to his warped mind . . ."

"Sorry, run that by me again."

"He's got a puzzler's mind, the kind that sees everything in terms of hidden answers, and deceptions, and references, and connections, and riddles, and word games. Hiding what's turned out to be fact in a great pile of fiction is exactly the kind of thing that would appeal to him."

"This degree they say you did, what was it in? Ornithology with psychiatry?" she said, half mocking, half complimentary.

"Geography," he said, adding, "with Economics," like a plea in mitigation. It didn't work.

"My God. You mean I'm getting involved with a bird-watcher with a geography degree? At least I won't have to worry about getting to sleep at nights."

He examined this, decided there was more in it to be pleased with than to take offence at, and went on, "Being a detective's like learning to use the reference library. It's all a question of knowing where to look. We had these guys down from the Uni, a trick cyclist and a linguist. I took notes. What I'm saying is that while everyone should take care, there's no group in particular we can advise as being at greater risk than any other. Saying everyone's in danger may sound like cold comfort, but if you look at it statistically, if everyone's in danger, the odds on you being the one are pretty long. So take care, but don't take to the hills. Not without company, anyway. Talking of which, are you going to be fit for our expedition this weekend?"

"No problem," she said, stretching back sinuously so that her T-shirt rode up from her jeans revealing a band of gently rounded belly which set all those alarms flashing and ringing along his arteries once more. "I'm feeling better by the minute. Who did you see at the library? Dick?"

"Yes," he said. If she'd wanted to flick a bit of cold water at him, introducing Dee's name at this juncture did the trick. "Talking of Dee, you ever hear of a doctor with that name?"

"Not unless you mean the Elizabethan astrologer and necromancer," she said.

"Yeah, that'll be the one," he said. Clever old Pascoe, ho ho ho.

"This the latest theory, the Wordman's a magician and Dick's a descendant of the doctor?"

"Well, you've got to admit he's a little bit weird," he said, adding quickly to dilute his criticism, "Must be the time he spends with Penn. When I went up to the Reference, they were in the office, playing that funny board game. Paronomania."

He looked at her closely to see if he'd got it right.

Rye laughed and said, "You do listen, then!"

"Depends who's talking. You said the word actually means an obsessive interest in word games?"

"That's right. It's a mix of paronomasia, that's word-play or a pun, and mania, with maybe a touch of paranoia thrown in. What are you looking at me like that for?"

"You realize you've just repeated more or less what I was saying about the Wordman?" said Hat.

"Oh, come on," she said with irritation. "What your tame experts said, you mean? Listen, these two have been playing this game ever since I joined the staff. It's no big secret vice. I asked about it and Dick explained the name, no problem. He even gave me a copy of the rules and so on. I've got it somewhere."

She started looking through a drawer.

"The two boards I've seen looked hand-painted, and they were different," said Hat. "Is it a real game? Or just one they made up?"

"What on earth would the difference be?" she said, smiling at him. "I know it started at school when they were playing Scrabble—"

"At school?" he interrupted. "Dee went to Unthank too?"

"Yes. That a problem?"

"Of course not." But it might be an answer. "So, Scrabble."

"That's right. It seems there was a dispute about some Latin word that one of them used, and it led to them playing a version in which you couldn't use anything but Latin. Things developed from that, they wanted something more complicated, with a bigger board, more letters, different rules, and the players take turns in choosing the language. . . . Oh, here it is—no, don't read it now, you can keep it, time I was clearing out some of this clutter."

Hat folded the sheets of paper she'd given him and put them in his wallet.

"No wonder I couldn't understand any of the words I saw," he said, reluctantly impressed. "How many languages do they speak, for God's sake?"

"French, German—Penn's fluent in that, of course—bit of Spanish, Italian, the usual stuff. But it doesn't matter. They don't have to know a language to play in it so long as there's a dictionary in the library. That's part of the fun, it seems. It's like poker. One will produce a word which looks like it might be Slovakian, say, then defy the other to challenge him. Is it a bluff or has he swotted up a bit of Slovak the day before, and is now trying to provoke a challenge? Then out comes the dictionary and it's lose a go and fifty points if it's a false word, and the same if it's an unsuccessful challenge."

"What a pair of sad plonkers," muttered Hat.

"Why do you say that?" she asked, looking at him curiously. "Two consenting adults, and they play in private, they're not trying to impress anyone."

"They seem to have impressed you. Ever try it yourself?"

"Wouldn't have minded, but I've never been asked," she said. "Story of my life, really. Lots of interesting games going on, but nobody asks me to play."

Was this a hint? An invitation? Or just a tease?

He drank some coffee to moisten his suddenly dry throat as he tried to work out whether the time was ripe for a move. His body certainly thought it was. He could feel his flesh beginning to overheat.

"You all right, Hat?" said Rye, looking at him with some concern. "You're looking very flushed."

"Oh yes, I'm fine," he said.

But even as he spoke, it occurred to him he was far from fine and that this heat had more to do with debility than desire.

"You don't look fine, not unless you always start flushing in patches at this time in the evening," she said. "In fact you look like what I felt like at work yesterday."

"You mean I've caught your lurgy?" said Hat, choking back a cough. "I knew we had a lot in common."

"Please. I hate a plucky trooper. You feel OK to drive home?"

It occurred to Hat that if he played his cards right, he could claim sanctuary here, then he recalled that Rye herself was only just recovering from the bug. In romantic fiction, the patient often got the nurse on to his bed. On the other hand, he suspected that all a pair of patients would get on was each other's nerves.

"Yeah, no problem. So what's the prognosis?"

"Well, you'll feel a lot worse before you begin to feel better, but the good news is that it may be nasty but it's short."

"So I should be OK for the weekend then?"

She smiled at him and said, "It's your show, Hat. But if we have to cancel again, I may start wondering if fate isn't trying to tell us something."

"You leave fate to me," he said, stifling a cough as he headed for the door. "Good night's sleep and I'll probably be back keeping Yorkshire safe for civilians first thing in the morning."

"I believe you," she said, kissing her index finger and placing it gently on his burning forehead. "I feel safer already. Goodnight, Hat. Take care."

And such is the power of a good woman's touch that he believed it himself as he went out to his car. Love can conquer everything and he knew he was truly, madly, deeply in love.

XXVII

Sometimes even a good woman can get it wrong and next day Hat felt truly, deeply, madly lousy. His first impulse was to go to work so that they could see how bad he was, but when he fell over trying to pull his underpants on, he abandoned the idea and rang in instead.

He got through to Wield who sounded if not sympathetic, at least neutral; then he heard in the background Dalziel's voice demanding who he was talking to and Wield explaining that it was Bowler who wasn't coming in because he was ill.

"Not coming in because he's *ill*?" said Dalziel with the amazement of a man who rated illness as an excuse for absence well below abduction by aliens. "Here, let me speak to him."

He grabbed the phone and said, "What's going off, lad?"

"Sorry, sir," croaked Hat. "You were right, I've got that flu-bug."

"Oh. My bloody fault, is it? What's that music I can hear? You're not in a night club with some totty, are you?"

"No!" cried Hat indignantly. "It's the radio. I'm in bed. By myself."

"Don't get uppity. Remember Abishag and David. Or mebbe not. He died, if I recall right."

"That's what I feel like," said Hat, playing for the sympathy vote. Then the faint bell he'd heard at Rye's rang louder. "Sir, there's something . . ."

"No last requests, lad. That's just gilding the lily."

"No, sir. It's just that, in that last Dialogue, wasn't there a bit about death at the end? Something about the best thing of all being never to be born?"

"Aye, that's right, got it here. So?"

"So, I know it probably means nothing, but I think that guy, Heine, the one Penn's translating, said something like that."

It was remarkable how distance lent courage. After Pascoe's discomfiture, he probably wouldn't have dared bring up poetry again to the Fat Man's face.

"Didn't realize you were a German scholar," said Dalziel.

"I'm not, sir. It's just that Rye . . . Miss Pomona at the library, well, Penn sometimes leaves stuff lying around where she can see it, by accident on purpose, so to speak . . ."

"Aye, I read that in the DCI's report. But I thought that were romantic stuff, trying to get his end away. How'd he get on to death?"

"Trying for the sympathy vote, maybe," said Hat.

This tickled the Fat Man's fancy and he laughed so loud Hat had to distance his earpiece.

"Aye, you can get a long way with the sympathy vote," said Dalziel. "But it only works on lasses, not on superintendents. Get well soon, lad, else I may come visiting with a wreath."

He put the phone down and returned to his office without speaking to Wield. There he sat for a little while deep in thought. He had to admit he was floundering. Well, he'd floundered before and always reached the shore, but this was more public than usual, and there were too many buggers out there eager to celebrate his drowning. Time to grasp a few straws.

He picked up his phone and dialled.

"Eden Thackeray, please. Nay, luv, don't give me crap about important meetings. He'll have just got into his office and he'll only be there 'cos it's quieter than home and he can smoke a cigar without his missus throwing a bucket of cold water over him. Tell him it's Andy Dalziel."

A moment later he heard the urbane tones of Eden Thackeray, Senior Partner though now officially semi-retired of Messrs. Thackeray, Amberson, Mellor and Thackeray, Mid-Yorkshire's most prestigious solicitors.

"Andy, you've been frightening my new receptionist."

"Part of the learning curve. How're you doing, lad? Still pulling the strings?"

"It gets harder. It's all right knowing, as you might put it, where all the bodies are buried, but the trouble is at my age it gets harder to remember."

"Trick is, not letting any bugger know you've forgot. Any road, I don't believe you. I'll give you a test. You're Lord Partridge's lawyer, right?"

"Indeed I am, but, Andy, as you well know, professional ethics do not permit—"

"Nay," interrupted Dalziel. "No need to lock your door and switch on your scrambler, I'm not after His Lordship. But, knowing you, I'd bet you'd know everything worth knowing about a big client like old Budgie, right down to his domestic staff, right?"

"Old Budgie? I didn't realize you were on such close personal terms with His Lordship, Andy."

"Old mates from way back," said Dalziel. "Now, what I'm interested in is, there's this German woman lives on the estate, used to be some kind of maid or cook or housekeeper . . ."

"You mean Frau Penck, mother to our own literary lion, Charley Penn?"

"That's the one. So, from your knowledge of her, how's she get on with Charley? OK to tell me that?"

"I suppose," said Thackeray judiciously, "that, as I act for neither of them, I am able, without commitment and off the record, to entertain such a question. Let me see. A fraught relationship, I would say. She thinks that Charley should be living with her, taking on the job of the head of the Penck household, vacated when her beloved husband died some twenty years ago. This would be the good old German way. She feels that he has forgotten his heritage and gone native. Not even his success as a writer counts too much. His books are not what in Germany is known as 'serious literature,' and besides, they are in English."

"She does speak English?"

"Oh yes, fluently, though with a strong accent which grows stronger if she does not wish to understand what you say."

"She got money?"

"Not that I know of. But she doesn't need any. The family place a high value on her, and she on them. She lives in a grace-and-favour cottage and seems content to remain there for the rest of her days."

"So how come Charley went to yon posh school, Unthank College? Old Budgie pay, did he?"

"His Lordship is not quite so profligate of his money," said Thackeray drily. "The boy won a scholarship. I'm not saying strings might not have been pulled, but he was, by all accounts, a bright child."

"And a rich one now, I dare say. Could easily set his old mam up in a nice house somewhere."

"Which I believe he has offered to do. I gather he regards the Partridge's grace and favour as cause for resentment rather than gratitude. His mother, however, tends to look upon England outside of the Haysgarth estate as an extension of the old East Germany, with people like yourself as lackeys of the English branch of the Stasi."

"So if a cop turned up asking questions about her Charley, how would she react?"

"Uncooperatively, I would guess. He would be transfigured into the perfect devoted son against whom she would not hear a word said, in English or in German."

"But if old Budgie or one of his chums spoke to her about Charley . . . ?"

"If it was implied that she should feel herself lucky to have mothered a son who'd done so well in the great outside world, she would very forcibly point out his shortcomings as a good German boy. I know this because when I first encountered her, I fell into this error."

"That's grand," said Dalziel. "Remind me I'm in the chair next time I see you at the Gents."

This was a reference not to an assignation in a public toilet, but to their common membership of the Borough Club for Professional Gentlemen.

"I don't suppose there's any point in my asking what you are up to, Andy?"

"Right as always, Eden. Cheers!"

Dalziel put the phone down, thought for a moment, then picked it up again and dialled.

"Cap Marvell."

"Hello, chuck, it's me," he said.

"Again? This is twice in a fortnight you've rung from work. Could I claim harassment?"

"No, them as I harass know they've been harassed," he said. "Listen, luv, got to thinking, I'm a selfish sod, not good for a relationship."

"Andy, are you feeling all right? You haven't had a fall, banged your head, seen a flash of very bright light?"

"And what I thought was, this hop of the Hero's out at old Budgie's, why don't we go? Long time since we tripped the light fantastic."

"Sorry, Andy. I'll have to sit down. I feel my vapours coming on."

"That's a date then? Grand. See you later."

He pressed the receiver rest, dialled again.

"Hello, Lily White Laundry Service, how can I help you?"

"How do, luv," said Dalziel. "Can you do a kilt for Saturday?"

When Pascoe arrived that morning, he reminded the others that Pottle and Urquhart were calling in later to review the latest Dialogue and give their considered judgment of the earlier ones.

"Oh God," said Dalziel. "Wish I were ill, too."

"Too?"

"Bowler's gone sick," explained Wield.

"It's a sick world," said Pascoe.

"Temperatures running high at home, are they?"

"Only metaphorically. Ellie and Charley Penn met to do the final judging for this short story competition last night. Sam Johnson should have been there too, so it wasn't exactly a cheerful occasion. She came home demanding to know why we hadn't got an inch closer to catching this madman."

"That's what you told her, was it?"

"She tends to go into a fit if I say things like enquiries are in progress and an arrest is expected soon."

"I thought they might have cancelled the competition," said Wield.

"Because one of the judges got killed? Doesn't work like that, Wieldy. All those aspiring Scott Fitzgeralds don't give a toss about Sam Johnson, whom they'd never heard of anyway. If it had been Charley Penn, it might have been different. As it is, far from cancelling the comp, Mary Agnew has been using the murder, all the murders, to get it a lot more publicity. Didn't you see last night's *Gazette*? She published the titles of the long short list—that's about fifty stories. And she's done a deal with John Wingate, the telly guy. All the short-list authors have been invited to the studio theatre in the Centre and the result is going to be announced in what used to be Jax Ripley's Saturday-night slot."

"Ripley's slot? God, bloody media will cash in on owt. They're probably going to charge folk for pissing in the bog where Stuffer Steel got topped!" exclaimed Dalziel. "I reckon if I live long enough, I'll see them bring back public hangings. Come to think of it, there's a few as I'd pay good money to see hanged."

Pascoe and Wield exchanged that blank glance through which over the years they had come to share amusement at the Fat Man's often outrageous illogicalities.

He appeared not to notice and went on, "Ellie tell you owt about the winner, did she? No doubt it'll be some blood-and-guts story, all about perves and kinky sex."

Putting aside the question as to whether this was a comment on public taste or his wife's predilections, Pascoe said, "Yes, she said that I'd probably be glad to hear that the winning story was a gently amusing little tale, almost a fairy story, which would leave children and adults alike feeling good about themselves."

"And Charley Penn went for that? Must have been sniffing lighter fluid. Who's the genius who wrote it?"

"That we shan't know till Saturday night when the winner's sealed envelope is opened. You coming along, sir?"

"You must be joking!"

"Not really. I just thought there could be a chance the Wordman might turn up."

"That's what you said about the preview."

"Actually it was Bowler who said that."

"Well, I hope he's not boasting about it," growled Dalziel. "And if chummy does turn up, you think this time he's going to wear his *I'm the Wordman* T-shirt, do you?"

"Who knows? Pottle said that as he gets more and more convinced of his invulnerability, he'll delight in taking risks. Anyway, I'll definitely be there, with Ellie being a judge."

"Oh aye? And you're worried the losers might turn nasty? Well, with the Wordman being so easy to spot, one pair of police eyes should be enough."

"Two pairs," said Wield.

"You're going?"

"Edwin likes to support local cultural activities."

This time it was Pascoe's and Dalziel's glances that met.

"If it's a local cultural activity," said Dalziel, "I've filled my quota for the month. Any road, Saturday night I'm going dancing."

"Dancing," said Pascoe, trying to keep all expression or interrogation out of the word.

"Aye. Man. Woman. Music. Rhythmic movement. If you've got your clothes on, it's called dancing."

"Yes, sir. And would that be salsa? Line? A rave? A hunt ball? A *thé dansant?*"

"That's for me to know and you to exercise your imaginations on," said Dalziel, rising. "Give us a shout when Pinky and Perky show up, will you? But if I'm dead, don't bother getting out the Ouija board."

He went out of the room.

"Not a happy man," said Wield.

"Probably saw that piece about him in the *Sun* this morning. Headline was 'WHEN DINOSAURS RULED THE WORLD.' He needs a result on this one pretty quick."

"Don't we all? You got any ideas?"

"Apart from herding everyone vaguely connected with the case into a field and beating them with a dead chicken till one of them confesses? No. Perhaps the dynamic duo from Academe will point us in the right direction."

"You reckon?" said Wield. "Think my money's on the dead chicken."

In the event, Urquhart turned up alone, Pottle having been overtaken by the rampaging virus which had laid low Rye Pomona and Hat Bowler. He sent in a written summary of his conclusions which didn't add a lot to what he'd said at the previous meeting. The Wordman was growing increasingly bold as each killing confirmed his sense of invulnerability. His purpose had clearly been to render Johnson defenceless by the drug before dispatching him by stifling. But when the lecturer had died without need of hands-on contact, this had been seen as yet another affirmation that he was on the right path.

"The Wordman is ruthless in performance, but not in retrospection," wrote Pottle. "The Dialogues are being held with three respondents. The first is the Underworld being who is at the same time both a shade of some individual and the Power which connives at this series of murders; the second is you, me, anyone reading the Dialogues, who will (he hopes) at the same time understand and approve his purpose, and admire and be baffled by his ingenuity; the third is himself. In the real world, as opposed to the timeless world of his ritual, he sees the victims as real people, not just necessary signposts on his mysterious path, and needs to persuade himself that they personally, or those who remain, benefit from their death."

Cautiously he refused to put down on paper any suggestion as to the kind of person they should be looking for but in a handwritten note invited Pascoe to give him a ring next week when he hoped to be recovered.

Urquhart appeared, more, it seemed to Pascoe, for the pleasure he got out of provoking Andy Dalziel than because he felt he had anything useful to contribute. Or perhaps it was that a lifetime of adopting anti-authoritarian attitudes had left him unable to offer assistance to the police directly so he slipped it in obliquely under the guise of mocking them.

And the Fat Man too, realized Pascoe in a flash of insight, actually enjoyed the bouts. His dismissal of the linguist as an over-educated underwashed blot on the Scottish escutcheon was an equally knee-jerk reaction. How much benefit he felt he derived from Urquhart's input was hard to guess, but he enjoyed the crack.

"So what've you got for us, Rob Roy?" he opened.

"Haud yer weesht, Hamish, and ye'll maybe find oot," replied Urquhart.

That was twice the Scot had shot *Hamish* at Dalziel like a custard pie, and twice Dalziel had looked momentarily spattered. Am I missing something? thought Pascoe.

What Urquhart had got for them wasn't much, and at least as literary as linguistic, which made Pascoe suspect his *wee hairie* in the Eng. Lit. Department was seeing more of the Dialogues than she ought to be. Well, as long as the leak stopped there and didn't trickle into the tabloids, no harm done, and they were getting two experts for the price of one.

"Pozzo said something about this guy and religion, didn't he? Not a religious maniac in the obvious sense, in fact probably totally a-religious on the surface. That's always the way with these trick-cyclists, isn't it? They give with one hand while they're taking away with the other, and in the end you're left with fuck all."

"Better a handful of fuck all than a handful of crap, which is all I'm looking at so far," growled Dalziel holding up a great paw as if in illustration.

"Me too," said Urquhart, staring hard at him. "Like I said, lots of religious language, both in tone and direct reference, but you've probably noticed that yourself, Mr. Pascoe."

Nice stress there, implying that I'm the police force's token literate, thought Pascoe.

"Yes, I did notice a few," he said.

"But one thing keeps on coming up. First Dialogue: 'the force behind the light, the force which burns away all fear . . .' Third: 'be the strength of my life; of whom then shall I be afraid . . .' Fourth: 'in the light of that aura, I had no one to fear . . .' Fifth: 'my light and salvation which is why I don't have to fear any sod.' I checked these out. And what I got was Psalm 27."

He produced a Bible and read, *"The Lord is my light and my salvation; whom shall I fear? the Lord is the strength of my life; of whom shall I be afraid?"* then looked around triumphantly, as if the silence which followed were tumultuous applause.

"Interesting," said Pascoe hurriedly. "May I see?"

He took the book from Urquhart and read the beginning of the psalm. Dalziel said, "And?"

"*And* me no *ands,* Andy," said Urquhart. "Except maybe I did wonder, looking at yon illustration in the First Dialogue, could that object in the bowl of the P be a book, maybe the Bible itself, or a missal in which you'd find the psalms?"

Pascoe put the Bible down and looked at the illuminated letter.

"You could be right," he said. "It could be the spine of book. But what about the design on it? Any thoughts on that?"

"Maybe it's meant to be the specific codex that contains the illuminated *In Principio* this is based on?" suggested Urquhart. "But you'd need a specialist to help you there."

Dalziel, who'd picked up the Bible to thumb through it, recited sonorously, " 'Of making many books there is no end; and much study is a weariness of the flesh.' Please, no more specialists."

"Aye, I can see how they'd be a bother to you," said Urquhart.

But he soon after brought his textual analysis to a conclusion.

"So it would seem to me that our wee Wordman could regard certain printed texts as a sort of coded gospel. *Here is wisdom. Let him that hath understanding,* sort of thing."

"That's Revelation, not a gospel," said Dalziel. "Let him that hath understanding count the number of the beast; for it is the number of a man."

"Now why am I not surprised you know that, Superintendent?" said Urquhart. "One last thing. In the Fifth Dialogue 'life became too great a bore . . .' that looks like a quote from the last letter that guy Beddoes poor Sam Johnson was researching wrote before he topped himself. 'Life was too great a bore on one leg and that a bad one.' Seems the poor sod had tried killing himself before and only succeeded in having a leg amputated. Him a doctor, too. Would have made a great NHS consultant from the sound of it!"

"That it?" said Dalziel. "All right, young Lochinvar, you can ride back into the west."

This time Urquhart let the Fat Man have the last word and as if in acknowledgement, Dalziel waited till the door had closed behind him before he said, "Another waste of fucking time!"

"I don't think so, sir," said Pascoe firmly. "We're building up a profile. And that last thing about the Beddoes quote, that tells us something."

"Oh aye? From what you said about your mate being a bit of a piss-artist, mebbe it means he died legless, too," said Dalziel.

"Very good, sir. But it means the Wordman must be quite well acquainted with Beddoes' writings. And I know someone who's deeply interested."

"Oh God, not Roote again!" groaned the Fat Man. "Give it a rest, will you?"

"Arrest?" said Pascoe. "That's exactly what I want to give him."

Dalziel regarded him sadly and said, "Pete, tha's beginning to sound like this Wordman. You ought to get out more. What is it the kids say nowadays? Get a life, lad. Get a fucking life!"

XXVIII

But getting a life isn't easy when there's so much death around.

On Saturday morning Pascoe woke, stretched, thought with pleasure, "I'm off duty."

Then recalled he was going to a funeral, his second of the week.

For a cop, weekends usually meant more rather than less work. Yet Pascoe, like a slave dreaming of home, had never lost an in-the-grain feeling that Saturdays were for football matches, odd jobs, partying, getting married, taking the family on a picnic, all that sort of good stuff. So, despite the fact that the pressures of the Wordman investigation were causing a huge contraction of official time off (without any proportionate expansion of official *paid* overtime), he'd clung on to his scheduled Wordman-free Saturday like a drowning man to a life-belt.

But Linda Lupin, Loopy Linda, had changed all that.

Murdered bodies, especially where poison is involved, are usually kept on ice until all parties with a forensic concern—police, coroner, DPS, and (if someone's in custody) defence counsel—are content that every last drop of evidence, incriminatory or exculpatory, has been squeezed from them. Fond relatives are advised to put their grief in cold storage too against the day of its proper obsequial display.

But when the fond relative is Linda Lupin, MEP, before whom even French officials have been known to quail, things may be arranged differently.

Her reasoning (which, as always, came carved on tablets of stone) was that her step-brother's death was already causing Europe to suffer one period of her absence and it was doubtful if it could survive another so soon following. Therefore the funeral must take place during her current stay, i.e. before next week when she purposed to return to her divine task of keeping the Continent fit for Anglo-Saxons.

And so it came to pass that Sam Johnson was buried on Saturday morning.

Linda would have preferred the finality of cremation, but here the coroner dug his heels in. The body must remain accessible. So the ceremony took place in St. Hilda's, the university church.

Official admission that Steel and Johnson were the Wordman's fourth and fifth victims was in itself enough to provoke the British media into a feeding frenzy of speculation and accusation, and the unexpected involvement of Linda Lupin was the ox-tail in the olio. The funeral could have degenerated into a cross between a pop-concert and an England away-match if the wise Victorian founders of the university hadn't extended the principle that any building likely to house students should be surrounded by high stone walls topped with shards of glass to include the church. University security guards, like a castle garrison in a siege, circumambulated the perimeter, pushing off the ladders by which the most depraved of invaders attempted to capture a view within, while a sharp radio message from the police soon took care of the helicopter which swooped, harpy-like, out of the low cloud cover above.

But local knowledge, like love, can o'erperch the highest walls, and as Peter and Ellie Pascoe made their way up the gravelled path towards the church door, what looked like a lapidary Death detached itself from a tombstone and revealed itself as Sammy Ruddlesdin.

"Time for a quick word, Peter?" he asked.

Pascoe shook his head and pressed on. Ruddlesdin kept pace with them.

"At least say if you're here in your official capacity or as a family friend," he insisted.

Pascoe shook his head again and went through the doorway into the church porch.

Ellie paused on the steps and hissed into Ruddlesdin's ear, "In which of his capacities would you like to be told to fuck off, Sammy?"

As she followed her husband, the reporter yelled after her, "Is that a quote, Mrs. Pascoe?"

She sat down next to Peter, kicked her shoes off and rested her feet on a hassock.

Pascoe murmured, "Thought I'd lost you."

"Just having a word."

"Oh hell. What did you say?" he asked in alarm.

"Nothing printable," she assured him. "I told him to fuck off."

"You didn't? You did. Bit rough, weren't you? It's only old Sammy."

She turned her head to look at him and said, "Peter, I don't know what capacity you are here in, but me, I've come to say goodbye to someone I'll miss, someone I regarded as a good friend, and that doesn't involve being polite to journalists, whether it's old Sammy or any of those other hyenas prowling around out there. So just let me get on with mourning, OK?"

"Fine," he said. "So you won't be assaulting Loopy Linda with a custard pie then?"

Linda Lupin was one of the Left's pet hate figures.

Ellie considered.

"No. Not till she's off holy ground, anyway."

One thing that even her many enemies had to acknowledge of Linda Lupin was that she had presence. Not even a coffin could upstage her. The solemn progress of the last remains of Sam Johnson up the aisle went almost unremarked as all gazes focused on the unexpected sister.

She was of stocky build, medium height, with cropped black hair, wide-set eyes which never seemed to blink, a long nose, a rubber mouth and a chin to break ice with. Yet she was not unattractive. Indeed a retired politician famous for his amours had confessed to getting more pleasure out of a recurring fantasy involving Linda and a cat-o'-nine-tails than real-life affairs with two or three women he most ungallantly named.

Her strength, thought Pascoe, was that in any company on any occasion she never for one moment showed doubt that she was the most important person present. Her current entourage, consisting of the university Vice-Chancellor and the senior members of the English Department all in their academic robes, looked like a Gilbert and Sullivan chorus doing their stiltedly intricate little routines behind the principal singer.

Indeed most of the chief mourners were university people, including several colleagues Pascoe had heard Johnson in his cups categorize as "plagiarizing plonkers who haven't had an original idea since they cut off their bollocks to see where their watery spunk came from." Two in particular he'd mocked for their alleged attempts to wheedle their way into his confidence so that they could gain access to his painstakingly acquired Romantic database. Well, perhaps now was their chance. He couldn't see Loopy Linda having much use for it, so presumably it would go to the most successful sycophant.

One absentee, whom he'd expected to see if not among the chief mourners, at least on the fringe of the group, was Franny Roote. He and Ellie were seated quite near the back of the church and the student/ gardener certainly wasn't in front of them. Odd, he found himself thinking. Then, recalling Dalziel's warning against obsessionalism, he firmly put the matter out of his mind.

The service got under way. The university chaplain, a young man who was almost brutal in his determination to avoid the old orotund style, gave an account of Johnson's life which, whatever it did to the traditionalists, moved Ellie to tears.

When he finished, the chaplain said, "And now, if anyone here would like to say something more about Sam, please come forward . . . We don't often get the chance to speak from the heart. Don't be afraid to take it."

He descended from the pulpit and took his seat below, gazing out with an encouraging smile at the congregation who, naturally, being British, lowered their eyes, shifted uneasily on their buttocks, and generally gave every sign of acute embarrassment.

Pascoe bowed his head in deep prayer, in fact in two deep prayers, the first being that Loopy Linda wouldn't seize the chance for one of her famous bring-back-the-bastinado rants. The second, and more fervent, was that Ellie wouldn't make a move. Believing that God helps those who help God, with his right foot he edged one of her discarded shoes out of her reach. Not that that would stop her. If the fit came on her, she was quite capable of advancing bare-footed, like a penitent of old.

He felt her muscles tense preparatory to rising. Then good old God at last showed his appreciation of his servant Pascoe's efforts to give Him a helping hand. Or foot. Somewhere behind them there was a susurrus of rising bodies and speculation as someone moved along a pew. Everyone turned to gawk, as if the "Wedding March" had just struck up to announce the bride's arrival in the church.

But Pascoe knew who it was before his eyes confirmed it.

Slowly, silently, the slim figure of Franny Roote advanced up the aisle and climbed into the pulpit. He was wearing his usual black, broken only by a tiny white cross which, despite its size, seemed to burn against his chest.

For a long moment, he stood looking down on the congregation, his pale face expressionless, as if gathering his thoughts.

When at last he spoke his voice was low, yet like an actor's whisper, it carried without difficulty to the furthermost corners of the silent church.

"Sam was my teacher and my friend. When I first met him, I was coming out of a bad time without any certain knowledge that a worse did not lie ahead. Behind me was a known darkness; before me was a darkness I did not know. And then, by human chance but, I am sure, by God's design, I met Sam.

"As a teacher, he was a light in the darkness of my ignorance. As a friend, he was a light in the darkness of my despair. He showed me that I had nothing to fear by going forward in search of intellectual knowledge and everything to gain by going forward in search of myself.

"I last saw him not long before his dreadful death. Our talk was mainly of matters academic, though as always other things were mixed in, for Sam didn't lock himself away in some elitist ivory tower. His domain was very much the real world."

He paused and his gaze flickered towards the array of academics surrounding Linda Lupin in the front pew. Then he resumed.

"I've tried to think of the things he said at that last encounter, for it is my belief that death, even when he comes—indeed perhaps especially when he comes—violently and unexpectedly, never comes without sending ahead messages that he is near.

"I know we certainly spoke of death. It is hard not to speak of him when discussing, as we were, Sam's favourite poet, Thomas Lovell Beddoes. And I know we spoke of death's mystery, and of the way our usual, though not our sole, medium of communication, language, by its very complexity often conceals more than it reveals.

"Did he have a premonition? I recall how he smiled, it seemed to me wryly, as he quoted a fragment from Beddoes:

> "I fear there is some maddening secret
> Hid in your words (and at each turn of thought
> Comes up a skull,) like an anatomy
> Found in a weedy hole, 'mongst stone and roots
> And straggling reptiles, with his tongueless mouth
> Telling of murder . . ."

(It seemed to Pascoe that as the man spoke the word *roots*, his eyes sought out Pascoe's and a faint smile flickered across those pallid lips. But perhaps he was mistaken.)

The man spoke on.

"Perhaps Sam was trying to tell me something, something he barely understood himself. Perhaps one day I will interpret that secret. Or perhaps I will have to wait till Sam himself interprets it for me.

"For though Sam did not subscribe to any organized form of religion, I know from our discussions that he had a deep belief in a life after death very different from but very superior to this grotesque bergomask we lumber through here on earth. In this, his soul was deeply in tune with that of Beddoes, and the book he was writing about him would have been a masterpiece of philosophy as well as scholarship.

"A few more lines of poetry, and I am done. Forgive me if they strike any of you as macabre, but believe me that they would not so have struck Sam. In fact he once told me that if he had the planning of his own funeral, he would like to hear these lines recited.

"So for his wish and my own comfort, let me speak them.

> "We do lie beneath the grass
> In the moonlight, in the shade
> Of the yew-tree. They that pass
> Hear us not. We are afraid
> They would envy our delight,
> In our graves by glow-worm night.
> Come follow us, and smile as we;
> We sail to the rock in the ancient waves,
> Where the snow falls by thousands into the sea,
> And the drowned and the shipwrecked have happy graves."

He stood as still as the carved eagle whose spread wings held the pulpit lectern, looking down at the congregation with a fierce intensity to match the bird's. The silence in the church felt more than mere absence of noise. It was as if they had drifted out of the main current of time into some byewater which promised a Lethean oblivion to any strong enough to reach over the side and drink. Then Roote himself broke the spell as he descended and walked back down the aisle, his shoulders hunched, his head bowed, no longer a commanding other-worldly presence but a waif and forlorn boy.

"Follow that!" whispered Ellie.

She was right, thought Pascoe, relieved. It would have taken an ego as insensitive as a politician's to stand up now and proclaim what must inevitably sound a more prosaic sorrow.

He saw Linda Lupin crane her head to follow Roote's progress down the aisle. Then she spoke sharply and urgently to the Vice-Chancellor.

Wanting to know who this weird creature is who's presumed to so disturb the even tenor of the funeral, thought Pascoe, wondering, not without a certain glee, what retribution for such impertinence she might be able to drop on to Roote from her political eminence.

After the interment, as people milled around the churchyard prior to running the gauntlet of journalists and cameramen lined up outside the gate, he saw that Loopy Linda had actually taken matters into her own hands and had Roote in her grasp and was pouring out her anger into his shell-shocked ear.

"See that," he murmured to Ellie. "I bet our Franny wishes he was back inside."

"What makes you say that?"

"Because anything must be better than oral acupuncture," said Pascoe.

But even as he spoke, the reason for Ellie's doubtful response penetrated as he saw Roote finally open his mouth in reply and something like . . . no, something that definitely was a smile broke out across Linda Lupin's face. They were having a conversation, not a row.

"I thought she'd be a straight up-and-down old-fashioned C. of E. Christian, help the deserving poor and sod the rest, no farting in church," he said, disappointed. "I was looking forward to seeing her tear Franny's head off."

"Where've you been, Peter? Our Linda is, naturally, a modern loopy touchy-feely, I-hear-voices kind of Christian. Her most recent loopiness is a deep involvement with the Third Thought Counselling movement . . . You have heard of Third Thought Therapy, haven't you?"

"Anything to do with Third Age, University of?"

"Only in terms of its target audience. Its subtitle is Hospice for the Soul. Some Belgian monk started it. Basically it's a raft of stratagems for coming to terms with death, bottom line being that you shouldn't wait till it comes looking for you but go out to confront it while you're still fit in mind and body."

"And Third Thought?"

"I know you rarely get past the sports page in your paper, but what happened to education?"

"Not Beddoes, is it?" said Pascoe.

That bugger kept on cropping up. The last line of Roote's tribute still echoed in his mind . . .

. . . and the drowned and the shipwrecked have happy graves.

Hadn't the First Dialogue talked about the drowned AA man having a happy grave?

"Don't be silly," Ellie said. "It's Big Daddy himself. Will the Shake. Prospero. 'And then retire me to Milan where Every third thought shall be my grave.' How could you not recognize that?"

"Not everyone had the advantage of playing Caliban in the school play," said Pascoe.

"Ariel," she said, punching him. "Anyway, Linda, it seems, met this monk and was bowled over by him, since when she has been advocating pumping large sums of Euro-dosh into the movement."

"But he's Belgian, you say?"

"Linda has nothing against foreigners so long as they don't want to tell us what to do, and of course acknowledge the superiority of the Brits, which this guy clearly did when he chose an English name for his therapy, though I suspect his reason was commercial, wanting maximum recognition on his website."

"A website in a monastery?"

"Peter, leave Dalziel's Disneyland for a while and try the real world."

"How come you know so much about Loopy?"

"Like the little red book says, know thyself, but know thine enemies a bloody sight better. But to get back to what we were talking about, far from dropping himself in deep doo-doo with Ms. Lupin by maundering on about graves and things, I think our friend, Roote, may have done himself a lot of good. You see, by a strange chance, the symbol of Third Thought is a tiny white cross, so Roote must be into it as well. Lucky boy."

"Lucky," spat Pascoe. "I doubt if luck had anything to do with it. Cunning little bastard!"

"Quote, Chief Inspector?" said Sammy Ruddlesdin, leaping out from behind a basalt angel. "You got a quote for me?"

"Sammy, why don't you fuck off?" said Peter Pascoe.

XXIX

By the time Saturday evening arrived, Pascoe would have paid cash money for the pleasure of stretching out in his favourite armchair and letting the inanities of weekend television lull him to sleep.

The call of duty demanding his presence at the short story result ceremony was growing ever fainter. Nothing was going to happen relevant to the Wordman enquiry and, in any case, Edgar Wield would be there to keep an eye on things. Even Ellie generously encouraged him to stay away.

"As a judge, I've got to go," she said. "No need for you to suffer though. Put your feet up. I'll cancel the baby-sitter."

He thought of all the tedious police social occasions she'd endured on his behalf and his conscience pricked him mightily.

"No, I'll go," he said. "It's not like it's the Oscars with acceptance speeches going on forever. How long is the TV spot? Half an hour?"

"That's it. Plus there's drinks before for distinguished guests and their undistinguished partners. Few snorts of the hard stuff and a bit of lively conversation might be just the thing you need."

"We'd better take a taxi then," said Pascoe.

But to start with, it looked like Ellie had got it entirely wrong. If anything, the atmosphere at the drinks party was slightly less lively than the university church that morning. The last time most of those present had been gathered together in the Centre, Councillor Steel had been murdered.

And enough of them had attended Sam Johnson's funeral for his death to darken their thoughts too.

But as with most wakes, two or three drinks eventually brought light and a dawn chorus of chatter, and though the first person to laugh out loud looked a little apologetic, soon the gathering was indistinguishable in jollity from any other party which isn't going to last long and where somebody else is paying for the booze. Who exactly, Pascoe didn't know. Probably the *Gazette*. It occurred to him that the only person to ask the question out loud would have been Stuffer Steel, keen to ensure the ratepayers weren't being ripped off. And Johnson might have been a little satirical too, though both of them would have made sure they got their share of what was on offer.

Not that anyone else seemed to be holding back. Nothing like the awareness of death for making folk grasp at life, thought Pascoe, looking round and counting heads. Yes, all the preview luminaries seemed to be here. Except of course those who were dead. And the dancing Dalziel. And the Hon. Geoffrey, or rather Lord Pyke-Strengler of the Stang, his full title now being due since, according to the papers, the sharks had left enough gobbets of his father to merit a small burial.

"So who's the winner, Mary?" Ambrose Bird asked the newspaper editor.

"I've no idea," said Agnew.

Bird cocked his head on one side, very bird-like, and said sceptically, "Come on, I'm sure you and dear Percy here have made damn sure no one's going to win who might bring a blush to your maiden cheeks."

This certainly made Follows flush, with irritation rather than embarrassment, but Mary Agnew laughed and said, "I think you're confusing me with some other Mary, Brose. It's true the winning story is a charming modern fairy tale, fit for children of all ages, but the two runners-up are a lot more gutsy. And it was Charley and Ellie here who selected them without interference from either Percy or myself."

"No interference from Percy? That must have been a blessing," said Bird.

"Some of us are capable of doing our designated jobs without sticking our long bills into other people's business," snapped Follows.

"Children, children, not in front of the adults," said Charley Penn.

Bird glowered at Follows, then forced a smile and said, "Charley, you certainly must know the name of the winner. How about a hint?"

"Wrong again, Brose," said Penn. "I know the name of the winning story and the pseudonym of the winner, but not his or her real name. Couldn't have found out even if I wanted to. Mary could make Millbank look like Liberty Hall, she's such a control freak. Seems every entry had to be accompanied by a sealed envelope with the story title and a pseudonym printed on the outside and the writer's real name and address inside. She kept the envelopes well away from the judges. In fact she's made rules about the rules. What it said in the *Gazette* was that no envelope would be opened till the decision had been made. But since the whole farce has turned into a mini-Booker with the results being announced live on the box, she and Spielberg there"—nodding towards John Wingate—"decided to screw up the tension by directing that none of the envelopes would be opened till tonight."

Pascoe and Wield exchanged glances. It wasn't strictly true. After the recognition that the Dialogues were fact, not fiction, every entry to the competition had been matched with its envelope, and in the half-dozen or so cases where the chosen type-face seemed to correspond with that of the Dialogues, the envelopes had been opened and the writers checked out. It had proved as fruitless an exercise as Pascoe had guessed it would be, but, like the PR handouts say, behind the apparent glamour of detective work lie hundreds of tedious hours spent in such necessary humdrum elimination.

The thought provoked a yawn and Wield said, "You should try sleeping a bit more often."

"I'd like to, but it's not in my job description," said Pascoe. "I'll maybe catch up when I retire."

"Like old George?"

"I think he's kept in practise. Sorry. That's not very charitable. And he's not been looking so well recently, has he? I hope he's not going to be one of those poor devils who look forward to retirement then when it comes, pffut!"

"Me too. I always had him down for a natural pensioner. Cottage in the country, potter around with his roses, write his reminiscences. Duck to water, I'd have said."

"Maybe it's started to hit him. Thirty-odd years it's been. Where did he see it all leading back then? Now here he is, wondering where it's all gone and how come all those paths of glory haven't led him to the gravy. He can't have planned to stop at DI."

"There are lower peaks," said Wield. "Like DS."

"Wieldy, I'm sorry, I didn't mean . . . hey, why am I apologizing, you know exactly what I meant and didn't mean! Like I know that some DSs are where they are because that's where they want to be."

For a long time it had been a matter of puzzlement to him that someone with Wield's abilities should show no enthusiasm whatsoever for promotion. He'd put the point to Dalziel many years back and got the terse answer, "Authority without exposure, that's what being a sergeant means," which only made sense when belatedly he became aware that Wield was gay.

"Mebbe George wanted to be where he ended," said Wield. "He's been a good cop. In fact, hearing what Mary Agnew said about them envelopes reminded me of what George said about the Wordman and the library. The Steel Dialogue was the first that didn't show up in a story bag sent round from the *Gazette*, right?"

"Yes, because the competition closing date had passed and there weren't going to be any more bags."

"But since then both the Steel and the Johnson Dialogues have been delivered direct to the library," persisted Wield, as if making a telling point.

"Which is why we've now installed our own state-of-the-art cameras to give us round the clock coverage of the library mailbox," said Pascoe, puzzled.

"I know that," said Wield patiently. "What I'm saying is we've assumed till now that the early Dialogues were all sent to the *Gazette* and only turned up at the library because they were taken to be entries for the story competition. If that's the way it was, and the Wordman's true choice of addressee for his Dialogues was the *Gazette*, why not keep on sending them there?"

"What's your point, Wieldy?"

"If George is right and there's a positive rather than just an accidental link between the Dialogues and the library, perhaps the early Dialogues were placed in among the entries after the bag got there."

"Maybe," said Pascoe. "But so what? Can't keep a watch on the bags now, can we, because there aren't any."

"No, but I'm thinking—the story competition closed on the Friday that Ripley did her broadcast and got killed. According to the *Gazette* post-boy, the last sack of entries was dropped off here about eight o'clock on Saturday morning. Yon lass with the funny name that Bowler fancies found the Dialogue in it at nine fifteen. Did anyone check the security videos for the time between?"

"Not on my instruction," admitted Pascoe. "Shit."

"Shit on all of us," said Wield. "But not a lot. If the Dialogue was put in the sack after it got here, chances are it was done during working hours by which time, courtesy the late Councillor Steel, most of the cameras would be switched off."

"Still should have checked, Wieldy," said Pascoe.

"Well, mebbe it's not too late. Think we'd be missed for a couple of minutes?"

Pascoe glanced round. Ellie was deep in conversation with John Wingate (probably kick-starting a telly career, he thought), while Edwin Digweed was refereeing what looked like the beginning of yet another schoolyard scrap between prancing Percy and the Last of the Actor–Managers.

"Shouldn't think so," he said.

They found the duty security man in his office which smelled strongly and illegally of tobacco smoke. At first he seemed disinclined to put himself out.

"Fortnight back, you say? No chance," he said. "Unless there's a reason not to, we just let the tapes run their course, then they rewind and get recorded over."

"Yes," said Pascoe. "But there's several hours of recording time on each tape, and unless there's something going on, like tonight"—he indicated the screen on which they could see a low-quality black and white image of the drinks reception they'd just left—"any individual camera might not be activated for days at a time."

"Yes, they will be," the officer defended. "We do our rounds, you know. Then there's the cleaners, they're here before the morning switch-off."

"Nevertheless," said Pascoe.

Beside him, Wield sniffed deeply and began coughing.

"You OK?" said Pascoe. "Funny how dry the air can get in these no-smoking buildings."

Five minutes later the security man had returned with a selection of tapes.

The tape covering the staff entrance to the Centre which was where the post-boy had delivered the sack was no help. This camera got activated so frequently—by people leaving the building late in the evening, and in the morning by cleaners, delivery men and early arrivals—that it only covered the previous week.

But they struck lucky with the tape from the reference library camera. The first date shown was over a fortnight ago, in the middle of the week running up to Ripley's murder. Pascoe watched the flickering screen closely and thought that Councillor Steel would have been pleased to see how conscientiously the security men and the cleaning staff performed their duties. The ratepayer was getting value for money here. And also from Dick Dee, it seemed. Twice he triggered the alarm as he emerged from his office well into the evening, once on the Thursday night and again on the Friday night when Ripley had been killed.

And now they were watching the cleaners on Saturday morning. They left. The camera switched itself off. And usually at some point shortly thereafter, as the security man explained, the whole system would be switched off till evening. But this time they struck lucky. When the picture crinkled back into focus, it was still Saturday morning, time 8.45.

"Sometimes the night-duty man forgets," said the security officer. "And it stays on till the day man notices. Doesn't happen often, but you get some dozy old boys in this game that really ought to be at home in bed."

He looked through the duty sheets, then hastily shoved them into a drawer. Pascoe guessed he'd found he was the dozy old boy in question.

But this could be a case of *felix culpa,* he thought as he watched the screen and saw Dick Dee appear with a mail tray in one hand and a plastic sack in the other. He put them on the counter and went into the office. The screen went blank.

"You still haven't got a camera in that office," he said accusingly.

"Not our fault, mate. Economies. Anyway, no one can get in there without going through the ref library. No windows, see?"

The picture returned as Dee emerged from the office. He pulled open the plastic sack, peered inside, made a wry face and turned his attention to the mail. But before he'd even begun to open anything, Percy Follows appeared. He didn't look pleased.

Pascoe recalled Rye Pomona's statement. The two men had been in the office, discussing Jax Ripley's broadcast when she arrived, she'd said, and she'd thought it best not to disturb them. Clearly the girl was a diplomat. Even without sound it was evident from Follows' expression that this was no friendly discussion. Dee on the other hand was unruffled and ushered his boss into the office, pushing the door almost shut and the camera was once more deactivated.

Then back to life. And now they hit paydirt. It wasn't, as he'd expected, Rye's arrival which started the tape rolling again. It was another figure, whom he recognized with what he was ashamed to acknowledge was a pang of delighted hope.

Franny Roote.

He stood by the counter, presumably listening to the heated debate going on within.

Now he reached into the battered briefcase he was carrying, took
something out—hard to see because it was on the wrong side of the
camera—glanced round as if to check there were no witnesses, pulled
open the plastic bag, and thrust it inside. Then he left. Total time elapsed,
fifty-one seconds.

"Calloo callay, oh frabjous day!" said Pascoe.

"Hang about," said Wield.

The picture had cut off. Now it came on again, time only a minute or
so later.

This time it was Charley Penn who'd triggered the camera.

He too seemed to listen, he too glanced round, less furtively than
Roote, his customary sardonic smile in place, then he too produced a sheet
of paper from his briefcase and placed it gently into the open plastic sack.

Oh shit, thought Pascoe. It never rains but it pours!

Now Penn moved out of shot, presumably to one of the work cubicles,
and the screen went black till it was re-energized by the arrival of Rye
Pomona.

She went behind the enquiry desk, paused as if listening to the row in
the office, stooped to place her shoulder bag under the counter, then
started opening the mail.

There didn't seem to be anything there which interested her and she
turned her attention to the sack. From it she took a single sheet of paper
which she examined for a moment before turning to look into the off-shot
body of the library. Her face was expressionless but she let the sheet slip
from her fingers which she then rubbed together, as if trying to rid them of
the traces of something noxious.

The picture went again with Rye still in shot and when it returned
they'd leapt forward to the security round on Saturday night.

"The day guy switched off," said the officer apologetically. "But you
look like you got what you wanted."

So much for my poker face, thought Pascoe.

"It'll do to be going on with," he said noncommittally. "Let's take another look."

They went through it again twice. It seemed quite clear that Roote had
put a sheet or sheets of paper into the sack, and with the kind of computer

enhancement available to them back at the station, they should be able to establish this beyond all doubt.

"Right, we'll take this with us, OK? You'll get a receipt."

"Sir," said Wield, as always sticking to protocol in face of even a single member of the public, "think we ought to be on our way."

Pascoe followed his gaze. It led to the screen showing the pre-awards reception. The room was now empty except for a couple of catering staff clearing up the glasses.

Pascoe's first instinct was to send Wield down to the studio to explain things to Ellie while he headed out in search of Roote, but as they hurried along the corridor away from the security room, the sergeant tried to dissuade him.

"You know what Roote's like, Pete," he said. "At least give Andy a bell first, get him on board. And there's Charley Penn to look at too, remember."

"Yes, but that looked like the sheet that the Pomona girl took out first and read," argued Pascoe. "Then she dropped it to the floor. She said something in her statement about finding some poem that Penn had translated, didn't she?"

"Yes, she did. And Penn said he must have accidentally left it on top of the sack when he went up to the counter. But it didn't look very accidental to me. And who's to say he couldn't have slipped the Dialogue in too and used the poem as a cover-story in case anyone did spot him?"

"Possible, I suppose, but unlikely. Anyway, we know where Penn is, he's here. It's the thought of Roote wandering round loose that bothers me."

But determined to show he was being sensible, Pascoe diverted to a part of the Centre where his mobile got a good signal. He tried Dalziel's home number. Nothing.

"Didn't he say something about going dancing?" said Wield.

He tried the Fat Man's mobile, still without success.

"Probably can't hear it over the clicking of the castanets," said Pascoe.

"He'll have to sit out some time, else the floor won't take it," said Wield.

This was calumny as they both knew that Dalziel's ability to trip lightly on the dance floor was indeed fantastic.

"We're wasting time," said Pascoe. "Roote could be out there killing somebody."

"What if he is? Where are you going to look?" asked Wield reasonably. "Best thing is to call up the station and get them to send someone round to check if he's in his flat and to keep a watch on it if he isn't. At least that 'ud save you a wasted trip."

"Very thoughtful of you, Wieldy," said Pascoe. "What you're really saying is I'm too partial and prejudiced to be allowed near him."

"No, but that's pretty well what Roote will be suggesting, isn't it?" said Wield. "Look, Pete, he's definitely got questions to answer. Maybe you shouldn't be the one asking them, not to start with, anyway."

"Bollocks," said Pascoe.

But he rang the station and did as Wield suggested, urging that he be contacted as soon as the officers sent had reported from the flat.

It took another ten minutes during which he and Wield didn't speak.

"No one there, sir," came the report. "How long do you want them to stay on watch?"

"As long as it takes," said Pascoe.

He switched off his phone, looked at the unreadable face of the sergeant and said with a sigh, "OK. You win. Let's go and make our apologies."

They'd arrived at the door of the studio. The tiered seats rose up steeply on three sides from the brightly lit shallow stage and it looked like a full house. Indeed the only empty seat he could see was at the front next to Ellie. She did not look pleased.

The length of time he'd been absent without explanation became apparent when suddenly there was a burst of applause and a cry of delight exploded at the back and a woman who didn't look much over sixteen jumped out of her seat crying, "It's me!" as the beam of a tight-focused spot swung across the audience till it picked her out.

She'd won third prize it emerged during a rambling and tearful thank you speech which out-Oscared the Oscars.

Wield said urgently, "Pete. End of row, left-hand wing, five rows back."

Pascoe counted.

"Thank you, God," he said.

Franny Roote was sitting there, dressed as always in black so that his pale face seemed to float out of the semi-gloom of the auditorium. An image came into Pascoe's mind from some poem read long ago of a condemned prisoner being led to his death through a press of spectators. Even at a distance it was impossible to mistake that pale face. So it was with Roote; except, if Pascoe had got it right, here was the executioner, not the executed.

On the acting floor, Mary Agnew was announcing the runner-up who had written a story which, if the judges were to be believed, plumbed the depths of man's inhumanity to man. The title and the pseudonym were read out, the envelope ripped open, and from the balcony came another delighted cry as a second woman, this one old enough to be her predecessor's great-grandmother, saw fame descend.

"Come on," said Pascoe as the audience applauded the newcomer onto the stage.

He hoped to slip unnoticed past Ellie, but failed. Her accusing gaze hit him like a sling-shot. He winced, smiled weakly, and pressed on up the aisle steps towards Roote.

"Mr. Roote," he murmured. "Could we have a word?"

"Mr. Pascoe, hello. Of course, always glad to talk with you."

The young man gazed up at him expectantly, the usual faint smile on his lips.

"I mean, outside."

"Oh. Couldn't it wait? This will be over soon. It's going out live, you know."

"I'd rather . . ."

Pascoe's voice faded under an outbreak of irritated shushing, and he realized the second-place winner was into her thank you speech. Fortunately age had taught her the value of economy and it had twice the style in half the length of number three's.

As she left the stage to renewed, and relieved, applause, Pascoe said firmly, "Now, please, Mr. Roote."

"Just a couple more minutes," pleaded the man.

Pascoe glanced round at Wield who shook his head slightly as if in answer to the unspoken question, How about I put him in an arm-lock and drag him out?

Below, Agnew was saying, "And now to our winner. The judges were unanimous in their choice. They said feel-good stories may not be popular in an age preoccupied with the seamier side of human experience, but when they are as beautifully crafted as this one, with a depth of humanity and a lightness of touch rarely found outside the great classical masters of the genre, then they are a reassuring affirmation of all that is best and most worthwhile in human experience. With a testimonial like that, I bet you can't wait to read the story—which you'll be able to do in the next issue of the *Gazette*. Its title is 'Once Upon a Life,' and its author's very fitting pseudonym is *Hilary Greatheart*, whose real name is . . ."

Dramatic pause while the envelope was torn open.

Roote stood up.

Pascoe, a little surprised by this sudden capitulation, said, "Thank you. Let's head out of the back door, shall we?"

Roote said, "No, no, I don't think you understand," and tried to push past.

Pascoe seized his arm, feeling a surge of deplorable pleasure that at last he was going to have an excuse to pass on some positive pain.

Then Wield seized *his* arm and said, "Pete, no."

And at the same time a great light exploded in both his face and his mind as the prize-winner's spot found them out and it registered that Mary Agnew had just proclaimed, ". . . Mr. Francis Roote of 17a Westburn Lane. Will you please come up, Mr. Roote?"

He let go and watched Franny Roote run lightly down the steps to accept his award.

"You OK, Pete?" said Wield anxiously.

"Never been better," said Pascoe, his gaze fixed unblinkingly on the brightly lit stage below. "At least we've got the bastard where we can see him. But I'll tell you one thing, Wieldy. If he mentions me in his thank you speech, I may run down there and kill him."

XXX

"... **putting on my** top hat, brushing off my tails," sang Andy Dalziel.

"Andy, you are not wearing tails," called Cap Marvell from her bedroom.

"Wasn't talking about me clothes," said Dalziel, looking down complacently at the kilt which encompassed his promontory buttocks.

Cap emerged from the bedroom.

"I don't like the sound of that. You *are* wearing something underneath that skirt, aren't you?"

For answer he lifted the kilt to reveal a pair of Union Jack boxer shorts and did a twirl.

Then he let his gaze run the whole length of the woman's body from the discreet diamond tiara in her hair down the deeply cloven wine-coloured silk evening gown to the silver diamante-edged shoes and said, "By gum, tha looks a treat."

"Thank you kindly," she said. "And you too, Andy. A treat. That I take it is your family tartan?"

"Doubt it. Don't think the Dalziels have their own so likely the old man chose this one to match his bonny blue eyes."

"So he wasn't a professional Scot, then?"

"No. A baker and a pragmatist. The kilt's the best garment in the world for three things, he used to say, and one of them was dancing."

"Dare I ask the other two?"

"Defecation and copulation," said the Fat Man. "Shall we go?"

"Yes, I'm ready. Andy, I'm really touched you said you'd come tonight . . ."

". . . but?"

"But nothing."

"I know a but when I hear one," said Dalziel. "But will I promise to behave myself, is that it?"

She laughed and said, "Don't be silly. Half the pleasure of going to my son's regimental ball is the chance to behave badly. I've been trying to embarrass him for years. I think he enjoys it. No, if there was a but it was: But I hope that for once there's no chance of work rearing its ugly head. This is one time I'd be really pissed off to find myself coming home early, or left to the tender mercies of baby-faced subalterns who treat me like their gran, or randy majors who think it would be a laugh to stick it to the colonel's mother."

"Any on 'em try that and it'll be piss-pots at dawn," said Dalziel. "I promised, luv, remember? No bugger knows where I'm at, and if you and the Hero don't mention what I do for a living, I certainly won't. Let the sojer boys think I'm your rich sugar daddy. As for being called out, I've not got a mobile or even a pager with me. You can search me, if you like."

He looked at her hopefully.

"Later," she laughed. "I look forward to searching you later. So that's a promise. You won't even be thinking about work."

"Nay, I never said that," he protested. "When I'm having the time of my life, you'd not deprive me of the pleasure of thinking about all those poor sods back here working their fingers to the bone."

"You don't really believe that, do you? When the cat's away . . ."

He smiled tigerishly.

"There's cats and cats," said Andy Dalziel.

As the taxi bearing Dalziel and his lady to the ball headed into the dark countryside, Peter Pascoe was feeling very much like a mouse, but a mouse being played with rather than playing.

After receiving his prize and making a touching little speech in which he dedicated his story to the memory of Sam Johnson, Franny Roote had returned to Pascoe and said, "I'm sorry I had to cut you short before. I'm all yours now if you still want me."

Tell him to sod off, thought Pascoe. Collect your wife and go home, there's nothing in this for you.

So the voice of experience spoke in his mind, but the mill of duty was grinding and could not so easily be switched off.

Ellie looked ready to hit him when he told her he had to go to the station, and when she realized it was on account of Roote, she turned and walked away, as if not trusting herself to speak.

Back at the station, Roote sat quietly while they played the security tape to him, then he smiled and said, "It's a fair cop. Does it mean I'm disqualified?"

"We're not talking driving offences here, Mr. Roote," snapped Pascoe. But his agile mind was already anticipating the man's explanation.

"Of course you're not. I meant from winning the prize. Look, it's silly, only I'd been shilly-shallying about putting my story in—you know how it is, you write something and it feels great at the time, then you look at it later and wonder how you could have imagined anyone would ever want to read it. I'm sure Mrs. Pascoe must have been through all this and more when she was writing her novel, which, incidentally I'm really looking forward to reading. Anyway, I woke up on Saturday knowing I'd missed the deadline and thinking what an idiot I was, and I got the idea of taking it round to the *Gazette* first thing and asking if I could have a special dispensation to add it to the others. Well, they told me there that the stories had already been sent round to the library for their initial sorting out by Mr. Dee and Miss Pomona. So I headed round to the Centre, I really don't know why, but I suppose I had some idea of throwing myself on Mr. Dee's mercy—he's such a nice man, isn't he? But when I got up to the reference library, I could hear him having a rather heavy discussion with Mr. Follows in the office, and there on the counter was this plastic sack, open, and I could see it was full of the competition stories. I think I went on auto-pilot then. I found myself thinking, Where's the harm, it's not going to win anyway, and I slipped mine in. I suppose that technically I broke the competition rules. On the other hand, the Friday night time limit was for submission at the *Gazette* office, and I wasn't submitting my story there, was I? Perhaps you could advise me here, Mr. Pascoe. I'm a child when it comes to the law and you're an expert, aren't you? I'm in your hands."

He held his own hands out before him as he spoke, as if to show there was nothing in them, and smiled ruefully.

Pascoe said, "Do you really imagine that I give a toss about this sodding short story competition, Mr. Roote?"

"It does seem rather strange. But I thought maybe because Mrs. Pascoe was involved in the judging, you felt a little protective of her reputation. I suppose, in a manner of speaking, this is her first professional engagement, and naturally you'd be very solicitous to see she got it right."

Leave it alone, Pete, urged Wield telepathically. *He's jerking you around like a hooked fish.*

He must have got through because the DCI, after a couple of the deepest breaths the sergeant had ever seen him take, terminated the interview and advised Roote that he was free to go.

"You did the right thing," said Wield after they'd seen him off the premises.

"Did I? I wish to hell I thought so," replied Pascoe savagely. "OK, he might have been slipping his story in late, but that doesn't mean he didn't put the Dialogue in too."

"True, but unless you can produce something to support that idea, all you've got here is the kind of daft story the press would go to town on. 'Cop bangs up wife's protégé. "A likely story," says top tec.' Plus everything from the past being raked up. That what you want?"

"You should have been a sub-editor, Wieldy," said Pascoe. "But I tell you, every time I see him walk away, I think, someone's going to pay because I found him too slippery to keep a hold of."

"You can't know that, Pete," said Wield. "But if you're right, he'll be back."

He *was* back, but a lot quicker than either of them anticipated.

Pascoe had just got home and was in the middle of a lively discussion about the evening with Ellie when the phone rang.

He picked it up, listened, said, "Oh Christ. I'll be there."

"What's happened?" said Ellie.

"I put a uniformed watch on Roote's flat and, in all the excitement, I forgot to cancel it. They've just brought him back in. They tried to release him again when they realized what had happened, but he's refusing to go till he gets my personal assurance that he can go to bed without fear of further disturbance. He says either I come or the press comes. This time I really am going to kill the bastard!"

At just about the same time, Dalziel was doing a Gay Gordons with enormous energy and a lightness of step which won universal applause.

"Don't know what he does to your ma, Piers," said Lord Partridge, "but he frightens the shit out of me."

Lieutenant-Colonel Piers Evenlode smiled a touch wanly, but at least he smiled. When he'd learned that his mother was bringing her frightful plod to the ball, his heart had sunk. On the whole she did her best to make sure that the, in his view, neo-Bohemian lifestyle she favoured did not impinge too much upon his military career. By reverting to her maiden name of Marvell, she drew no attention to him on the occasions when her various protest activities got her into the papers, and, to be fair, since she and this ton of lard had become an item, though unchanged in her attitudes and activities, she no longer seemed to seek the limelight in the old way. No, what he feared, more for her sake than his own, he reassured himself, was that Andy Dalziel's presence at the ball would render her an object of pity and ridicule.

And, he also admitted because he was a basically honest man, that some of the muffled laughter would be directed at himself.

His worst fears had seemed to be realized when he saw the kilt.

But in the event, the man had proved able to carry it, and he'd fielded all the attempted jokes at his expense with good humour and enough sharp wit to make the would-be mockers wary, and above all, far from looking ludicrous on the dance floor, he had moved with such grace and lightness that he was rapidly the partner of choice amongst the women who preferred real dancing to the close-quarters foreplay favoured by the increasingly tipsy soldiery.

That was another thing. Eschewing champagne, the man had consumed what must have been a whole bottle of malt without showing the slightest diminution of speech or motor control.

So perhaps, unless it turned out he'd got the stately home ringed by bobbies with their Breathalyzers at the ready, it was going to be all right after all.

The dance finished and Dalziel led Cap off the floor to where her son was standing.

"Refill, luv?" he said.

"No thanks, I'm fine," she said.

"Summat to eat, then?"

"No, really."

"Think I'll have another nibble," he said. "Need to keep my strength up if I'm going to be searched later."

With a wink at Piers, he moved away.

"Searched?" said Piers, alarmed, recalling his fantasy about a ring of cops watching the house. "What's he mean?"

His mother looked at him fondly.

"Darling, you don't want to know," she said.

In the buffet room, Dalziel looked around till he saw what he was looking for, a white-haired woman with a strong-jawed, rather severe face who was keeping a close eye on a flock of young helpers.

"How do, luv," said Dalziel, approaching. "Any more of that lovely *Sahnetorte?*"

She looked at him with interest and said, "*Sie sprechen Deutsch, mein Herr?*"

"Just enough to ask for what I like," he said. "And I like that cream cake. Best I've had since last time I were in Berlin. Where do you get it round here? It 'ud be worth a long trip."

"We do not get it," she said scornfully in heavily accented but perfectly clear English. "I make it."

"Nay! Well, blow me. You make it yourself! Now, hang on, I bet you're Frau Penck, the treasure old Budgie was telling me about."

"His Lordship is very kind."

"Didn't he say you were Charley Penn's mam?" Dalziel went on. "By God, making cake like that and being Charley's mam, you've a lot to be proud of. Always talking about the lovely cakes his old *mutti* makes, is our Charley."

"You know my son?" she asked.

"Aye, do I. Often have a drink with him on a Sunday lunchtime, but he usually has to cut it short, to go and see his old mam, he always says. Well, I can see why he rushes off now. It must do you good to know that someone as important as Charley puts you top of his list when it comes to choosing what to do. He's a big man, tha knows. He can pick and choose his company. It's incredible the way he's succeeded. More British than the Brits! You'd never know he weren't a bred-in-the-bone Yorkshireman. You must be right proud to think you can get a man like this to come running just by snapping your fingers."

She did not reply to this but gave him what Dalziel thought of as the universal female significant look which implied that her lips were sealed but if they weren't, then she might have something to say which would bowl him over.

He pressed on.

"Last Sunday, I recall, it were my birthday and I was pushing the boat out a bit, and I tried to persuade Charley to hang on a bit longer to have a spot of lunch in the pub. They do a lovely sticky toffee pudding there, but when I tried to tempt Charley, he said it couldn't compare with the sweets his old mam would have ready for him. He's always talking about the grub he gets every Sunday when he visits you. Well, now I know why. Go on, make me mouth water, what did you give him?"

"Last Sunday? Nothing," the old woman said.

"Nothing? Not even *Sahnetorte*?" said Dalziel, amazed.

"Nothing at all. He did not come. It was no matter. I do not expect him. He comes when he will."

"You're sure he weren't here last Sunday?" said Dalziel, looking at her doubtfully.

"Of course I am sure. You think I am senile?"

"Nay, missus, I can see you're not that. My mistake, he must have said he was going somewhere else. Now, about the cake . . ."

"I think you'll find it's over here, Andy," said Cap Marvell.

He turned. She was standing regarding him with the kind of expression he'd expect to be printed on his own face if he heard a known villain, caught with his hand in a church poor-box, claiming he was making a contribution.

"Oh aye. So it is. Nice talking, missus. I'll give your love to Charley."

"So," said Cap as they moved away, "this is how you leave your work behind, is it?"

"Nay, lass, I were just passing the time of day . . ."

"Lying about your birthday? That's bollocks, and I've got a great eye for bollocks."

"Well, you've had the practice . . . Jesus, that hurt!"

"Next time it won't be your ankle I kick. Let's have the truth."

"It's nowt really . . . just a notion I got about Charley Penn. He said he were out here visiting his mam last Sunday afternoon when Johnson got topped. Young Bowler checked her out and she seemed to say that Charley were never away. Just thought when I bumped into her that I'd have a little chat, double check. No harm in that, is there?"

She considered then said, "Bollocks again. I don't think you bumped into her because you came to the ball, you came to the ball so that you could bump into her. And that was because you reckoned that with her background when Frau Penck found herself being questioned by the police about her son, she probably clammed up tighter than a virgin's valve. On the other hand, talking to an old chum of *Budgie's* who's escorted the colonel's mama to the regimental ball, she could let all her resentment at being neglected by her Anglophile son hang out."

"Virgin's valve? Don't know where you pick these expressions up from," said Dalziel reprovingly.

"Sod the expression. What I've said is the truth. Admit it or I'll push that *Sahnetorte* into your face."

Dalziel looked down at the huge portion of the cream cake he'd just helped himself to and said, "Funny, but that's just what I were going to do. Nay, hold on there, I'm admitting, I'm admitting. OK, it mebbe helped tip the balance, but I'm bloody glad it did. I'd not have missed this for the world. I'm having the best time of my life."

"That's as maybe, but you've used me, Andy."

"Well," he said judiciously through a mawful of whipped cream, "you've never complained before. Any road, it's nearly the sabbath. Good day for forgiving is the sabbath."

"Oh, I forgive, but I won't forget. You owe me one, Andy Dalziel."

"Don't worry, luv," he said. "Afore the night's out, I intend giving thee one. Hey, listen, they're playing a tango. Let's go and show these tin soldiers how to do it!"

And as Dalziel escorted his lady on to the dance floor, Peter Pascoe escorted Franny Roote out of the police station.

"Let me say again how sorry I am about this misunderstanding, Mr. Roote," he said. "A simple breakdown in communication, I'm afraid."

"That's what lies at the root of most human problems, isn't it, Mr. Pascoe?" said the man earnestly. "A simple breakdown in communication. If only words always did what we want them to. Goodnight."

He climbed into the police car provided to take him back to his flat, smiled up at Pascoe through the window and gave a little wave as the vehicle moved off into the darkness.

Pascoe watched it go.

"I think words always do exactly what you want them to do, Franny, my boy," he murmured. "*The root of most human problems.* Oh yes, that fits you to a tee. But I shall pull you up out of the earth before I'm finished and consign you to the bonfire like any other noxious weed. I shall. I shall. Believe me, I shall!"

He went to his own car, climbed in, and drove home.

XXXI

"My God," **said** Rye Pomona as she opened the door. "The birdman cometh!"

"What?" said Hat Bowler, his face darkening.

"What *what*? It's called a joke. Or is there some rule which says twitchers' gear mustn't be a source of merriment?"

Hat, though he felt rather dashing in a Great Outdoors windswept sort of way, was more baffled than offended by this reference to his camouflage forage cap, RSPB tanktop and moleskin breeks. Then his error dawned on him.

"Sorry. You said *birdman*. I thought you said *Wordman*, which I didn't think was very funny. . . ."

"Which indeed it would not have been, had I indeed said it," replied Rye coolly. "Is there anything else I haven't said which you would care to be offended by?"

This wasn't the start he'd hoped for, thought Hat. Time to regroup.

"You look great," he said, running his eyes down her yellow top and burgundy shorts. "The birds will be watching you."

She made a face like she'd just sucked a lemon, which was not the optimum reaction to what had in the past been a pretty successful chat-up line but nonetheless preferable to chilly reproach.

"You'd better come in before someone sees you and sends for help," she said. "As I suspect you've guessed, I'm not ready. You're early, aren't you?"

He followed her into her flat. There were old movies, he recollected, where a guy drove up to a girl's front door, blew his horn, and watched her come running down the steps, big smile on her face, hoping she hadn't kept him waiting. But this was a recollection he thought better to keep to himself, as was the observation that no, he wasn't early, but so dead on time you could have set a nuclear clock by him.

He sat down and said, "Hey, I saw you on telly last night."

"You did? You must have sharp eyes."

"Twitchers' eyes," he said. "Spot a redwing at three hundred paces. By the way, don't know if it's the same for girls, but my mother used to tell me to be careful pulling funny faces or I might stop like that."

That worked. The renewed sour-lemon look vanished to be replaced by a broad grin.

"You think it's easy scowling when what I planned was . . ."

"What?"

"Something like this."

She stooped over him and kissed him on the lips, lightly but with a definite hint of tongue.

This was even better than smiling girl running down the steps to the car.

She said, "I'll be with you in a couple of minutes."

He watched her go into what he presumed was the bedroom and fantasized about following her. Decided no. That kiss was encouraging but not an invitation. Besides, these moleskin breeks were hell to get out of in a hurry, and in the distant future he wanted their first time to be replayable for passion not for laughs.

The distant future.

Why was he so certain they were going to have a distant future together in which to remember a first time?

Because he couldn't imagine any kind of future apart.

"So what was that all about last night?" she called to him through the partially open door.

"All what where who?"

"Don't be coy. All that with your two colleagues, Dorian Gray and the attic."

He worked this out.

"DCI Pascoe and Sergeant Wield," he said. "You mean at the presentation?"

He'd seen it on TV. And he'd got a detailed background when he called in at the station that morning, thinking, with the kind of logic he'd have probably laughed at in a woman, that after a couple of days on sick leave it might be well to establish that he was recovered sufficiently to take his day off.

"You see, you do know all what where who," Rye said from the bedroom. "When that creepy guy Roote came up to get his prize, I saw beauty and the beast watching him like they'd have preferred to be massaging his extremities with a cattle prod. At least, that's how the good-looking one looked. The other always looks like that, I guess."

"Well, there's a bit of a history there," said Hat.

She came out of the bedroom. The top and shorts had been replaced by jeans and a chunky brown sweater and her crown of hair tucked into a drab green beret.

"Will the birds still be watching me?" she said challengingly.

"Only if they've any sense," he said.

She nodded and said, "Good answer. So what's this history, and what had been going on last night to hot things up? Was it something to do with the security cameras?"

"How the hell do you know that?" he demanded.

"That ugly sergeant started asking me questions again about the morning I found the Ripley Dialogue. But what he seemed particularly interested in was me finding Charley Penn's translation of 'Du bist wie eine Blume.' It felt like he'd been watching me and the only way I could figure that was, the camera must have been on. If that's right and you lot have only just realized, it looks like someone's been sleeping on the job, eh?"

"What did Wield say about Penn?" asked Hat, trying to keep his voice neutral.

"Not a lot. He's not exactly effusive, is he? I suggested leaving poetry lying around was an oblique form of sexual harassment which he might care to investigate, and I think he smiled but it might just have been wind."

"But he didn't actually mention the tapes?"

"No. I worked that out all by my little self."

"Clever," he said. "Really. I'm not taking the piss."

"Yeah. Well, I did sweet-talk Dave, the security man, just to be sure," she admitted. "So come on. Fill me in on Franny Roote and your DCI."

It did not seem a good time to plead police confidentiality, and besides he was in so deep sharing Wordman stuff with Rye that it was easier to go on than pull back, so he told her about Pascoe's fraught relationship with Franny Roote.

"When I saw him going up to the stage last night, I was gobsmacked," he said. "Especially after what they'd said about the winning story. Didn't sound like him at all. . . ."

"Like your Mr. Pascoe's version of him, you mean?" she said.

"I have met him myself a couple of times," said Hat defensively. "And you called him creepy."

"Yeah, but I meant it sort of literally. He gets in the library sometimes, and he moves so lightly, you never know he's there till suddenly he's next to you. So Pascoe fancies him for the Wordman? Hey, I've just thought. His wife was helping Penn to judge, wasn't she? Co-operating with one suspect to give the prize to another! I bet Pascoe was delighted about that. I bet they lay awake all night chuckling about it."

"She wasn't to know, was she?" said Hat, who was an Ellie Pascoe fan. "You must have read the story. How did it sound to you?"

"Good," she admitted. "Dick thought it was the tops. I wasn't quite so enthusiastic, but I did think it was good. Moving, you know. Lot of uplift. Not really my thing."

The seed of a quip about a girl with a figure like hers not needing a lot of uplift spurted across his mind but died before it got close to ejaculation.

"Well, it seems what actually happened last night was this . . ." said Hat, who when he gave his trust didn't care to stint.

It was Wield who'd filled him in. He'd have probably preferred to keep the whole business low-key but the way things panned, this hadn't been an option. The story of Roote's return visit was being told all over the station with advantages, and it seemed sensible to give Bowler a full account, to help set the record straight.

"It's not CID at its best, but it's a lot better than some of the versions that are fluttering about," concluded the sergeant. "You hear them, you stamp on them, OK?"

"OK," said Hat. "What's the super's reaction to all this?"

"Mr. Dalziel must have danced himself off the ground," said Wield. "He's not been seen yet. But no doubt he'll appear shortly. And if you want to enjoy your day off, lad, I'd advise you to make yourself scarce. The super has a tendency to count days spent on sick leave as normal rest days."

All this Hat now told Rye who frowned and said, "He does sound a bit weird."

"Roote?"

"No. This Pascoe. I thought when I met him that this was one tightly held together guy."

"Perhaps he needs to be. He feels threatened."

"That's it, isn't it? He *feels* threatened. From what you say, there haven't actually been any threats, have there?"

"No. But this Roote's something else. I can see how he could threaten you without actually threatening you, if you know what I mean."

She looked at him quizzically and said, "You're a loyal man, Constable Bowler. Decided what you're going to do about Georgie Porgie yet?"

That had been something else Wield had said. There'd been two or three more phone calls from Angela Ripley. Wield himself had taken one and, according to him, she didn't sound altogether persuaded that Hat was really sick. The sergeant paused to allow explanation but when it didn't come, he didn't press. And he'd said absolutely nothing about talking to Rye about Charley Penn.

Discretion or distrust?

"Cat got your tongue?" said Rye.

"Sorry. Nothing is what I'm going to do about the DI," said Hat defiantly. "Angela Ripley will be on her way back to the States today. I don't see any reason to muck up George's retirement party."

Suddenly she kissed him again.

"And you're a very nice man too," she said. "Let's go and look at some birds."

It was a day of sun and light showers with a brisk west wind driving clouds down the sky and swirling leaves across the road in the MG's path. He'd kept the hood up because of this but Rye had said, "Can't we have it down?" and now as they sped along, she pulled off her beret and leaned her head back with eyes closed and such an expression of sheer delight on her face that now the dancing leaves seemed to Hat like rose petals scattered before a marriage procession.

Watch it, son, he mocked himself, or she'll have you writing poetry next, you whose appreciation of verse never got much beyond "The Good Ship Venus."

The thought was mother to a couplet.

> *I went out with Raina.*
> *By God, you should have seen her.*

He laughed to himself but she noticed.

"Come on," she said, having to shout above the rushing air. "Today we share."

He told her. It didn't sound all that funny but it got a full-throated laugh.

Encouraged, he said, "Seeing it's share time, how about the story of your life? How come you're a librarian?"

"What's wrong with librarians?" she demanded.

"Nothing," he assured her. "Bit of an image problem, maybe. All I meant was you, with your background and looks and everything, how come you didn't end up in the theatre? I mean, Raina Pomona, if ever a name looked custom-built for bright lights, that must be it!"

She said something but the wind caught it and whirled it away.

"Sorry?" he shouted.

"I said, once upon a time, maybe . . . but that was in another country and besides, the wench is dead."

She laughed as she said this, not like before, but this time with an edge as bright and sharp as the wind that was rippling the silver blaze in her hair like a pike in a dark mere.

"You OK?" he said. "Do you want the hood up?"

"No," she cried. "Of course not. Doesn't this thing go any faster?"

He said, "How fast do you want to go?"

"Fast as you like," she said.

"OK."

They were off the main road now and on to narrow country byways. He leaned his weight into the accelerator and sent the hedgerows blurring by. He was a good driver, good enough to know that he was driving too fast, not for the bends in the road—those his technique could deal with—but for the unexpected which might lie in wait around any one of them.

But Rye was leaning against him, her right arm round his shoulders, her left hand gripping his forearm tight, her mouth so close to his cheek that he could feel the warmth of her breath mingling in the cold blast of air which their speed was driving in their faces.

He took a long left-hand curve, shallow enough to present no problems or even require any diminution of speed, but as the car came out of the bend, a deer jumped over the hedgerow on the right, paused long enough to register their approach, then bounded effortlessly into the field on the left.

Probably there was no risk of collision but instinctively his foot hit the brake, only for a second, but with the car still off-line and a scatter of wet leaves on the road, it was enough to set up a skid. As skids go, it was nothing, the kind of thing he could control in his sleep. But the road was narrow and the offside wheels were on to the grass verge in the brief moment before he regained full control. Fortunately the ground wasn't boggy and there was no ditch, but it did make the whole thing a little more dramatic as hawthorn branches whipped across the windscreen and their faces before he brought the car to a halt which threw them forward against the seat belts.

"Well, that was fun," said Hat. "Thank you, Bambi. Shit! Rye, are you OK?"

For the girl's response to his attempted lightness was to let out a piercing cry of pain and collapse forward, sobbing convulsively.

He released his seat belt and turned to her.

"What's happened? Where's it hurt?" he demanded, looking for but not finding any signs of bleeding.

"It's all right," she gasped. "Really . . . there's nothing . . ."

Gently he raised her head and looked into her face. There was no colour in her cheeks and her eyes were full of tears, but he felt no physical response as his fingers touched her neck and collarbone in search of damage.

She took several deep breaths, knuckled the tears from her eyes, and said, "Honestly, before you start getting too gynaecological, I'm OK."

"You didn't sound OK."

"Shock."

"Yeah?" He looked at her doubtfully.

"What?"

"A little skid. Over in a second. You don't seem . . ."

"The type?" she completed. "So suddenly you know all about me, do you, Detective?"

"No. But I'd like to. After all, it was you who said that today was for sharing."

"I said that? Yes, I believe I did."

She opened the door and got out and stood there, stretching as if it were bed she'd just got out of.

Then she turned to him and said, "Didn't you promise to provide the provisions for this expedition? Would that include coffee? Because if it does, that's certainly something I've no objection to sharing."

XXXII

They climbed through the hedge into the little copse that the deer had emerged from and sat drinking their coffee with the gnarled bole of a beech tree between them and the wind.

Hat said nothing, but suddenly she started to talk as if in response to a question.

"Yes, I did want to be an actress. Like you said, what else would I want to be, you know, born in a trunk, all that crap? Serge—my twin Sergius—he reacted the other way. He wanted to be a lawyer. All the drama, he used to say, and twenty times the money. I suppose I looked at the great stars while he just looked at Mum and Dad."

"They weren't all that successful, then?" said Hat.

"They seemed to work pretty steadily while we were young. And they always talked about the past as if they'd been really big once and, with a bit of luck, would make it to the top again. But by the time I got into my teens, even the steadiness was going. There were long periods of resting, which they seemed to do best with a glass in their hands. Every couple needs a common interest to keep them together. Theirs was drinking."

"Seriously?"

"They were drunks," she said flatly. "It was good in one way. Being neglected by your parents simply because they're so self-centred you don't rate is hard for a kid to take. But being neglected because they've got a drink problem makes some kind of sense. Anyway, I was stage-struck and planning to go to drama college after I left school, and I did a lot of ama-teur stuff and I even got a toe-hold on the pro theatre, crowd scenes and walk-on juvenile parts. What I thought of as my really big break came when I got the part of Beth in a stage version of *Little Women* being done as a summer show in Torquay which was where my parents were resting at the time."

"A big break?" said Hat. "How big?"

"I was only fifteen, for God's sake," she snapped. Then, realizing belat-edly his query rose from genuine interest and had nothing of sneer in it, she smiled apologetically and said, "I mean, it seemed huge to me. And it was a nice part, long way off a lead, but I got to be interestingly ill."

"I can vouch you're pretty hot stuff at that," said Hat, recalling her opening the door to him when he paid his sick-visit.

"Thank you kindly," she said. "Anyway, my big opening night came and my father was supposed to be driving me to the theatre but he sud-denly announced that he couldn't make it and my mother would have to take me instead. Serge got into a shouting match with him, asking him what the hell could be more important than going to my first night and Dad gave him some hammy speech about how nothing but the most ur-gent business affecting the prosperity of the whole family could make him miss such an occasion and if there was any chance of his getting away to catch even the briefest glimpse of his little girl on the stage, he would do it. Then he was gone."

"That must have made you happy."

"To tell the truth, Serge was a lot more fired up about it than I was. I wasn't going on the stage to impress my dad, it was all those other people, those strangers, that I wanted to bowl over with my talent. But I did need a lift, and when the time came and I found Mum stoned out of her mind, then I really blew my top. Serge calmed me down and rang a mini-cab. The time came, and it didn't. We rang again. There'd been some kind of traffic hold-up, it would be with us soon. It wasn't. Now I *was* getting hysterical. And Serge appeared with my mother's car keys and said, no problem, he'd drive me."

Hat began to see where the story was going.

He said softly, "He was how old? Fifteen?"

"That's right. My twin and by coincidence the same age. You ought to be a detective."

"Sorry. I meant, he couldn't have a licence. Could he drive?"

"Like all fifteen-year-old boys, he thought he could," said Rye. "We set out. I was late, not so late it was a real problem, but in my state of mind I played up like I was some prima donna late for a Royal Command Performance. I yelled at him to drive faster. It was a wet murky evening. Faster, I screamed, faster. He just grinned and said, 'Fasten your seat-belt, Sis. It's going to be a bumpy night.' Those were the last words I heard him say. We went round a bend too fast, got into a skid . . . it all came back just now when you had to brake . . ."

Hat put his arms around her and held her. She leaned into him for a while then straightened up determinedly and pushed him away.

"We went straight into a car coming the other way," she said in a flat voice, speaking very quickly as if this was something she had to say but wanted to get over. "There were two people in it. They were both killed. Serge died too. As for me, I remember the skid, and I remember lying there on a pavement—outside a churchyard, would you believe?—looking up at the night sky . . . then I don't recall another thing till I woke up in hospital over a week later."

Hat whistled.

"A week? That must have been heavy damage you took."

"Yeah. Broken this and that. But it was my head that caused the most concern. Fractured skull, pressure on the brain. They had to operate twice. By the time they got that sorted, the rest of me was just about knitted to-gether."

As she spoke her hand had gone involuntarily to the silver blaze in her hair.

Hat reached out and touched it.

"Is that when you got this?" he asked.

"Yes. I was shaved completely bald, of course, but they assured me it would all grow back. Well, it did. Except that for some reason which they explained without explaining their explanation, if you know what I mean, the hair over the scar came out like this. They suggested I should dye it, but I said no."

"Why?" asked Hat.

"Because of Serge," she said flatly. "Because I hate visiting graveyards, all that morbid crap, but as long as I've got eyes to see myself in the mirror, I'll never forget him."

Hat looked at her with troubled eyes and she said, "I'm sorry, I'm mucking up our day. I shouldn't have told you any of this, not now anyway. I've never talked about it to anyone else, except Dick."

Even in the midst of her unhappiness and his empathy, some selfish gene felt that as a blow.

He said, "You told Dick?"

"Yes. He's like you, not pushy. Questions are easy to duck, but the weight of non-questions from people you like becomes unbearable. He just listened, and nodded, and said, 'That's hard. I know about losing someone young, you're never happy again without recalling they're not there to share your happiness.' He's very wise, Dick."

Me too, thought Hat. Wise enough not to let my jealousy show!

But he must have looked pretty unhappy because suddenly she smiled broadly and said, "Hey, it's OK. That little skid back there shook me up a bit, but really, I'm fine now. My own fault for showing off to myself that fast cars don't bother me. Which they don't. And to prove it, let's get going before all those birds head south for the winter."

She stood up, reached down her hand and hauled him to his feet too.

He didn't let go of her hand but held it tight and said, "You're sure? We can easily head back to town, spend the day watching telly or something."

"I won't ask you to interpret *or something*," she said. "No, I promised to twitch and twitch I will, as soon as I get my hand back."

They got back into the car.

As they pulled away, Hat said, "So what did happen to the acting career?"

"Career's putting it a bit strong," she said. "Thing was, when I finally got back to normal after about six months, I found it had all gone, all that ambition, all those dreams. I'd lost Serge and now I could see beyond all doubt what a sad pair my parents were. Incidentally, it came out later that the urgent business my father had to attend to that night was banging away with some stage-struck groupie who believed all his name-dropping big-time luvvie stories. It wasn't a life I wanted to have anything to do with any more."

He said, "So this is why you sounded so cynical when you were telling me about your name?"

"About finding out they'd lied about the parts they were playing? Yeah, that just seemed to confirm it. Even their real life was an act and the only way they could deal with their children was by making them bit players."

"So you chose another role entirely."

"Sorry?"

"Librarian. Traditional image is about as anti-luvvie as you can get, isn't it? Quiet, demure, rather prim, glaring at noisy readers over horned-rim specs, staidly dressed, a bit repressed . . ."

"This is how you see me, is it?"

He laughed and said, "No. All I mean is, if that was what you were aiming at, someone ought to tell you you've missed by a Scots mile."

She said, "Hmm. I'll take that as a compliment, shall I? So now we've got me sorted, let's turn the spotlight on your interesting bits."

"I'll look forward to that," he said. "But tell you what, we're nearly there. So rather than risk frightening the birds, let's leave my interesting bits till after lunch, shall we? Then I'll be happy to let you pick over them to your heart's content."

"OK, but just tell me one thing first," she said as the car turned down a track marked by an ancient finger post which read *Stang Tarn*. "Do you cops learn innuendo during your probationary year or is it a prerequisite of joining?"

XXXIII

"Andy, you look like you've just come back from a trip to the underworld in every sense. Hard night on stake-out, was it?"

"You could put it like that," said Andy Dalziel.

It was a hard thing to admit, but the days were past when he could drink and dance till dawn, take a taxi home, live up to his vainglorious sexual promises, snatch an hour or so's sleep and be in The Dog and Duck at opening time without some evidence of his energy-sapping activities being inscribed upon his face.

"But it's nowt that another pint won't put right. How about you, Charley?"

"Nay, but I've just come in. Give us a chance to wash my teeth with this one," said Charley Penn.

Dalziel went up to the bar, noting with approval that the barman, observing his approach, stopped serving another customer to pull the anticipated pint. Marvellous what a few kind words would do to set a man on the straight and narrow, thought Dalziel complacently.

He returned to the table and sank a gill.

"That's better already," he said.

"So what's going off?" enquired Penn.

"Eh?"

"Come on, this isn't your usual watering hole," sneered the writer. "You're here for some special reason."

"I hope there's not a pub in this town where I'm not known and welcome," said Dalziel in an injured tone.

"You've got that half-right," said Penn. "Last time I saw you in here, it was definitely business. Me and that lad, Roote, and Sam Johnson . . ."

His face clouded as he spoke of Johnson and he said, "Last Sunday. Christ, it's hard to credit it were only last Sunday. And now the poor sod's in the ground. That felt like indecent haste. What happened, Andy? Loopy Linda jerk your wires?"

"She's a strong woman, Charley, hard to gainsay," said Dalziel. "Or so I gather. Never met her myself."

"I noticed you weren't at the funeral," said Penn.

"Well, bury one you've buried them all," said Dalziel. "Went OK, did it? I gather young Roote did a turn."

"He spoke from the heart, nowt wrong with that," said Penn.

"Oh aye, most things he does come from the heart, I don't doubt it," said Dalziel. "You sound impressed, Charley."

"He seems a good lad. He's put the past behind him. Something a lot more of us should try to do, maybe. And he's got talent. You heard he won the short story competition?"

"Aye."

There'd been a message, or rather a series of messages on Dalziel's answering machine, in which Pascoe had brought him up to speed on the events of the night.

"Good story, was it?"

"About the only one," grunted Penn, who was notorious for stinting praise. "When I saw some of the crud on the short list, I was glad I hadn't had to read the stuff that didn't make it. But Roote's story would have shone in any company. It was a good night for the lad, pity your lackeys had to try and spoil it for him."

"Lackeys? Don't recall noticing I had any lackeys last time I looked. Must have drunk some genetically modified ale."

"Yon DCI, Ellie Pascoe's man. She's a grand lass. You'd've hoped, being wed to her, he'd know better. And that one with the face. God, take him round the maternity ward, you'd not have to waste time and drugs inducing labour."

"You should be careful what you say, Charley. Likely there's an Ombudsman and a tribunal I could report you to for nasty remarks like that."

"I'd not be surprised. Anyway, Andy, shall we get down to it, then you can go home and crawl back into bed which is what you shouldn't have got out of?"

Dalziel finished his pint and looked with surprise into the empty glass.

With a sigh, Penn finished his drink and went to the bar for replacements.

"That's kind," said Dalziel.

"Self-interest. You'd not arrest a man who'd just bought you a drink. Would you?"

"Well, I'd be mad to arrest the bugger afore he bought it, wouldn't I?" said Dalziel. "Charley, I want you to think hard before you answer this. Last Sunday you said you had to go off because on Sundays you always went to visit your old ma. When you were asked later in the week where you'd been that's what you said, visiting your ma. And that's more or less what your ma said too."

"You've been talking to my mother?" exclaimed Penn.

"Nay, Charley, did you think we wouldn't check up? We check out everything anyone tells us, especially if they make their money inventing things."

"And my mother, what does she say?"

"She says her Karl is a good boy, a perfect son."

"There you go then," said Penn. "So what are you saying, Andy?"

"I'm saying I can see where you got your talent for fiction from," said Dalziel. "Where were you last Sunday afternoon, Charley?"

Penn took a long slow draw on his beer. Wondering whether I'm bluffing, thought Dalziel. Wondering whether he should call it.

"Is this about Sam Johnson?" said Penn, postponing the moment.

"What else?"

"You think mebbe I'm this Wordman?"

"Well, it sounds like a trade description of your job, Charley."

"You think I may have murdered—how many is it?—five people, and you can still sit there having a drink with me?"

"Love the 'how many is it?', Charley. Innocent, guilty, you know exactly how many it is. Writer like you's probably got a little notebook where you jot down owt of interest that comes up. Unless you're not interested in murder."

"Only as a fine art," said Penn.

"That a confession? 'Cos I get the impression that's how this lunatic keeps himself going, got his head bent round some daft idea or other in which killing isn't wrong, or at least is necessary for the sake of something more important."

"No, it's not a confession. But yes, you're right, I've been keeping a close eye on these killings. That's what writers do. Bit like being a detective, taking note of what makes people tick, especially the oddities, which means most of us."

"So, have you drawn any conclusions, Charley?"

"Only that there's a lot more mileage in it."

"Why do you say that?"

" 'Cos he's obviously a clever sod, and if the sharpest brain in our CID has got to waste time suspecting me, then you can't be within a moonshot of catching him."

"Charley," said Dalziel softly, "there's one way you can stop me wasting time. Make up your mind if you're going to come clean or try to tough it out. Last Sunday afternoon . . . ?"

"And if I tell you I went to see my mother, what then?"

"Then I invite you down the nick where the refreshments aren't half as good as this and the service is twice as lousy," said Dalziel.

"Oh well, if you'd put it like that to start with . . . I was with a friend. A female friend."

"They're the best kind," said Dalziel. "But, let me guess, she's married and being a true gent, you can't possibly give me her name."

"Andy, I don't know why we bother to have conversations when you know everything in advance."

"Because it's words that make the world go round," said Dalziel.

"I thought it was love."

"Same thing. Nowt that doesn't come down to words."

"You're getting too deep for me, Andy. So what do we do now?"

"You? You do nowt. Me, I'll tell you what I'm going to do. I'm not going to press you to reveal a name, Charley, because I respect your loyalty and delicate feelings in this matter. But you're right about us being alike. I keep a little notebook too where I jot down oddities. And I reckon when I go through my notes, I'm going to come across—it might be a couple, it might be half a dozen, it might even be more—names of women who could be the *femme* I'm *cherche*zing. I'll put 'em in alphabetic order then I'll call round to see each of them in turn, preferably at night just when they're serving up supper to hubby and the family, and I'll ask 'em, 'Were you fucking Charley Penn last Sunday afternoon? I need to know else he's in big trouble.' And I'm sure that the lady in question will stand up and be counted rather than let you stay in that trouble. In fact, if she's tired of her old man and fancies getting together with you on a more permanent basis, she might jump at the chance to get this out in the open. Could even be that more than one will see this as too good a chance to miss and I may be stuck with a superfluity of admissions, which could be awkward. But that's a risk I'll just have to take. Unless you care to save me from it."

He nodded as if to affirm his readiness to undertake such a perilous mission and drank his beer.

"Fuck you, Dalziel," said Penn.

"I take it that's a 'yes,' " said Dalziel.

XXXIV

Hat Bowler's lunch had passed with much less drama.

He had taken Rye first of all into a wooded gully where they spotted enough birds to justify the expedition. She listened to his expert commentary with apparent interest but he was careful not to go on too long and risk boredom setting in. Also he was aware that the clouds were getting ever lower and wanted to make sure that their lunch at least was not spoilt by the inevitable rain.

They found a sheltered spot under a huge outcrop of rock from which several loose boulders had detached themselves over the years. He set about kicking it clear of sheep droppings and, when he caught her watching him with some amusement, he said apologetically, "Yeah, I know, it's like eating in a sheep's toilet, but they know a thing or two about shade in summer and shelter in winter."

"Where there's shit there's shelter, isn't that what the shepherds say?" laughed Rye.

"I'll have to remember that. OK, that does it, I think."

They sat and ate the assortment of sandwiches he had provided. Despite his promise to be founder of the feast, Rye produced from her knapsack a chocolate-iced sponge cake which she sliced in two.

"Hey, this is good," he said. "You bake it?"

"That's not surprise I hear, I hope?"

"Gratitude and delight," he said.

Things were going well, he felt. She gave every sign of enjoying his company as much as he was enjoying hers, but any hope he had of their growing closeness easing itself into a bit of al fresco grappling vanished when as they drank the rest of the coffee, the rain began, not much, more an undeniable moistness of the air than real spots, but enough he guessed to dampen ardour if applied to naked skin.

Quickly they packed up.

"What do you want to do?" he asked.

"I haven't come all this way to leave without taking a look at the famous tarn," she said. "And I've not forgotten your interesting bits."

The rain still hadn't really taken a hold by the time they reached the tarn, with the dampness in the air manifesting itself in the form of a general mistiness rather than a downpour. They stood at the water's edge, straining their eyes through the vaporous air towards the further bank where a low stone building was just visible.

"Isn't that the view that Dick painted?" said Rye.

"More or less. Slightly different angle, and a lot better visibility. But that's certainly Stangcreek Cottage."

He put the binoculars to his eyes and added, "Looks as if there's someone there. I can see smoke coming from the chimney."

"Oh, good. Somewhere to shelter if this gets any worse."

"Look, we can head back to the car now if you want," he said anxiously.

"Worried your make-up might wash off?" she mocked. "I thought you were the tough outdoor type. Can we walk right round the lake?"

"Well, it's all right as far as the cottage but then it starts to get a bit boggy as you get near to Stang Creek itself. That's the main feed stream for the tarn, but all the water that comes running off the hills back there is looking to find a way out too, and the ground's full of little creeks and inlets. No way you aren't going to get your feet wet . . ."

"You must have been bitten by a rabid duck, all this hydrophobia," she cut him short. "Come on. Let's move!"

He followed her, mentally noting that macho protectiveness cut no ice with Rye.

As he'd promised, there was a track of sorts round the northern side of the mere, dangerous to a car's springs but easy terrain for walkers.

The mist thickened as they walked, cutting visibility down to about twenty yards with occasional tantalizing glimpses across the water, and wrapping them in a grey but not unpleasing cocoon. There was very little sound and what there was came mysteriously as from a great distance. No birds sang and the gentle lapping of the lake water in the reeds was more a foil against which to measure silence than a noise in its own right. After a while Hat let his hand brush Rye's and she took it and locked her fingers in his, and so they walked on, hand in hand.

Neither spoke. It felt to Hat that there was a spell on them which words could only break and if it remained unbroken, they might walk on like this forever. Was it possible to make vows without speaking? he wondered. And the strangely unconstabulary thought flitted across his mind that perhaps it was the vows made without words that were kept forever. In fact a wordless world might in many respects be a better place. Men name things to have power over them. Leave them nameless and we cannot dominate but may still love them.

Part of his mind thought with horror of the reaction among his peers of the CID if he tried enunciating any of these ideas in the nick. Another part wanted to tumble them all out in front of Rye and invite her reaction. But to do so would require words. And words in this silence were sacrilege.

And then came a sound unholier than any words, a sound that ripped through the silence, whirring and grating, now harsh, now edgy, rising and falling, now metal, now stone.

"What kind of bird is *that*?" asked Rye in a hushed and fearful tone.

"No bird that I've ever heard," said Hat. "It sounds more like . . ."

He hesitated, not at all sure what it did sound more like.

Then, so sudden it was almost as if the sound had taken shape before them, the squat black shape of Stangcreek Cottage leapt out of the mist a few yards ahead.

The sound was coming from behind the cottage. They went round the side and saw a mud-spattered Fiesta parked outside a timber-framed lean-to which rested against the building's rear wall like a drunk against a charity worker.

Under the minimal shelter of the lean-to a man stooped over a foot-driven grinding wheel against which he held the head of an axe. The wheel turned, sparks flew, the metal screamed.

"Goodness me," said Rye. "It's Dick. Dick, hello! *Dick!*"

At the sound of her raised voice, Dick Dee turned and stood still for a moment, the axe held tight in both hands, regarding them blankly.

Then the slow rejuvenating smile spread across his face and he said, "Well, this is a pleasant surprise."

In a surprisingly fluent movement for one whose comfortable shape gave little promise of athleticism, he swung the axe high in the air, letting his hands slide from the head to the shaft, then brought it down with sufficient force to bury it in one of several heavy logs scattered around the lean-to floor.

"So here you are. How wise I was to light a fire. But let's not hang around out here. As we say in rural Yorkshire, won't you step in-by, you'll have had your tea?"

XXXV

The next hour passed very comfortably, a little too comfortably in Rye's case for Hat's peace of mind.

That easiness between her and Dee which he had observed before was even more apparent outside the workplace. As they talked and laughed together, he felt, if not excluded, at least cut adrift and moving ever further from that blessed closeness he and Rye had shared during their mist-wrapped walk around the lake.

Dee had made tea and toast for them on the very welcome woodfire which crackled and sparked in the grate. The tea was a bit smoky, but the toast—thick slices of white bread impaled on a long thin carving knife and held up to the heat till they were almost black then generously loaded with cool fresh butter and apricot jam—was delicious.

Dee sat on the floor, Hat perched on a three-legged stool, while Rye sat in the only chair. This was a lovely thing, carved out of oak, with lion-head armrests and claw feet, all possessing that deep patina which only age and the polish of use can give.

"Found it in the barn," explained Dee. "One of the arms was broken and someone at some time had thought a coat of whitewash would improve it. So I neglected my painting for a while on the grounds that putting this back to what it was made a greater contribution to art and beauty than anything I could do."

"It's lovely, Dick," said Rye.

"Yes, isn't it. And at last there is someone here worthy to sit in it. No doubt about it, eh, Hat? Rye must be our chairman. 'Queen and huntress chaste and fair . . .' "

As he spoke he took her hand and urged her to take her seat.

Hat, resenting the contact and thinking to earn some Brownie points by a quick flash of linguistic correctness, said, "Chair*woman*, I think you mean. Or at least Chair*person*."

"That's what you think I mean, is it?" said Dee pleasantly. "Yet *man* in its origins was never gender specific. There are those who derive it from the same Indogermanic source posited for *mind*, that is *men* or *mon*, to think or remember, thus referring to that power of rational thought which differentiates us from the beasts. Whatever the truth of this, it's certain that its reference to the male of the species is a much later development, and therefore to say that those instances where it still retains its original sense of *human being*, such as *mankind*, demonstrate masculine arrogance and exclusivity is as absurd as saying that the internal combustion engine was invented because Henry Ford started making motor cars. However, I acknowledge that among ignorant people I cannot forever be giving my little lecture, so yes, back there in the land of *hoi polloi*, I usually observe the conventions of the new ignorance. But here, among friends, no need to hide our lights under bushels! Rye, you shall be our chairman, Hat, you shall be our stoolie, and I as usual shall take the floor."

Hat felt he ought to feel patronized but found it hard not to feel flattered instead. It was a rare art, he reluctantly admitted, to be able to rattle on like Dee without getting right up your nose. Remove the element of sexual jealousy, and he guessed he'd be really impressed by the guy, who gave the impression of being not unimpressed by Hat. At every opportunity he went out of his way to offer cues for him to display his ornithological expertise, showing what seemed a genuine rather than just a polite interest, and being modestly self-deprecating when Rye drew attention to several of his paintings which included birdlife.

There was no doubt about it, he might not be a bird painter in the Aubusson or even the Hon. Geoffrey style, but his touch when it came to painting the *feel* of a bird in flight was indisputable, and Hat was able to join his praise to Rye's with, he hoped, no discernible element of grudgingness.

It was some comfort to see that this apparent closeness between the two librarians didn't extend to details of Dee's private life. Rye was clearly as surprised as he was to find her colleague in residence. Not that residence seemed the right word. The cottage was primitive in the extreme with no modern utilities.

"I used to come up to the tarn to paint," explained Dick, "and I took shelter in here one day when it started raining, I mean really raining, not this soft breath of god stuff. And it occurred to me that I would find it really useful to have a place like this where I could store some gear and work inside when the weather was inclement. So I made enquiries, discovered that it all belonged to the Stang estate, that's the Pyke-Strengler family property, and I was able to use my slight acquaintance with the Hon. Geoffrey to persuade them to let me take out a lease on the place for a nominal rent. I take care of basic upkeep, it's in my own interest of course, and everyone's happy."

"Do you actually stay here?" asked Rye.

"I occasionally camp out overnight," he admitted. "I've got a sleeping bag and a camping stove and various bits and pieces. I've tried to avoid nest-building. I don't want a rural retreat, just a workshop. But it's amazing how the stuff builds up! And, as you can see, I am nesh enough to like a fire when things get a little too chilly or damp."

"But a place like this on the open market would surely bring a good price," said Hat.

"Oh yes. And Geoffrey's father, the famous absentee, would have dearly loved such a good price. He sold off everything he could, but the bulk of the estate land and its properties are entailed. The revenue comes from letting. Now Stangcreek Cottage refurbished and modernized would be a desirable holiday rental, but that costs money and the late lord wasn't about to spend hard cash on anything but his own interests. What Geoffrey will decide to do remains to be seen, but I think that on the whole he so loves this bit of the estate for his own activities, whether artistic or atavistic, that he won't want to encourage trippers."

"Like us, you mean?" said Hat.

"Genuine bird-watchers he doesn't mind, though it must come as a shock to some of them to see the duck they were just admiring through their glasses explode before their eyes. More tea?"

Hat glanced at Rye, trying desperately not to look too eager to be up and off. She put her mug down and said, "No thanks, Dick. Not for me. I came out to enjoy the fresh air and see some birds, though Hat here might like to hang around in the dry for the rest of the day. He seems to be allergic to water."

Dick Dee smiled at him. The fact that there was more of sympathy than mockery in the smile didn't help. He stood up and said brightly, "Ready when you are."

Outside the rain was no longer dismissable as romantic mist.

Dee said, "Going back along the track, are you?"

"No," said Hat firmly. "All the way round."

"Oh. Bit wet along there, you'll find. And there's a lot of water in the Creek. You know the crossing, do you?"

"Yes," said Hat shortly. "No problem."

"Good. I'll get back to trying to put an edge on that damn axe. See you tomorrow, Rye."

"Can't wait," grinned Rye, giving him a peck on the cheek.

Hat turned away and set off at a rapid pace. Male chivalry didn't seem to cut much ice with her so let's see what a bit of physical equal opportunity did! Behind him he heard the screel of the axe-grinding resume but it was soon drowned in the noise of running waters.

The curve of steep hills to the west formed a natural watershed, funnelling rapid becks down through narrow gills with enough force to continue carving deep passages through the peaty ground levelling off to the tarn. The smaller streams were easily crossable, often with a single step or at most a bit of help from some natural stepping stone, but he deliberately chose a route which required maximum strength and agility. From time to time he glanced back to check Rye's progress and always found she was matching him stride for stride, so he tried smiling encouragingly in an attempt to imply that he was holding himself in check for her benefit. His reward for such silent braggadocio was just. His foot slipped off a greasy rock into a tumult of icy water and, as his boot filled, she swept past him, laughing, and took the lead. If anything, her chosen route was more difficult than his and soon she'd opened up a gap between them. Eventually, however, not without satisfaction he saw her come to a halt as she reached the bank of Stang Creek itself, the most significant of the many water courses running into the mere. Crossing it was a problem if you didn't know the exact location of the stepping stones, which weren't easy to spot, most of them hiding beneath a couple of inches of water, except at times of greatest drought. Your first sight of someone crossing probably got you as close as modern agnosticism could manage to what the disciples felt on the Sea of Galilee after the feeding of the five thousand.

Looking forward to a bit of miracle-making, Hat called out as he approached, "So what's the hold-up? Top athlete like you, I thought you'd just leap across."

She turned to look at him and he immediately regretted his frivolous words. Her face was set, her eyes wide and startled. After her previous showing he couldn't understand why such a small obstacle should cause such a strong reaction, but he hurried forward to reassure her there really wasn't any problem.

Before he could speak she pointed and said, "Hat . . . down there . . ."

He looked downstream, his brain anticipating a distressed animal . . . a fox with a gangrenous trapped leg perhaps . . . or a drowned sheep . . .

And at first he saw nothing.

Then he made it out.

In the water, mostly submerged, held by the fast moving current against the hidden stepping stones over which he had planned to run so miraculously, was a body.

Or perhaps it wasn't a body. The eye is easily deceived. Perhaps it was just some green plastic farm-feed bag, blown here by the autumn gales, bulked out by trapped air and floating vegetation.

He ran along the bank, hoping to be able to turn to Rye and with his laughter at her error bring the colour back to her face. But as he stepped out along the hidden stones and bent down for a closer look, he saw there was no cause for laughter here.

Rye was on the bank alongside him.

He looked up at her and said warningly, "I'm going to pull it out."

She turned away with affected indifference and said, "There's a boat down there. I'll take a look."

He glanced downstream. Thirty yards or so, just before the creek entered the tarn, a flat-bottomed boat was moored.

The policeman in him wanted to say, *No. Don't go near. This could be a crime scene and the less we contaminate it the better.*

Instead he said, "Yeah, why don't you do that?"

He'd only seen one drowned body before, but that had been enough to demonstrate what water without and decay within could do to weak human flesh. Rye looked shaken enough already without that.

She moved away, and he stooped and with both hands took hold of what looked like a waxed outdoor jacket. It was difficult to get a grip but finally he succeeded and began to drag the body out of the water.

"Oh shit," he said as he got the torso on to the bank.

It was a body all right, but not all of it. Or not all a body. Or only part of a body. Or a body with a bit missing. In fact, was a body a body if you didn't have all of it?

Which questions of semantics were only occupying his mind to divert it from the fact that the corpse had no head.

He forced himself to concentrate.

From the look of it, the head hadn't been detached through the depredations of water life. In fact he doubted very much if this fast-flowing freshwater stream harboured denizens capable of inflicting such damage.

No, if he had to make a quick pathological guess based on the evidence of his eyes, he'd say that it had been chopped off. And it had taken several blows.

He dragged the corpse fully out of the water and stood up, glad to put even the distance of his height between himself and the monstrous thing at his feet.

He looked to see where Rye was.

She had clambered aboard the moored boat and was stooping over something.

Now his police training got the upper hand. This was beyond doubt the scene of a crime. He recalled the advice of a police college training officer. "At a crime scene, put your hands in your pocket and play with your dick. That way you won't be tempted to touch anything else."

"Rye," he called, moving towards her.

She stood up and turned to him. Even in these circumstances he could admire the graceful balance of her body as she adjusted easily to the gentle rocking of the boat beneath her feet.

She was holding something, a basket of some kind, the sort that fishermen use, what was it called? A creel, that was it. And she was pulling the straps from the buckles that held the lid down.

She shouldn't be doing that. And not just because of the risk of contaminating the scene.

No, there was something else.

Precognition, instinct, detective work, call it what you will, but he knew beyond all doubt what was in that basket.

"No!" he cried running towards her. "Rye, leave it!"

But it was always going to be too late.

She pulled up the lid and peered inside.

She tried not to scream or perhaps it was just that her vocal cords were too constricted to produce anything more than a dim echo of the grate of the grindstone on the axehead. For a moment he thought she was going to topple backwards into the water, but her weakening knees flexed, and as if in acknowledgement that something had to go, either herself or what she held in her hands, she hurled the basket from her on to the bank.

It hit the ground, bounced, turned over, and out of it rolled a human head.

Even before it came to a halt at his feet, Hat had recognized that in one sense at least it was not out of place in this setting. If a man has to die, then let him die on his own land.

This was beyond all dispute the head of Geoffrey, Lord Pyke-Strengler of the Stang.

XXXVI

the sixth dialogue

Hello again.

Me too. What a wondrously varied path this is you've put me on! A Right to Roam Bill which did not need an Act of Parliament to make it law.

Winding through private properties and public buildings, tracking ancient highways and rural byways, and now leading me far from the populous city to the dark heart of the countryside. For it is the path that leads, not I who lead my chosen ones along the path. Indeed it is the path that does the choosing, letting them think always that they advance of their own accord. I myself am merely an instrument.

Or a French horn, maybe. I like the idea of being a French horn.

Seriously, my role as simple instrument has never been clearer than it was today. The chosen one answered his cues like one who had spent long hours conning the part. Never at the Athenian bouphonia *did ox approach the sacrificial altar more willingly. All the necessary instruments he provided himself, even putting the guilty weapon into my hands with his own.*

And in that moment time stopped. Nothing gradual, no slow slowing down as often before. Time is . . . time isn't.

And the burbling of the creek around the moored boat joins with the twarting of a whaup into one long melancholy line of sound stretching up from the dimpled tarn into the vast inane of the sky, like a phone-line to the Gods.

How comforting to think of Them reclining up there, listening with solemn approval to all that goes on here below.

In my hands the oiled steel column trembles and throbs towards its spontaneous climax. And now its seed spurts out, as black and round as sturgeon roe, fanning through the air to plant immortal life in this mortal flesh before me. His mouth gapes wide in the ecstasy of that moment of ultimate penetration, but not as wide as this new red orifice about his throat out of which I see his soul fly like a bird escaping its cage. Off it goes, winging its way across the glimmering tarn, rejoicing in its sudden freedom, while here on the dull earth its empty cage collapses beside the laughing creek.

The guilty weapon I hurl into the cleansing waters.

No arm rises up to take it.

I have work still to do. The head, half-severed from its fleshy stalk by the shotgun blast, must be completely plucked and set in its container. The axe is at hand—where else would it be? Three blows complete the work, no more, no less. For this is a truly trinal day, three in one, the trinity completed as I roll the corpse into the sounding stream.

What of the axe? I heft it in my hand and contemplate the inscrutable waters. But it bears no guilt. It is an instrument of my path not his departure. So let it be.

Bearing it with me I move away, and with each step I feel time's drag return.

Oh, let me come soon to that safe haven where I shall mark time forever. And time will lose power to mark me.

XXXVII

The *bouphonia*," said Drew Urquhart, "which can be translated as 'the murder of the ox,' was an Athenian rite aimed at bringing an end to a period of drought and its associated deprivations. You'll likely have read about it in *The Golden Bough*. . . ."

He paused and directed a smile at Dalziel, who said, "I don't do much reading in pubs. Just give us the gist."

"Frazer describes the ritual thus. Barley and wheat were laid on the altar and oxen driven close by. The animal that went up to the altar and started eating was sacrificed by men using axe and knife, which weapons they immediately threw away from them and fled. Ultimately everyone concerned in the animal's death stood trial, each passed on the blame till it came to be laid completely at the door of the knife and the axe which were judged guilty, condemned and hurled into the sea."

Pascoe, who had been listening closely—unlike his master who had cupped his great hands round his great face and was groaning softly into the resultant funnel with a sound like a rising westerly echoing through Fingal's Cave—asked, "So you think this is why the Wordman threw the gun away but not the axe? The Hon. was dead when his head got chopped off so the axe wasn't guilty."

"That's right. You'll have noticed how he talks about the weapon more or less firing itself, just as he talks about the victim selecting itself, like the Athenian ox. By the by, did the PM find any sign he'd been eating anything?"

Pascoe glanced at Dalziel who was the arbiter of how much information they gave non-officials, but before he could get eye contact, Dr. Pottle (back to full smoking strength after his recent illness) said, "More significant than all these word games he clearly likes playing could be the strong sexual imagery he uses here. It's what's happening in his psyche that will give us the clue to track him down, not his warped rationality. That is an area over which, by its very nature, he still has some control. It's the emotions, the passions, running out of control which will betray him in the end. At the very least, they may result in the deposit of significant physical traces. You've checked the ground thoroughly for signs of semen, I presume? It reads to me as if ejaculation almost certainly took place either during or immediately after the event."

Dalziel's head emerged from its cavern and he said coldly, "I'm not right sure what your job is, Dr. Pottle, but one thing I'm sure it's not is telling me mine. By a stroke of luck which was long overdue it were one of my own officers who was first on the scene, so as far as possible it's been kept uncontaminated. Yes, we've gone over every inch of that terrain for half a mile in all directions. Yes, everything there was to be recorded, removed, examined and analysed has been taken care of. We've dragged the tarn and found the gun and a deal of rubbish beside, none of which looks like it might be relevant. We've got the axe from the cottage and found traces of blood on it which show it was the same as was used on the Hon. Geoffrey. And, yes, Mr. Urquhart, the post mortem found traces of cucumber sandwich in his mouth and on the bank by the boat we found a sandwich, wholewheat bread, by the bye, with a single bite out of it. All this is confidential police information which I'm telling you just to show how far I'm willing to go to catch this lunatic. If any of it helps either of you two jokers to tell us owt useful, speak now or forever hold your pieces."

He regarded the visiting experts with the open expression of a man who had laid all his cards on the table. Except of course, thought Pascoe, he hadn't mentioned that Bowler had confessed to allowing his bit of skirt to seriously contaminate the scene, he hadn't mentioned that they'd turned Stangcreek Cottage upside down and questioned Dick Dee for five hours straight off (during which time he hadn't asked for his solicitor and at the end of which time he'd looked a lot fresher than his interrogators) before releasing him, and he hadn't mentioned that a very alert forensic examiner had noticed faint traces of blood on the fish hook on one of the rods in the boat, which on examination had proved to be human and AB, unlike the Hon.'s which was A. And he certainly hadn't mentioned that the Hon.'s

Land-Rover, which they'd alerted police forces nationally to look out for, had just been discovered in the police car-pound to which it had been removed for illegal parking behind the railway station.

The Dialogue hadn't turned up till Monday morning when it was discovered among the library mail, but from the moment Bowler had rung in on Sunday with news of his grisly discovery, they'd treated it as a Wordman killing.

Not, as Wield had observed, that this made them feel like they were one step ahead of the game, only that the bugger now had them all playing it according to his rules.

Now, on Tuesday morning, Pascoe had persuaded a reluctant Dalziel that it was time to hear what the "experts" had to say.

"Well?" growled Dalziel.

Urquhart scratched his stubbly chin with a noise which sounded like a challenge to the heavyweight champion of carnal frication who sat before him and said, "Trinal, trinity, in three parts. Find out what he's on about there and you might be in sniffing distance of what makes the bugger tick."

"Doesn't it just refer to the three blows used to chop the head off?" suggested Pascoe.

"That certainly reinforces it," said the linguist. "But a head and a body make two parts not three, so it's not that. And why roll the body into the water and put the head into the fishing basket? There's something going on here that we're missing."

"That it?" said Dalziel. "There's summat we're missing? Well, thank you, Sherlock. Dr. Pottle, owt you can add to that, or mebbe you feel your colleague's said it all?"

Pottle lit a fresh cigarette from the one he was smoking and said, "He's really getting into his swing. I don't know how far away the proposed end is, but he's completely sure he's going to get there now. This is by far the shortest Dialogue yet. The further he gets, the shorter they're likely to become. Reliving the last experience in words is merely occupying precious time which could better be devoted to looking forward to the next one. Now he's certain he's on the right path, his dialogue with his victims and with his spirit-guide can just as easily continue in his mind as on the page."

"You think he might stop writing altogether?" said Pascoe.

"No. That part of the writing which is part of the game he's playing with us will remain. It's in the rules, so to speak. And he enjoys it. I said last time that his growing confidence is likely to be his downfall. I think that more and more he will be dropping little clues into his Dialogues. He's like a squash player who is so certain of his vast superiority that he'll start playing with the racket in his wrong hand, or boasting all his shots off the back wall. But the subconscious self-revelations which I am looking for will be much harder to find. Though it hurts me to say it, I think that from now on Mr. Urquhart's skills are going to be more useful than mine."

Dalziel let out a sigh so redolent of tragic despair he could have sold it to Mrs. Siddons. As if in response, his phone rang.

He answered. With most people it's possible to gauge something of their relationship with a caller from tone of voice, vocabulary, body language, et cetera, but Pascoe had never found a way of working out whether Dalziel were speaking to the Queen or an estate agent.

"Dalziel," he snarled. Listened. "Aye." Listened. "Nay." Listened. "Mebbe." Dropped the receiver on to the rest so that it bounced.

Cap Marvell perhaps asking if he fancied a bout of violent sexual activity in his lunch hour? The PM offering him a peerage? The Wordman threatening his life?

"That it, gents?" said Dalziel hopefully.

Pottle and Urquhart looked at each other, then the Scot said, "Way I see it, words are the key. This is like breaking a text-based code. You can do it the long way, by sheer hard work, or you can hit lucky and find the significant text, or texts."

"Or you can hope his growing arrogance results in a clue that someone can solve before rather than after the event," said Pottle.

"I'll make a note of that," said the Fat Man dismissively. "Thanks, gents. Work to do. DC Bowler here will see you out."

Pottle and Urquhart gathered their papers together. Pascoe said effusively, "Good of you both to come. Please don't hesitate to give me a ring if anything occurs."

At the door Urquhart said with heavy irony, "Don't know why it is, Superintendent, but whenever I leave these meetings, I sometimes get to worrying just a wee bittie how much you really think I've managed to help you."

"Nay, Mr. Urquhart," said Dalziel with a fulsome orotundity, "I'd be real sorry to think I'd left you in any doubt about that."

"Plonker," he added as the door closed, or maybe just a moment earlier.

"Then I don't really see why you bother to sit in on these sessions," said Pascoe, letting his irritation show.

"Because if I weren't ready to spend time with plonkers, I'd likely be a lonely man," said Dalziel. "Any road, I didn't say he were a useless plonker. And if Pozzo says we ought to listen to him, then mebbe we should. He sometimes puffs out a bit of sense."

This was a roundabout concession to Pascoe, who had a good personal relationship with Pottle, and knowing it was the closest he was likely to get to an apology, the DCI put aside his irritation and said, "So where do we go from here, sir?"

"Me, I'm going to see Desperate Dan. That were him on the phone. You, if I remember right, have got a date with the vultures. Don't know what Wieldy here has got on. Mebbe he can find time to do a bit of police work if some bugger doesn't want him to judge a bonny baby competition."

Desperate Dan was Chief Constable Trimble. The vultures were the media. Interest in the Wordman killings had increased exponentially with each new death and this latest killing had rocketed it into an international dimension. Not only was the Hon. a peer of the realm, but one of the tabloids had worked out that there was a distant royal connection which put him at something like three hundred and thirty-seventh in line to the throne. American and European interest had exploded. One German TV company had dug up a would-be telly don whose claim that a Pyke-Strengler had been beheaded during the Civil War sparked speculation that a left-wing revolutionary movement was behind the killing. Attempts to fit the earlier killings into such a political pattern were proving ludicrous, but journalists haven't reached the depths of their profession by allowing ludicrosity to get in the way of a good story.

Pascoe, who had ambiguous feelings about being regarded as the acceptable face of policing, had been elected spokesman at the forthcoming press conference. His ambiguity rose from a reluctance to accept the kind of type-casting which, while it might be good for his career, could also take it in directions he was not yet ready to go. The world of policy committees and high-level political contacts might get a lot of scrambled egg on your shoulders, but it was far removed from that other world of practical investigation which got a lot of honest dirt under your fingernails. Like St. Augustine and sex, he knew he'd have to give it up one day, but preferably not yet.

"Mr. Trimble wants an update, does he?" he asked.

"Update?" said Dalziel. "Nay, the bugger wants a result and he wants it yesterday. Someone up there's giving him a hard time."

He spoke with the grim satisfaction of one who knows what a hard time is. Pascoe observed him with a sympathy he was careful not to show. Dalziel drove his troops mercilessly when the occasion demanded, but he took his own bumps and rarely passed them on to his underlings. Going up or coming down, the buck stopped with Andy Dalziel, and Pascoe could only guess at the strain the Wordman case was putting the Fat Man under.

Hat came back into the room. His reaction to the discovery of the body had won grudging praise from Dalziel, though he had advised for future consideration that on the whole it was best not to let your bit of fluff play netball with the victim's severed head.

In particular, Hat's immediate return to Stangcreek Cottage where he'd promptly secured the axe and taken a preliminary statement from Dick Dee had been approved, not because of anything it produced but because it kept the librarian in situ as a witness. That he must also be classed as a suspect, Bowler had known from the minute he saw the body, and if Dee hadn't been in the cottage when he and Rye got back to it, the DC would have put out a call to pick him up. Similarly if he'd tried to leave before the troops arrived, he would have arrested him which would have started the custodial clock ticking.

Not that it was just professional satisfaction at not wasting any precious senior officer interrogation time that he felt. The way that Rye had accepted Dee's comforting on their return to the cottage had made him very aware that if she got a sniff he was treating her boss as a serious suspect, the smooth course of their relationship might have hit a rock. She'd probably got the message by now, but at a sufficient remove for the blame to be heaped on Pascoe or the Fat Man rather than his lowly self.

The good news (if the removal of a possible perp from the frame could be called good news) was that they'd found nothing positive to link Dee with the Hon.'s death.

It was true that his prints were all over the axe which Forensic had confirmed was the instrument used to sever the Hon.'s head, but as he'd been using it to split logs in Hat's presence, this was hardly surprising. He did have a small cut on one of his fingers, but when his claim that his blood type was O was confirmed by a check of his medical records (written permission to see which "for elimination purposes" he readily gave), hope of tying him in to the AB blood spots on the fish hook faded.

Dalziel, who felt that anyone found using a bloodstained axe near a headless body was at the very least guilty of wasting police time, seemed inclined to blame the messenger, but Pascoe's slim shoulders had grown professionally broad over the years and he was able to ignore the accusatory grunts and snorts and carry on with his meticulous summation of the lack of evidence against Dee.

"The path. report suggests the Hon. had been dead between two and four days. Dee's alibi'd at work for most of the relevant daylight hours. After work with the evenings drawing in, seems less of a possibility. The time it would have taken to get out there means it would have been dusk when they arrived—"

"They?" interrupted Wield.

"The killer must have driven the Hon.'s Land-Rover back from the tarn, ergo he must have gone out there in it," said Pascoe. "However, we do know that the Hon. often spent time out there fishing at night. In fact, interestingly, it was Dee himself who told us that. He has been most helpful and co-operative throughout."

"That's a mark agin him," said Dalziel hopefully. "Member of the public trying to help the police has got summat on his conscience, that's my experience."

"Perhaps you should widen your social circles, sir," murmured Pascoe. "But it makes little difference as Dee is alibi'd for the nights too."

"Oh aye? Shagging someone, is he?" said the Fat Man.

"He didn't volunteer any details of his emotional life," said Pascoe. "But he spent one of the evenings in question at a county librarians' meeting in Sheffield to which he drove with Percy Follows, getting back here after midnight. The other he spent at Charley Penn's flat where, having drunk very freely of Penn's Scotch, he spent the night on the sofa. Penn confirms."

The phone rang. Dalziel picked it up, listened, then said, "If I were on my way, I'd not be answering the sodding phone, would I? Soon!"

He banged it down again.

"Mr. Trimble?" said Pascoe.

"His secretary. If it had been Dan, I'd not have been so polite. Pete, I'm letting you rabbit on like this in the hope you're keeping the good news till the last. Should I hold my breath?"

"No, sir. Sorry."

"Then sod it, I might as well go and help Dan find where he's hid his Scotch," said the Fat Man, rising and making for the door.

"Sir," said Hat.

"What sir's that, lad?" said Dalziel in the doorway.

"Sorry, sir?"

"Is it 'Mr. Dalziel, sir, please don't leave 'cos I've got summat very perceptive to say'? Or is it 'Mr. Pascoe, sir, now the old fart's gone, I've got summat very perceptive to say'?"

Hat knew that there were some questions better unanswered.

He said, "I was just thinking, what if there were two of them?"

"Two bodies you mean? Wieldy, you were at the PM. Didn't the loose bits match?"

Wield said, "Think he means two killers."

"Jesus. Why stick at two? If we're into invention, let's make it a mob."

"Two would mean that neither of them actually needed to have travelled out to the tarn with Lord Pyke-Strengler," said Hat. "And there'd have been a spare driver to bring his Land-Rover back."

"To what end?" enquired Pascoe.

"The Land-Rover would get noticed from a distance out there," said Hat. "The body where it was could have lain there a lot longer if we hadn't happened to stumble on it. The longer it lies, the less there is for us to find. Or maybe the idea was to shift it. Maybe that was what Dee was up to, but he saw us wandering around on the far side of the tarn and when we started out towards the cottage, he got back there fast to intercept us. He didn't seem very keen for us to go on."

"In your statement all you say is he remarked it got a bit boggy further along the shore," said Pascoe.

"Well, there's different ways of saying things," said Hat, blushing slightly.

"Especially if they don't fit a thesis, eh?" said Pascoe. "Where's this leading, Hat? Are we still talking about Dee? Like I just told you, he's alibi'd."

"Not if Charley Penn's the other half of the pair, he isn't," said Hat.

Dalziel said, "Still fancy Charley, do you, lad? I'll say this for you, once you get someone in your sights, you keep the bugger there."

There wasn't the usual force in his mockery, however, and Hat felt encouraged enough to go on.

"And if they were both in it, then it doesn't matter that Penn's got an alibi for the Johnson killing."

"Which you established by interviewing his mother," said Dalziel. "I were going to talk to you about your interview techniques, lad."

His tone was now distinctly unfriendly.

"Something come up, sir?" said Pascoe.

"Nothing important. Just that Sherlock here got it all wrong and it seems Charley weren't anywhere near his ma's place that Sunday."

Hat felt both crestfallen and elated at the same time.

Pascoe said, "He admits this?"

"He does now," said Dalziel. "But don't start oiling your handcuffs. He says he's got another alibi. Claims he spent the afternoon on the nest with a ladyfriend."

"And what's the ladyfriend say?"

"Nowt. Turns out she's on holiday in the Seychelles for three weeks. With her husband. So we need to tread careful."

"Why's that?"

"Seems the lady in question is Maggot Blossom. That's right. Help-meet and comfort to Joe Blossom, the Lord of the Flies, our beloved mayor. So we'll need to wait till they get back afore we make enquiries."

"Not like you to be so diplomatic, sir," said Pascoe provocatively.

"Not diplomatic. Careful. Yon Maggot's got a leg-lock could break a man's spine." Then in face of Pascoe's sceptical moue, he added, "Also, she's got a tattoo somewhere Charley couldn't know about unless . . . Any road, unless young Bowler here can come up with summat more than a funny feeling, looks like Penn's right on the edge of the frame."

Hat looked around desperately as if he hoped a messenger might arrive with a freshly penned confession.

Pascoe said encouragingly, "Nothing wrong with informed speculation, Hat. You must have something going through your mind to suggest the possibility that Dee and Penn might enter into a conspiracy?"

Hat said, "Well, they went to the same school."

"So did Hitler and Wittgenstein," laughed Pascoe. Then recalled where he'd got this bit of information. From Sam Johnson's account of his first meeting with Charley Penn. He stopped laughing.

"And they play this weird game together," Hat went on. "I saw them at it."

"At it? You talking game as in rumpty-tumpty?" said Dalziel, interested.

"No, sir. It's a board game, like Scrabble, only a lot harder. They use all kinds of different languages and there's a lot of other rules. We saw a board when we were round at Penn's flat, sir."

"So we did," said Pascoe. "Some odd name, what was it?"

"*Pa-ro-no-mania,*" said Hat carefully.

"Not *paronomasia?*" suggested Pascoe.

"No. Definitely mania. The other means word-play or punning, doesn't it?" said Hat, happy to show Pascoe that he wasn't the only clever bugger around.

"So it does," said Pascoe. "And what does your word—which I must say I've never come across—mean?"

"It's a real word, sir," averred Hat, detecting a hint of dubiety. "It was Miss Pomona who told me about it after I saw them playing. Hang on, I've got a copy of the rules . . ."

He began to search through the wallet into which he'd put the papers Rye had given him before he'd taken to his sickbed.

"Here we go," he said triumphantly, handing the tightly creased sheets to Pascoe who unfolded them carefully and read them with interest.

"OED, Second Edition. I stand corrected."

"And I'm standing like a spare prick at a wedding," said Dalziel. "This is worse than listening to yon pair of epidemics."

"Sorry," said Pascoe. "Hey, now, how about this. The OED always gives the earliest known usage of the word and in this case it's, wait for it, Lord Lyttelton, 1760, *Dialogues of the Dead.* How's that for coincidence?"

"I don't know. How is it?" said Dalziel. "And what's it mean, this word?"

"Well, seems it's a factitious word, formed from a union of *paronomasia* and *mania* . . ."

Dalziel ground his teeth and Pascoe hurried on.

". . . and it means basically 'an obsessive interest in word games.' Since 1978, it's also been the proprietary name of this board game Penn and Dee are so fond of."

"Never heard of it," said Dalziel. "But I lost interest in board games after I found you got more rewards for climbing boring ladders than sliding down lovely slippery snakes."

Pascoe avoided Wield's eye and said, "Looking at the rules, I'm surprised anyone has ever heard of it: 'language of shuffler's choice . . . double points for intersecting rhymes . . . quadruple points for oxymorons . . .' Jesus! Who'd want to play this?"

"Dee and Penn play it all the time evidently," said Hat.

"Miss Pomona told you that too, I presume?" said Pascoe. "And how long have you been nursing this interesting information to your bosom?"

He spoke with studied politeness but Hat caught his drift instantly and said, "Not long. I mean, I only found out about it last week, and then I went sick, and really it didn't seem to mean much, not till I heard Dr. Urquhart and Dr. Pottle going on today, then Mr. Pascoe said about Penn giving Dee his alibi for one night last week, and I thought . . ."

"Nay lad, wait till you're in the dock afore you start summing up for the defence," said Dalziel, not unkindly. "Likely it's a load of nowt anyway. I mean, you can't go to jail for playing games, not even two fellows having a romp together, so long as it's between consenting adults in private, eh, Wieldy?"

"Yes, sir," said the sergeant. "Except if you call it rugby football, when you can sell folk tickets to watch, so they tell me."

Emotion always found it hard to get a fingerhold on the sergeant's face but this was said with a lack of expression that made Charles Bronson look animated.

"Rugby," said Dalziel. "Aye, that's a point. The Old Unthinkables. Nice one, Wieldy."

To be complimented on his attempted gibe at Dalziel's favourite sport did bring a look almost recognizable as surprise to the sergeant's features.

"Sir?" he said.

"The Old Unthinkables," repeated Dalziel. "That's what they call Unthank College's Old Boys' team. Not bad for a bunch of pubic school poofters, saving your presence. Not afraid to put the boot in, that's one thing they've learned for their daddies' money."

He spoke approvingly.

Wield said, "Missing your point, I'm afraid, sir."

"Penn and Dee went to Unthank, and so did John Wingate, yon telly belly, Ripley's boss. I know 'cos he used to play for the Unthinkables. Scrum half. Nice reverse pass."

The phone rang again.

"And?" said Pascoe.

"He must be about the same age as Penn and Dee. Might be worth a chat, Pete. Find out what they got up to as kids. Christ, I must be desperate, can't believe I'm saying this. I've spent too much time listening to your mate Pozzo."

The phone was still ringing.

Pascoe said, "Shall I answer that? Could be the Chief's office again."

"Then he'll think I'm on my way," said Dalziel indifferently.

He glanced at his watch.

"Tell you what, Wingate'll be at your press conference with all the other vultures. Reel him in when it's over. Knowing your style, Pete, that should be about half twelve. These telly bellys like shooting the questions, let's see if he can take his own medicine."

"You'll be finished with the Chief by then?"

"Unless he opens a new bottle of Scotch," said Dalziel. "Bowler, you be there too. After all, this is your idea."

"Thank you, sir," said Hat, delighted.

"Don't get carried away. Likely it'll turn out a waste of time, and I just want you close so I don't waste my energy kicking summat inanimate."

He left. Hat turned to the others, smiling, inviting them to share Dalziel's joke.

They didn't smile back.

Pascoe said thoughtfully, "Not like the super to chase rainbows."

"Not unless he's got an itch in his piles . . ."

They contemplated the Fat Man's famous haruspical piles for a moment, then Pascoe said, "Wieldy, the OED's online now. Ellie's a subscriber, if I give you her details, can you whistle it up on the computer?"

"You authorize it, I can whistle up the PM's holiday snaps," said Wield.

They followed him to his computer and watched as he ran his fingers over the keyboard.

"Right," he said. "Here we are."

"Great. Now find *paronomania*," said Pascoe.

But Wield was ahead of him.

"*Paranomasia* we've got. And *paromphalocele* we've got too, which from the sound of it we could do without. But no sign whatsoever of *paronomania*. So unless the great Oxford English Dictionary's missed a bit, there's no such word."

"And yet," said Pascoe, "we have all seen it, and its definition. Interesting. While you're at it, Wieldy, try *contortuplicated*."

"That's what the super said," said Hat. "I thought he just made it up."

"No," said Wield. "It's here. 'Twisted and entangled.' But it's obsolete. Just one example and that's 1648."

"Not attributed to A. Dalziel, is it?" said Pascoe. "Let that be a lesson to you, Hat. Never underestimate the super."

"No, sir. Sir, how did Mr. Dalziel know about Mrs. Blossom's tattoo?"

"Can't imagine," said Pascoe. "Why don't you ask him yourself?"

XXXVIII

The press conference lasted a good hour.

The technique preferred by most policemen when dealing with the gentlemen of the press, hungry for information, is the response mono-syllabic. *Yes* and *no*, as appropriate, blossoming into an euphuistic *No Comment* when neither of these will do.

Pascoe, however, favoured the sesquipedalian style. As Dalziel put it, "After thirty minutes with me, they're clamouring for more. After thirty minutes with Pete, they're clamouring to be let out." Tyro reporters had been known to leave one of his sessions with several pads crammed with notes which on analysis had not rendered a single line of usable copy.

Only once on this occasion did anyone come close to laying a finger on him and that was Mary Agnew, editor of the *Mid-Yorkshire Gazette*, whose personal attendance signalled the importance of the story.

"Mr. Pascoe," she said, "it appears to us out here that these so-called Wordman killings are systematic rather than random. Is this your opinion also?"

"It would seem to me," said Pascoe, "that the sequence of killings plus the associated correspondence, details of which I am, for obvious reasons of security, unable to share with you at this juncture, predicates what for the want of a better term we might define as a system, though we should not let the familiarity of the term confuse us into apprehending anything we would recognize as a logical underpinning of the perpetrator's thought processes. We are dealing here with a morbid psychology and what is systematic to him might well, when understood, appear to the normal mind as disjunctive and even aleatoric."

"I'll take that as a yes," said Agnew. "In which case, given that we have here a madman killing according to some kind of sequential system, how close are you to being able to give warning to those most at risk of becoming victims, whether as individuals or in a body?"

"Good question," said Pascoe, meaning in Westminster-speak that he had no intention of answering it. "All I can say is that if these killings *are* systematic, then the vast majority of your readers can have nothing to fear."

"They'll be pleased to know it. But looking down the list of victims, I can work out for myself that from Jax Ripley on, all of them have had something to do with the Centre, either directly or indirectly. Have you put everyone who works in the Centre or has any strong connection with it on alert?"

Pascoe, feeling himself harried, switched tactics abruptly, said, "No," then directed his gaze towards a *Scotsman* reporter whose accent he knew to be thick enough to baffle at least half of those assembled and said, "Mr. Murray?"

Afterwards he wondered, as he'd often done before, what would happen if he'd opted for sharing rather than evasion. Let them have all the disparate bits and pieces which were cluttering up his mind and his desk, and perhaps there was someone out there, someone with special knowledge or maybe just some enthusiastic reader of detective novels to whom such exegetics were but a pre-dormitory snack, who'd look at them and say, "Hey, I know what this means! It's obvious!"

One day perhaps . . .

The right to make such a choice could be one of the compensations of that rise to place which he sometimes feared—and sometimes feared would never come!

"Peter, hi. Am I about to be offered a scoop or am I just double-parked?"

John Wingate was coming towards him escorted by Bowler, whom Pascoe had told to extract the TV producer from the departing media mob with maximum discretion.

"Definitely not the first. As for the second, that's between you and your conscience," said Pascoe, shaking the man's hand. They knew each other, not well, but well enough to be comfortable with each other. Being a cop meant many relationships which in other professions might have matured into friendships stuck here. Pascoe recognized the main hesitation was usually on his side. Other people soon forgot you were a cop, and that was the danger of intimacy. What did you do when you were offered a joint in a friend's house, or found yourself invited to admire his acumen in having picked up a crate of export Scotch, duty-free, from a contact in the shipping trade? He'd seen the expression of shocked disbelief in friends' faces when he'd enquired if these were wise things to be sharing with a senior CID officer, and that had often been the last totally open expression he'd seen in those particular faces.

Now he contemplated an oblique approach to the question of Dee and Penn but quickly discounted it. Wingate was too bright not to realize he was being pumped. The direct route was probably the best, not directness as Andy Dalziel (who happily had not yet appeared) understood it, but something much more casual and low-key.

"Something you could help us with maybe," he said. "You went to Unthank College, didn't you?"

"That's right."

"Were Charley Penn and Dick Dee there at the same time?"

"Yes, they were, as a matter of fact."

"Good friends, were they?"

"Not of mine. I was a year ahead. A year in school's even longer than a week in politics."

"But of each other?"

Wingate didn't reply straightaway and Pascoe felt the just-a-friendly-chat smile on his face begin to freeze into a rictus.

"John?" he prompted.

"Sorry. What was the question?"

Good technique that, thought Pascoe. By forcing me to repeat the question in a much more positive form, he's upped the atmosphere from chat toward interrogation.

"Were Dee and Penn close friends?" he said.

"Don't see how I'm qualified to answer that, Peter. Not sure why you'd want to ask me that either."

"It's OK, John, nothing sinister. Just part of the usual business of collecting and collating mile after mile of tedious information, most of which proves totally irrelevant. I certainly don't want you to feel used."

This was offered with a rueful you-know-all-about-this-too twist of the lips.

"Oh, I don't, because so far I haven't been. And I don't think I will be, not unless you can give me some better reason, or indeed any reason at all, for interrogating me about my merry schooldays."

"It's not an interrogation, John," said Pascoe patiently. "Just a couple of friendly questions. Can't see why someone in your job should have any problem with that."

"My job? Let's examine that. Basically I'm still what I started out as, a journalist, and in that game you don't get Brownie points for jumping into bed with the police."

"Didn't do Jax Ripley any harm."

Dalziel had done one of his Red Shadow entrances; you don't know he's there till he bursts into song.

"What?" said Wingate, turning and looking alarmed. Then, recovering, he smiled and said, "Superintendent, I didn't see you. Yes, well, Jax, God bless her, had her own techniques."

"Certainly did," said Dalziel. "Don't want to interrupt, Pete, but just wanted to check with Mr. Wingate if his missus was going to be at home this afternoon. Thought I might pop round and have a chat."

This produced a shared moment of bewilderment with Pascoe which might be to the good.

"Moira? But why should you want to talk to Moira about Dee and Penn?" asked Wingate.

"No reason, 'cos I don't. No, it's just a general chat I had in mind."

"Yes, but why?" insisted Wingate, still more puzzled than aggressive.

"I'm conducting a murder investigation, Mr. Wingate," said Dalziel heavily. "Several murder investigations."

"So what's that got to do with her? She had no special connection with any of the victims."

"She knew Jax Ripley, didn't she? I can talk to her about Jax Ripley and what she got up to. All right, I can probably tell her more than she can tell me. But I'm clutching at straws, Mr. Wingate, and I might as well clutch at your missus, seeing it doesn't look like there's going to be owt to clutch at here. Is there, Mr. Wingate?"

He smiled one of his terrible smiles, lips drawn back from savage teeth, like the jaws of a mechanical digger about to seize and uproot a tree.

Pascoe was long acquainted with the Fat Man and all his winning ways and his mind had whipped, computer quick, through a wide selection of possible scenarios and opted for the one which made most sense.

The Fat Man was telling Wingate he knew that he'd been banging Jax

Ripley and was offering him the simple choice all detectives at some time offer most criminals—bubble or be bubbled.

Wingate's mind clearly moved as fast, or even faster as he had also to work out the best response. Not that there was much real alternative.

He caved in instantly but to do him justice he caved in with style, turning back to Pascoe and saying with a good shot at urbanity, "Where were we? Oh yes, you were asking me about my schooldays. And Dee and Penn. Now let me see what I can recall . . ."

It wasn't a very edifying story, but then the behaviour of schoolboys rarely has much to do with edification.

Penn and Dee had arrived at Unthank on the same day without previous acquaintance but soon found themselves thrown together by a common cause, survival.

Unlike the majority of pupils whose parents paid the school's fees, they were scholarship kids, known to the fee-payers as "skulks," who were admitted under a system by which, in return for a modicum of support from the public exchequer, the college undertook to educate three or four scions of the commonalty each year.

Schoolchildren love elected victims—the strong to have a legitimate target for their strength, the weak to help divert persecution from themselves.

Most victims, said Wingate, were localized by year, first-year skulks suffering at the hands of first-year bullies and so on. But some became a general target, usually because of some particularly distinguishing feature, like colour or a speech impediment.

"Penn got singled out when we found out he was German," said Wingate. "His first name is Karl, not Charles, which was pretty suspicious. Then someone saw his mother when she visited the school, a large lady, very blonde who spoke with a heavy Germanic accent. His father's real name, we soon found out, had been Penck, Ludwig Penck, which he'd changed to Penn when he got naturalized. I heard later that they'd got out of East Berlin when the Wall went up and kept going to the UK because Penck had an uncle here who'd been a p.o.w. in Yorkshire and stayed on after the war. Penck would have been sent back to West Germany, but his uncle was working on the estate of Lord Partridge, looking after his horses. Partridge was a Tory MP then, in the Cabinet, and he quickly took up the Pencks' cause. With old Macmillan in charge, liberal credentials could still do a Tory a bit of good back then, not like the present bunch where you need to kick two foreigners before breakfast to establish you're the right stuff. So he got permission to stay plus a job. Good heart-warming stuff, but of course at school no one was much interested in the political background, except maybe to think that if anyone had been persecuted once that was very good reason to persecute them again!"

"Kraut," said Hat suddenly, his first contribution to the conversation. They all looked at him.

"I heard Dee call Mr. Penn *Kraut,"* he explained.

"That's right, that's what he used to be called at school. Karl the Kraut," said Wingate.

"And he called Mr. Dee something back . . . it sounded like *whoreson?"*

"It would have been. Karl the Kraut and Orson the Whoreson," said Wingate. "Dee's mother came to the school too. Everyone was always very interested in everyone else's parents. Anything you could use to embarrass anyone with was avidly seized upon. Mrs. Dee was dead glamorous in a rather flashy way. Miniskirts were in then and she wore one right up to her bum. To add to the poor kid's other troubles, he had this birthmark, a sort of light brown patch of skin running down his belly into his groin. Some bastard suggested it was a symptom of some nasty disease he'd caught from his mother, and christened him Orson the Whoreson."

"You can always tell a well brought-up boy by his manners," said Dalziel. "Why Orson?"

"That was one of his names," said Wingate. "His mother hadn't done him any favours, had she? I presume she was a movie fan."

"Sir," said Hat excitedly, "you remember when I found . . ."

Pascoe shut him up with a glance. The Pascoe glance might lack the Big Bertha impact of Dalziel's facial artillery, yet it had a Medusa-like quality which served just as well.

"So," said the DCI to Wingate, "we've got a couple of kids being bullied rotten by their social superiors, what happened next?"

"Let's not make this a class thing," said Wingate equably. "OK, they were skulks, but it wasn't just that. You'll find just as much bullying in your local comp. Even at Unthank you didn't have to be a skulk to get picked on. There was another kid Penn and Dee were pretty thick with. Little Johnny Oakeshott. He was no skulk, in fact his family could probably have bought and sold most of the rest of us—"

"Any connection with the Oakeshotts out of Beverley?" interrupted Dalziel. "Them as own half Humberside?"

"That's the family," said Wingate. "Didn't stop Johnny from getting bullied. He was small, a bit girlish, lovely curly blond hair and the poor kid had a bit of a lisp. And his real name was Sinjon, which didn't help."

"Sinjon spelt St. John?" said Pascoe.

"That's right. He became Johnny when Dee and Penn took him under their wing. Not that that was much protection to start with as the hunt was very much up for them. They were both pretty small too, not as small as Johnny but small enough to be easy meat. Plus they were both pretty odd in their different ways. And that's what really sets off the bullies."

"So what happened? Were they bullied all the way through school?"

"Far from it," said Wingate. "By the time I was in the fourth year and they were in the third, things had changed."

"They'd started to fit in, you mean?"

"Hardly. But not fitting in isn't the point at school. It's the way you don't fit in. Penn's route to acceptability was the more conventional. He'd shot up and bulked out. He was never a heavyweight, you understand, but when he fought, he fought to kill. When he beat up the boss bully in his class, we all took notice. When he sorted out the tough guy in my year too, it was universally agreed that Penn was not a suitable target any more."

"And Dee?"

"Well, first of all he benefited from Penn making it clear that any attack on his mate, Dee, was an attack on himself. But at the same time his oddity developed along lines which entertained rather than alienated his classmates. He was obsessed with words, the more weird and wonderful the better, and he started using these during lessons. It was a marvellous form of piss-taking because the teachers couldn't really complain about it. They either had to admit their ignorance or try to bluff it out. Some of them tried to ignore him when he put his hand up to answer a question but the other kids caught on and made sure that often Dee's was the only hand that went up."

"In other words, he had to perform to be accepted?" said Pascoe.

Wingate shrugged.

"We all find our own ways to survive, at all ages," he said, glancing at Dalziel.

The Fat Man yawned widely. Indeed hippopotamicly, thought Pascoe. If such a word existed.

He said, "How about making up words?"

Wingate smiled coldly and said, "How like the police to know more than they let on. Yes, he did that too, which added a new element to this game he played with the staff who now also ran the risk of pretending to understand a word which didn't even exist. But it wasn't just a case of *épater la pédagogie;* he used to put these collections of words together into his own personal dictionaries, each one devoted to a special area. I recall there was a European dictionary, and an Ecclesiastic, and an Educational—that was quite fun. But the one that really confirmed his status in the adolescent intellectual world was his Erotic dictionary. He had, I seem to recall, over a hundred words related to female genitalia. I don't know whether it was a real word or one of his own, but if you ever hear a man of my age refer to his woman's *twilly-flew,* you know he's an old Unthinkable."

"Ee," said Wield.

"Eh?" said Wingate.

"All the examples you gave began with an E. European, Educational, Erotic."

"Oh yes. That was part of the joke. It was our Head of English who started it, I think. He was one member of staff who wasn't at all fazed by Dee's little games. In fact he joined in, often managing to cap him. And it was him that drew attention to the significance of Dee's initials. O.E.D. And after that Dee started finding E-words for all his collections so they could be OED's too. Like *Orson's Erotic Dictionary.*"

"But where's the Richard?" enquired Pascoe.

"What? Ah, Dick, you mean? No, that was the English master's joke. He started calling him Dictionary Dee, and it stuck. Dick is short for Dictionary. Gerrit?"

"I see," said Pascoe. He could also see Dalziel yawning again.

He said, "So it was exit Karl and Orson, enter Charley and Dick, right?"

"And enter Johnny too. No more taking the piss out of Sinjon."

"So now they belonged?"

"They were accepted rather than belonged," said Wingate judiciously. "They never let the rest of us forget how we'd once treated them. They started a magazine called *The Skulker,* only two copies of each edition, one for themselves, one they rented out. It was real samizdat stuff, so outrageously subversive that everyone wanted to read it, even though it was us as much as the staff who were being subverted."

Pascoe recalled his visit to Penn's flat and said, " 'Lonesome's loblance,' that mean anything to you?"

Wingate looked at him curiously and said, "You have been doing your research. Lonesome was Mr. Pine, Head of Dacre House. Everyone hated him."

"Dacre House . . . known as Dog House?" guessed Pascoe. "And *loblance?* Let me guess. One of Dee's names for the male organ?"

"Don't recall it precisely, but it sounds likely."

"Simpson? Bland?"

"Head Prefect of Dacre and his second-in-command. Dee and Penn's greatest enemies. They had a running battle with them."

"Who won?"

"It was no contest by the time they got to the Fifths. Dee and Penn were in pretty well total control. From time to time they would even call each other Kraut and Whoreson very publicly, though no one else dared, of course. It was like they were saying, *Just because we condescend to coexist with you lot doesn't mean we've really got anything in common. We're still different, and different means better. Anyone care to argue?*"

"And did anyone?"

"Occasionally. But by the time Dee had sorted them out verbally and Penn physically, they realized the error of their ways."

"And little Johnny Oakeshott, did he stay part of the team?" asked Pascoe.

"Johnny? Sorry, didn't I say? He died."

"Died? Just like that? Christ, I know they're all stiff upper lip, these places, but I'd have thought they took notice of dead kids!" said Dalziel.

"How did he die?" asked Pascoe.

"Drowned. Don't ask me how. There were all kinds of stories but all that ever came out officially was that he'd been found early one morning in the school swimming pool. Midnight bathing was a favourite rule-breaking sport. It was assumed he'd gone in by himself, or joined some group and got left behind. We don't know. Penn and Dee went ballistic. They brought out a special edition of *The Skulker.* Front page was all black with *J'ACCUSE* scrawled across it in white."

"Who did they accuse?"

Wingate shrugged.

"Everyone. The system. Life. They claimed to have got in touch with Johnny through a Ouija board and promised that all would be revealed in the next edition."

"And was it?"

"No. Someone told the Head and he came down hard. Told them what they'd written already was enough to get them expelled. Anything more and they'd be finishing their education in a pair of crummy comprehensives, miles apart. That was a clincher. Together they could survive, even prosper. Apart . . . who knows?"

"So they caved in and conformed?"

"Caved in? Perhaps. Conformed? No way. From that time on, the pair of them refused to have anything at all to do with the formal structures of the school. They never became prefects, refused to accept prizes, had nothing to do with organized sports or any other extra-mural activities. And as far as I know they've never attended any Old Boys' get-together or responded to any Appeal. They went through the sixth form, got university places, did their exams, walked out after the last one, and were never seen at Unthank again."

"Did they go to the same university?"

"No. They went their separate ways, which surprised a lot of people. Dee went up to John's, Oxford, to read English and Penn went off to Warwick to do modern languages. I meet them both occasionally through my job. We get on fine. But if I ever refer to our schooldays, they look at me blankly. It's as if they've wiped that part of the slate clean. You won't even find any mention of it in Penn's publicity material."

Now Wingate fell silent as if his memories had stirred up stuff he'd sooner have forgotten.

After a while Pascoe asked, "Anything else you can tell us, John?"

"No, that's it."

"You sure?" said Dalziel. "Not holding owt back, are you?"

"No, I'm not," retorted Wingate angrily.

"If you say so," said Dalziel. "But I can't think why you made such a fuss about talking in the first place if that's all you had to say."

"Oh, there were several reasons, Superintendent," said Wingate. "Let me list them if it will make you feel happier and hasten my departure . . . First because what I had to say doesn't show me or my fellows in a particularly good light; secondly, because I see no reason why I should retail personal details of people's lives to the police unless I feel they are truly relevant to some matter of importance; and thirdly, as a journalist, I am in the business of collecting rather than dispensing information, unless I feel there is some positive professional *quid pro quo*."

"Seems to me secondly and thirdly must sometimes trip over each other," said Dalziel. "Any road, you can run along now—so long as you remember that, while it weren't much of a *quo*, you've had your *quid* for it.

Any mention of owt about this in any of your little programmes and I'll be asking for a refund. Bye now."

"Goodbye, Superintendent," said Wingate.

Pascoe, trying for a conciliatory tone, said a touch over effusively, "Thanks a lot, John. That was really most helpful."

The producer looked at him for a long moment then said, "And goodbye to you too, Detective Chief Inspector."

Bang goes another nearly friend, thought Pascoe.

When the door had closed behind the departing man, he said to Dalziel, "So, how did you know about Wingate and Ripley?"

"Lucky guess," said the Fat Man. "Not mine. Young Bowler here said summat."

"Is that so?" said Pascoe, giving the DC a not altogether friendly glance. "Well, I don't think we'll be getting much co-operation from our local TV station from now on."

"Nay, I think we'll be getting all the co-operation we ever want," said Dalziel, grinning sharkishly. "Shouldn't waste your sympathy there, Pete. Married man who can't control his own loblance has to be a right twilly-flew. Question is, was it worthwhile squeezing his goolies? Did we get owt useful? Young Bowler, you looked like you were wetting your knickers to say summat back there."

"Yes, sir," said Hat eagerly. "Two things really. First, this boy Johnny who drowned, in this game Penn and Dee play, even though it's just for two players, they set up a third tile rack and when I saw them playing—when they called each other Kraut and Whoreson—the letters on this rack were J, O, H, N, N, and Y. Also, they've both got this photo of the three of them at school, at least I presume the third one's the dead boy."

"They've got a picture of themselves with a dead boy?" said Dalziel, interested.

"No, sir. I mean, he wasn't dead when the picture was taken."

"Pity. Go on."

"And his real name's St. John, and that drawing that came with the First Dialogue, didn't Dee say it was from the Gospel according to St. John . . . ?"

He felt himself running out of steam.

Dalziel said, "That your first thing finished then? Let's hope you're working upwards. Next?"

"It just struck me, with Dee's real name being Orson, it made me think of what Councillor Steel said before he died which sounded like *rosebud*—didn't someone say that was the last word that someone said in that film *Citizen whatsit* which Orson Welles directed and starred in . . . isn't that right . . . ? I never saw it myself . . ."

He looked around hopefully, not for applause but at least a shred of interest.

Pascoe gave him an encouraging smile, Wield remained as unreadable as ever, and Dalziel said, "What's your point, lad?"

"It's just the association, sir . . . I thought it might be significant . . ."

"Oh aye? I suppose if Stuffer Steel were a film buff, which he weren't, and if he were an old Unthinkable, which he weren't, and if he knew Dee's real first name, which I doubt, then it might come in sniffing distance of significant. Don't cry, lad. At least you're trying. What about you two big strong silent types? Wieldy?"

"This thing about the dead boy sounds a bit odd, but I don't see that it adds up to much," said the sergeant.

"More than just a bit odd, wouldn't you say?" said Pascoe.

"Mebbe. But it's not something Dee and Penn try to keep hidden, is it? Photo's on display, name on the tile rack which anyone can see. It's what folk want to hide that usually means most. And it seems to me we're getting bogged down in words here, not real stuff."

"The Wordman is all about words, Wieldy," said Pascoe gently.

"Aye, but about words playing around inside him. Seems to me Dee and Penn in their different ways let their words out, don't trap them inside where they might fester."

Dalziel, in face of this unexpected psycho-linguistic analysis, let out an *et tu Brute* sigh and turned to Pascoe.

"Pete, you think we might be on to something here, do you? Makes a change not to hear you badmouthing Franny Roote, who I hear is like to turn out the next Enid Blyton. But it 'ud be nice to know what's really going on in that mazy mind of thine."

"I don't know . . . it's just that I can't believe that in Dee's case all these coincidences of place and time and opportunity and interest don't add up to something significant."

"So let's talk to him again. Not you, but. If he is the Wordman, he's a clever bugger with it and he'll have got you sussed by now. You talk to Charley Penn, see if you can shake him on this lads'-night-in alibi. Me, I'll see how Mr. Dee reacts to a bit of basic English. Bowler, you come with me."

"Me, sir?" said Hat unenthusiastically.

"Aye. Any objection? From what I've heard you spend more time round at that library than you do here, so why so shy all of a sudden?"

Then the Fat Man let out a derisive laugh.

"Got it. Your bit of stuff, Miss Ribena, thinks a lot of her boss and you're scared it might queer your pitch if she catches you holding him down while I stamp on his goolies! Test of character, lad. She's going to have to choose between you and him some time, might as well force the issue afore you buy the ring. Now let's get some forward progress on this case, right? We've been running across the pitch far too long, lots of fancy footwork but no territorial gain. If this bugger wants to play games with us, let's at least start playing in his half of the field!"

Such a rallying cry, probably even more forcibly expressed, might have had some effect on a bunch of muddied oafs playing rugger, thought Pascoe. But none of those present in the CID room seemed fired by it.

He said, "Chief complaining about lack of progress, was he, sir?"

"He knows better," said Dalziel. "Though it's evident Loopy Linda's still banging heads in the Home Office. But Desperate Dan's got things closer to home to worry about."

"Like what?"

Dalziel glanced towards the doorway where Hat and Wield stood in deep confabulation.

"Like who's going to make the presentation at George's farewell tonight, me or him."

"I should have thought, in the circs, it's got to be top man there," said Pascoe, surprised. "Much as George loves you, I think he'll be expecting Mr. Trimble's honeyed words and firm handshake to accompany the clock or whatever it is we're giving him."

"Fishing tackle, they tell me," said Dalziel. "Well, we'll see."

Wield and Bowler had stopped talking and were looking to Dalziel expectantly.

Pascoe had a sense of something unsaid, but if he were right, it was going to stop unsaid, for the time being anyway.

"Can't hang around here all day," declared the Fat Man. "Not when there's goolies to stamp on. Come on, lad. We're off to the library. Where I hope you'll remember the first two rules of good detection."

"What're they, sir?" said Bowler.

"First's no groping on the job!" chortled Dalziel. "I'll tell thee the second on the way."

XXXIX

Despite the Fat Man's promise, most of the short journey to the Centre passed in silence, which Dalziel finally broke by saying accusingly, "Cat got your tongue?"

"Sorry, sir, I didn't want to disturb you."

Hat had decided that on the whole it wasn't a good idea to enquire further about Mrs. Blossom's tattoo.

"It's not talk as disturbs a good cop, lad, it's lack of it," said the Fat Man significantly.

"Yes, sir. Is that the second rule, sir?"

"Eh?"

"Of good detective work. You said you would tell me the second on the way."

"The second is don't take the piss out of anyone big enough to cause you grief," said Dalziel. "No, I just thought, you and me being together all cosy like, good chance for you to tell me owt you felt I ought to be told."

Oh shit! thought Hat. Even with poor Jax dead, he's still going on about me being the leak! The old sod can't bear not to be right. He's convinced I did it, but he won't be happy till he hears me say it. I could really pull his plonker here, tell him, *Yes, sir, I've got something to say about that info that was leaked to Jax the Ripper.* And when he's got himself all ready, sitting there all smug and know-it-all, expecting my confession, I'll let him know the leak was his randy old mucker, George Headingley, whose farewell party he's attending this evening, and what's he going to do about it?

And what would he do about it? That was the question. Presumably, once he knew something like that, he couldn't just let it go. There'd have to be a proper investigation and instead of sailing into the sunset, poor old Georgie Porgie would be . . . well, he'd rehearsed sufficiently already the possible consequences for Headingley.

He said, "Well, there was one thing . . ."

"Aye?"

"You know Charley Penn writes books? Well, I was thinking about what Dr. Urquhart said . . ."

"Should watch that, it could send you blind," said Dalziel.

". . . about the Wordman being so hung up on word games and stuff, he probably regards certain printed texts as a sort of coded gospel, and I wondered if it might be worth taking a close look at Penn's novels . . ."

"Oh aye? You volunteering to read 'em? We're going to the right place to get a start."

"No, sir, no way," said Hat. "I mean, I don't go in for that sort of thing, I thought maybe talk to someone who knows about these things . . ."

"You got someone in mind? Not your ladyfriend from the library, by any chance?"

Christ, it's like your mind is a goldfish bowl and this big cat dips his paw in whenever he fancies, thought Hat.

"Yes, she might be OK," he said. Then because this sounded a little lukewarm, he added, "She's been very helpful in getting my ideas sorted already."

And saw his error even as the words came out.

"Already? Make a habit of discussing confidential police matters with pretty young things, do you?" said the Fat Man. "I hope not, lad, 'cos that's the second rule I were going to tell you. When someone takes a hold of your bollocks, whether to twist 'em or to stroke 'em, just lie back and think of me. There's not enough pleasure or pain in the world to cover what I'm likely to do to any bugger I catch talking out of school. You with me, lad?"

"Yes, sir. I'm with you," said Hat, wishing with all his sinking heart he wasn't.

But that naturally ebullient organ rose again when as they got out of the car the Fat Man said, "That weren't a bad idea about Charley Penn's books. Have a chat with that lass of thine. From the sound of it, she owes you one. And I don't mean a jump. That you negotiate with your own coin, not mine."

And things got even better when they arrived in the reference library to find Rye alone, looking very fetching in a low-cut sleeveless top and clinging hipsters.

"How do, luv," said Dalziel. "Bossman around?"

"Sorry, no. He just popped out," said Rye. "Can I help?"

"Not really. Need to talk to him. Any idea where he's gone?"

"I'm sorry, I'm not allowed to give members of the public . . ." She broke off and looked at Dalziel more closely. "Oh, it's Mr. Dazzle, isn't it? Sorry, I didn't recognize you. Is it police business? Then I'm sure it'll be OK. He's gone along to the Heritage Centre, he shouldn't be long if you'd like to wait."

Behind Dalziel, Hat grinned broadly, especially at Rye's studied mis-pronunciation of the holy name.

But the Fat Man was untroubled by such bird-bolts as this and replied courteously, "Thank you, Ms. Pomona, but I'll just go and find him. Glad to see you so chipper after your nasty experience at the weekend. Lot of lasses these days would have needed a month off work and counselling for life. Thank God there's still some of the old stock around. But if you do need to talk to anyone, DC Bowler's a good listener."

With a hint of a wink at Hat, he wandered off through the door.

"You like living dangerously, do you?" said Hat.

Rye smiled and said, "Not so dangerous, just your normal nean-derthal. I caught him clocking my cleavage."

Hat, who had been enjoying an eyeful himself, averted his gaze and said, "So how're you keeping?"

"I'm OK. Didn't sleep too well, but that'll pass."

"I'm sure, but look, don't try to be too relaxed about it. That was a nasty shock you had, the head and all. These things can get to you in unex-pected ways."

"You were there too. You have some kind of immunity?"

"No. That's how I know about how it can hit you."

They regarded each other gravely, then she smiled and reached out and touched his hand and said, "OK, so let's counsel each other. Like a cof-fee?"

"If you're not too busy."

She gestured round at the almost empty library. A couple of pallid students were working in the reading bays, a wild-haired woman was sitting at a table behind a wall of the bound *Transactions of the Mid-Yorkshire Archaeological Society*, there was no sign of Penn or Roote or any of the regulars.

"Not exactly overworked, are you?" he said.

"We do other things than deal with the public," she said. "And with Dick busy elsewhere, I'm glad things are so quiet."

"So what's so important in Heritage?" he asked as she led him into the office.

"It's the Roman Experience. It's due to open tomorrow. Councillor Steel's death tipped the balance and the money was voted through at the next council meeting."

"They haven't hung about spending it then."

"Everything was set up, it just needed the announcement that bills would be paid."

"And what's it got to do with Dick?"

"Nothing really. But you know this power struggle I told you about, between Prancing Percy and the Last of the Actor–Managers? Well, they're both desperately trying to take the credit for the Roman Experience, and as Dick knows infinitely more about classical history than Percy, he's been commanded along to give gravitas to Percy's pronouncements. The trouble is, from Percy's point of view, that Dick is so honest and even handed, Ambrose Bird raises no objection."

"What about this woman, whatsername, the one who's been ill? Is she still off the scene?"

"Shh," said Rye, lowering her voice. "You mean Philomel Carcanet and that's her out there, hiding behind that wall of *Transactions*. She came in this morning to supervise the dress rehearsal. She knows more about Roman Mid-Yorkshire than anyone alive. Trouble is, she can't bear to talk to anyone alive for more than five minutes, which makes for a big communication problem. She came up here to pull herself together an hour ago. She's still pulling. While those two are down there, dividing the spoils and jockeying for position when they advertise the post of Centre Director. Can you switch that kettle on?"

"So who's your money on?" asked Hat.

"They'd both be disastrous," she said, spooning instant coffee into mugs. "All they want is to make sure their own corner's protected. Anyway, you're not here to discuss Centre politics, are you? What's Billy Bunter told you to ask me about? I think the kettle's boiling."

I must be made of glass, thought Hat. Everyone reads me like a book.

"Books," he said, passing her the kettle. "You said you were a fan of Penn's novels."

"I enjoy them," she said, pouring water into the mugs and passing one to Hat. "Though since he started being a fan of me, rather less so. Every time Harry Hacker says something smart or suggestive, I hear Penn's voice. A pity. The lionization of authors is a chancy business. It's like eating, really. While you're enjoying a nice piece of rump steak, you don't want to think too much about where it came from."

Hat, who had so far in his life not allowed such a consideration to trouble his digestion, nodded sagely and said, "Very true. But to get back to Penn's books, I saw one of them once done on the telly and gave up after ten minutes, so can you give me a brief tour through them?"

Then, to pre-empt the question he guessed her quizzical gaze was leading up to, he added, "The thing is this linguist guy from the Uni reckons that the Wordman's so hung up on words, if we can get a line on the kind of stuff he reads, we raise our chances of getting a line on him."

"Or the kind of stuff he writes, you mean," said Rye. "You're not interested in whether he reads the Harry Hacker novels, but whether he writes them."

"We've got to follow all lines of enquiry," said Hat.

"Yeah? That's what Billy Bunter's doing hounding Dick, is it? If you're not getting anywhere chasing the guilty, keep bashing away at someone innocent in the hope that you'll terrorize or trick them into a confession?"

"You may be right," said Hat. "But that's for top brass only. Me, I'm not even qualified to use the cattle prod yet so I've got to stick to old-fashioned methods like terrorizing people at long distance by asking questions when they're not there."

She thought about this, then said, "Harry Hacker is a sort of mix of the poet Heine, Lermontov's hero, Pechorin, and the Scarlet Pimpernel, with a bit of Sherlock Holmes, Don Juan (Byron's rather than Mozart's) and Raffles thrown in . . ."

"Hold on," said Hat. "Remember you're talking to a simple soul whose idea of a good read is a newspaper that's got more pictures than words. If we could cut out the literary padding and just stick to straightforward facts . . ."

"To the educated mind," she said coldly, "what you term padding acts as a form of referential shorthand, saving many hundreds of words of one syllable. But if you insist. Harry is a Jack-the-lad, bumming around Europe in the first few decades of the nineteenth century, getting embroiled in many of the big historical events, a bit of a con artist, a bit of a crook, but with his own moral parameters and a heart of gold. His background is uncertain and one of the connecting threads running through all the books is his quest to find out about himself, psychologically, spiritually and genetically. Such introspections could be a bit of a drag in a romantic thriller, but Penn livens it up by putting it in the form of encounters with Harry's *doppelgänger*, that's another version of himself. Sounds daft but it works."

"I'll take your word," said Hat. "This Harry sounds a right weirdo. How come the books are so popular?"

"Don't get me wrong about Harry. He's a real Romantic hero. He can be the life and soul of the party, pulling the birds almost at will, yet at other times he has these fits of Byronic (sorry, I can't think of any other way of putting it) melancholy in which all he wants is to be by himself and commune with Nature. But his saving grace is a strong sense of irony which enables him to send himself up just when you think he's taking himself far too seriously. The books are full of verbal wit, lots of good jokes, passages of exciting action, good but not overdone historical backgrounds, and strong plots which often include a clever puzzle element which Harry is instrumental in solving. They are not great works of art, but they make very good not unintelligent recreational reading. Their televisation, as so often happens, manages to disguise, dilute or simply dissipate most of those elements which make the novels special and give them their unique flavour."

She paused and Hat put down his coffee mug to applaud, not entirely ironically.

"That was good," he said. "Fluent, stylish, and I understood nearly all of it. But just to cut to the chase, is there anything in them which might connect directly to what we know about the Wordman?"

"Well, that depends on how you're using *we*. I dare say the full harvest of police knowledge and what I've managed to glean from your furrow are two very different things. But from my lowly point of view, the answer is possibly, but not uniquely."

"Eh?"

"I mean, if it turned out the Wordman had written something like the Harry Hacker series, it wouldn't be amazing. But I can think of a lot of other books it wouldn't be amazing to find he'd written, except of course that it would be, as some of the authors are dead and none of those who aren't lives in Mid-Yorkshire."

"Which is just the point. Penn does live in Mid-Yorkshire," said Hat. "What about this other stuff he's interested in, the German thing?"

"Heinrich Heine? Nothing there I can think of except insofar as he's a model for Harry Hacker. Harry was Heine's given name, you know."

"Harry? Thought you said it was Heinrich."

"That came later. One of Penn's translations called him Harry and I asked about it and he told me that at birth Heine was named Harry after an English acquaintance of the family. It gave him a lot of grief as a kid, particularly as the sound the local rag and bone man used to yell to urge his donkey on came out something like *Harry!* Heine changed it to the German form when he converted to Christianity, aged twenty-seven."

Now Hat was very attentive.

"You mean the other kids used to take the piss out of him because of his name?"

"Apparently. I don't know if there was anti-Semitism there too, but the way Penn told it made it sound pretty traumatic."

"Yes, it would," said Hat, excited. "Same kind of thing happened to him at school."

He told her what they'd found out about Penn's background.

She frowned and said, "You're digging deep, aren't you? I presume you've been checking out Dick in the same way."

"Yeah, well you've got to get all the relevant facts about everyone in an enquiry. In fairness to them really."

His weak justification got the scornful laugh it deserved.

"So what relevant facts did you discover about Dick?" she demanded.

Why was it when he was talking to Rye there always came a point when, despite the rasp of Dalziel's injunction in his mental ear, *remember you're a cop!,* it seemed easiest to tell her everything?

He told her everything, picking up the framed photograph on the desk when he came to Johnny Oakeshott's death and saying, "I presume that's him in the middle. Penn's got the same picture in his flat. Obviously he meant a lot to them both."

Rye took the picture and stared at the angelically smiling little boy.

"When someone you're close to dies young, yes, it does mean a lot. What's sinister about that?"

He recalled her brother, Sergius, and said, "Yes, of course it must, I didn't mean there was anything odd about that. But the attempts to get in touch with him . . ." Then just in case it turned out that Rye had tried making contact through a spiritualist, or some such daft kind of thing that girls might do, he pressed on, "But this stuff with the dictionaries, that's got to be a bit weird, hasn't it?"

"It's no big deal," she said dismissively. "Everyone who knows him well knows about the dictionaries. As for his name, all you had to do was look at the electoral register. Or the council employees list. Or the telephone directory. The fact that he's known as Dick is no more significant than you being Hat or me being Rye."

"Yes, but *Orson* . . ."

"No worse that Ethelbert. Or Raina for that matter."

"No, I meant, Orson *Welles* . . ."

She looked baffled for a moment then began to smile and eventually laughed out loud.

"Don't tell me. Orson Welles . . . Citizen Kane . . . *rosebud!* I've heard of drowning men clutching at straws, but this is going out to sea in a colander. I mean, where does it lead next? *Touch of Evil* maybe? Though come to think of it, when I look at your Mr. Dalziel, you may be on to something there . . ."

He didn't get the reference but didn't think it sounded a useful line to pursue.

"These dictionaries of Dee's, you knew about them then?" he said.

"Yes. I've seen some of them."

He thought instantly of what Wingate had said about the Erotic Dictionary and said jealously, "Which ones?"

"I really can't remember. Does it matter?"

"No. Where did you see them? Here?"

He looked around the office in search of the offending tomes.

"No. At his flat."

"You've been to his flat?"

"Any reason why I shouldn't have been?"

"No, of course not. I was just wondering what it was like."

She smiled and said, "Nothing special. A bit cramped but maybe that's because every inch of space is crammed with dictionaries."

"Yeah?" he said eagerly.

"Yeah," said Rye. "Not because he's obsessed or round the twist or anything like that, but because they are at the centre of his intellectual life. He's writing a book about them, a history of dictionaries. It will probably become the standard work when it's published."

She spoke with a sort of vicarious pride.

"When will that be?"

"Another four, five years, I'd guess."

"Oh well. I'd probably wait for the movie anyway," said Hat. "Or the statue."

He sat back in his chair and sipped his coffee and looked at the pictures hanging on the wall. Once more it struck him that they were all men. But he wasn't about to remark on it, not even neutrally. Previously any hint that Dee was in the frame had provoked angry indignation. By contrast, this rational debunking he was hearing now was affectionate banter and had to indicate that he'd made progress in his quest to win her heart. No way he was going to risk that by what might sound like a homophobic sneer!

He said, "This the Dee ancestral portrait gallery?"

"No," said Rye. "These are all, I believe, famous creators of or contributors to dictionaries. That one's Nathaniel Bailey, I think. Noah Webster. Dr. Johnson, of course. And this one here might interest a man in your line of work."

She pointed at the largest, positioned right in front of the desk, a sepia-tinted photo of a bearded man sitting on a kitchen chair with a book on his knee and on his head a peakless cap which gave him the look of a Russian refugee.

"Why's that?"

"Well, his name was William Minor, he was an American doctor and a prolific and very important contributor of early instances of word usage to what eventually became the Oxford English Dictionary."

"Fascinating," said Hat. "So what's his claim to fame as far as the police are concerned? Found the first use of the word copper, did he?"

"No, I don't think so. It's the fact that he spent the best part of forty years, the years in which he made his contributions to the OED, locked up in Broadmoor for murder."

"Good God," said Hat staring with renewed interest at the photograph.

Contrary to received opinion that there is no art to read the mind's construction in the face, many of the faces that he'd seen staring back at him from official mug-shot albums seemed to have criminality deeply engraved in every lineament, but this serene figure could have modelled for the Nice Old Gent in *The Railway Children*.

"And what happened to him in the end?"

"Oh, he went back to America and died," said Rye.

"You're missing the best bit," said a new voice. "As indeed was poor Minor."

They turned to the doorway where Charley Penn had materialized like Loki, the Aesir spirit of malicious mischief, his sardonic smile showing his uneven teeth.

How long had he been in eavesdropping distance? wondered Hat.

"Can I help you, Mr. Penn?" said Rye with enough frost in her voice to blast a rathe primrose.

"Just looking for Dick," he said.

"He's in the basement. They're working on the Roman Market Experience."

"Of course. *Per Ardua ad Asda,* one might say. I think I'll go and see the fun. Nice to see you again, Mr. Bowler."

"You too," said Hat, who was working out whether Penn wanted to be asked what was the best bit Rye had missed out, or whether his intention was to provoke the question direct once he'd departed.

He made up his mind and called after the retreating writer, "So what was this best bit I haven't heard?"

Penn halted and turned.

"What? Oh yes, about Minor, you mean? Well, it seemed that, despite his advancing years, the poor chap had constant erotic fantasies about naked young women which he found incompatible with his growing belief in God."

"Yeah? Well, it must happen to a lot of older men," said Hat with what he felt was commendable sharpness.

But Penn didn't look wounded.

On the contrary he grinned the saturnine grin and said, "Surely. But they don't all sharpen their penknives and cut off their dicks, do they? Have a nice day."

XL

"**Oh God, the** smells, the smells!" cried Ambrose Bird, pinching his aquiline nose. "They are overdoing the smells. They always overdo the smells."

"Smells are evocative, perhaps the most instantly evocative of all our human sense impressions," retorted Percy Follows.

"Is that so? And evocative, as no doubt you are aware from the vast depth of your classical knowledge, derives from Latin *evoco, evocare,* to call forth. I see from the programme that one of these alleged smells is that of roasting dormouse. Putting aside the question of where in this ecologically sensitive age you would obtain a dormouse to roast, we must ask ourselves what it is this odour is supposed to be evoking? You cannot call forth that which is not there. How many of our visitors do you imagine will have had any experience of roast dormouse? Therefore as a stimulus of latent memory, such a smell can hardly be called evocative. *Sic probo!*"

"I see the floorshow's started," said Andy Dalziel.

Dick Dee turned and smiled.

"Superintendent, how silently you arrive. But I shouldn't be surprised at such lightness of movement from one who only last Saturday evening was the terpsichorean star of the Fusiliers' Ball."

This was top-level intelligence. OK, he'd teased Pascoe and Wield with vague reference to his Saturday night dance date but even they would have been hard put to find where he'd been, so how had news of any of this reached Dick Dee?

The answer was obvious.

Charley Penn who must have hot-footed it down to Haysgarth to check out how Dalziel had broken his alibi.

He said, "You're well informed for a man who does nowt but read old books. And talking of old books, why've you left 'em to come down here? Refereeing job, is it?"

Down here was the basement of the Centre, intended purely for storage until the discovery of the Roman floor during the digging of the foundations. The decision to incorporate the floor into the Centre as part of a Roman Reality Experience had seemed a brilliant compromise between the archaeologist camp and the council pragmatists who wanted to get the Centre finished as soon as possible. It hadn't worked quite like that. Stuffer Steel had opposed every penny of the extra expense involved, and the extra strain placed on Philomel Carcanet had been a large factor in her breakdown.

"As always, you put your finger on it, Superintendent," said Dee. "My modest reputation for being well informed brings me here as an arbiter between our disputing gladiators."

"Why are they here anyway? Not their patch. Thought I saw Phil Carcanet up in your library just now."

"Yes, indeed. It's such a shame. It was her baby, the Experience, you know. She worked so hard getting everyone on board, the archaeologists and the council. She had to do it practically single-handed—no one else cared to take on Councillor Steel. It ran quite against the grain of her personality and in the end it broke her. She's been on sick leave, but Mr. Steel's demise removed the last obstacle to the project, suddenly the money was there, and with the opening so imminent, she made an effort to come in today, but I fear she found her fellow triumvirs reluctant to withdraw from the field. You see, that's another thing the councillor's death has done. It's cleared the way to the appointment of an overall director, and it is his bays our heroes are apparently struggling for. At the first sign of dispute, dear Philomel fluttered away. Before you lie the fruit of her labours, but not for her the harvest. Oh dear."

He put his hands to his ears in response to an explosion of noise.

"Turn it down, turn it down!" screamed Follows.

The noise declined and became recognizable as a babble of voices intermixed with horses neighing, cocks crowing, dogs barking, bells ring-ing, children laughing, and the occasional strains of a faintly oriental mu-sic, with brass notes blaring at a distance and plucked strings resonating much nearer.

"That's better," said the librarian.

"You think so? You must attend a lot of very quiet markets. They're not like Sainsbury's, you know, all Muzak and the swish of plastic. They are very noisy places," said Bird.

"Ah, your famous crowd expertise," mocked Follows. "Which must, I presume, have come from a previous incarnation as you can't have picked it up from your theatre audiences. But that language—isn't it supposed to be Latin and Anglo-Saxon these people are speaking? That doesn't sound like anything I've ever heard."

"Why should it be when all you ever heard was some old fogey in a dusty gown declaiming Cicero or *Beowulf*? This, as far as the best palaeo-demoticists can assess, is how it must have sounded in its vernacular form."

Dalziel, observing Dee, thought he caught a flicker of self-approval and said, "That pally whatsit one of yours, then?"

It was good pay-back for the Fusiliers' Ball. Dee's features registered surprise which he tried to cover not by concealment but by exaggerating it into comedy.

"Ooh, what a sharp old detective you are, Superintendent. Indeed, I did drop the neologism into a conversation I had with Mr. Bird and it's pleasing to learn that, with his finely tuned actor's ear, he has added it to his word-hoard. I should add that it seems to me a perfectly logical com-pound and one I would not be surprised to find already existent. What else, I wonder, has your own sharp ear extracted from these exchanges?"

Dalziel said, "Well, it's confirmed what I knew, that they're a right pair of mutton-tuggers. At a guess, I'd say that when poor old Phil took badly, Ambrose put himself in charge of sound effects and Percy took smells. Seems about right."

"Spot on again," said Dee. "I like *mutton-tuggers*, by the way. An evolved usage, but much apter than the original. Do you want to watch the rest of the shall we call it performance? Or shall we make a small tour while we talk?"

The internal interrogative was offered with a small smile which Dalziel stored up for future ingestion along with a lot of other stuff which was rais-ing interesting questions.

"Talk about what?" he said.

"About whatever it is you've come to talk to me about," said Dee. "Though at a guess I'd say it was the sad death of Lord Pyke-Strengler, and its place in the wider context of your pursuit of the Wordman."

As he spoke he led the way around the market between the various stalls. Most were pure artefacts, as realistic as lighting and sound effects could make them, but with the goods on display and the traders selling them all ingeniously moulded out of plastic. There were, however, three or four stalls which were stocked with real articles and attended by real people. Dee paused before one of these which was selling small articles made of metal, weights, cups, ornaments and so on. The stallholder, a handsome dark-haired woman in a simple brown robe which complemented rather than concealed the sinuous body moving beneath it, smiled at him and said, "*Salve, domine. Scin' Latine?*"

Dee answered, "*Immo vero, domina,*" then picked up a brass cat and rattled off a whole sentence in Latin to which the woman replied ruefully, "Oh shit. We're not going to get a lot like you, are we?"

"No, I'm probably a one-off," laughed Dee. "What I said was, I liked the pretty little pussy-cat but I liked the one in the brown robe a lot better."

"Did you now? I see I'd better learn the Latin and Old English for cheeky sod if I'm going to survive here."

Dalziel watched this little piece of by-play with interest, noting the ease with which the librarian joked along with the woman and her readiness to slip into flirt mode. No one had suggested to him that Dee might be a ladies' man, but maybe that was because he hadn't been questioned by a woman.

As they moved away he said, "So what were that all about?"

"In the interests of verisimilitude, some of the stalls are manned by real people. Ambrose Bird supplies them from his company, actors who aren't in the current production and who fancy making a bit of extra cash. They're taught enough Latin and Anglo-Saxon to say hello and ask any potential customer if they speak either language. When, as in most cases, they get a blank look, they relapse into a sort of broken Shakespearean English."

"Except now and then they'll get some clever bugger who does speak the lingo."

"What would the world be without clever buggers?" asked Dee.

"A sight happier," said Dalziel. "And do they actually sell that gimcrackery?"

"Very high quality reproductions," corrected Dee primly. "Yes, when you enter the experience, you can purchase a *follis* full of *folles* . . ."

"Eh?"

"*Follis* means money bag, but it also came to refer to the coins, particularly the small-denomination copper and bronze coins, that the bag holds. These can be used to make purchases from the active stalls or in the *taberna* over there."

"That's like a pub, is it?" said Dalziel with interest.

"In this case more like a café," said Dee. "But it might be a good place for us to have our talk. Note, however, the *calidarium* or bathhouse as we pass."

He indicated a door which had a glass panel in it. Peering through, Dalziel saw a small pool of steaming water with a naked man sitting in it, reading a papyrus scroll. Beyond and only dimly visible through the wreathing steam stretched other expanses of water in which and along whose tiled edges disported figures, some draped with towels, some apparently naked, though the swirling steam kept all within the bounds of Mid-Yorkshire decency. It took him a moment to work out that what he was looking at was the first small pool multiplied by cleverly placed mirrors and backed by a video projection probably culled from some old Hollywood Roman epic.

"Clever, isn't it?" said Dee.

"Not really," said Dalziel. "Not when you've seen the big bath down the rugby club. And they know all the verses to 'The Good Ship Venus' down there too."

The taberna also fell well short of the rugby club in its provision. There was no service and when there was, as Dee explained, the choice would be between a sweet more or less authentic fruit drink or a totally anachronistic cup of tea or coffee.

"A concession to Councillor Steel who had to be persuaded that there was going to be a strong self-financing element in the project," said Dee.

"You'll not be sorry he's out of the way then?" said Dalziel as they sat on a marble bench.

"I might find that question provocatively offensive if I weren't persuaded that it is your intention to provoke," said Dee. "In any case, Superintendent, you should understand that the success or failure of this project means very little to me. On the whole, despite the educational arguments, it all verges a little too much on the kitsch for my taste. In these days of interactive user-friendly fully automated hi-tech exhibitions, I still feel nostalgic for the old-style museum with its musty smells and its atmosphere of reverential silence. The past is another country and I sometimes feel we are visiting it more like football hooligans on a day out than serious travellers. How about you, Mr. Dalziel? How do you feel about the past?"

"Me? You get to my age, you don't want to be looking back too much. But professionally speaking, it's somewhere I spend a lot of time," said Dalziel.

"But not, I'm sure, in any glitzy hi-tech way like the modern Heritage industry?"

"Oh, I don't know. You mind that old TV science-fiction series, *Doctor Who*? Fellow travels around in a time machine that looks like a police box from the outside? Load of old bollocks, most of it, but I always felt that bit were right. A police box. 'Cos that's what I do with the past. Like yon Doctor, I spend a lot of time visiting bygone days where villains have done things to try and change the future, and I don't much care how I get there. It's my job to mend things as far as I can and make certain the future's as close to what it ought to be as I can get it."

Dee regarded him wide-eyed.

"A time-lord!" he exclaimed. "You see yourself as a time-lord? Yes, yes, I think I get it. Someone commits a murder, or robs a bank, it's because they want to change the future as they see it, usually to make it more comfortable for themselves and those they are close to, right? But by catching them, you restore the status quo, so far as that's possible. Naturally if someone has been killed, there's little you can do by way of resuscitation, is there?"

"I can't bring folk back to life, that's for sure," said Dalziel. "But I can keep them living. This Wordman, for instance, how many's he killed now? Started with Andrew Ainstable, if you count letting someone die, then there was young David Pitman and Jax Ripley, and after that . . . who came next?"

"Councillor Steel," said Dee readily. "Then Sam Johnson and Geoff Pyke-Strengler."

"They tripped nice and easy off your tongue, Mr. Dee," said Dalziel.

"Oh dear. Was that a trap? If so, let me make a suggestion, Mr. Dalziel. I have up till now been happy to play my part in the charade that I was being questioned as a witness. But your continuing interest makes me wonder if it might not be time for both of us to come out in the open and acknowledge that I am a suspect."

His expression now was one of eager almost ingenuous enquiry.

"You want to be a suspect?" said Dalziel curiously.

"I want to have the opportunity to remove myself from your list—if, as I fear, I'm on it. Am I on it, Mr. Dalziel?"

"Oh yes," said the Fat Man, smiling. "Like Abou Ben Adhem."

"Thank you," said Dee, smiling back. "Now let's try to discover some single point of fact that will prove to you I'm not the Wordman. You may ask me anything you like and I will answer truthfully."

"Or pay a forfeit."

"Sorry?"

"Truth, Dare, Force or Promise. Used to play it a lot when I were a kid. You had to choose one of them. Or you could pay a forfeit, like taking your knickers off. You've chosen Truth."

"And I intend to keep my knickers on," said Dee.

"Oh aye. You bent?"

"Bent as in crooked, or sexually deviant?"

"Both."

"No."

"Never?"

"Well, I have in my time committed various offences, like breaking road traffic regulations, shading my expenses, and using library stationery for my own purposes. Also there are one or two small amatory idiosyncrasies which I enjoy if I can find a willing partner of the opposite sex. But I believe that all of these fall within the margins of normal human behaviour, so I feel able to answer *no* even though I am not strictly able to answer *never*."

"So you and Charley Penn never pulled each other's plonkers?"

"As young adolescents, yes, occasionally. But only as, if you'll forgive the expression, a stop-gap strategy to fill that anguished period between the onset of puberty and access to girls. Once girls appeared on the scene, our friendship became nunlike in its chasteness."

"Nunlike? Not monklike?"

"After the bad press many of the Catholic male Orders have been getting in recent years, I think I'll stick to nunlike."

"Could Charley be the Wordman?"

"No."

"How so sure? 'Less you're the Wordman yourself, of course."

"Because, as I'm sure you have already ascertained, on the first of the two evenings you questioned me about, when I was enjoying the company of Percy Follows, Charley was culturally engaged with his literary group. And on the second evening he was with me."

"Who says the killing took place in the evening? OK, that second day, you gave each other alibis in the evening, and your work means you've got an alibi for the day. But not Charley. He's very vague about what he was doing that day. Says he thinks he probably went to the library but nobody seems able to confirm this. Not unless you're suddenly going to remember seeing him there?"

"Now why should I do that?"

"One good turn, mebbe. But like mutual masturbation."

"You mean in return for the good turn he has done me by alibiing me for that evening? But that would only make sense if we were both the Wordman."

"That's an interesting thought."

"And one which I doubt has just sprung ready-formed into your mind, Superintendent. A *folie à deux,* is that the way you're seeing things? Oh dear, and here was I thinking it was only myself I had to remove from your hook."

"Hook. Like in fishing. Do any fishing yourself?"

"I have done, yes. Why?"

"The Hon. Geoff had a couple of rods with him. Like he'd mebbe gone out to fish with a mate."

"I think perhaps you are mistaking our relationship."

"Oh aye? How about your relationship with that lass of yours. You banging her?"

"Sorry?"

"Her with the silver flash and the funny name."

"Rye. I assumed it was Rye you were referring to. It was the participle I had difficulty with."

"There's these tablets you can take. I said, are you banging her? whanging her? slipping her the yard of porridge? stirring her custard with your spoon? twiddling with her twilly-flew?"

That got a reaction but it was only a faint almost complimentary smile.

"Am I having a relationship with Rye, you mean? No."

"But you'd like to?"

"She is an attractive woman."

"That a yes?"

"Yes."

"Got anything going at the moment?"

"A sexual outlet, you mean? No."

"So how do you manage?"

"Manage what?"

"Manage not to embarrass yourself every time you stand up. Man in his prime, all parts working, getting horny whenever you look at your assistant, and you and Charley have grown out of giving each other a helping hand, so what do you do? Pay for it?"

"I don't get the drift of your questions, Mr. Dalziel."

"We never said owt about drift, just that I could ask anything I wanted and you'd answer truthfully. You got a problem with that?"

"Only an intellectual one. I understood there'd been no sexual overtones in these killings, so I'm curious why you seem concerned to focus on my sexuality."

"Who said there'd been no sexual overtones?"

"You'll recall I have in fact read three of the five Dialogues so I can draw my own conclusions from them. Only one woman has been attacked and there was nothing in what I read in that episode which suggested a sex motive. In fact there is, how shall I put it, an almost sexually sterile atmosphere about the whole affair."

"You're sounding a bit defensive."

"Am I? Ah, I'm with you. You're being provocative again. If I am the Wordman and my motive is completely non-sexual, then all these questions about my sex life might trigger a reaction at being so grossly misunderstood, is that the idea?"

"Reaction like this one, you mean?"

"Not being the Wordman, I could not be so precise. But I should say the impression I got from my reading was of someone clever enough to see through your little stratagem earlier than I did, and not let himself be provoked."

"Or clever enough to appear slightly less clever than he really is."

"Now that would be really clever. But surely such a paragon of cleverness would never let himself fall into your clutches for close questioning anyway?"

"Put your finger in it there, Mr. Dee. *Let himself fall.* Seems to me the fellow I'm thinking of might actually enjoy a little chat like this, face to face with the enemy and running rings round him."

"It would, I think, be a long run. I speak metaphorically, of course. Forgive me if I seem to have erred towards over-familiarity, but I do feel that anyone trying to run rings round you, Mr. Dalziel, had best come equipped for a marathon. But how am I doing in my puny effort to persuade you I am not your man? I must confess I feel my strength failing."

He did a little mime of exhaustion and, as if in sympathy, all the lights went out and the hubbub of sound effects which had provided a foil to their conversation ceased.

The ensuing silence was short. The voices of Bird and Follows rose in angry unison demanding what the hell was happening, then parted into contrapuntal duet as each sought to find a way of off-loading responsibility on to the other.

Dalziel and Dee felt their way out of the dark taberna into the market place where people were striking matches or flashing torches to give a dim illumination. The door of the *calidarium* opened and a man wearing swimming trunks and dripping water stepped out followed by a puff of smoke.

"Enter Dagon, downstage, left," murmured Dee.

"What the hell's going on?" demanded the man angrily. "Something electrical blew up in there and I'm sitting over my arse in fucking water!"

He had good reason to be angry, thought Dalziel as he made his way back towards the market centre where Bird and Follows were positioned. En route he stubbed his toe against various objects which he kicked aside with great force.

"Who's in charge?" he demanded.

For once, neither of the two men seemed eager to assume the primacy.

"Well, I'll tell you both summat for nowt—you'd best get this sorted else I'll make sure the local Fire and Safety Officer closes you down permanent. That bastard in the bath could have been electrocuted. And why's it so fucking dark? Imagine what it 'ud be like down here with a few dozen people, a lot of them kids, milling around. Where's your back-up system, for God's sake? Get it sorted quick or I'll start thumbing through the big book to see what I can find to charge you with. And if I can't find owt serious enough, I'll mebbe just bray you with the book!"

He strode away, finding the stairs and the exit back to the regions of light and air by dead reckoning. When he got there, he paused and found Dee at his side.

"You know, Mr. Dalziel," said the librarian with a smile, "after that performance, I think if I were the Wordman, I'd put my hand up now and confess."

"That right, Mr. Dee?" said Dalziel indifferently. "And I'll tell you what I think, shall I? I think you're fuller of crap than a knackered septic tank."

Dee pursed his lips and looked pensive as if this were a statement worthy of close examination then said, "I'm sorry to hear that. Does it mean our little game of Truth, Dare, Force or Promise is over?"

"*Your* little game. When there's folk lying dead, I don't play games. I'll see you around, Mr. Dee."

He moved away with mastodon tread. Behind him, still as a primeval hunter, Dick Dee watched till he was out of sight.

XLI

Detective Inspector George Headingley may not have scaled the promotional heights, but he had performed the feat unusual in police circles of achieving his modest eminence without standing too hard on anyone's face.

Therefore as his colleagues, CID and Uniformed, gathered in the Social Club that night to say their farewells, the atmosphere was more than usually cordial. Pascoe had been to farewell parties where the attendance had been meagre, the jokes sour, and though the banners read *Good Luck!* the body language spelled *Good Riddance*. But tonight everyone had made an effort to attend, the contributions to the leaving present had been generous, and the laughter already rising from the assembled men, especially those at Headingley's crowded table, was good humoured and full bellied.

There'd been a special cheer of welcome and some spontaneous applause when the door had opened to admit Detective Constable Shirley Novello. This was her first public appearance since the shooting which had put her out of commission since the summer.

She looked pale and didn't move with her usual athletic spring as she advanced to take the seat offered her next to George Headingley, who won another cheer by standing up and greeting her with a kiss on the cheek.

Pascoe went to the table and leaned over her chair.

"Shirley, it's good to see you. Didn't know you were coming."

"Couldn't miss the chance of making sure the DI really was leaving, could I?" she said.

"Well, don't overdo it," he said. "You know what they say about too much too soon."

"Yes, dead before twenty," said Headingley.

Beneath the roar of laughter which this evoked, Wield said in his ear, "Pete, Dan's here, but still no sign of Andy."

"Great."

Though Headingley's popularity was great enough for Uniformed to be there in numbers too, this was essentially a CID party, and Dalziel's absence meant the duties of host devolved upon him.

He went forward to welcome the Chief Constable.

"Glad you could make it, sir," he said. "Looks like everyone's determined it's going to be a great night."

Even as he spoke his eyes told him that he was wrong. Trimble's features had the cast of a man who'd come to bury someone rather than praise him.

"Where is he?" asked the Chief curtly.

"George?"

"No. Mr. Dalziel."

"On his way," said Pascoe. "Let me get you a drink, sir."

On his way wasn't a positive lie as, presumably, wherever Dalziel was, he purposed at some point to arrive at the Social Club, therefore, whatever he was doing, he could be said to be on his way there.

But the positive truth was that Pascoe hadn't the faintest idea where the Fat Man was. He had seen him briefly on his return from the Centre but a phone call had taken him away before he could enlarge upon his comment in response to the question of how he'd got on with Dee: "Yon bugger's too clever by half."

While being too clever by half was not in itself a guarantee of criminality, it was certainly true that several men so categorized by Dalziel were currently doing *The Times* crossword before breakfast in one of Her Majesty's penitentiaries.

Bowler hadn't been able to add much more about Dee, but he was voluble about his own discoveries and was clearly hurt just this side of the sulks by Wield's reduction of them to a self-mutilating lexicographer and a German poet who changed his name 'cos he got the piss taken out of him, neither of whom seemed to have any discernible relevance to the case in hand.

For a small man, Dan Trimble had an authoritarian way with a large drink and had downed three of these with no apparent effect on his frame of mind when Pascoe glanced at his watch and murmured, "Show time, I think, sir. The natives are getting a little restless."

"What? No, no, what's your hurry? The DI seems to be enjoying himself. Another few minutes won't hurt. No word from Andy yet?"

" 'Fraid not, but any moment now, I'm sure . . ."

And as if he'd been waiting for his cue, the Fat Man erupted through the main door, emanating good cheer like the Spirit of Christmas Present. Making his way across the room towards Trimble, he paused to smite Headingley on the shoulder, ruffle Novello's hair, and utter some good thing which set the table on a roar. Then he arrived at the bar, accepted the large Scotch which materialized there, downed it in one, and said, "Made it then! Would have hated to miss your speech, sir."

"Miss my . . . ? Andy, you said you'd ring."

"I know I did, and I would have done, only things got a bit complicated. . . ."

He put his arm round Trimble's shoulders and drew the Chief aside and spoke earnestly in his ear.

"Like Lord Dorincourt giving some friendly advice to Little Lord Fauntleroy," murmured Pascoe to Wield.

"At least it's stopped him looking like he'd had his budget cut," said Wield as Trimble's expression first of all relaxed, then eased itself into a positive smile as the Fat Man smote his hand to his breast in a histrionic gesture of reassurance.

"I think he's just sold him a used policeman," said Pascoe thoughtfully.

Dalziel came to join him as the Chief Constable wandered over to Headingley's table and put his hand on the DI's shoulder and made a joke which won a laugh as loud as Dalziel's had.

"Dan's going to make the presentation then?" said Pascoe.

"Always was," said Dalziel.

"Am I going to find out what's been going on?"

"Why not? Read that."

He pulled some creased papers out of his pocket and handed them over. Trimble had moved into the centre of the room, there were cries for order, and after the inevitable responses of "Mine's a pint" had won their inevitable laughs, he began to speak without notes. He had an excellent public manner and as he rehearsed the highlights of the retiring detective's career with wit and eloquence, it was hard to believe that he'd had any re-luctance to be doing so.

Pascoe, who didn't need to be told of Headingley's virtues, glanced down at the papers Dalziel had given him. His glance soon became fixed, and after the first reading he went through them again, then gave Dalziel's ribs, or at least that stratum of subcutaneous fat beneath which he guessed they were situated, an insubordinate poke and hissed, "Where the hell did these come from?"

"You recall Angie, Jax Ripley's sister, at the funeral? These are copies of e-mails from Jax to her."

"I'd gathered that. I mean, how did you get hold of them?"

"Angie rang Desperate Dan afore she left for the States on Sunday. When she told him what she were on about, he said he'd like to see copies so she put 'em in the post. No lift on Sunday so he got 'em this morning."

Their muttered conversation was attracting attention so Pascoe took the Fat Man's sleeve and drew him away from the bar to the back of the room.

"Watch it," said Dalziel. "That's as nice a piece of worsted you're pulling as you'd see on the Lord Mayor of Bradford."

"You see what this means? Of course you bloody well see. Georgie Porgie. A fat, cuddly senior officer. Ripley's Deep-throat was Headingley not Bowler!"

"Aye," said Dalziel complacently. "Always a bit of a swordsman, George. Hung like a donkey. Resemblance didn't end there, but."

The Chief Constable was warming to his task and talking about old-fashioned virtues like loyalty to one's colleagues and utter reliability.

"You knew!"

"Not till he went sick after she got topped. Then I got to thinking, maybe I'd done young Bowler an injustice. I mean, Ripley were a smart lass. If it's information you're after, you don't start snogging the office boy."

"And the Chief . . . no wonder he was having kittens about making the presentation. Doesn't look good if the officer you've praised up to the heav-ens one day goes down for corruption the next!"

"Corruption? Now there's a big word for a little thing like dipping your wick. Have you clocked George's missus lately? Like a bin liner stuffed with frozen broccoli. Man like George was sitting there, just begging to be taken for a ride by owt with big ambitions and tits to match. I should have taken greater care of him."

This display of paternalistic guilt should have been comforting, but Pascoe wasn't in the market.

He said indignantly, "He's been selling us out for a quick jump!"

"Lots of jumps, if you read between the lines, and some on 'em not so quick either. Teach us all a thing or two, could George."

"I'll skip the lesson, thank you," said Pascoe primly. "What on earth made Angie Ripley want to share these rather sordid details with the Chief? I mean, they don't exactly reflect well on her sister."

"She weren't thinking of her sister's reputation, she were thinking of her murder," said Dalziel.

"Her murder . . . Jesus! You mean she reckons that wanting to shut her up could have been a good motive for killing her? George Headingley killing her? She must be crazy!"

"She didn't know George, did she? In fact after we met at the funeral, it seems she decided the description fitted me! Minute Dan read them but, he knew it must be George. Silly cow."

He sounded indignant. On the other hand, thought Pascoe, having mistaken the Fat Man for her sister's lover, it was very easy to see how she took the step of suspecting him to be her sister's killer!

He kept the thought to himself and asked, "But what's going to happen . . . ? In fact, what *has* happened? What did you tell the Chief to make him so happy?"

Trimble was retailing George Headingley stories with great zest and rolling his audience in the aisles. He did not sound like a man who had any fear that his valedictory encomium might one day be presented as evidence of his poor judgment and lack of managerial control.

"Told him that in my opinion any resemblance between Jax Ripley's roly-poly Georgie Porgie and our George were purely coincidental, or at worst, Ripley based the fantasies she invented for her sister's entertainment on George because he was the officer who did a lot of our media briefings. Told him that I'd checked out George personally and that I could give my personal assurance there were nowt in it. And finally I told him that the stuff about a motive for killing Ripley was totally irrelevant and there'd be no come-back from sister Angie because in a very short while we'd be charging someone with the Wordman killings, including Jax's."

"Will we?"

"You want to tell Dan we won't?"

They were interrupted by a crescendoing round of applause shot through with cheers and whistles as the Chief Constable reached the climax of his address and a flushed and beaming George Headingley rose and went forward to receive the state-of-the-art fishing rod and associated tackle which had been his chosen gift.

"Oh, and one other thing," said Dalziel as he clapped his hands together thunderously. "Seems that Desperate Dan weren't the first police officer Angie confided in. Seems she took her suspicions first of all to young Hat Bowler and it were only when she thought he was dragging his feet that she decided to ring Dan afore she took off home."

"Hat? But he hasn't said anything, has he?"

"No. Gave him plenty of chance to, but he kept mum."

"But why? When it would have cleared him of suspicion?"

"Mebbe he looked at George and thought, Here's a guy, long years of honourable service, sailing into retirement, do I want to be the one who torpedoes him? Mebbe he thought that sometime in the future he might be dependent on someone turning a blind eye to something he'd got up to too."

"And which of these made you decide to keep quiet?" asked Pascoe.

"Me? I didn't have to decide," said Dalziel. "Let's go and congratulate George, shall we? Looks like he's getting a round in."

As they made their way back to the bar, Pascoe said, "Have you told Hat yet?"

"Told him what?"

"That he's off the hook."

Dalziel roared with laughter.

"Don't be daft. Why should I do that?"

"Because . . . well, because he deserves it. He's got the makings of a good cop."

"No argument there," said Dalziel. "He's bright and he's keen and he's proved he's dead loyal. He could go far with the right incentive, and that's what I'm giving him."

"How?"

"Well, every time he thinks he can relax on the job, I'll just need to give him that fish-eyed look which says I've still got doubts about him and he'll be doing double-overtime without pay just to prove me wrong, won't he? And one thing I'll never have to worry about is him letting his gob be ruled by his bollocks rather than his brain."

Oh, Andy, Andy, thought Pascoe, you think you're so clever and you may even be right. But you've forgotten, if you ever knew it, the absolute power of young love. I've seen the way Bowler looks at Rye Pomona and

I'm not sure that even the fear of the Great God Dalziel is enough to keep him quiet if she asks something nicely.

The Fat Man, unaware of these treacherous doubts about his infallibility, had gone through the crowd at the bar like Lomu through an English defence.

"George, lad," he cried, "congrats, you've made it at last, out into civvy street, safe and sound."

"Andy, I was wondering where you'd got to. What are you drinking?"

"Only two minutes out of the job and the bugger's forgotten already!" declared Dalziel plaintively. "I'll have a pint and a chaser. So, George, you take care of yourself, eh, it's a wilderness out there."

"I'll be careful," said Headingley.

"I'm sure you will, wandering round the countryside with that lovely new rod of thine. Just one bit of advice from one old angler to another."

Dalziel took Headingley's hand as he spoke and pressed it tight.

"What's that, Andy?"

The pressure increased till the blood could hardly reach the DI's fingertips and at the same time the Fat Man stared unblinkingly into his watering eyes as he said softly, "Don't go dipping it in any forbidden waters, George, or I may have to come looking for you."

They stood there looking at each other for several seconds. Then behind the bar a phone rang.

The barman picked it up, listened, then called, "Is there a policeman in the house?"

Through the laughter he added, "It's the station. Would like to speak to someone in CID. Mr. Dalziel or Mr. Pascoe preferred."

Pascoe said, "I'll get it."

He took the phone, listened for a while, then said, "On our way."

He put the receiver down. Dalziel was watching him. He jerked his head to the door.

Out of the press around the bar, the Fat Man said, "This had better be good. I've got a pint and a gill back there surrounded by bastards with the scruples of a starving gannet."

"Oh, it's good," said Pascoe. "It was Seymour."

DC Seymour had drawn the short straw and been left to look after the CID shop.

"He's just had a call from the security guard at the Centre," he went on.

"Oh fuck. Not another body."

"No," said Pascoe, pausing long enough for Dalziel to look relieved before going on. "Another two bodies. Ambrose Bird and Percy Follows. Dead in the Roman Experience bathhouse."

"Oh shit," said Andy Dalziel. "Shit and double shit. How dead? Drown-dead?"

"No. Electrocuted-dead," said Peter Pascoe.

the seventh dialogue

Do you recall how at the beginning I said my heart fainted at the distance I saw stretching between my setting out and my destination?

Yes, that's exactly how I felt. Oh me of little faith, wherefore did I doubt? How far have I come and how quickly, a quarter of my way now in the blink of an eye, striding out with braggart step, measuring my path not in miles, but in leagues!

No plan is needed when you are part of a plan, and when I beheld him who was equally a part of the plan, though his time seemed some way still removed, descending like one who hurries to a longed-for assignation, without thought I followed—happy word!

In the darkness I lost him for a while, then suddenly the torches flickered to life, the sounds swelled, the odours drifted across my flaring nostrils, and I found myself deep in the past of the Roman market. Two figures moved towards each other between the stalls, one clad in a courtier's purple and gold tunic with jewelled clasps, clutching in his hand a leather bag from which he took coins as if to make a purchase, the other in the plain dignified toga which denotes a senator.

"Ho, Diomed, well met! Do you sup with Glaucus tonight?" cried the first.

"I know not," said the senator. "What a fearful night is this! There's two or three of us have seen strange sights."

"And shall see stranger still. Will you walk with me into the bathhouse where we may hear ourselves talk above this fearful babble?"

"Gladly, for the stink of this place rubs my nostrils raw!"

Side by side they moved into the calidarium.

Through the viewing port I watched them, still not knowing what I was called to do or indeed, with the middle step still not clear, not certain I was called to do anything.

Then as the tunic was unclasped and the toga slid to the ground, I felt time, already by artifice here displaced, begin to slow like cooling lava running down Vesuvius's side which in its last embrace grips fragile flesh and makes it live forever.

They step into the water, the courtier first, his long gold hair catching the light from the images of naked bathers projected on the wall, his trembling limbs slender and white; the senator behind, his black ponytail jutting out jauntily, the muscles of his sturdier browner body taut with desire. There is no pause for foreplay. The strong brown arms go round the slim white body as, like a full-acorned boar, a German one, the senator cries "O!" and mounts the courtier.

Unnoticed, because lava itself bursting through the walls would in this condition go unnoticed, I open the door and step inside.

Like a surgeon who need not look for his instrument because he knows it will always be there to hand, or in this case to foot, I feel no surprise as my toe catches on a cable and sends an electric soldering iron snaking across the floor to plop into the pool like a questing vole. Nor does thought play a part in sending my hand along the cable to its source where my fingers find and press a switch.

They twist and tauten in one last orgasmic spasm and then go still. From the courtier's discarded tunic I take the dagger and make the necessary mark on his white flesh, while from his bag I take the necessary coin and place it in the senator's open mouth.

Now it is done. I step back into Roman time and without haste mount the stairway to my own.

I feel a deep peace. I know now that I can proclaim myself from the mountaintops, yet none will hear and understand and lay traps to prevent me. Never has the way ahead seemed so clear.

A path In VIew, I neVer stray to Left or rIght.
A weDDIng was, or so It seems, but wasn't whIte.
A Date I haVe, the fIrst In fun, though not by nIght.

XLIII

"They were still—how shall I put it?—*coupled* when we got there," said Peter Pascoe.

"Fused together," growled Dalziel. "Don't be mealy-mouthed."

"Coupled," repeated Pascoe. "The maintenance man claims that he disconnected the soldering iron from the extension lead and disconnected the extension lead from the socket on the floor above, which was where he'd had to plug it in because of course all the electrics in the basement had cut out when the fault down there developed. He admits, because he can hardly deny it, that after going upstairs to check the repaired circuits at the main power box, he omitted to return to collect the iron. He says he left it in situ because he intended doing another check on the basement circuitry first thing this morning to make sure all was well for the official opening. A conscientious worker."

"A lying bastard," said Dalziel. "He switched the iron off at the switch on the extension plug, went upstairs, checked the power box, then one of his mates yelled, 'Coming for a pint, Joe?' and he forgot all about it."

Pascoe gave him a tightly weary smile and wondered why, as they'd both had the same sleep-curtailed night, the Fat Man looked so alert and vigorous while he felt ready to keel over?

But keeling over wasn't an option when he was giving a briefing to his CID team, plus the Chief Constable who'd decided that in view of the seriousness of the situation, he himself would monitor the next conference, plus the Doctors Pottle and Urquhart, whose presence had also been Trimble's idea as soon as he heard that the Seventh Dialogue had been found next morning in one of the Centre mailboxes—not the library box which the police were monitoring, but the unmonitored Heritage box on the far side of the building.

Dalziel had objected, making the point that details of advanced investigative procedures and likely suspects ought not to be made available to civilians, to which Trimble had replied somewhat acidly that if he did not trust his co-opted experts then perhaps he shouldn't have recruited them in the first place, and if they were to be of any use to the team, then they must be as fully briefed as everyone else. The Fat Man had got a bit of his own back when the Chief had commented on the presence of DC Novello. "CID rule, sir. If you're fit enough to drink, you're fit enough to work," he'd said. He'd answered Pascoe's own reservations on the DC's presence rather more humanely by saying, "I gave her a ring, asked if she felt up to sitting in for an hour. Break her in gently's best after what she's been through. Also, could be useful getting a female slant on things. Can't be any dafter than the crap we're likely to get from Oor Wullie and Smokey Joe."

"Maybe they won't have much to say," Pascoe tried to reassure him.

"They never do. Doesn't stop the buggers from prattling on, but. Just try not to encourage them, eh?"

But it was Trimble who gave the first cue.

In response to Dalziel's interjection, he asked, "Does it really matter at this juncture if the maintenance man is trying to cover his back or not?"

"Not really," said Pascoe.

"Except," said Dr. Pottle, "insofar as what he says throws doubt on to the Wordman's version in the Dialogue."

He paused, weighed Dalziel's menacing glower against the Chief Constable's encouraging nod, decided that in this case rank counted, and went on, "The Wordman's version as always stresses his sense of being the instrument of some superior power, a very active instrument of course, but nonetheless one whose certainty of invulnerability is based on the provision by his guiding power of that conventional trinity of crime investigation: motive, means and opportunity."

"What motive?" demanded Dalziel. "There ain't none, that's the point when you're dealing with madmen!"

"You're wrong, Superintendent, though I won't irritate you with psychological analysis at this juncture. But motive in the sense that these killings are clearly sequential not even you will deny."

"Meaning he only kills people who fit some crazy pattern he's working to? Well, thanks for that insight, Doctor. It 'ud be a lot more useful if you could work out the pattern for us, but I dare say that's not on offer yet?"

"I regret the basis of the sequence still escapes me, but I'm working on it," said Pottle, lighting his fifth cigarette since arrival. "What is clear is that the Wordman looks to his guiding power to point out his next victim or victims, then to bring them into the killing situation, and finally to provide the means."

"Took his own knife along to sort out Jax Ripley," said Wield.

"True, but he still makes it clear that the weapon was somehow provided for him in some manner he could fit into his grand plan. And similarly with the drug used to poison Sam Johnson."

"So what are you saying, Doctor?" enquired Trimble.

"Only that, if the maintenance man's version is true, it means that the Wordman is rearranging the facts of the incident to fit in with his fantasy, or even to persuade us of its reality. Which would be very interesting."

"Interesting!" groaned Dalziel. "Like it's interesting if you're waiting for a bus and a giraffe walks down the street, only it doesn't get you anywhere!"

Pascoe hid a smile and went on, "Whatever the truth of that, the two men were certainly electrocuted in the Roman Experience . . ."

"Sounded more like a Greek experience, from what I heard," grunted Urquhart who looked even more wrecked than Pascoe felt and had been struggling to find a dormitory position on an upright plastic chair.

"As always, I bow to expertise," said Pascoe. "Anyway, they were in the Centre basement area—"

"Sir," interrupted Hat Bowler, "had they arranged to meet there to, you know, do it? Like a date, I mean. Or had it just happened? Or was it a sexual assault?"

"I think, in view of the dressing-up element, and unless we discount the Dialogue completely, it was all planned and voluntary," said Pascoe. "The duty security man says that Bird had warned him that he would be testing the basement effects early that evening for about an hour to make sure that all was well. The security videos were as useless as ever. A fire door wedged open at the head of the main stair down to the Experience effectively cut out the corridor along which Follows must have approached from the library and therefore cut out the pursuing Wordman too. There is no video camera in place yet in the Experience area. I presume Bird and

Follows knew this otherwise they'd hardly have rendezvoused there. You look doubtful, Hat."

"It's just that, well, those two didn't seem the type . . ."

Pascoe raised an eyebrow, Wield scratched his nose, and Hat stumbled on, ". . . sorry, I didn't mean not the type to be gay, because I don't know what that would be, but they didn't seem to like each other, in fact the few times I saw them, they seemed to be getting right up each other's noses."

"Not their noses you should have been watching," muttered Dalziel.

Pottle said, "This apparent antagonism was almost certainly their way of concealing the relationship, though it may well be that a real antagonism actually played a significant role in it too. There are certain kinds of lovers' quarrels which add a positive spice to heterosexual relationships. The vigorous verbal battles we so often find being joined between men and women in Shakespeare are nearly always a prelude to their eventual coupling."

"I should add," said Pascoe, "that the security man does recollect other occasions when Bird used the theatre for what he called lighting rehearsals, just him and allegedly the lighting director, though the security man once glimpsed what he called this lanky blonde in an off the shoulder dress before a door was shut in his face. I suspect they had been taking advantage of Bird's access to props and costumes to play out their fantasies for some time and the completion of the Roman Experience had seemed like an opportunity not to be refused."

Trimble said hopefully, "This killing couldn't be just a bit of good old-fashioned gay-bashing, could it? That would make things such a lot simpler."

Pascoe opened his mouth to make a sharp response to this crass comment, but Wield came quickly in with, "Sorry, sir, but there's nothing in the Dialogue to suggest the Wordman disapproves. He may be mad but that doesn't mean he's got to be bigoted."

Then he glanced at Pascoe and dropped an eyelid as if to say, *I'm a big boy now, I can look after myself.*

Pottle added, "I agree with the sergeant. Indeed so far I have found little to suggest that the Wordman disapproves in moral terms of any of his victims. Certainly there are no traces of homophobia."

"Yes, of course. Sorry," said Trimble. "Mr. Pascoe, please go on."

"Yes, as I was saying, the pathologist has confirmed that death was by electrocution. After death the bodies were interfered with in a curious way . . ."

"After!" grunted Dalziel.

". . . with Follows having a mark scratched on his forehead. Scratches on skin are difficult but the best guess is it was intended to look like this."

Pascoe went to the drywipe board and drew: $

"It's a dollar sign," said Trimble.

"Possibly," said Pascoe. "And certainly if that's what it is meant to be, there is a link of a kind with what was found in Ambrose Bird's mouth."

He produced a plastic evidence bag in which a small metal disc was visible.

"It is a Roman coin, copper or bronze. We showed it to Ms. Carcanet, the Heritage Director. As you may know, she's been unwell and the news of what had happened in the Roman Experience didn't do her state of mind any good. But she managed to tell us that the head stamped on the coin is probably that of the Emperor Diocletian, though it's very worn, far too badly for the inscription to be legible."

"But it is genuine?" asked Trimble.

"Oh yes. Most of the coins in the tourist bags like the one Follows was carrying are replicas, but for authenticity they decided to include a few examples of the real thing, well-used Roman coins too worn to have any value to a collector. Did the Wordman select it deliberately because he wanted the real thing, I wonder. And perhaps too we should recall that the classical Greeks used to place an obolus or small coin in the mouth of the dead so that they could pay Charon to ferry them over the Styx."

"Karen?" said Dalziel. "Over the sticks? Grand National's not been the same since they invented women jockeys."

Pascoe, who'd heard it all before, ignored this provocative philistinism and concluded, "Anyway there we have it, a dollar sign and a Roman coin. I suppose it could be some kind of statement about money being the root of all evil?"

He looked hopefully towards the two doctors.

Pottle shook his head.

"I doubt it. As I say, I find little evidence of any warped moral schema here. He's not killing people because they are prostitutes, or black, or Arsenal supporters. No, I'd guess that the coin and the sign are riddle elements rather than psychological indices. Perhaps our semiotic expert can help."

He blew a wraith of smoke towards Drew Urquhart who had apparently overcome all the gymnastic problems inherent in going to sleep on a hard office chair.

The linguist opened his eyes, yawned, and scratched his stubbly face.

"Thought about it," he said. "Not a fucking clue what they mean."

Dalziel rolled his eyes like ten-pin bowls but before he could knock the Scot over, he continued, "But there is a couple of wee things that did strike me. I'll go through the Dialogue bit by bit if that's OK, Mr. Trimble?"

He looked deferentially towards the Chief Constable. The sly sod's sending Andy up! thought Pascoe. With an embarrassed glance at his Head of CID, Trimble nodded.

"First para takes the form of a question, establishing a dialogue between him and us. Second starts biblically, 'me of little faith,' version of Matthew 14.31. Then note 'a quarter of the way.' Eight deaths so far, implying another twenty-four to go, though not necessarily, as I shall explain later."

"Can't wait," said Dalziel.

"Cross your legs and think of Jesus, my old gran used to say," said Urquhart. "Something else here, same para, you must have noticed it with your guid Scots ancestry, Mr. Dalziel. 'Braggart step.' Now how does it go?"

He started humming a tune, then interpolated the odd word as though having difficulty remembering, the whiles looking imploringly at Dalziel who suddenly amazed them all by breaking forth in a not unpleasing baritone and singing, *"If you're thinking in your inner hairt the braggart's in my step, ye've never smelt the tangle o' the Isles!"*

"Bravo," said Urquhart. "Guid to see you've not gone completely native."

"So the Wordman knows the song. So what?"

"By heather paths wi' heaven in their wiles," murmured Urquhart. "It all builds a picture. Next para: 'Happy word.' Presumably *followed* because of course he is following Follows. Well, we knew he was a word freak, but more interestingly, note the bit which says that Follows is equally part of the plan, 'though his time seemed some way removed.' Question, how so? Presumably it means that Follows wasn't the next in sequence. The next but one, maybe? Then why say *some way removed*? Also notice half a dozen paras on, 'the middle step still not clear.' As if to say that even with the real next target, which must be Bird, available, there's still an intermediary step between Bird and Follows."

"Like last time," said Pascoe, who'd been listening with intense interest. "He talked about three steps, didn't he? Even though there was only the one body."

Urquhart nodded approvingly as though at a favoured pupil and went on, "Makes me wonder if the coin and the dollar sign might not have something to do with this middle step. But fuck knows what. Let's move on. Next para, nothing. Then they start talking. This felt literary to me. I checked it out with my wee hairie. 'What a fearful night is this! There's two or three of us have seen strange sights,' is *Julius Caesar*, Act One Scene Three. But Diomed and Glaucus don't seem to be in Shakespeare."

"Bulwer Lytton, *Last Days of Pompeii*, Chapter One," said Dalziel. "Thought everyone knew that."

It was a show-stopper for everyone but Pascoe, who knew that this volume was a pretty well permanent feature of Dalziel's bedside table. His knowledge did not come from any personal acquaintance with the Fat Man's sleeping arrangements but because on one of the rare occasions Ellie had been in his house, she had "inadvertently" wandered into the bedroom when looking for the bathroom, an "error" she repeated on the next two rare occasions. The book remained in place, but the bookmark she noticed in it had changed places, suggesting either a very slow or a cyclic reading.

She'd also noted that the volume was stamped *Property of the Longboat Hotel, Scarborough* and the bookmark was a folded copy of a bill for a week's stay directed to the account of Mr. and Mrs. A.H. Dalziel. Little was known, or perhaps self-preservation ensured little was said, about Dalziel's ex-wife. But Ellie, noting the date on the bill, declared, "This must have been their honeymoon! And he's kept the book he stole by his bed all these years. How romantic!" and immediately went out and bought a second-hand copy. Pascoe had tried to read it but gave up after a couple of chapters so had to be content with his wife's psychological exegesis.

All this flitted across his mind, plus an epiphanic revelation of the significance of that second initial which he'd never known the Fat Man use anywhere else as he heard Urquhart say, "Don't know it, Hamish. What's it about?"

"About the eruption of Vesuvius that destroyed the city way back in Roman times."

"Well, that fits with all that stuff about lava later on. And the *Julius Caesar* quote might suggest that a tyrant is about to be overthrown . . ."

"Hang on," said Pascoe. "These aren't the Wordman's words but what Follows and Bird said to each other."

"We only have the Wordman's word for that," said Urquhart. "And I did say *might* suggest. I'm just trying to strike a few ideas here. On a bit. 'Middle step, lava,' done that. Ah yes, the para about them getting down to it in the water. Bit of excitement here. No moral disapproval, I'd agree with

Pottle there, but I think the Wordman got a wee bittie titillation here, maybe. 'Like a full-acorned boar, a German one . . .' "

He looked invitingly at Dalziel who said, "Nay, lad. Tha's had all the help tha's going to get from me. I don't keep pups and yap."

"Shakespeare again. *Cymbeline*. Posthumus imagines the supposititious coupling of his wife, Imogen, with her alleged lover, Iachimo."

"Like a full-acorned boar, eh?" savoured Dalziel. "Not bad. So what do you make of that, dominie?"

Urquhart grinned at the appellation and said, "Fuck all. On we go. Para starting 'Like a surgeon,' note the little play on *hand* and *foot*. This cunt really lives in a world where words and their relationships mean more than people and theirs. 'Questing vole' is a bit odd . . ."

"Evelyn Waugh," said Pascoe.

"Oh, *her*," said Dalziel.

"Feather-footed through the plashy fen passes the questing vole. *Scoop*," said Pascoe.

"Significant?" wondered Urquhart.

"It's parodic. And of course comic. I suppose it reinforces what you said about the Wordman's preference of words to people. Yet wasn't there in the first couple of Dialogues anyway some sense of genuine, I don't know, almost affection for Mr. Ainstable and young Pitman?"

They all considered for a moment then Novello said, "Maybe the difference was, he didn't know them. Not personally."

This was her first contribution. She really didn't look well, thought Pascoe, determined that she was going to be dispatched home the minute this lot was over.

Hat Bowler checked out his colleague's pallor with less sympathetic eyes. What the fuck was she doing here anyway? he asked himself. This case was his big chance to establish himself firmly as a player in the Holy Trinity's game and he didn't care to see an old favourite coming up on the rails.

But you don't shoot old favourites down, not in public anyway.

He said brightly, "That's right. He seems to have got started on this by chance. But after those two, all the others seem to be connected in some way, either with the investigation or with the library. How about if he knew the others and had reasons for not caring about them?"

"Or reasons for not letting his acquaintance with them get in the way of killing them. Word-play, jokes, quotation can be useful distancing devices," said Pottle.

Dalziel made a noise like an old iron pier undermined by the suck of the sea and said wistfully, "Are we near done?"

"Not quite. The best is still to be," said Urquhart. "Last prose para. Thought you might have had something to say about this, Pozzo."

"His sense of peace, you mean? His belief that he is invulnerable, invincible? I hardly feel it necessary to point out the obvious. As I've said before, eventually it is this belief that he can tell us anything about himself and his purposes with no risk of either prevention or detection that will be his downfall. But of course we need your linguistic skills, Dr. Urquhart, to interpret these nods and winks."

"Well, thank you kindly. OK, the wee bit of verse at the end, it's a riddle of course. Right wee Jimmy riddler, this guy. And when you find answers, they usually just ask more questions."

"Which is what the press out there are waiting to do," said Trimble sourly.

Poor old Dan, thought Pascoe. He came along hoping that rabbits were going to be plucked from hats by the burrowload. Instead, the end of the expert evidence is in sight and he doesn't feel he's even glimpsed a vanishing rump!

"Aye, well, if the guid Lord had gi'en us the airt to see the morn today, we'd all be farting through silk, as my auld Kirkcaldy grannie used to say. But dinna despair. Pozzo's right, he's giving us clues and I'm the boy to grasp 'em. Anything strike you about this wee doggerel?"

They all looked at their copies of the Dialogue, then Bowler and Novello said simultaneously, "The print," and looked at each other speculatively.

"That's right. The print. All them capitals. Could they mean something, I asked myself," said Urquhart.

"Like he's a lousy typist," said Dalziel.

"Not anywhere else, he's not," said Urquhart. "No, I reckon this is a chronogram."

He looked around triumphantly. The returned gazes were blank.

"A chronogram," he explained, "is a piece of writing in which certain letters are made to stand out to express a relevant date or epoch. Mostly it used Roman numerals because of course they are expressed in letters. For example, Gustavus Adolphus, the Swedish king killed during the Thirty Years War, had a medal struck to commemorate a victory in 1632 with this inscription."

He went to the drywipe board and wrote:

ChrIstVs DVX: ergo trIVMphVs

"Which of course means . . ."

He paused expectantly, playing up to the dominie role that Dalziel had mocked him with.

"With Christ in charge, we'd solve this in no time," said Novello pertly.

They all laughed, even Trimble, and Urquhart flashed her the louche smile which probably pulled any number of female students, thought Hat maliciously.

"That'll do nicely," said the linguist. "Now, think Roman numerals and check out the upper case letters. In Latin inscriptions, U's are normally printed as V's of course. Which gives us—" he wrote 100+1+5+500+5+10+1+5+1000+5—"which equals 1632. This also works in English. A famous example is . . ."

He wrote again.

LorD haVe MerCIe Vpon Vs

"Add this up and you will see we get 1666. The reference incidentally isn't to the Great Fire but to the other great event which Dryden celebrates in his *Annus Mirabilis*, the naval warfare between Britain and Holland."

It was interesting, thought Pascoe. The more he got into his teaching mode, the less marked his Scots accent became.

"This one uses U's as V's too, though it's not in Latin," said Wield.

"A licence carried over from the craft of lapidary inscription," said Urquhart. "Before they got power tools, it was a lot easier for masons to carve straight lines and angles than curves. Our Wordman, however, is a purist. In his triplet, only V's count numerically. And you will note that as in all the best chronograms every numerically significant letter is capitalized and therefore counts. It's much easier if you just pick out those that add up to the sum you want. Anyway, let's see what we have."

He wrote:

$$1+5+1+1+5+50+1+500+500+1+1+1+500+1+5+1+1+1 = 1576$$

"Well, there you go," he said complacently, returning to his seat.

They all sat looking at the board like Belshazaar's courtiers staring at the wall.

"And that's it?" said Andy Dalziel.

"Unless my arithmetic's wrong."

"But what the fuck does it mean?"

"Hey, man, I'm just the language man, you're the fucking detectives. But when he says 'a date I have,' I take that to mean with his next victim, so 1576 has got to be some kind of pointer."

"I'm sorry, my history's pretty lousy," said Peter Pascoe. "Did anything significant happen in 1576?"

"I expect shit happened, it usually does," said Urquhart indifferently. "Look, that's it for me. Unless you've got any questions I can answer, I've got a lecture to give."

"I too have promises to keep," said Pottle. "So unless there is anything else . . ."

"*Else!*" echoed Dalziel under his breath but not that far.

Pascoe looked around the room then said, "No that looks like it for now. Again, many many thanks, both. I'll be in touch. And of course, if anything occurs to you, don't hesitate to contact me at any time."

The two academics left. After an uncomfortable moment, the Chief Constable said, "Well, that solves at least one problem, Andy. Now we can get down to all those details of advanced investigative techniques and likely suspects you didn't want to share with civilians."

"Right," said the Fat Man. "Peter?"

Well, thanks a bunch, thought Pascoe.

He said, "Sir, we're throwing everything at this. Forensic, computer records, plus all the manpower we can muster interviewing everyone who got within half a mile of the library yesterday evening. All the library security tapes and all the tapes from everywhere else in the shopping precinct are being gone over inch by inch. And as you've seen with Dr. Pottle and Dr. Urquhart, we're drawing on every kind of outside help we can think of."

"Suspects?" said Trimble.

"Yes, sir. Immediately upon establishing that a crime had been committed last night, we sent officers to ascertain the whereabouts and movements of the three men we have in the frame."

"Who are . . . ?"

Pascoe drew a deep breath and said, "Charley Penn, Franny Roote, Dick Dee."

The Chief Constable had to know there were no others, yet he still managed to look disappointed.

"I see," he said. "So after eight deaths your thinking doesn't take you past this trio whom I understand you have already looked very closely at. Charley Penn, the nearest thing we have in the area to a media celebrity. And Franny Roote, in whom I gather you have a strong personal interest, Mr. Pascoe. And Dick Dee, the man who was instrumental in getting us to take this matter seriously in the first place."

He raised his eyebrows at Pascoe who felt like saying, "Well, thank you kindly, sir, for pointing out the sodding obvious to us poor dumb detectives. Now why don't you piss off back to your big office and leave us to get on with our underpaid jobs?"

Instead he said mildly, "The Wordman too is a media celebrity. And I have a strong *professional* interest in Mr. Roote. As for Dee, fire investigators advise taking a close look at the guy who reports the fire, also the main man on the spot when you arrive."

Trimble considered this, seemed to spot the subtext, smiled faintly and said, "I do hope we're not anticipating arson attacks too. Any joy when you checked them out?"

"Nothing positive. But none of them had a firm alibi for the early part of the evening."

"Well, that's something, I suppose. Though, come to think of it, I don't think I've got a firm alibi either."

Trimble stood up suddenly and the others rose too.

"I won't keep you back from your work any longer. I don't need to impress on any of you how urgent it is we bring this business to a rapid and satisfactory conclusion, just as I didn't need our local Member of Parliament impressing it on me this morning. Andy, be sure to keep me up to speed on progress, won't you?"

"Anything happens, you'll be the first to know," assured the Fat Man.

As the door closed behind the Chief, they all slumped back into their chairs and studied the floor and/or ceiling as if in hope that someone else was going to burst forth with an inspired insight.

Finally Dalziel said, "Nowt for it, we're going to have to arrest Dan. You heard him say he hadn't got an alibi. Unless young Bowler can help us out."

"Sir?"

"Well, you're sitting there pursing your lips like a cat's arsehole. It's either wind or words that are trying to get out. So do we listen or duck?"

"Sorry, sir. I was just looking at that date he wrote on the board—1576. Seems it ought to mean something to me."

"Oh aye? You got O-level history?"

"I took it," said Hat evasively.

"Good enough. You bugger off down to the library and check out everything that happened in that year. If you do nowt else, you'll be letting Dee and likely Charley Penn too know we've got the message."

Doing his best to conceal his delight at being given an excuse to see Rye, Hat made for the door.

But his joy was pricked a little when Dalziel called after him, "And make sure that's the only date that's on your mind in yon library. Young women can seriously damage a young detective's career."

The Fat Man winked at Pascoe then said, "How about you, Ivor? Owt strike you?"

"Sorry, sir, were you talking to me?" said Novello with a histrionic little start.

It had taken her some time to find out why Dalziel called her Ivor and when she did, she affected an isn't-it-sad indifference to yet another example of male infantilism. But secretly, particularly after the correct Pascoe's injunction to all others against using this sobriquet left the Fat Man as its sole source, she had to admit a certain pleasure in being so singled out. After all, when Samuel heard God calling him in the Temple, he didn't retort sourly, "It's *Mr.* Samuel to you."

"That bullet sent you deaf as well? Christ, you look terrible. Time you went home."

It occurred to her to suggest that if looking terrible were reason for sending people home, Dalziel and Wield would never leave the house, but of course she didn't. Truth was she didn't feel too clever but admitting it in this company wasn't an option.

"There was something," she said. "The coin in Bird's mouth. But there wasn't one in Follows. Maybe the Wordman didn't mind Bird getting over the Styx to heaven, but disliked Follows so much, he wanted to keep on hurting him beyond the grave."

Pascoe nodded approvingly. The smart bastard's been there already, thought Novello, but doesn't reckon there's much in it.

The smart bastard said, "It's a thought, though of course we should be careful not to confuse the classical underworld with a Christian heaven. And it still leaves us with the problem of the dollar sign."

"The almighty dollar, maybe?" suggested Novello. "Could be the Wordman thinks that hell is something like America."

Pascoe grinned, showing real amusement. Made a nice change from the patronizing encouragement of his smile, thought Novello. Though, paradoxically, she felt encouraged enough to add, "I've got this feeling that while the coin might somehow represent the middle step he refers to, the dollar sign has got a significance to do with the choice of victim. I read through all the Dialogues and there was that other instance of scratching something on the head, Councillor Steel, wasn't it? Only one step there, so far as we can make out, so what did the scratching mean?"

"RIP in Cyrillic script, wasn't it?" said Pascoe. "A joke, it looked like, given he was called Cyril. The Wordman likes a joke, particularly if it's to do with words."

"Yes, sir. That's something we shouldn't forget, isn't it? We should never lose sight of the words, any words, when we're dealing with the Wordman. I mean, words aren't just useful labels. Like in religion, when you speak certain words, things happen or are supposed to happen. Magic too. Or in some cultures, you don't tell people your special name because names are more than labels, they are actually you in a special way. I'm sorry, I'm not putting this very well. What I'm saying is that words, maybe a special arrangement of words, seem to have a special significance to the Wordman, each word marks a step forward, and sometimes he can link separate words to individuals and then they get killed, but maybe sometimes he links more than one word to an individual and then we get only one corpse but a trinity of steps, like he says in the Dialogue where he describes killing Lord Pyke-Strengler."

She paused, wondering, Am I babbling? Dalziel was certainly looking at her as if he reckoned she was delirious.

She got help from an unexpected source.

Wield said, "You mean his reason for chopping the Hon.'s head off could be something to do with words, with these steps you're talking about, rather than with the Wordman's state of mind. External, not internal?"

"That's right," she said. "Like he thought, all right, I've got a body, that's a step. Now if I do this and this with it, that would be another two steps. He's eager to be moving forward along this path he keeps talking about and when something like this occurs, whatever it was, of course he puts it down to divine intervention or something."

"So what are you suggesting?" asked Pascoe.

"Maybe instead of concentrating on clues in the conventional sense, we should start collecting words. Listing them in every way we can until one of the lists makes some kind of sense."

"Examples, please," said Pascoe encouragingly.

Dalziel would have growled, "Money where your mouth is, luv, else keep it zipped." She felt that she would have preferred that, then glanced at him, saw his expression, and changed her mind.

"Well, Pyke-Strengler's body was found in the stream, right, and his head in a fishing basket in his boat. So words like stream, water, beck, brook, river, and boat, basket . . . wickerwork . . . creel . . ."

She was starting to feel very tired and these swirling ideas which had seemed on the verge of coalescing into something solid were beginning to dissipate like morning mist, but she pressed on.

"And this latest, Bird and . . . whatsisname . . . words like coin . . . and dollar . . . and money . . ."

She felt something like a sob gathering in her throat and tailed off into silence because it seemed a better alternative.

Dalziel and Pascoe exchanged glances then the Fat Man said, "Ivor, that's grand. You keep working on that, eh? I really appreciate you coming in like this, and the Chief'll have noted it too. Now I reckon it's time you headed off home for a bit of a rest."

Cue to say, No, I feel fine, but speech felt even more treacherous in face of this lumbering sympathy, so instead she stood up, nodded curtly, and made it out of the door without a wobble.

Dalziel said, "Wieldy, see she's all right. Don't know what you were thinking of, Pete, pressing her like that when she's still convalescing."

"Hang about," said Pascoe indignantly. "It wasn't my idea having her here."

"Wasn't it? All right. Back to the case. What other ideas are you not having?"

"Keep banging away at Penn, Roote and Dee, I suppose."

"Sound like a firm of dodgy solicitors. That it?"

"Yup. Sorry. How about you, sir?"

"Me?" Dalziel yawned widely and scratched his crotch like it had offended him. "Think I'll go home and read a good book."

And I can guess which one it's likely to be, *Hamish,* thought Pascoe.

But being a sensitive man, with a wife, child, child's dog, and mortgage to support, he didn't say it.

XLIV

Hat Bowler's unproductive schoolboy flirtation with History had left him with a vague notion that the sixteenth century was a period which most of the English nation spent at the theatre.

It was at first a comfort when Rye Pomona pointed out that there'd been quite a lot of real-life action too.

Henry VIII had told the Pope to take a hike while he carved his way through six wives, though, disappointingly, it emerged he'd only executed two of them. Next Bloody Mary had disfigured, dismembered, disembowelled, and in sundry other ways disposed of large numbers of her subjects on the very reasonable grounds that she didn't like the colour of their religion. Marginally less extreme on the religious front, Elizabeth had not spared to use the axe as a political statement even when it involved removing the heads of her Scots cousin and her Essex lover. And of course there'd been wars on land and sea, mainly against the Spanish whose great Armada was repulsed and scattered by a combination of English seamanship and English weather.

With such a record of bloody violence throughout the century, Hat had high hopes of finding something pertinent to the Wordman's plans in the year 1576.

Alas, even when Rye had moved out of her own memory into that of the computer, it soon became apparent that of all years, this had been one of the least eventful. He tried to work the information that James Burbage had built the first playhouse in Shoreditch and that the explorer Martin Frobisher had made the first of his three voyages up the North American coast in search of the Northwest Passage into some kind of significant metaphor of the Wordman's intentions, but it was beyond his ingenuity.

Appeal to Rye's greater imaginative powers had no effect. He had, as usual, told her everything on the grounds that half knowledge is more dangerous than complete ignorance but for once she had shown little interest in his indiscretion. She seemed as thrown down in spirits as the rest of the library staff, among whom the huge buzz initially generated by the news, manner, and circumstances of Percy Follows' death had rapidly faded to a pall-like silence under which individuals brooded on the meaning of these things. Even the chatty students in the reference library seemed subdued by it and took little advantage of the absence from his customary cubicle of Charley Penn whose snarling remonstrances usually kept them in order.

Nor was Dick Dee to be seen, so the second of Dalziel's stated objectives—letting two of the prime suspects know that one of the Dialogue's puzzles had been penetrated—had failed as completely as the first.

"How about something more local?" suggested Hat. "Was anything special happening in Mid-Yorkshire in 1576?"

"I've no idea," she said. "Look, there's the computer. You want to play around with the history archives, be my guest. With Dick not here, I've got plenty to be getting on with."

"So where is he?" asked Hat.

"Senior staff crisis meeting with the chair of the Centre Committee," said Rye.

"So you're the bossman," he said. "Congrats. Why don't you use your authority to give yourself an extended coffee break."

He smiled at her, he hoped winningly.

Vain hope.

She said, "For God's sake, can't you get it into your head that I've got a job to do too? And it strikes me you might be better employed doing yours somewhere else instead of wasting time hanging around here, asking about a stupid date. There are people dead, Hat, don't you understand that? You seem to be treating it like it was some sort of game."

Oh but it is! the retort formed in his mind. But now his eyes were telling him what his heart ought to have spotted much sooner, that here was a young woman who, only a few days after finding a severed head in a basket, had once again been brought in close contact with the monster, death.

He said, "Rye, I'm sorry . . . I thought, telling you everything like I do, well, I think I was beginning to think of you as another cop . . . I don't mean . . . what I mean is, coping the way we do . . . the way we have to because it's our job . . . but it's not yours . . . I'm sorry."

She looked at him for a moment, then said, "We all have to cope, Hat. Look under *Local History Legal Chronology*," before turning away and retreating into the office.

As offers of olive branches go, that, he reckoned, was about as good as it was going to get.

He sat himself down at the computer, recalling with amusement pretending to be baffled by it as an excuse to make contact with Rye just a few short weeks ago. As a ploy, it hadn't worked, except to put him handy when they needed a cop. In fact, come to think of it, if anything had brought them together, it was the Wordman. An uncomfortable basis for a relationship? Why so? No reason not to be grateful if good came out of evil.

The Local History site revealed that 1576 had been a very good year in Mid-Yorkshire for boundary disputes, cattle theft, and blasphemy, for which the penalties ranged from a big fine for taking the Lord's name in vain, to having a hole burnt through your tongue with a red-hot iron for suggesting that, according to the Scriptures, the vicar ought to be giving tithes of his goods and produce to impoverished parishioners rather than the other way round. The vicar in question was called Jugg and the man with the holey unholy tongue was called Lamperley. Hat looked for a clue in this, found none, but nonetheless made a note of the names.

He went through all the other chronologies, social, cultural, religious, and found nothing to his purpose.

Now he had no more excuse to stay in the library, but he found himself lingering, or even, self-envisaged with a policeman's eye, loitering around the desk. But Rye, whom he could see through the partially opened office door, kept her eyes steadfastly on her work. There was a bell to press if you required assistance, and he was steeling himself to press it when a voice said in his ear, "Hello, Mr. Bowler."

He turned to find himself looking at a pleasantly smiling Franny Roote with, a little way behind him and staring at the computer screen which he had not cleared, Charley Penn who looked completely wrecked.

"Hello, Mr. Roote," said Hat very formally, resolving in light of Pascoe's warnings about the young man's cleverness to give nothing away.

"Into local history now as well as birds?" said Penn, joining them. "Or are you just after the first sighting of the Lesser Nippled Tit in the sixteenth century?"

"Ornithological history can be very interesting," said Hat, trying to work out if the man was sick or merely hungover.

"Is that right? In the old days, but, when you lot spotted an interesting new specimen, didn't you used to shoot it so as you could take a closer look? Bit extreme that, I'd say, killing something for the sake of a hobby."

He spat *hobby* out like a loose filling, then reached between Roote and Hat to press long and hard on the bellpush, at the same time shouting, "Shop!"

Rye emerged, her expression as blank as Hat was trying to keep his.

"Hello, luv," said Penn. "Where's thy gaffer?"

"Mr. Dee is at a meeting. I don't know when he'll be back."

"A meeting? Of course, they'll be debating the succession. Should we look for white smoke going up?"

"I think in the circumstances that's a pretty crass and offensive remark, Mr. Penn," said Rye, staring at the writer unblinkingly.

"You do? Well, as long as it's pretty, eh? I just wanted to try out a new version of *Der Scheidende* on him. You'll do, though. What do you think of translating it as 'Man on his way out?' Too free, maybe?"

As Penn thrust a sheet of paper at Rye, Hat turned away to remove himself from the temptation to interfere which he was certain would provoke only the man's mockery and the woman's resentment.

"I shouldn't pay any heed to Charley, Mr. Bowler," murmured Roote, following him. "He's not too well today. Anyway, it's all words with him. Words words words. They don't mean anything. Or perhaps they just mean whatever he wants them to mean. So cheer up, eh?"

Furious at being offered comfort from this source, Hat said aggressively, "I notice you're looking pretty cheerful yourself, Mr. Roote. Got something to be happy about, have we?"

"Oh God, does it show?" said Roote in alarm. "I'm sorry, I realize that after what happened last night, it must seem most inappropriate, especially here. But maybe it's only your detective skills which have spotted it, and I look the same as ever to the layman's eye."

Is piss being taken? wondered Hat. And if it is, what the hell can I do about it?

He said, "So what's making you happy, Mr. Roote?"

The young man hesitated as if debating how trustworthy his interlocutor was, then seemed to make up his mind and said in a low voice, "It's quite remarkable considering the circumstances, you know, with me coming back here because of Sam, Dr. Johnson, then poor Sam dying like that, and suddenly I've lost my dearest friend, and also I've lost my tutor, the one man who could help me hold my studies together. I felt pretty low, you can understand that, I'm sure, Mr. Bowler. Then out of the blue I won the short story competition, and that was a much needed little perk. And out of that . . . well, it's early days, but Charley, Mr. Penn, liked the story so much that he showed it to his publishers who liked it as well, and next time his editor comes up to see him, Charley's going to introduce me with a view to maybe talking about some more stories, a whole bookful, for children, you understand. Isn't that marvellous?"

"Great," said Hat. "Congratulations."

"Thank you, but that's not all. You know Sam Johnson was working on a book about Beddoes . . . the poet," he explained in response to the blank look which must have passed over Hat's eyes, "early nineteenth century, fascinating writer, the last Elizabethan, Strachey called him, he figures in my study, in fact I'd grown more and more fascinated by him which was one of the things that brought Sam and me so close together. Well, Sam didn't leave a will, it seems, so his only close relative, his sister, that's Linda Lupin, MEP, inherits everything, and she's been so pissed off with academics flocking around like vultures, each claiming to be Sam's best buddy and the one he'd have wanted receive his research material and finish the book, that she's told them all to get stuffed! And she invited me to see her and after we'd talked a while, she said that Sam had written a lot about me in his letters, and from what he'd said, it seemed to her if I was willing that I was the person he'd have wanted to finish the book! Isn't that marvellous?"

"Yeah, great," said Hat, to whom the prospect of finishing someone else's book was about as appealing as the prospect of finishing someone's else's soup. "Congratulations."

"Thank you, Mr. Bowler. I can see you understand. A lot of people might think it funny that I can be so happy so soon after losing such a dear friend, but it's as if Sam's death has turned my life around. Suddenly I can see before me a path leading to a future that's got some shape and meaning. It's almost as if it were meant to be, as if there's someone out there, perhaps even Sam himself, who likes me and is looking after me. I went to the burial ground first thing this morning and offered thanks at Sam's grave, and for a while it felt like I was down there with him, chatting away like we did in the old days."

Hat looked into Roote's eyes which shone with a born-again fervour and resisted the temptation to say, *Why don't we try to arrange that on a permanent basis then?* and instead said, "Great. Excuse me now."

He turned back to the counter and saw that Rye and Penn seemed to have finished, or at least she had finished with him.

The writer moved away from the counter and gave him an encouraging wink as they passed.

Rye was re-entering the office.

He spoke her name but she didn't pause. He stood at the counter and watched her through the open door as she sat down at the desk once more.

There was a sheet of paper on the counter. He looked down and read what was written on it.

Man on his way out

Within my heart, within my head,
Every worldly joy lies dead,
And just as dead beyond repeal
Is hate of evil, nor do I feel
The pain of mine or others' lives,
For in me only Death survives!

At least, unless these literary folk had their own erotic code, it didn't read like sexual harassment. Perhaps clever old Pascoe and his weird Uni mates could riddle something out of it, and out of Roote's euphoria too.

He raised his eyes from the poem.

At her desk in the office, Rye was watching him.

He spoke her name again and she stretched out one elegant leg and kicked the door shut.

XLV

On the day of Percy Follows' funeral, the library was closed.

Officially this was to permit his colleagues to attend the ceremony.

"Wrong," said Charley Penn to Dick Dee. "It's to *force* his colleagues to attend the ceremony."

"I think for once your cynicism misses the mark, Charley," said Dee. "Percy had many good qualities, both as a man and a librarian. He'll be genuinely missed."

"Yeah?" said Penn. "Either way, it's fucking inconvenient. I can't work in my place with all those hairy workmen banging and shouting and competing whose ghetto-blaster is the loudest. Any road, with the funeral at one, I don't see why the place needs to be shut all afternoon."

"It was felt that as a mark of respect . . ." He saw he wasn't impressing the writer so quickly added, "Also there will be some light refreshment on offer afterwards at the Lichen Hotel, a chance to talk about Percy and celebrate his life. By the time that's over . . ."

"Everyone'll be well pissed. But you'll be coming back, I would have thought. A glutton for punishment but not for lunchtime booze. So why don't I come round about three, say . . ."

"No," said Dee firmly. "I've got things to do."

"What?"

"If you must know, I thought I'd go out to Stangdale and clear my stuff out of the cottage."

"Why? New landlord giving you grief?"

"Hardly, as they're still looking for him, it seems. Some cousin who went out to America in the sixties looks the best bet. No, I just haven't felt any desire to go back there since . . . since what happened happened. It might wear off, of course, but until it does, it's silly to leave all my gear lying around for some passing rambler to nick. I wouldn't mind some company. Fancy an outing?"

"You must be joking!" said Penn. "You know what I feel about the fucking countryside. Once was enough. No, it'll have to be the Uni library, I suppose. All those gabby undergrads. I may run amuck."

Dee sighed and said, "All right, Charley, you can use my flat. But you don't touch my espresso machine, is that understood? Last time you left me with the choice of brown water or solids."

"Cross my heart," said Penn.

Percy Follows had been (and presumably, if all had gone according to plan, still was) a devout member of the Church of England at its apogee, a step beyond which could see a man tumbling into Rome. Not for him the simple worship of a day. If it didn't involve incense, candles, hyssop, aspersions, processions, genuflections, soaring choirs and gilded vestments, it didn't count. His parish priest being naturally of the same mind pulled out all the stops and did not miss the opportunity to deliver a meditation upon death and an encomium upon the deceased in what he fondly imagined was the style of Dr. Donne of St. Paul's.

Pascoe, admiring but unable to follow the example of his Great Leader, whose head was bowed and whose lips from time to time emitted a susurration not unlike the sound of waves making towards a pebbled shore, thumbed desperately through his prayer book in search of distraction. The Psalms seemed the nearest thing to light relief he was likely to find there, full of nice turns of phrase and good advice. How pleasant it might have been if the priest, for instance, had taken the hint of the first of the two appointed to be read at the burial service (only one was necessary but they'd got them both), the second verse of which read, 'I will keep my mouth as it were with a bridle; while the ungodly is in my sight.'

With Andy Dalziel snoring away before him, he could hardly have any doubt about the presence of the ungodly!

Pascoe riffled through the pages, letting them open as they would, and found himself looking at words he'd read recently.

*The Lord is my light, and my salvation; whom then shall I fear: the Lord
is the strength of my life; of whom then shall I be afraid?*

Psalm 27 which the Wordman seemed so fond of, finding assurance
therein (if Pottle had got it right) that his sense of acting on instruction
from the Other World made him invulnerable.

Not quite the same words, his excellent (though unlike Wield's, not
quite eidetic) memory told him. There'd been no *thens* in the version he'd
read in the Bible. And it had been headed by the legend *A Psalm of David*,
while here in the Prayer Book you got the first couple of words of the Latin
original *Dominus illuminatio*. No, not the original, of course. A Latin translation of the Hebrew, presumably in St. Jerome's *Vulgate*. From *vulgatus*—
made public.

Odd to think of an age when things were made public by translating
them into Latin!

Did any of this have any bearing on the hunt for the Wordman? None
whatsoever. It was like hunting the Snark. Who, as the Baker feared, would
probably turn out to be a Boojum.

The Baker. Funny how these things came back. There'd been a guy at
university, a slight inconsequential fellow who made so little impression
that some wag doing Eng. Lit. (that natural home of waggery) had christened him Baker because—how did it go?—

He would answer to "Hi!" or any loud cry,
Such as "Fry me!" or "Fritter my wig!"
To "What-you-may-call-um!" or "What-was-his-name?"
But especially "Thing-um-a-jig!"

In the end everyone called him Baker, even the tutors. Did he write
Baker at the head of his exam papers and take his degree in the name of
Baker? Was he happily settled down now as Mr. Baker, the civil engineer or
actuary, with a Mrs. Baker and a whole trayful of little Bakers?

Weird thing, names. Take Charley Penn. Christened Karl Penck. Karl
the Kraut. How hurtful it must be to have your own name hurled at you in
derision. Like his poetic hero, Heine. Named Harry. Mocked with donkey
cries. Till he changed it and his religion, both. But you can't change the
scars inside.

Or Dee. Another one with problems. Orson Eric. Not names to be ignored by the little savages at their play. But at least they gave him the

initials which ultimately provided an escape route. OED. Dick the Dictionary. But what baggage did he take with him along that escape route?

Escape route. Escape Roote. He wished he could. No change of name there, except the familiarization of Francis to Franny. But he still recalled that poem read out at Johnson's funeral, ". . . there is some maddening secret hid in your words . . . 'mongst stones and roots . . ." and how the reader's eyes had sought him out, mockingly, as he put a subtle stress on the word *roots*.

Or had he just imagined that? And was his attempt to read something significant into these name changes merely a symptom of his own personal paronomania? After all, a conscious shift from an unwelcome given name was common enough. He didn't need to look further than the young man at his side who seemed to have a touching belief that attendance at murder victims' funerals was de rigueur for an ambitious detective. Normally it was probably a source of some irritation for anyone called Bowler to be addressed as Hat, but when your real name was Ethelbert, you embraced the sobriquet with much relief! And then there were the more private and intimate forms of name change, like Jax (another!) Ripley calling Headingley "Georgie Porgie." None of which meant that either Bowler or the DI got on to the suspect list!

Though, come to think of it, the way George Headingley had kept his involvement with Ripley under wraps demonstrated what to a CID man should need no demonstration—that human beings were of all animals the most unreadable and unpredictable.

The vicar's sonorous seventeenth-century periods finally rolled to an end. According to him, if ever a man deserved to sit on the right hand of God, it was Percy Follows.

Though, from the sound of it, he'd probably much prefer sitting on either hand of Ambrose Bird.

It was one of those thoughts you suddenly feel you've spoken out loud and he glanced guiltily around, but no one was looking indignant. Dick Dee was sitting on the other side of the aisle, his eyes fixed on the pulpit, his expression either rapt or traumatized. Beside him was his assistant, Rye Pomona. Whose presence was probably the true reason for young Bowler's keenness to attend the funeral! He'd got a hint that things hadn't been moving too well on that front since their ill-fated expedition to Stang Tarn. If asked, he could have spoken some wise words to the DC. Police work can fascinate some civilians, especially a case like this involving mysterious communications and puzzles and all kinds of twists and turns. He'd no doubt that Bowler had, consciously or subconsciously, used this God-given turn-on, sharing more information with the girl than a young cop should, especially one who worked for Fat Andy whose attitude to sharing info with civilians was, tell 'em only what they need to know, and the buggers don't need to know much! But when you're young and in love, even the mountainous Dalziel could shrink to a molehill.

There was, however, another obstacle much harder to overcome because unforeseen. That sense of being special which came from being privy to the inner life of an investigation was a very intimate thing. But it was a narrow line to tread, and if something happened to bring your confidante face to face with the brutal realities of the case, her fascination could rapidly turn to revulsion.

Rye Pomona had been dragged over that line twice in rapid succession, the first time most brutally when she had been present at the discovery of Pyke-Strengler's corpse, followed very soon after by the murder of Percy Follows and Ambrose Bird, which, though her involvement was not so direct, must have strongly reinforced the effect of that day out in Stangdale.

So now, guessed Pascoe, poor Hat was finding that the confidences which had hitherto seemed the key to her heart were merely unwelcome reminders of his essential otherness from which she wanted to retreat.

If asked, he would have said something like, if she really likes you, Hat, she'll get over it, and though she may not like what you have to do, she'll respect you for doing it.

But this, like most wisdom, was banal in expression and retrospective in effect, so he kept it to himself, though noting how, after the service, as the mourners filed past the grave, Hat's eyes never left Rye who was some way ahead of them in the queue, talking quietly to Dee. At least they were free from the close attention of the media which had so infuriated Linda Lupin at her step-brother's funeral that she'd put in an official complaint about "insensitive behaviour bordering on the depraved." Result, a combination of editorial diktat and police street closures which had kept the hordes of Gideon at a distant prowl.

"Not a bad send-off," said Dalziel. "Good turn-out. What is it they say? Give the punters what they want and they'll turn up in their thousands. Why are you screwing up that skinny face of thine? Bad taste? At least I listened to the sermon while you were leafing through the prayer book, looking for the mucky bits."

Dalziel asleep missed less than many men awake.

"I was meditating on the psalms," said Pascoe. "Psalm 27 to be precise. *'The Lord is my light, and my salvation; whom then shall I fear?'* The Wordman's favourite."

And it was still with him, still working away in his mind . . .

"You OK?" demanded Dalziel.

"Yes, sorry." He came back to here and now, aware that the Fat Man had said something that he'd missed.

"I were saying, it seems to work for him."

"What?"

"The Twenty-seventh psalm," said Dalziel longsufferingly. " 'For in the time of trouble he shall hide me in his tabernacle: yea, in the secret place of his dwelling shall he hide me, and set me upon a rock of stone.' Bugger's certainly well hidden. Mebbe even when we're looking right at him. See our friend Dee's here. No sign of Penn or Roote, but."

"I hardly think that's significant," said Pascoe. "Follows was Dee's boss."

"Never said it was significant, did I? Well, there you go, Percy. Let's hope that angel's haircut of thine is standing thee in good stead. See you around!"

They'd reached the grave and Dalziel stopped to seize enough earth in his great fist to plant an aspidistra and hurled it on to the coffin-lid with a loud crash.

It was a good job, thought Pascoe, that Follows hadn't left instructions for an ecologically correct cardboard coffin or they might have seen him sooner than expected.

As they headed out of the graveyard towards the line of parked cars, he saw Dee and his assistant get into their vehicles, then drive off in convoy. When they reached the main road junction, neither turned left towards the Lichen Hotel where funeral meats awaited, but both went straight over towards the city centre. Paid Prancing Percy their respects then straight back to work. The queen is dead, long live the queen. Or king. No doubt the battle for succession in the library was already on.

Dalziel watched them too, then as if taking this as a hint, he said, "Think I'll give the wake a miss. I've seen the grub at the Lichen. Makes you understand how it got its name. But funerals always make a man thirsty. There's The Last Gasp round the corner. Weird sense of humour some of these breweries have. You can buy me a pint and a pie there. Both of you."

Reluctantly Pascoe and Bowler, both of whom had other things on their mind, followed their Great Master.

Dalziel's stated purpose was only half fulfilled. After his first pint (Bowler's treat) he postponed the pie, and halfway through the second (Pascoe's) he opined loudly, "This ale's almost as flat as the company. I'll not risk the grub here. Let's move on to the Black Bull. At least Jolly Jack knows how to keep beer."

But now, having obeyed the dictates of duty and self-preservation, Pascoe was ready to be obstinate.

"No thanks. Lots to do," he said firmly. Which was true but not the truth. What he really wanted was to be somewhere by himself and think.

"Jesus wept," said Dalziel, amazed. "How about you, young Bowler?"

"No," said Hat shortly, taking courage from Pascoe's example. "I'm busy too."

He too had noticed Dee and Rye driving off in convoy and wanted to brood on this and other matters.

"Well, I'll go to the foot of our stairs," said Dalziel, recognizing finality. "I'll mebbe have to change me after-shave. But think on, I'll be looking forward to seeing the outcome of all this busy-ness."

Back at the station Pascoe got a cup of coffee and a chocolate bar from the machine and slumped in his office chair, while the steam died from the liquid and the confection stayed unwrapped.

Out in the CID room, Hat sat in a posture so like the DCI's that anyone seeing both of them simultaneously might have started wondering about *doppelgängers*.

There was no one else on the CID floor. Elsewhere in the building, normal busy life was going on but here its attendant noises touched the ear with that sense of remoteness and distance you get when standing on a misty beach on a windless day, or in a snow-filled wood in winter.

Pascoe wanted to think about the strategy of the Wordman investigation and why it had failed. Hat wanted to think about Rye Pomona and whether she was still with Dee. But these troublesome thoughts seemed to lose their pace and energy as they ran up against the invisible barrier of this zone of calm elsewhereness.

It's like, thought Pascoe (and even this thought did not set his pulses racing), it's like those moments described in the Dialogues when time slows towards a halt . . . it's as if the Wordman has trailed his aura and I am on the edge of his dimension, that passive world in which he is the only active element.

This is where I should be looking for him, not out there in the busy world of routines, and elimination, and forensics. *This* is the secret place of his dwelling.

He let his body relax even more.

Psalm 27. He is back in church reading Psalm 27. The Lord is my light. He tries to move elsewhere, that part of his mind which is still a Detective Chief Inspector wanting to use this weird feeling to range over the whole of the case but not finding any response to the controls. This is what the Wordman must feel, he thinks. Whatever I do in this timeless time is what I have to do, not what I want to do.

Still in the church reading the Psalm, but also in his office at the station, he reaches out to pull the Wordman file across his desk towards him. He intends to open it and look at the psalm references that have been isolated. But instead he opens it at the very beginning, at the strange drawing, the *In Principio*. His fingers have no strength to turn further. What am I looking for? he asks himself. The twin oxen. The two *alephs*. The AA man. This I know already. What else?

In principio erat verbum.

The opening of the gospel according to St. John.

Dee was at St. John's College.

Roote is in the St. John Ambulance Brigade.

Johnny Oakeshott's real name was St. John.

St. John, the "son of thunder," St. John, symbolized by the eagle, St. John who bored his followers by his too often repeated exhortation to them to "love one another" because if you do that "you do enough"; who came close to being dumped into a cauldron of boiling oil under the persecution of the Emperor Domitian but escaped to die a natural death of ripe old age at Ephesus where he'd had a run in with a high priest of the goddess Diana, whose worship also brought a lot of trouble Paul's way . . .

Very interesting but not relevant, not at the moment anyway—or rather not at the non-moment, not in this segment of non-time. Something else, he knows there is something else.

And outside his door, in the CID room, less self-consciously perhaps, Hat Bowler too sits on this shore of time and feels its mighty turbulent ocean recede. Rye, Rye, he wants to think of Rye but all he can conjure up is that date in the Dialogue: 1576. Fifteen seventy-six. It means something to him . . . Once more he rehearses all that he has been able to discover about it but nothing cries out to him . . . or rather nothing stops crying, for that's what it feels like . . . like hearing a baby crying in a big empty house and rushing from room to room but finding them all empty . . . and still the baby cries . . .

One more door remains . . . behind this last door must lie the truth . . . The door bursts open . . .

"Sorry, did I wake you, lad?" says Sergeant Wield. "Mr. Pascoe in?"

And without waiting for an answer he crashes just as unceremoniously into Pascoe's office and with him comes surging back the relentless tide of time.

"Wieldy," said Pascoe, reaching for his cold coffee. "No need to knock. Just come right in. Make yourself at home."

With a confidence of welcome that put him beyond the reach of irony, Wield said, "Something you ought to see. First off, that partial on Ripley's mule, we've got a match."

"A match? I don't follow. They reported no match on record."

"Aye, but that was before the matching print was part of the record," said Wield. "You recall we took Dee's prints to match them with the prints on the axe that topped the Hon. . . ."

"Dee. You're saying we've got a match with Dee?"

"Not a complete, but ten points, which, considering what little there was to work with, is a big step," said Wield, laying a couple of sheets of paper in front of Pascoe.

"Ten's a long way from sixteen," said Pascoe disappointedly. "And how the hell did this come up anyway? Officially, Dee was never anything but a witness and his prints were taken purely for elimination, because he'd been using the axe."

The rules were very clear. All fingerprints provided voluntarily for purposes of elimination had to be destroyed the minute the elimination process was complete.

"Don't know what happened," said Wield. "Must somehow have got put in the system for cross-checking against the record and by the time they reached the top of the queue, that partial from Ripley's mule was part of the record. Something like that, I expect."

When a master of precise detail starts being vague, it is best to look the other way, especially when the possible illegalities have a smell of Dalziel about them.

Pascoe looked the other way and said, "OK, but I can't get excited, Wieldy. It's not usable in court and even if we had a full sixteen-point match, with the bad press prints have had recently, we'd need a hell of a lot more."

Wield said with just a hint of reproof, "Worked that out for myself. I thought, what else? And I remembered the bite."

"The bite? Ah, yes. We had forgot the bite. And . . . ?"

"I've been round to see Mr. Molar. Had to get him out of a lecture, he weren't best pleased. But it was worth it. He compared Dee's dental record with the bite and he says that it's a definite maybe verging on a possible definitely that those teeth made that bite."

"Dee's dental records . . . ?" Pascoe's mind was spinning. "How the hell did you get hold of Dee's dental records?"

"All above board," said Wield briskly. "He gave us written permission to see his medical records when we were talking to him about the Hon.'s death, remember? Almost fell over himself to do it. Well, dental comes under medical, and as the permission was still on the file . . ."

There were more potential illegalities floating around here than in a Marbella swimming pool, thought Pascoe.

Sod them!

He shook them out of his head, opened his mouth to shout for Hat, then saw it wasn't necessary.

The DC was standing in the doorway, his face aglow at the thought of getting Dick Dee into the middle of the frame.

Pascoe said, "Right. Let's talk to Mr. Dee again, but softly, softly. No point in putting the boot in till we know what we're kicking. All this could mean owt or it could mean nowt."

The use of Dalzielesque phraseology emphasized the point he was making. There'd been too many instances recently of policemen going in hard with too little evidence and either warning off the guilty or provoking official complaints from the innocent.

"We'll need someone to stay here and co-ordinate matters. And try to raise the super at the Black Bull."

He looked at Hat, saw the disappointment and the pleading in his eyes, and said, "Better be you, Wieldy. There's a trail here which could need some tidying up if it leads anywhere, and you're best equipped to do it."

No doubt about that. At the moment what little they had could be dispersed instantly by one indignant snort from a smart lawyer's nostrils.

"Hat, you come with me to the library."

"But it's closed today. Mark of respect."

"Hell, I'd forgotten. But that doesn't mean the staff won't be there. Dee and Rye Pomona drove straight off after the funeral. Clearly they weren't going to the Lichen."

"No, sir," said Hat unhappily.

Pascoe thought a moment then said, "Tell you what, you try Dee's flat, see if he's there. I'll do the library, which still seems the best bet. OK?"

"Fine," said Hat.

They got into their respective cars simultaneously but the little sports car was burning rubber out of the car park before Pascoe had fastened his seat belt.

He still felt pretty sure of finding Dee at the library and when he reached the Centre and saw the main doors were open, his confidence seemed justified. A security man stopped him to tell him the Centre was closed to the public that day. Pascoe showed him his ID and discovered that, as he'd suspected, a lot of staff were taking the chance to catch up on jobs that under normal workaday pressures got pushed to the back burner.

He made his way to the reference library, rehearsing the sweet words which were going to lure Dee down to the station. But he found the place empty except for a young female library assistant he didn't know who was painstakingly checking the shelves to make sure that all the reference books had been returned to their rightful positions and order.

He showed his ID again and asked if Dee had been in. She said she hadn't seen him, but she'd just arrived herself. Pascoe went behind the enquiry desk and tried the office door on the remote chance that the man was working inside, too rapt to hear conversation without.

The door opened and suddenly Pascoe had a vision of discovering Dee sitting there with his throat cut.

The office was empty. Pascoe went in and sat behind the desk to collect his thoughts.

He must be getting hard. He felt relief that his absurd imagining had turned out to be just that, but it wasn't relief that a human being wasn't dead, but rather relief that a promising line of enquiry hadn't been nipped in the bud—or nicked in the jugular!

Just how promising was this line anyway?

Dee was a good fit for the profile Pottle and Urquhart had produced between them. There was the obsession with word games, the delight in his own cleverness, and if he wanted the other world focus which the Dialogues seemed to illustrate, then perhaps he didn't need to look further than this photograph on the desk. The three boys, two of them bright and sharp and fighting their way out of adolescent adversity into premature adult control, the third still childish, innocent, in need of love and protection.

He recalled that poem again, the one on the page opened in the book in Sam Johnson's dead hands.

> *If there are ghosts to raise,*
> *What shall I call,*
> *Out of hell's murky haze,*
> *Heaven's blue pall?*
> *Raise my loved long-lost boy*
> *To lead me to his joy . . .*

But these were not the kind of ideas the CPS liked to be presented with. They wanted something with much more shape and substance, hard physical evidence, preferably accompanied by a water-tight confession.

And he had . . . a thumbprint and a bite mark. Neither definite. Both of doubtful admissibility. He closed his eyes and tried to ease his way back into that state of timelessness in which the answer had seemed almost within his grasp . . . the Twenty-seventh psalm: "God is my light . . ." *Dominus illuminatio mea . . .*

Then he opened his eyes and he saw everything.

Hat's heart leapt up as he dragged the MG round the corner of the street in which Dee's apartment was situated. He had been frightened he would find Rye's car parked outside, lending weight to a fantasy he fought against but could not resist of Dee's door opening in response to his frenzied knocking to reveal over the man's bare shoulder a bedroom, and a bed, and Rye's tousled chestnut hair with its distinctive blaze of grey spread out across the pillow. . . .

But of course there was no sign of the car. No, she'd be safe at home. He thought of ringing her number, then decided that contact was better delayed till Dee was safely down the nick and he could see which way things were going. With luck she need never know that he himself had done the arresting.

Not the arresting, he corrected himself. Pascoe wanted this played cool. A smiling invitation to have a friendly chat.

No frenzied knocking then. None needed at the front entrance, which was open. He went sedately up the stairs and tapped gently on the door.

It opened almost at once.

"What's this? A raid?" said Charley Penn. "Don't tell me. Andy Dalziel's lying out there with a Kalashnikov, right?"

"Mr. Penn. I was looking for Mr. Dee . . ."

"Well, you've come to the right place, but not at the right time," said Penn. "Step inside before someone shoots me."

Hat went in.

"Mr. Bowler, how nice."

Franny Roote was smiling up at him from a chair placed before a table on which lay an open Paronomania board.

There was no one else in the room.

Unhappily, Hat let his gaze turn towards the bedroom door.

"Is Mr. Dee . . ."

Penn went and threw the door open.

"No, not in here. Unless he's under the bed. Nor in the kitchen or the bog either, take a look. Sorry."

Hat pulled himself together and said, "Mr. Penn, what are you doing here?"

"Teaching my young chum, Roote, the rudiments of Paronomania. I'd ask you to join in, but only two can play."

Hat's gaze flickered to the third rack on which he could see the name *Johnny*, then returned to Penn's mocking mask.

"I meant, why are you here, in Mr. Dee's flat?"

"Because at present my pad is, as you'll recall, uninhabitable. The workmen from hell are still creating pandemonium. The library is closed to celebrate its release from the dead hand and limp wrist of poor Percy. So Dick kindly allowed me the use of his humble property to pursue my studies. But I ran into young Roote on my way here and let him inveigle me into initiating him into the rites of the second greatest game known to man."

Hat listened with growing impatience.

"So where is Mr. Dee?" he demanded.

"Ah, that's what you want to know? Why didn't you ask?" said Penn. "Mr. Dee is, to the best of my knowledge, out at that rustic slum which for some reason he so enjoys. Or used to. Recent events have changed his perception, I gather. *Et in Arcadia ego*. Since his landlord's unfortunate death, Dick no longer feels at ease out there and he has gone to retrieve his gear."

"You're saying he's gone out to Stangcreek Cottage?"

"I'm glad you agree that's what I'm saying because that is certainly what I was attempting to convey," said Penn.

The man's face was twisted into that cross between a smile and a snarl

Rye called his *smarl*. He's got something else to say, something, Hat guessed, he thinks I won't be pleased to hear.

His heart jolted as his thoughts outdistanced Penn's words. But he still had to hear them.

"Yes," said the writer. "Really bugs him, that place now. Didn't even fancy going out there by himself. Also the stuff he's got there would overflow that jalopy of his. So he dropped a hint or two I might like to give him a hand. But I had to say no. Bad back, my car's on the blink, and I hate the fucking countryside anyway. Still, it all worked out for the best. He came back from Percy's funeral full of the joys of spring."

"Why was that?" asked Hat unnecessarily. There was a singing in his ears, the air seemed dark with foreboding, and through the murk he could see Franny Roote regarding him with an expression of grave concern.

"Seems he asked young Rye if she'd hold his hand and she jumped at the chance. Yes, old Dick dragged off the funeral blacks, got into his track-suit and trainers, and headed off to rendezvous with young Ms. Pomona. Who knows? Perhaps in such pleasant company he'll get back his feel for nature. Hadn't you better answer that? It might be Andy Dalziel wanting to know if it's time to throw the stun grenades."

And Hat realized that part at least of the singing in his ears was the sound of his mobile ringing.

From his place in the library office, through the open door, out across the enquiry desk, Pascoe could see them, twenty dark blue volumes, standing as straight and smart as guardsmen on parade. And he knew beyond doubt the meaning of that mysterious shape in the bowl of the P of the *In Principio* at the head of the First Dialogue.

Not a Bible or a missal as Urquhart had suggested, but a volume of the great Oxford English Dictionary.

No lettering on the drawing, of course—that would have made things too easy—but the narrow band across the top of the dust jacket spine was there while the white disc at the bottom represented the university coat of arms. From this distance he couldn't make out the letters of the motto it contained, but he'd seen it often enough on his own OUP books to know what they spelled.

Dominus illuminatio mea.

The contents of the volumes were indicated by the first and last words each contained.

These he could read from here, but nevertheless he rose and went out to the shelf.

The first volume was easy.

A—Bazouki

The AA man, Andrew Ainstable. The boy who played the bazouki. Next:

BBC—Chalypsography

Jax Ripley. And the other?

He took the volume down to check.

Steel engraving.

Oh, dreadful pun! Councillor Steel killed with a burin. And the Cyrillic letters engraved upon his head just to underline the joke.

The third volume.

Cham—Creeky

Cham. Illustrative quotation from 1759:

". . . that great Cham of literature, Samuel Johnson."

Then **creeky** . . . ?

Stang Creek? Skip to the next volume.

Creel—Duzepere

Creel. Body in the creek, head in the creel. And **duzepere?**

A singular variant of douzepers meaning illustrious nobles, knights, or grandees.

Poor Pyke-Strengler. Perhaps if your father had not died . . .

The fifth volume.

Dvandva—Follis

Dvandva. *A compound word in which the elements are related to each other as if joined by a copula.*

Actor–manager.

Follis. *A small Roman coin,* like that found in Ambrose Bird's mouth. And the first word in the next volume.

Follow

The **$** hadn't been a dollar sign, but merely the removal of the letter **S**.

Bird and Follows. Who died, to make the whole thing even more complete, joined in a copula.

He went back into the office for privacy, closed the door, and pulled out his mobile.

The case was altered. Before, he hadn't really been able to get his head round the idea of the gentle quiet librarian being in the frame for all these killings. Now all he could think was that he'd sent a solitary young constable out looking for a man who had leapt to the terrifying eminence of being prime suspect.

"Answer, sod you, answer!" he yelled at the phone.

"Hello?"

"Bowler, where are you?"

"At Dee's flat, but . . ."

"OK, don't go in . . ."

"I'm in."

"Shit. OK. Smile sweetly and say you've got to fetch something from the car. Then get out. No buts. Do it!"

He waited. Then to his relief he heard the youngster's voice saying, "Sir, what's going in?"

Quickly he ran through what he'd seen, what he was guessing, adding, "It may be quite wrong or nothing to do with Dee but I want you to wait till . . ."

But Hat was screaming at him.

"Sir, what's the next word? Tell me the next fucking word!"

Pascoe frowned, decided this was no time for a lecture on chain of command, went out of the office into the library and read, "**Follows—Haswed,**" pronouncing it as spelt, voicing the **w**. "*Has wed* . . . that's it! A *wedding was* in the last Dialogue. Though in fact it might be pronounced *Hasued* . . ."

"I don't give a fuck how it's pronounced, what's it mean?"

Once more Pascoe reacted to the urgency not the insubordination and checked.

"*Marked with grey or brown,*" he said. "The Dialogue poem said '*but wasn't white,*' remember? Now if only . . . Hat? You still there? Are you all right? Hat!"

But Hat wasn't hearing. He was seeing a head of rich chestnut hair marked by a flash of silvery grey. And something else he saw too, trembling on his retina like the filaments of light presaging a migraine.

1576

Not a year. A date.

I have a date, the poem had said.

1.5.76.

The first of May, 1976.

Rye's birthday.

The bastard had told them she was next and he'd been too blind to see it!

"Hat? What the hell's going on? Is Dee there? Hat!"

"No, he's not," yelled Hat, going down the stairs five at a time. "He's out at Stangcreek Cottage. And he's got Rye with him. She's haswed, her hair's haswed, and she was born May the first, seventy-six—1576, remember?"

"Hat, wait there, I'm on my way. Wait there, that's an order."

"Fuck you," screamed Hat into his phone.

He flung it on to the passenger seat of his car without switching it off and Pascoe, now moving down the Centre stairs at a speed almost equal to that of his young colleague, heard the crash of gears, squeal of tyres, and roar of an engine as the MG took off.

XLVI

The chair she sat in like a burnished throne gleamed in the firelight.

Sensuously she let her fingers trace the serpentine grooves of the intricately carved arm rests till she came to the sudden hard swell of the lions' heads.

She smiled down at Dick Dee who squatted before her on the three-legged stool. Between them lay a Paronomania board, which, fully open, looked like some exotic medieval map of the cosmos.

"Will you take it with you?" she asked. "The chair, I mean?"

"Strictly speaking, it isn't mine," he said.

"And are you always a strict speaker, Dick?"

"Strict," he mused. "From *strictus,* past participle of *stringere,* to draw or bind tight. It's a synantonym, of course . . ."

He paused and looked at her invitingly.

Taking her cue, she said, "A what?"

"A synantonym. One of those interesting words which can be their own opposite. Like *overlook, impregnable, cleave.*"

Rye considered, then said, "Those I can see, but *strict?*"

"There is a Scottish usage, meaning swift or rapid, particularly in relation to running water. So yes, I feel I can say I'm a strict speaker in one way or another."

"But will you keep the chair?"

"In the sense of preserve it, yes. Indeed when I showed it to poor

Geoffrey one day, he implied in his bumbling way that I might consider it a gift, though I doubt whether in law my unsupported recollection would be title enough. I fear you are in danger of being deflowered, my dear."

Rye looked at the board. She had just laid, not without some complacency, *azalea.* Now Dee crossed it at the l with *genitalia,* then carefully removed the rest of her tiles.

"I did mention the rhyming rule, didn't I?" he said. "Cross one of your opponent's words with a rhyming word and you score both words and also win the right to remove your opponent's tiles for your own use, if so desired."

"But that means you could put my *azalea* back down on your next go," she said with pretended indignation.

"Just so. It might be wise therefore to seek a way to block my *genitalia.*"

"Oh, I shall, never fear. If I'd known you invited me here to deflower me, I would never have come."

In fact she almost hadn't.

After Percy Follows' funeral, when Dick Dee had told her he was going to clear out Stangcreek Cottage, she'd said, "You're giving it up? Trouble with the new lord?"

"As they're having difficulty establishing who it might be, no, not yet. Just trouble with my relationship with the place. I've only been back once since it happened and I got straight back in the car and returned to town. I no longer feel at ease there."

"I'm sorry," she said. "You seemed so much at home. Have you got a lot of stuff?"

"Enough. Even camping out, it tends to accumulate." A pause, then, "Look, you wouldn't care to come along and give me a hand? Two hands, in fact, and an extra car, would be very useful."

She would have said no straight off if he hadn't gone on in a rush, "And to tell the truth, I'm not very keen on going back there by myself."

Now she hesitated, but still with the odds on refusal, till suddenly he said, "Oh hell! Rye, of course, you've got even more reason than I have for being reluctant to go out there again. My fears are all associative. You actually found the poor devil. It was crass of me to ask you. I'm sorry."

Which worked better than any persuasion.

"And it's craven of me to hesitate," she said. "Of course I'll come."

He looked at her doubtfully.

"You're sure? Please don't feel you've got to."

"Because you're my boss?" She laughed. "I don't believe I've ever done anything I didn't want just because you were my boss."

"I'm glad to hear it. What I meant was, because you're my friend."

She thought about this then smiled and said, "Yes, I am. And yes, I shall come. But first I'll have to go home and get out of these sad rags. It's the only outfit I've got fit to wear at funerals, and they seem to be the big social occasion this season."

"That's OK. I want to change too. Do we need to make our apologies for skipping the meats?"

"Who to? I think we just go, and them as miss us will miss us, and them as don't, won't."

"I couldn't have put it better myself."

And now, an hour later, here they were at the cottage and so far Rye had felt none of the feared oppression, nor so far as she could see, had her companion.

They hadn't made much progress with the packing up. It had felt damp and chill in the cottage and Dee had riddled the ashes in the grate, lit a whole packet of firelights and tossed on a couple of logs.

"I chopped 'em," he said. "We might as well benefit from them."

"Good idea." She warmed her hands at the rapidly blazing fire and drew in the smell of the burning wood.

"I love that smell," she said.

"Me too. Ash, I think. The best. Ashes to ashes makes more sense if you view it as a process rather than rubbish disposal. To burn and die, giving off warmth and sweet odour, is not a bad image of life, don't you agree?"

"Does that still include sure and certain hope of resurrection?" asked Rye, smiling.

"You're asking whether I'm comfortable with the notion that poor Percy might return to us?" he said, returning her smile.

"We shall be changed, remember?"

"In that case . . . But enough of metalinguistics. To work. I've got plenty of bin liners and some cardboard boxes. Just shove the stuff in. Nothing to worry about, except the paintings, and they're not exactly Old Masters."

"The young master's maybe?" said Rye.

"Thank 'ee kindly, miss," he said.

They'd started the packing but had been at it only a few minutes when Rye had happened on the game board. Even folded it was an object of exquisite design, with ornate brass hinges gleaming gold against polished rosewood.

"May I open it?" she asked.

"Of course."

"Oh, but it's lovely," she exclaimed as she saw the intricate zodiacal designs winding their way among the letter squares. "I've seen the one you and Charley play on in the office, but this is even more ornate."

"Yes, they're all different," he said. "But this I regard as the masterboard. The star signs on it mean that certain words can gain added value if they're entered in certain significant locations. For instance—I'm sure I know it, but it is best always to be sure with a lady—remind me of your date of birth."

"The first of May 1976."

"May the first, seventy-six. Mayday, Mayday. Yes, now I recall. That's Taurus, of course. So if you had the tiles to lay your own name in your own star-sign, then you would gain extra points. If first, however, you were able to place significant planets in the sign according to their conjunction on the date, and better still, at the time of your birth, then your point score would be, if you will excuse the trope, astronomical. But forgive me. I am intoxicated with the distillations of my own fermented fancy. Nothing more boring than the ramblings of a drunk!"

"Not boring," she assured him. "But maybe a touch baffling. I've looked at that copy of the rules you gave me, but to be honest they just left me more confused than when I started."

"Always the case," he said. "The best games are like the best lives—you only learn by living them. But let me try to elucidate . . ."

It was a simple progression from elucidation via demonstration to play.

When he set up the third tile rack with the letters spelling Johnny on it, she looked a question at him.

"A young schoolfriend who died," he said.

"The boy in the photo?"

"That's him. Little Johnny Oakeshott. He had the sweetest nature of any creature I ever knew. Charley Penn and I were a good working team but Johnny somehow made us complete. Before, we were a very effective combination of intellect and imagination. To which Johnny added a human soul. Does that sound mawkish?"

"No," she said. "No, it doesn't."

He smiled at her and said, "I always thought you would understand.

We played the game three-handed in those days. Johnny was never any good at it, but he loved to feel he was taking part."

"Then he died?"

"Yes," he said sombrely. "Stolen by some envious god. Since then we've always kept a rack for him. And there's a rule which never got written down which permits a player to use the letters in Johnny's rack if by adding them to his own letters he can form a whole word in any language."

"Then what? He wins outright?"

Dee shrugged and said, "Who knows? It hasn't happened yet. I sometimes fantasize that if it did, we would find Johnny sitting there in his place, ready to play. A real spell, in every sense, you see. But this is morbid. Let me initiate you into my mystery."

And so the game began. Dee clearly enjoyed the role of patient teacher, though it did seem to Rye that every time she thought she was getting the hang of it, he introduced a new and still more complex element. Not that she felt this as competitive. Indeed she soon began to get a sense that the mature experience of the game would have more of the partnership of dancing in it than the clash of competition. The rich designs glowed on the board and the letter tiles, made of smooth ivory, slipped through the fingers like silken fish when you dipped your hand into their container to replenish your store. This container itself was a thing of beauty, no plain tin or battered cardboard box, but a heavy gold-hinged casket carved from rubeous crystal.

"My mother's sole heirloom," he said when she asked about it. "How her mother got hold of it I don't know, nor indeed, considering the circumstances of the family, how she held on to it when everything else of value must have gone to the saleroom or the pawnshop. It held what little jewellery she possessed, gimcrack stuff, mainly. Now it holds something far more precious. The seed of words waiting for their creator. All language is here, which means life itself, for nothing exists till these seeds are sown."

And he had shaken the crystal casket so that the pieces of ivory slid and rustled and seemed to syllable her name.

Gradually, irresistibly, an erotic subtext had entered their game, a sort of sexy flirtation with sly innuendoes, hot-eyed side-glances, verbal caresses, entirely free from menace. She always felt that any time she wanted to step back, she need send only the slightest signal and, without fuss or recrimination, the normal friendly decorum of their working relationship would be restored. But she sent no such signal. Bathed in the shifting chiaroscuro of the fire, her body felt warm and relaxed. Where this game was leading, she did not know, nor yet how far she wanted it to go. At some point Dee had produced a bottle of dark red wine and a pair of tumblers, and the peppery liquid slipping down her throat was like the early throes of love-making, at the same time satisfying and increasing the drinker's appetite. The world of rock and water and vegetation outside the small weather-darkened windows seemed a long way away, and more distant still seemed that other world of people and buildings and engines and technology. If their memory seemed dark and comfortless it was because all their warmth and light and comfort and pleasure seemed concentrated in this narrow room. As for the airy infinities of the great mysterious universe in which all worlds exist, what need to go out and stare at the skies when all its beauty and wisdom was contained here on this magic game board which lay at her feet like the cosmos under the gaze of God?

And far away, still in that furthermost world, Hat Bowler was driving his car through the afternoon traffic like a mad thing while some way behind and falling further back, Peter Pascoe was heading in the same direction with rather more concern for his own life and limb as well as those of other road users.

The logs on the fire burnt swiftly, domed, then collapsed into a tumbled bed of glowing ashes whose red heart pulsated with consuming heat.

"A great fire for toast," murmured Rye. "When I was a kid, I remember sitting before a fire like this, and we toasted thick slices of white bread till they were almost black and spread butter over them till it melted through the airholes in the dough. I thought of it last time I was here . . ."

"Toast," echoed Dick. "Yes, toast would be nice. Later, perhaps. When the game is done."

And he threw more logs on the fire and soon the seeds of heat in the ashes blossomed once more into flames which embraced these new limbs of wood so that they shifted and sighed and moaned as the fire within them grew hotter and hotter till the room turned unbearably warm.

Dee reached down and pulled off the old tracksuit top he was wearing, revealing a short-sleeved vest which strained against an unexpectedly muscular and athletic body. Rye followed suit, pulling the chunky woollen sweater she was wearing against the anticipated rural chill over her head.

It was only as the heavy fibres rubbed across her face that she recalled she didn't have a top on underneath, only the flimsy silk bra she'd worn with her funeral outfit. Or was she perhaps pretending that it was only now that she remembered this? Certainly there was no perceptible pause as she drew the sweater off completely and let it fall alongside the chair, then leaned forward to make the word *joy*.

Dee neither averted his eyes nor ogled her bosom, but nodded as if in approval and said, "And now, if we were playing the poets' convention whereby crossing a word with another which either follows or precedes it in a poem which must of course be accurately quoted, I could score well here by crossing *joy* with *crimson*."

"Blake," she said. "So I could do the same by crossing your *secret* here with my *love?*"

"Still Blake. Excellent."

"Actually I was thinking of Doris Day," she said.

He threw his head back and laughed, and she laughed too, but somehow, instead of easing the sexual tension between them as she had intended, this shared laughter sent another line of contact snaking out which drew them even closer, affirming their mutual fondness and pleasure in each other's company without one wit diminishing their newly discovered physical attraction.

Why not? she thought. I'm a free agent, no commitments existing and as far as Dick goes, none intended. So why not gather a few rosebuds while I may?

But at the same time, her future working alongside Dee came into her mind. Would things be changed? She felt she could rely on him to keep things the same, if that's what she wanted. Yes, she was certain of his discretion, yet could even the greatest discretion resist the probing gaze of Charley Penn? The thought of those knowing eyes, that insinuating smarl, the ambiguous remarks implying a vicarious intimacy, was not pleasant to her.

And also into her mind, despite her genuine confidence of being a free agent with no commitments, came an image of Hat Bowler.

Who was now free of traffic on the quiet country roads and moving so fast that his passage hardly allowed time for the sheep grazing in the fields to raise their heads before he was out of sight, leaving only a wisp of exhaust smoke as evidence they hadn't been dreaming. Still some way behind him but, now that he was out of the city, keeping pace, came Pascoe with, a little way further back, the siren and lights of the patrol car which had picked up Andy Dalziel from the Black Bull.

The Fat Man came on his mobile now.

"Where are you at, Pete?"

Pascoe told him.

"And Bowler?"

"Not in sight yet."

"Well, stop driving along like an old woman! Get up there with him. Owt happens to the lad, I'll hod thee responsible."

"It's more what's likely to happen to Dee when Hat catches up with him that I'm worried about."

"Him? Turns out he's the Wordman, who's going to care?" said Dalziel dismissively. "No, it's young Bowler we've got to look out for. Another couple of years shaking that college education out of him, he could make a good cop. What the fuck are you doing with this thing? Pedalling it?"

The last two sentences, Pascoe assumed, were addressed to the driver of the patrol car, but he felt their power too and pushed his foot even harder on to the accelerator so that the same sheep which a little earlier had been disturbed by the passage of the MG twitched their ears again, but, being, contrary to their image, quick learners, this time did not bother to raise their heads.

So, thought Rye, will I, won't I?

She was aware that while her mind vacillated, her body was independently sending out much more positive signals.

She had stretched herself out in the chair, waiting for Dee, in every sense, to make his move. Her left bra-strap had slipped down over her shoulder and her breast had almost escaped from its silken cup, but she made no effort to recapture it. Indeed sensing, and perhaps slightly piqued by, a degree of hesitation in Dee himself, she relaxed her shoulders so that the nipple of the errant orb came fully into view.

Now she had his attention. But it wasn't on her swelling nipple that his eyes were fixed.

He was looking at her head.

She said, "What?"

He reached across the board and touched the silver blaze in her hair.

"I've always wanted to do that," he said.

"To check it doesn't come off on your fingers?" she mocked. " 'Tis in grain, sir. 'Twill endure wind and weather."

"I never doubted it," he said. And now he let his gaze slip down to her bosom.

He said, "Rye . . ."

She said, "Yes?"

He said, "Rye?"

She said, "Yes."

It was that easy.

He stood up so suddenly, one of his feet jolted the Paronomania board, shuffling the letters from the places so that now they made no sense.

He said, "I'll just get . . . I've got . . . excuse me . . ."

He turned and went out of the room.

Smiling, she now rose and undid her bra, letting it fall to the floor as she slipped out of her jeans and pants.

She went to the window. It took an effort of focus to get her gaze beyond the patina of rain stains and lichen which darkened the glass, but finally the grey mysterious surface of the tarn trembled into view.

Nothing moved. No wind crimpled the water. Not a bird in sight.

Birds made her think of Hat again. Dear sweet Hat, so knowingly innocent so innocently knowing. He need never know about Dick. Except, of course, that some men had an instinct for such things as sensitive as some women's. And in any case, she suspected Charley Penn, if he found out, would make sure Hat did so too.

Was it still too late to say no to Dick? Depended on your point of view. A woman has the right to say no at any time, at any stage; that was right, that was how it should be. But to be standing here, naked, when Dick came back into the room was to shout a YES! at him which she guessed for many men might drown out a simple spoken no.

For God's sake, if you're going to say no, put your clothes back on, woman, she urged herself.

Too late. She heard the door open behind her.

So be it, she thought, with hardly a pang of regret. Enjoy!

As if in affirmation of her decision she now saw a faint effulgence lighten the murky air which obscured the furthermost bank of the tarn. The setting sun breaking through to bless this union, she told herself only half-mockingly.

Except, of course, it was still mid-afternoon and she was looking east not west.

Also the sun sank, it didn't come rushing towards you!

So much for free will and independent decision. Just when you made up your mind to one course, fate coughed in your ear and set you on another.

For now it was clear the effulgence was in fact caused by the headlights of a car bowling merrily along the track which ran round the tarn towards the cottage. And there was sound too, a horn blaring as if the newcomer were desperate to announce his coming. And finally even at this distance she recognized the vehicle as Hat's sports car and smiled at the aptness of thinking of it as *bowling* along. Except now it was no longer bowling, it was bouncing and bumping over the potholed and rock-strewn track without diminution of speed. What desperate errand did Hat imagine he was on so to abuse his beloved MG?

Whatever it was it meant the end or at least the postponement of promised joy.

Preparing a rueful grimace, she turned to retrieve her clothes and get dressed.

But what she saw froze her in place.

Dee was standing there. He'd come forward so that his feet were on the game board. He too was stark naked, his arms held wide, with something in his left hand, she didn't work out what, for in his right hand he held a long thin knife. And she felt her gaze drawn down across his belly towards his crotch where his cock steepled out of a tangle of blond hair.

The car horn was blaring more loudly now, the headlights must be visible through the dirty glass behind her, Hat was almost here, but he was going to be too late. As she stared fixedly at the rampant figure before her, she knew beyond all doubt that he was going to be too late.

The MG got within fifty yards of the cottage before it hit a pothole too deep for even its sturdy suspension to bounce out of. The engine gave one last gasp and died. But it didn't give way to silence.

Hat heard the screams as he vaulted out of his seat.

Shouting something, he had no idea what, he sprinted towards the cottage whose windows glowed with a dull flickering red like Hellmouth in a Miracle play.

Behind him, approaching the tarn, there were other lights and the screech owl wail of a siren. Help was on its way, but to Hat it was help as meaningless as prayers for the dead and the comforts of religion. Keep screaming! he thought. Keep on screaming. The screams were the most dreadful sounds he'd ever heard, but as long as he could hear them he knew that Rye was alive.

Through the grubby window he glimpsed two figures grappling, a hand held high, in it a long thin knife, glistening red . . .

He ran down the side of the cottage, smashed through the door as if it were plywood, and plunged into Hellmouth.

Lurid in the shifting light of a high-leaping fire, the two naked figures wrestled in the middle of the room, close locked above the Paronomania board as if this defined the area of their struggle like a wrestling mat. The lion chair had been knocked over into the grate and already its back was beginning to char. But Hat had no eyes for this. All he saw was the knife raised high . . . the knife already dripping with blood . . .

He hurled himself forward and seized Dick Dee from behind, one arm round his neck, the other grappling the knife arm, and tried to drag him away from Rye. He came with such ease that Hat was taken by surprise and fell backwards. But he didn't release his grip and without the use of his arms to break his fall, he crashed heavily to the ground, his head whiplashing against the crystal tile dish. The flames of the fire seemed to dance into his mind, filling it with smoke and shifting shadow. He felt a gush of liquid over his already misting eyes, blood, tears, he didn't know what except that it stung and blinded. The weight of Dee was pressing down upon him. He threw it off and as he tried to sit up, he felt something run like a soldering iron along his left ribcage. Rye was screaming again. Not for herself this time, because he could still feel Dee's body close by his side. It must be for him, and the thought gave him strength. He tried to rise again. Something smashed against the side of his head. He flailed out blindly, his fingers touched metal—grasped—straightened as a blade cut into flesh—adjusted.

And now they tightened around a bone handle.

He had the knife.

But his assailant had something almost as lethal in its place which came crashing once more against the side of the detective's head.

Minimum force. For some reason this phrase came into Hat's mind from his not so distant training days. Force may be used to effect an arrest, but it must always be the minimum force commensurate with the lawful restraint of a suspect.

When you were on your back, and blind, and wounded, and losing consciousness, and grappling with a homicidal maniac, minimum was hard to define.

He swung his arm up high then drove the knife down hard. That felt like minimum. And again. Still felt like minimum. And again . . . yes, still well within the limits . . . and again . . . if this were minimum, what in this case would be maximum. . . ?

The question danced in and out of the flickering flames and shifting shadows in his mind, pursuing an elusive answer among broken definitions and the shards of words. Then the rising ululation of what he knew was a siren but still sounded to him like that ill-omened bird of night rose to a climax.

Then stopped.

And darkness fell.

XLVII

The darkness lasted a long time.

Or perhaps a short time. He couldn't know. It was punctuated by flashes of cognition in which his senses worked but in a mixed-up way. He smelt movement, felt colours, saw sounds. None of these impressions made any sense or seemed related to any other. Whether they belonged to real time or to that dream-time which can pack infinity into a grain of sand, he didn't know.

So when he finally awoke, he was ready to find himself still helpless on the floor of Stangcreek Cottage.

His eyes weren't functioning properly but at least they were register-ing images albeit dimly on his retina and he could make out someone standing over him.

Oh shit. He was right. It was still the cottage . . .

He tried to move. Couldn't. This got worse. He was bound down.

He tried to speak. His mouth was dry as . . .

There were half a dozen laddish similes in common canteen use but he couldn't recall any of them.

The looming figure stepped closer.

The features came into focus. They were frightful, contorted, menacing.

The dreadful lips moved.

"She's all right, lad."

And the ogreish features dissolved and resolved themselves into the comfortable because familiar dissonances of Edgar Wield's face while at the same time the bonds which held him down turned into the starched and tightly tucked sheets of a hospital bed.

"She's all right," repeated Wield.

If Wieldy said it, then it must be true. And he knew he'd be eternally grateful to the sergeant for knowing the one question his disfunctional tongue had wanted to ask.

He closed his eyes again.

Next time he opened them, Pascoe was there.

The DCI called a nurse who helped him raise his head, which he only now realized was heavily bandaged, and gave him water.

"Thanks," he gasped. "My throat was dry as a screech owl's crotch."

Vulture's, he meant. But it was coming back.

The nurse said to Pascoe, "Don't overtire him. Don't let him move too much. I'll let the doctor know he's awake."

Hey, I'm not only awake, I'm here! thought Hat. But he was too weak in body and will to protest.

"Where . . . ? How long . . . ?" he croaked.

Pascoe said, "You're in the Central Hospital. You've been here for eleven days."

"Eleven . . . ? I've been out of it for eleven days?"

Eleven days was worrying. Eleven days was a huge step on the way to brain death.

Pascoe smiled.

"It's all right. Mr. Dalziel allows a fortnight before he tells them to switch everything off. In any case, you were never comatose. But you do have a depressed skull fracture and there was pressure on the brain. It's OK. They've got you sorted. You'll be able to do *The Times* crossword again."

"Never could before," said Hat. Then thought, Christ! don't relapse into plucky little trooper mode, you're fucking terrified!

He said, "You're not bullshitting me, sir? I mean, eleven days . . ."

Pascoe said, "Relax. The reason you've been out of it so long is mainly because of the sedation. Trouble was, whenever you did wake up, you were so confused that they were worried you'd do even more damage to yourself."

"Confused?"

"Delirious, if you like. Thrashing around like you were in a mud-bath with Sharon Stone."

Sharon Stone? thought Hat. No thanks, I'll pick my own fantasies.

This reaction cheered him up more than the DCI's reassurances. Time to forget about himself and ask about Rye, put some detail on Wield's assurance that she was OK. He heard her screams and saw again her naked body being mauled by that bastard Dee and wondered how much detail he was ready for. But he had to find out.

Not yet, though. Pascoe was still speaking.

"And the things you were shouting . . ." The DCI shook his head as if still unable to believe them.

"Like what?"

"Don't worry, we've got them all taken down so they can be used in evidence against you when you get back to work."

Comforting words. He was good, Pascoe. Nice bedside manner. Should have been a GP. But not a Georgie Porgie, no, couldn't see him as that . . .

"This morning Sergeant Wield said you were back with us. Said you were asking about Ms. Pomona."

Wield. Knew what you were thinking before you thought it.

He said, "The sarge said she was OK, right?"

"She's fine. A few bruises and scratches. Nothing else."

"Nothing?"

"Nothing," said Pascoe emphatically. "You got there in time, Hat. He didn't have time to do anything to her, believe me."

He's telling me the bastard didn't rape her, thought Hat. Why doesn't he just come out and say it?

Maybe because I don't just come out and ask it.

And what if Dee had raped her? What difference would it have made?

To me? Or to her? he asked himself with angry revulsion. A hell of a difference to her. And who gives a toss if it makes any difference to me?

It's because I'm ill, he tried to reassure himself. Being sick makes you selfish.

He said, "Is she in hospital too?"

"No way. One night for observation. Then she discharged herself. She doesn't seem fond of hospitals."

"No, I think she had a bad time once . . . so she wouldn't want to hang around . . ."

"She's been in to see you every day," said Pascoe, grinning. "And I gather that the first thing she does every morning and last thing at night is ring to check you're OK. So you can get that neglected look off your face. Hat, that's some girl you've got yourself there. When you were rolling around with Dee she broke a bottle of wine over his head. He'd dropped his knife, we gather, and was trying to beat your brains in with this crystal dish that weighed a ton. She got it off him and started to give him some of what he was giving you. Some girl."

"And I got the knife," said Hat, frowning with the effort of memory. "And I . . . what's happened to Dee? Is he . . . ?"

He wanted him dead, yet he wanted him alive, because if he were dead . . . He recalled the knife rising and plunging, rising and plunging. Minimum force.

"He's dead," said Pascoe gently.

"Shit."

"Saves the cost of a trial," said Pascoe. "And saves Rye the trauma of a trial."

"Yeah."

"There'll be an enquiry, of course," Pascoe went on lightly. "Always is when an officer is involved in a death. Nothing to worry about in the circs, just a formality."

"Sure," said Hat.

He knows as well as I do that nowadays there's no such thing as a formality, thought Pascoe. Dead man, cop involved, sod the circumstances, there's a whole percussion band out there ranging from civil rights activists through religious nuts to fuck-you-all anarchists waiting to beat their different drums in the hope that when the cacophony stops, a cop's career will lie mortally wounded.

With luck in this case the media would be blaring out the triumphant notes of celebration loud enough to drown the dissenters. The Wordman erased. The killer of at least seven people himself killed. Damsel in distress rescued by heroic young officer. Rumours of romance in the air. This boy deserves a medal!

Pascoe hoped he'd get it. One thing none of the interested parties on either side had seen was that room in Stangcreek Cottage as he saw it when he'd finally burst through the door.

Blood everywhere. Hat, wounded in his side and his head, lying unconscious on his back. The naked girl, stained with gore like an ancient Pict with woad, kneeling by him, cradling his bleeding head. And Dee, sprawled across the Paronomania board like some sacrificial ox, his body rent by so many wounds that the blood from them had joined to cover him in a scarlet cloak, and all across that body, gleaming like stars in some alien red sky, and scattered across the floor like the Milky Way, were the game's letter tiles, bearing some arcane message for any who could read.

To a neutral observer it might look as if it was Dee who'd been the victim of a maniacal attack.

Dalziel when he arrived hot on Pascoe's heels had taken this in at a glance.

After they'd called for an ambulance and ministered to Hat and Rye as best they could, the Fat Man had said, "Best try some resuscitation here."

"Nay, sir, he's gone," said his driver with the authority of one who'd attended more major traffic accidents than he cared to recall.

"Even so, can't have folk saying we didn't try," said Dalziel firmly. "Pete, give us a hand."

Pascoe knew what they were doing. It was called interfering with a crime scene. It was also called making sure that when the enquiry team sat in judgment in some nice clean conference room with pads of pristine paper to make notes on and jugs of crystal water to refresh their throats when they became dry from asking too many dusty questions, no one would be able to pass around photos of an abattoir.

No way they could alter the pathologist's report, of course. But verbal description of the wounds wrapped in formal medical language, or even photographs of the cleaned-up body on a mortuary slab did not begin to convey the scene at Stangcreek Cottage.

These morbid reflections were driven from his mind by a disturbance in the corridor.

"Where's he hiding at?" cried a familiar voice. "In here? Keep it quiet, tha says, luv? Nay, I've dealt with more malingerers than tha's had hot flushes."

The door burst open and Dalziel filled the room.

"I knew it. Up and talking. No wonder the NHS is short of beds with fit buggers like you filling them."

Behind him an indignant staff nurse fluttered till Dalziel put her out of sight and mind by shutting the door.

"So, howst'a doing, lad? What fettle?" said the Fat Man, sitting on the edge of the bed which responded with the outraged squeak of a goosed matron.

"I'm OK, I think, sir," said Hat.

"He will be OK in a few weeks, I imagine," said Pascoe firmly.

"A few weeks?" said Dalziel incredulously.

"No, honestly, I think I'll be out and about before that," said Hat.

Dalziel regarded him closely, then shook his head.

"No you won't," he said. "The DCI's right. Couple of weeks at least. Then a couple more convalescing."

"No, really . . ." said Hat, this volte-face taking him by surprise.

"Fuck really," said Dalziel. "Listen, lad, out there while you're in here, you're a wounded hero. So in here you'll stay till we get that made official. Then when you do come out, them as wonder why you needed to stab Dee the Dick thirteen times can mutter all they like. Can't touch a hero."

"Why did you need to stab him thirteen times, Hat?" asked Pascoe.

"Wasn't counting," said Hat. "And maybe I didn't need to, but I certainly wanted to."

"First bit, good answer. Second bit, lousy answer," said Dalziel. "Best is no answer. Look pale, little wince of pain, then say it's all a blur, you remember nowt but this monster trying to kill this helpless innocent lass. All you knew was you had to stop him, even if it meant putting your own life on the line. And if you get a gong, say you reckon it's the lass as should have it, all you did was your job, they'll love that."

"Yes, sir," said Hat. "Sir, what about Penn?"

"What about him?"

"He alibi'd Dee for the Stang Creek killing, remember?"

"Maybe he got the night wrong. Maybe he was doing his mate a favour. Or maybe Dee bamboozled us about what he were doing the other possible times. Not your worry, lad. Leave Charley Penn to me."

"Yes, sir," said Hat, closing his eyes momentarily and wincing.

"You OK?" said Pascoe, concerned.

"Fine," said Hat. "Didn't realize it was such hard work being a hero."

"Expensive work too," said Dalziel. "First round in the Black Bull's on you when you get back. Come on, Pete. Lad needs his rest and some of us have got work to do."

Out in the corridor, Pascoe said, "Do we need to worry about Penn?"

"Only if he feels he don't need to worry about me. Hello, what's this? Don't usually see folk running into these places, just out."

The door at the end of the corridor had burst open to admit Rye Pomona at a run. She didn't look as if she would have stopped, but Dalziel's body was an obstacle not easily ignored.

"I got a message saying he's awake," she gasped.

"Awake, compos mentis, and asking about you," smiled Pascoe.

"He's OK? Truly OK?"

She spoke to Dalziel. Fair enough, thought Pascoe. I'm good enough for *reassurance,* but for *assurance,* Fat Andy's your only man.

"He's grand, luv. Bit weak still, but sight of you'll have him standing up in no time. How about yourself? You OK?"

She looked OK. Indeed, with her golden skin flushed from running and her rich chestnut hair with its distinctive silver flash becomingly dishevelled, she could have modelled for a pre-Raphaelite picture of Atalanta diverted from her race by Aphrodite's golden apples. Except there were only three of them and with Andy Dalziel as diversion, the artist would have need to paint a whole barrelful.

"Yes," she said impatiently. "I'm fine. Went back to work today."

"What? Miserable buggers. Should have thought they'd give you a month at least."

This indignation from one who believed that wheelchair access to police stations had been provided in order that convalescing cops could get back to their desks as soon as possible amused Pascoe.

He saw it amused the young woman too.

"To do what?" she said. "I've seen the quacks and the counsellors, I've taken the long country walks, I've got the victim T-shirt. I'm better off at work, and they're a bit short-handed there at the moment. We lost a couple of librarians recently, or haven't you heard? Now, if you'll excuse me, I'll go and see Hat."

She pushed past and went into the room.

"Good lass, yon," said Dalziel. "Bit lippy, but I don't mind that in a woman long as she's got the tits to go with it. Reminds me a bit of your Ellie when she were a lass."

Making a note to pass this intimation of senescence on to Ellie, Pascoe glanced through the glass panel.

Rye was kneeling by the bed, clasping one of Hat's hands in both of hers and looking into his eyes. They weren't speaking. Pascoe did not know where they were, did not know about that magic mist which had wrapped itself round them the time they walked along the margin of Stang Tarn, but he knew they were far away in some private place where even his distant gaze was an intrusion.

"Takes you back a couple of years, eh?" said Dalziel, who was peering over his shoulder.

"Further than that," said Pascoe. "Takes you right out of time. Come away. We're strangers here."

"Nay, lad. Not strangers. Just too busy to visit very often," said Andy Dalziel.

XLVIII

the last dialogue

DICK DEE: *Where am I?*

GEOFF PYKE-STRENGLER: *Dick Dee, by all that's wonderful! How are you, old chap?*

DICK: *I'm . . . I'm not sure how I am. Geoffrey, is that you? I'm so sorry . . .*

GEOFF: *What on earth for? Not your fault we're here.*

DICK: *Isn't it? I thought that . . . what is this place . . . ?*

GEOFF: *Hard to explain, old boy. Not really a place at all, if you get my drift. How did you get here, anyway?*

DICK: *It's all mixed up . . . there was this tunnel with a very bright light at the end of it . . .*

SAM JOHNSON: *How very conventional. I had bells and explosions and birdsong, bit like the 1812 re-orchestrated by Messiaen.*

DICK: *Dr. Johnson . . . you too . . . I'm sorry . . .*

SAM: *You will be. Oh yes, you will be.*

GEOFF: *Ignore him. He's a bit down. The tunnel thingy, that's just an impression of the process of getting here. Quite a popular one, as it happens. I meant, what happened to start the process?*

DICK: *I can't remember . . . there was . . . no, it's gone.*

GEOFF: *Not to worry. It generally takes a bit of time before memory comes back.*

SAM: *Enjoy it while you can. It's when you start remembering that the pain starts. Oh God, here it comes. We may have left the stage but we still have the pantomime horse.*

PERCY FOLLOWS ⎫
⎬ *Hello, Dick.*
AMBROSE BIRD ⎭

PERCY: *How are things back there? Who's got my job? I half expected it might be you.*

BROSE: *Can hardly be him when he's down here with us, can it?*

PERCY: *You know what I mean.*

BROSE: *Only because my powers of interpretation compensate for your inadequacies of expression. How on earth you got to be borough librarian I cannot imagine.*

PERCY: *By the same process as a pipsqueak blowbag like yourself got to be the Last of the Actor–managers, I dare say. Where do you think we are going?*

BROSE: *For a walk by the river.*

PERCY: *But we went for a walk by the river this morning.*

BROSE: *That was when it was your choice. Now it's mine and I choose to go there again. Anyway, there's nowhere else. Come on, no dawdling.*

PERCY: *Don't poke. You're poking again. I promise you, if you start poking, I'll start jerking.*

DICK: *I wanted to say something to them but they didn't give me the chance to get a word in. And why are they walking so close together like that?*

GEOFF: *That's how they arrived, sort of joined up. And the way you arrive is the way you stay, it seems, at least till you cross the river. You may have noticed I'm having to hold my head on, for instance.*

DICK: *Yes, I'm so sorry . . .*

GEOFF: *Bad habit that, always apologizing.*

DICK: *But your poor head . . .*

GEOFF: *I know. But look, old boy, there's you bleeding all over the place and I'm not apologizing, am I?*

ANDREW AINSTABLE: *'Scuse me, gents, but I'm looking for a bridge. Couldn't tell me if it's upstream or downstream, could you? I've got a Home Start waiting and I was due there . . . can't recall when exactly, but I know he's waiting.*

GEOFF: *Try upstream, old boy.*

DICK: *Who on earth was that?*

GEOFF: *On earth he was an AA man. He's still a bit confused even though he's been down here longer than any of us. Spends all his time looking for a bridge.*

DICK: *Bridge? I'd say he's tried to swim across, from the look of him.*

GEOFF: *Not an option, old boy. No, that's the way he came, dripping wet. He wants to find this bridge 'cos that's where he left his van.*

DICK: *This is very confusing. And I keep on hearing music . . .*

GEOFF: *Oh yes, that's young Pitman. He just lies around on the bank all day playing his bazouki. Seems perfectly happy and he can't frighten the fish because there don't seem to be any. Disappointing that. I know it's not real—not in the real sense—but if you're going to have a not-real river, you might as well stock it with not-real fish. Instead we've got that odd-coloured mist. Sort of purply. Looks industrial to me, like there's some big plant with furnaces and such quite close. And that spells pollution with a big P. That's what I used to love about the tarn. Creek ran into it straight from the hills. Nothing up there to pump chemicals and sewage into the water. Miss it, you know. Hope when we get across we might find somewhere a man can cast a line and hope to hook something more than an old bedstead.*

SAM: *My God, will you listen to him? It's over, old boy. All that stuff belongs somewhere else. Here it's done with, finito, kaput. The nearest you're ever going to get again to that creek you keep on going on about is being right up it, without a paddle. Oh shit, here she comes, I'm out of here.*

GEOFF: *Poor chap, it's hit him bad. You never know how people will take it. Me, remembering how things were keeps me going. Poor Sam it just drives mad. That's why he can't stand Jax. All she wants to talk about is the past. Jax, my dear, how are you? Look who's just arrived.*

JAX RIPLEY: *Dick, is that you? Lovely to see you. Is my Wordman story still running? Do I still get a credit whenever anyone does a piece? What about movie rights? Or a TV drama-doc? It rates a drama-doc, at least. Who have they got to play me? God, I hope it's not that girl in EastEnders, you know, the one with hair. I know she's the right size, but everything else about her is so wrong. That mouth . . . !*

DICK: *I couldn't really say. Jax . . . what happened . . . I'm sorry . . .*

JAX: *Are you? That's not much of a compliment. I seem to remember really enjoying it.*

GEOFF: *He's still a bit confused.*

JAX: *No use to me then. Unless you managed to smuggle a mobile in. No? Thought not. God, what wouldn't I give for a mobile! Catch you later, Dick. Be good.*

GEOFF: *Lovely girl. Interviewed me once, you know. Thought I might have a chance afterwards, things going really well, then that blasted phone of hers rang. How about you? She seemed genuinely pleased to see you. Did you ever . . . ?*

DICK: *I'm not sure . . . I seem to recall something . . . but I can't be sure . . .*

GEOFF: *You are in a bad way, aren't you?*

DICK: *I'm trying to get my head round all this. We are dead, right?*

GEOFF: *Got it in one, old chum. Yes, there's no getting away from it. That's what we are. Dead.*

DICK: *And this place . . .*

GEOFF: *I've thought a lot about that. Conclusion—it's not really a place, it's more a sort of state. Not like Mississippi . . . except insofar as it's got this bloody great river . . . but like I just said, it's not a real river either . . . more a sort of visible metaphor . . . hark at me, talking like a critic! . . . but you know what I mean . . . it helps our minds keep a hold on things . . . rather like you seeing dying as a tunnel . . . it's all a bit hard to grasp at first . . .*

DICK: *But you seem to have grasped it better than anyone, Geoff. Why's that?*

GEOFF: *Born to it, I suppose.*

DICK: *You mean, because you've got a title?*

GEOFF: *Good lord, no. Load of bollocks, all that stuff. It's just that, well, I'm connected, you know. Sort of divinely.*

DICK: *You mean you're God?*

GEOFF: *Of course not. Don't say things like that. Got one of my ancestors into a lot of bother way back. No, but I am family, so to speak. Sort of fourth cousin, x times removed. It's the fallen angels, you see. Some of them got the option of turning human rather than spending an eternity in hell. Hard choice to make, I should think. Back on earth, the connection's not much help, but down here, it seems to give us descendants a bit of an inside track on things. Not that I know much more than here we are and here we'll stay till we're all here, then we'll go across.*

DICK: *Who's all? And where's across? And how long do we have to wait?*

GEOFF: *Forget how long, old boy. No time here. Time's away and somewhere else. Don't know where that came from, must have been something I learned at school, but it's true. As for all, I mean all those that the Wordman kills.*

DICK: *The Wordman . . . but aren't I the Wordman?*

GEOFF: *You? My dear Dick! What on earth put that notion in your head?*

DICK: *I don't know . . . just something . . . I feel responsible somehow . . .*

GEOFF: *And that's why you're apologizing left and right! My dear chap, rest easy. You couldn't hurt a fly. I recall the first time I gave you a pair of trout and you realized you had to clean them out yourself. You turned white! No, you're like the rest of us, a victim here. Look at you, all chopped about like a baited badger. Councillor, you tell him.*

STUFFER STEEL: *Tell him what?*

GEOFF: *The dear chap thinks he's the Wordman.*

STUFFER: *So he is. All them buggers as work in yon poncy Centre, all sodding wordmen, never done an honest day's work between 'em.*

GEOFF: *May have got something there, Councillor. But I mean Wordman with a capital W, the one who's been doing all these killings.*

STUFFER: *Oh, yon bugger. No, Mr. Dee, you may be a lot of things, most on 'em useless, but you're definitely not that Wordman, not if that's the bugger who killed me.*

DICK: *Thank God, thank God. But if it's not me, then who is it? Who was it who killed you, Councillor?*

STUFFER: *You really don't know? Aye well, fair do's. Took me some time to twig even after I got here. I mean, you're standing there washing your hands in a gent's bog and you look up and see a bonny young lass in the mirror, you don't think straight off, she's come to top me!*

DICK: *A young lass . . . oh my God . . .*

STUFFER: *Coming back, is it now? Aye, well, I looked at her and she looked at me, this big reassuring smile on her face. And I said what the hell are you doing in here, lass? And she said, I just wanted to tell you I've got that dinner you asked for sorted. You know, rib beef and Yorkshire pudding and lots and lots of roast spuds. And I thought, well that sounds all right. Then I felt sum- mat at the back of me neck and next thing I'm on the floor and it's all getting dark. Then there was this young fellow-me-lad bending over me and asking if I were all right and I knew I weren't all right, I knew I were on my way out, and I'd no idea why, that's what bothered me.*

DICK: *And you said* rosebud *to him. Why did you say* rosebud?

STUFFER: *Don't recollect saying owt, but if I did, I know it bloody weren't rose- bud! No, it 'ud be roast spuds! You see, what I couldn't get my head round was why she'd been going on about me dinner. But I've worked it out since. She wanted me to die happy. Aye, that must have been it. She didn't want me to die thinking, 'Oh Christ, there's someone here going to kill me.' She wanted me to go thinking I was about to get me dinner. Not much bloody hope of that down here, far as I can see, but it was a kindness, aye, I'll give her that. It was kindly meant.*

DICK: *And this was definitely Rye? This was Miss Pomona?*

GEOFF: *You know it was, Dick. It's coming back now, isn't it? Like the coun- cillor says, takes a bit of getting hold of. When I saw her pointing the Purdy at me, I just said, careful, my dear. Not good form to point a gun at anyone. It might go off. Then it did. Still thought it was an accident when I found myself here, but once I got talking to the others . . . Well, I should have known, pretty young lass like that fluttering her eyelashes at me and saying she was really interested in night fishing and she'd heard I'd got this boat out at Stang Creek—must have heard that from you, I suppose, Dick—no, it didn't make sense, I thought, not unless maybe she fancied me. Don't suppose that made sense either, but I have been fancied in my time, and an old cavalry horse don't pay much attention to anything else when he hears the bugle playing! Who knows, out in the country, snag a couple of trout, bake them over a fire, bottle of vino, anything can happen. And it did!*

DICK: *It's coming back now but I still can't believe it. We were getting on like a house on fire. She sent out all the signals. They seemed unmistakable, but I still needed to be absolutely sure. No way I wanted to risk our working relationship by giving her cause to think I was taking advantage. So I left her alone to give her time to think things over, cool off, if that's what she wanted, but when I peeped through the door, she was standing at the window taking her clothes off. Well, that was it. Couldn't be clearer, I thought. I slipped out of my kit in a trice, then just to keep it all light and easy, I grabbed a loaf of bread and a knife . . . we'd been talking about how nice toast tasted made over an open fire . . . and I went back in and said that I thought we'd have some toast afterwards. But she looked at me as if she wasn't listening . . . well, to tell the truth it was my erection she seemed to be looking at . . . I was well aroused, and she seemed to be really focused on it . . . quite flattering, really . . . and she came towards me, and I felt her take the knife from my hand, and next thing I had this feeling in my stomach, oddly it wasn't a pain, not at first, just a very strange and not at all distressing feeling which got somehow all mixed up with my desire for her, and she held me very close to her, and I felt myself beginning to go. I'd read about young women swooning with desire in Charley Penn's books and I recall thinking, I must tell Charley it happens to fellows too, and Rye was screaming with passion, at least that's what I took it to be though it did seem a bit strident, then suddenly it was as if I'd been grasped from behind and dragged backwards to the floor, and after that I've no idea what happened . . .*

GEOFF: *You got used for target practice by the look of you. Hello, what's all that noise down by the river?*

STUFFER: *I'll go and see.*

GEOFF: *Notice anything about the councillor?*

DICK: *Apart from that hole in the back of his neck? No.*

GEOFF: *His breath. No pong. One of the few advantages of this place. Lots of sensory switch off. All these wounds, no pain. And no smell. Plus you can see that damned attractive telly girl running around in the next-to-nothing and not get randy, though you may not feel that as an advantage. They really are making a din down there. Must be something happening. Let's go and see.*

DICK: *I can't get over it. Rye Pomona. But why . . . ?*

GEOFF: *No doubt there'll be answers by and by. Councillor, what's going on?*

STUFFER: *It's these two. They say they saw something out there on the river in the mist.*

PERCY⎫ *We did, we did. It's a boat, it's a boat, and we can see someone stand-*
BROSE⎭ *ing in it. They're coming to rescue us. Hooray! Hooray!*

SAM: *They're right, you know. Look, there it is, looming through the mist. But let's not be too quick to attract attention. There's no telling what plans this guy might have for us.*

JAX: *Who cares as long as he's got a mobile? Yoo hoo! Yoo hoo! Over here!*

ANDREW: *Is someone coming? Maybe they've seen my van. Oh yes, now I see him. But is it a him? I don't believe so. This could be very helpful. I'm sure it's that lass whose car I fixed. She must know where the bridge is. Miss! Miss! This way!*

DICK: *Dear God, he's right. It's her. It's Rye, it's Rye Pomona. There, I knew she couldn't be the Wordman, else what's she doing down here. Rye! Rye! Over here.*

STUFFER: *Aye, get yourself over here, my girl, I want a word with you.*

GEOFF: *Hold on. Hard to see with all this mist, certainly looks like Miss Pomona, but can't spot any, you know, bumpy bits. And that funny mark she's got in her hair, where's that?*

SAM: *If it's that girl and she's not dead, I'm going to kill her. Rye Pomona, is that you?*

SERGIUS POMONA: *Pomona certainly, but not Rye. Sergius of that ilk. Raina's twin.*

SAM: *Sergius . . . Raina . . . oh bizarre.*

STUFFER: *What's he laughing at?*

GEOFF: *Don't know but it's good to see him a bit more cheerful. Mr. Pomona, have you come to take us across?*

SERGIUS: *Yes, but before I come in to the bank and you start embarking, can we get any silly antagonisms out of the way? This isn't a large ferry and there's quite a lot of you, so we'll be pretty low in the water and the last thing we need is anyone rocking the boat. You do not want to end up in this river, believe me. So if you've got any questions, ask them now.*

DICK: *Yes, I've a question. Rye's actions, going around killing people, has this got anything to do with that accident when you died?*

SERGIUS: *She told you about that?*

DICK: *Yes. It started with her hair. I didn't ask but she must have seen I was curious and it all came out, how you crashed the car and two other people got killed, and you yourself of course . . .*

SERGIUS: *Ah, that's the version she gave you, was it? A few minor inaccuracies. It wasn't me driving, for a start. It was Rye. She was so desperate to get to the theatre for her potty little role that she'd have done anything. When I realized she was setting out in Mummy's car, I ran after her and because she was having trouble changing up, I managed to jump into the passenger seat. She caused the crash. She killed me and those other two people. But you're right about one thing. That was where all this started.*

SAM: *You're saying because she feels guilty about accidentally killing three people all those years ago, she started bumping us off now? I hope you've got Beddoes over there. He'll have loved this. It's really Gothic!*

SERGIUS: *It's a little more complicated. We were very close, real twins, to the point where we often seemed to share thoughts, and if anything happened to the other when we were apart, both of us felt it. So she was naturally devastated when I died, particularly as it was her fault, and when she wanted to ask my forgiveness, it didn't seem silly to try and contact me via our shared thoughts as we used to when I was alive. Well, we got a dialogue going in her mind, but she was never sure if it was real or she was just making it up . . .*

GEOFF: *And was it real?*

SERGIUS: *How should I know? I wasn't sure either if the dialogue I thought I was having with her was real or just my imagining. I mean, when you're both alive and can meet to exchange notes, you can cross-check, right? But with me down here, her up there, how could either of us tell? Unless of course, we got a sign.*

SAM: *A sign? Oh, God preserve us from signs!*

STUFFER: *Aye, one thing I've learnt in politics is any bugger looking for signs is sure to find 'em, and there's none of 'em to be trusted!*

SERGIUS: *You may be right, Councillor. Certainly once she started looking they came thick and fast. In fairness, you've got to understand her psychological state. It wasn't just guilt at my death that was screwing up her thinking. It was the way her whole life had been stood on its head. Her acting career had been all she ever thought of before the accident, but after she recovered, she gave it up completely. What she told people—indeed what she told herself— was that she did it out of revulsion against the artificialities and pretences of the stage. In fact it was rather more basic. You see, she found she could no longer remember the words!*

DICK: *But she always had a marvellous memory for quotation.*

SERGIUS: *Off the stage, everything was fine, near perfect recall. But once she trod the boards, it all went.*

BROSE: *How awful! I once recall drying up when I was playing Mirabell opposite Dame Judi at the Garrick . . .*

PERCY: *Oh, do shut up, Brose, and let the man finish. The sooner we get across this dreadful river, the sooner we'll be released from this most embarrassing position.*

SERGIUS: *Thank you, Mr. Follows. You should understand, Mr. Bird, it wasn't just her learned lines that went, it was all vocabulary. Can you imagine what it's like to be in a world devoid of words? Where nothing you see has a label? Nothing you feel can be expressed? Nothing you think . . . well, in fact, you can't think! This is what going on the stage meant for her. This is why she became a librarian, so she could spend her life in places where they treasured words and kept them stored safe for future generations. But all the time she wanted my forgiveness. She had a memory of me lifting her from the driver's seat of the wrecked car and laying her on the pavement, then reaching up to*

pluck a spray of cypress from a tree overhanging the churchyard wall and plac-
ing it on her breast and whispering a loving reassuring word in her ear before
going to take my place by the driver's door so she wouldn't be blamed for the
crash.

DICK: *That rings a bell . . .*

SERGIUS: *Indeed. I expect you're thinking of one of your friend Mr. Penn's*
translations which he used to leave lying around in what was always a vain ef-
fort to engage Rye's affections. It's from the poem which begins "All night long
when dreaming I see your face . . ."

DICK: *That's right. How does the last verse go?*

> *A word in secret you softly say*
> *And give me a cypress spray sweetly.*
> *I wake and find that I've lost the spray*
> *And the word escapes me completely.*

SERGIUS: *Well remembered. Pity Rye's memory didn't work as well. She got*
thrown out of the car and I was in no state to get out after her. I just slumped
across into the driver's seat and died. And it wasn't a churchyard wall we hit,
but a garden wall, and the nearest thing to a cypress tree in it was one of those
ghastly leylandii hedges. But Rye had such a powerful false memory that when
she read this particular effort of Mr. Penn's, she immediately saw it as one of
these signs she was always looking for. There were plenty of others. You yourself
bear some responsibility in this, Mr. Dee. You made her aware of that game of
yours, Paronomania, and she worked out for herself long before you told her
what was the significance of the third tile rack bearing the name Johnny.
Here, it seemed to her, was a perfect example of bringing someone back to life
through the power of words.

DICK: *But it was never like that with Johnny . . . I refuse to accept any re-*
sponsibility here . . . it's only a game . . . was . . .

SERGIUS: *Of course it was. With Rye, too, it was only a game to start with.*
But before we leave your game, Mr. Dee, you should be aware that in fact its
very name was one of the most significant triggers of her subsequent course of
action. In the beginning was the word, remember? And the word in this case
was PARONOMANIA.

DICK: *I don't understand. How could a name . . . ? Ah . . .*

SERGIUS: *I think you're getting there. After all, you too are a wordman. That's right. Try rearranging the letters.*

DICK: *Oh God . . . Paronomania . . . Raina Pomona! But I can't be blamed for an anagram!*

SERGIUS: *Why not? You have taken power from words and their construction, deconstruction, and reconstruction all your life. The man who splits the atom must bear some responsibility for all that springs therefrom, surely? Dear Rye saw in these and many other small signs evidence that I was trying to show her a path which would lead to direct communication with me.*

GEOFF: *By killing people? Don't get it, old boy.*

SERGIUS: *That was still to come. The nearest thing to an unmistakable sign came the day the shelf collapsed during the grand tour of the library. Most of you were there, which of course seemed significant later on. You remember the occasion, Mr. Dee?*

DICK: *Indeed. It was quite comic really the way everyone scattered as the books came tumbling down.*

PERCY: *I didn't think it was comic. I've never been so embarrassed in my life.*

BROSE: *Not even now, dear boy.*

PERCY: *This hardly counts as life, does it? So there!*

DICK: *But what . . . oh yes. It was the OED. All twenty volumes. What a crash they made! And it was this that . . . ?*

SERGIUS: *Yes. Rye didn't see an accident. She saw all the words in the language come flying off the shelves to send the great and the good of Mid-Yorkshire into undignified flight. In the beginning was the Word, and the Word was with God, and the Word was God. The path to communion with me must, she felt, lead through all these words, but how? So many, so very many . . . how to traverse such vast distances . . . she needed a chart to show her the path . . . and then it came to her . . . what if the OED was her chart . . . what if the limits of each volume were signposts . . . ? A to Bazouki . . . BBC to Chalypsography . . . but how? And now she told herself, or imagined she heard me telling her, that messages to and from the dead require messengers, and for these messengers to be efficient, they must leave her living and come to me dead. These ideas were all swirling madly in her mind, and might still have come to nothing had she not driven out that fatal morning, and broken down, and saw you come bowling merrily along the road, Mr. Ainstable.*

ANDREW: *This is all beyond me. Is my van on the other side then, mate?*

SERGIUS: *Of course it is. Everything any of you need is over there. After your death, Mr. Ainstable, which she merely observed, she was almost convinced. After Mr. Pitman's, which she contributed to but not necessarily fatally—he might after all have kept control of his bike and continued on his way home, cursing lady drivers—she felt sure that this was the path I had mapped out for her. And when you, dear lady, went on television, and practically invited her to prepare another Dialogue, everything seemed clear.*

JAX: *What a story! You say everything we need is on the other side. Computer terminals? Fax machines? Mobiles? That's great! Come on, let's not waste any more time. Let's go!*

STUFFER: *Hold your horses. I want to know what she meant by scraping away at my poor old head. I mean, killing me were bad enough, that were adding insult to injury!*

SERGIUS: *Oh yes. That was quite amusing really. She had to mark you to get the sense of steel engraving across. But the police experts interpreted it as an attempt to inscribe RIP, in Cyrillic script. They were right about the script—a macabre little joke on my sister's part—but in fact all she was writing was her initials, R.P., as an artist might inscribe a work of art. This was part of her desire for confirmation of my protection, for assurance of her invulnerability. Tell the world it was her; even as in your case, my lord, lead the police to the body. It didn't matter what she did, she felt she couldn't be caught, no matter what clues she left.*

SAM: *And that makes it all right, does it? So what clues did the cow leave after she did for me?*

SERGIUS: *Well, she left the book open at that poem about the loved, long lost boy. That was me, of course. And then there was the chocolate bar . . .*

SAM: *What chocolate bar, for God's sake?*

SERGIUS: *The Yorkie bar. Yorkies have the letters of its name printed on them, one on each segment. She broke it up and rearranged it on the mantel shelf above the fire. If anyone had found your body before the chocolate melted, they'd have read her message.*

SAM: *Message? What message? Some reference to* The Chocolate Soldier? *Very subtle!*

SERGIUS: *Oh no. Much clearer than that. The letters read* I RYE OK. *Surely even Mid-Yorkshire's Thickest would have got that? Perhaps not. I mean, none of them spotted that the illuminated* **P** *at the beginning of the first Dialogue represented a tree and there were apples among the pile of letters lying alongside the roots. Pomona, the goddess of fruit trees, remember? From the start she was telling you who she was. Later you even gave a little lecture to that young constable on why* **man** *in combinations like* **chairman** *need not be gender specific, and neither of you transferred it to* **wordman**. *But why should we be surprised? Even when the police more or less caught her in the act of slaying you, Mr. Dee, she still got away with it. Of course, love is blind, and when that poor young constable rushed in, what he saw was you assaulting his beloved. Happily for Rye, when he fell backwards in pulling you off her, he hit his head so hard, he was rendered almost senseless, a condition she maintained by breaking a bottle over his skull and blinding him with wine. It was easy then for her to make sure his hand found the knife which he proceeded to stick into you with such great enthusiasm. Not that it was necessary. You were going to die from Rye's first blow to the stomach anyway.*

DICK: *But why? Why did she do it? We were going to make love. She felt the same way as I did, I'm sure.*

SERGIUS: *You're right. She liked you; and she felt extremely randy; and being a modern young woman, saw no reason not to enjoy herself. But naturally on seeing the approach of the young man she really loved, she changed her mind. She's not that modern! Then she saw you naked, and that was it. But I'm afraid it wasn't your rampant loblance that so compelled her gaze, Mr. Dee, it was the rather large reddy-grey birthmark running across your belly. If ever a man was* haswed, *it was you. This was a sign from Serge, she thought. Time stopped for her. Which meant, of course, that very soon time had to stop for you also. Don't take it personally. Do take it as a comfort, if you will, that your death affected her more than anyone else's. And, of course, it had the bonus of giving the constabulary the best kind of ready-made culprit, a dead one who spared them the inconvenience and expense of a trial.*

DICK: *Oh God. You mean that's what I'm going to be remembered for? Being a serial killer?*

SERGIUS: *Well, it was always your ambition to make your mark as a word-man, wasn't it? And you did contribute to your own downfall. She wouldn't have come to the cottage if you hadn't asked her. And she wouldn't have seen your birthmark if you hadn't set out to seduce her. And the police wouldn't have had you so firmly in the frame if you'd come forward to admit you'd been in bed with Miss Ripley the day she died. That was an amusing irony, really. Rye had actually covered up your presence there by removing your watch which you'd left under the pillow! She did it out of affection for you. But if the police had found it and therefore questioned you earlier about your relationship with Miss Ripley, who knows? Perhaps the whole course of events may have been changed. Well, that's fate. Now, unless there are any more questions, let's start getting you aboard. You first, Messrs. Bird and Follows, as you are potentially the most awkward . . .*

PERCY: *We will get separated on the other side, won't we?*

SERGIUS: *Oh yes. Nothing Dante-esque about the place where you're going. Now, Miss Ripley . . . excellent . . . Mr. Ainstable, perhaps you could give Mr. Pitman a hand . . . he's a bit broken up . . . you'll love it over there, Mr. Pitman. Very Greek. Mr. Steel . . .*

STUFFER: *What's the nosh like, mate?*

SERGIUS: *Ambrosia. With chips. Dr. Johnson . . .*

SAM: *I don't know about this . . .*

SERGIUS: *Just think of it as sailing to the rock in the ancient waves, Doctor. And there's a young friend of yours waiting to see you. That's right. He may have a couple of things to tell you which you'll find surprising. There we go. Now, Mr. Dee . . .*

DICK: *Do I gather that we'll get the chance to meet people we once knew . . . ?*

SERGIUS: *Don't worry. Young Johnny knows you're coming. He's very excited. Last but not least, you, my lord.*

GEOFF: *Oh gosh, not so much of that lord stuff, eh? Not the place to be putting on the style from the sound of it.*

SERGIUS: *You may be surprised how hierarchical we are. And of course when you're connected . . .*

GEOFF: *So long as there's a bit of good sport. Shall I push off then? Right. Here we go. Just one thing that bothers me, as they say in the tec novels. Has all this worked out for Rye? I mean, was it really you leading her on all the time? And if her motive was getting in touch with you, why can't we hear her? Or did she have to get right through the whole twenty volumes of OED before she wrapped it up? In which case, sounds like she's got a long way to go? And won't the police get a bit suspicious when the Wordman killings carry on even with Dick here dead? Left hand down a bit, I think, old thing. Don't want to hit that rock or whatever it is out there . . . can't see a thing in this mist . . . oh yes, I can . . . it's getting a bit clearer . . . it's . . . it's . . . Oh my God . . . !*

And so their voices fade in the mist, or rather in my head, which is maybe the same thing, with Geoff's questions unanswered.

Silence. The same silence which began as I stepped back into time and looked down at dear Dick's ripped and bloody corpse, and dearer Hat's pale and bleeding face.

Oh, Serge, Serge, why have you deserted me? In all the other dialogues, I heard you, sometimes faint, sometimes loud and clear, always unmistakably you. In this one I have invented words, for you, for all of them, hoping like a nurse giving the kiss of life, that eventually my breath would give you strength once more to take your own.

But here I sit in what used to be Dick's chair, with all those old wordmen staring down at me from the walls, and I know that I am alone. Except for my memories.

Such memories.

How can I live with them?

I am of course mad by any normal standard of judging sanity.

And will be mad in my own judgment if I conclude that this has all been delusion, all done for nothing.

The questions I put into Geoff's mouth need to be answered.

Perhaps others will answer them for me. Even if the police are so blind that they let me get away with this, theirs are not the only eyes that I have to fear.

Through the open door into the library, I can see Charley Penn sitting at his table, looking towards me with a gaze by turns speculative and sceptical and accusing, and always angry.

Beside him is that strange young man, Franny Roote, who whenever he catches my eye gives me a small, almost complicitous smile.

Or is it guilt that makes me see these things?

Something else that I can see through my open door is real enough, nought realer.

The twenty volumes of the Oxford English Dictionary sitting proudly on its high shelf.

I set out on a path signposted by the forty words on those twenty volumes.

Haswed *has brought me up to the end of Volume VI.*

What of the other fourteen? Do I really need to labour over that long and tortuous path to discover the truth of it all? Must I press on into Volume VII?

Or have the six brought me to my destination?

Is this silence your final message to me, my beloved Serge, saying that I need no longer strain my ears to have a dialogue with the dead because I now at last have a sufficient dialogue with one of the living?

It's very important to know. And not just for me.

I look at the first word of the two defining the limits of Volume VII and my heart aches with love, and with fear.

For I know I have to decide very soon whether those three simple letters signpost a direction, or a destination.

Hat Hat Hat Hat

Is this the start of a new game?

Or is it simply **The End**?